ċ

WITHDRAWN

THE SILENCE

The new book in the Viennese Mystery series.

Vienna, 1900. Lawyer Karl Werthen is puzzling over the suicide of a local councilman when he is assigned by Karl Wittgenstein, a powerful industrialist with many enemies, to find his recently missing son, Hans. Werthen quickly discovers that the young man appears to be alive and well in another country. But when a friend of Hans – a journalist who wrote a number of articles claiming the councilman who committed suicide was corrupt – is found dead, also from a self-inflicted gunshot wound, Werthen fears that sinister forces are at work...

Recent Titles in this series by
J. Sydney Jones

THE EMPTY MIRROR
REQUIEM IN VIENNA

THE SILENCE

A Viennese Mystery

J. Sydney Jones

Severn House Large Print
London & New York

This first large print edition published 2013
in Great Britain and the USA by
SEVERN HOUSE PUBLISHERS LTD of
19 Cedar Road, Sutton, Surrey, England, SM2 5DA.
First world regular print edition published 2011 by
Severn House Publishers Ltd., London and New York.

British Library Cataloguing in Publication Data

Jones, J. Sydney. author.
    The silence. -- Large print edition. -- (A Viennese mystery
    ; 3)
    1. Werthen, Karl (Fictitious character)--Fiction.
    2. Lawyers--Austria--Vienna--Fiction. 3. Private
    investigators--Austria--Vienna--Fiction. 4. Suicide--
    Fiction. 5. Vienna (Austria)--Social conditions--19th
    century--Fiction. 6. Gross, Hans, 1847-1915--Fiction.
    7. Criminologists--Fiction. 8. Detective and mystery
    stories. 9. Large type books.
    I. Title II. Series
    813.6-dc23

    ISBN-13: 978-0-7278-9623-0

Severn House Publishers support the Forest Stewardship Council™
[FSC™], the leading international forest certification organisation. All
our titles that are printed on FSC certified paper carry the FSC logo.

Printed and bound in Great Britain by
TJ International Ltd, Padstow, Cornwall.

For my children – Evan and Tess

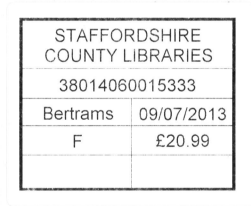

Acknowledgements

Thanks go first to my agent, John Talbot. Amanda Stewart, formerly of Severn House, took this project on, Edwin Buckhalter, Chairman of Severn House, and James Nightingale, Managing Editor, further shepherded it through production. My thanks to them and to their excellent production staff who have helped to make this a much better book than it was in manuscript. And as always, thanks go to my wife, Kelly, for being the heart of our family. She makes it all possible.

Whereof one cannot speak,
thereof one must be silent.

Ludwig Wittgenstein,
Tractatus Logico-Philosophicus

One

A lone figure stood high up in the central spire of Vienna's Rathaus. At the observation window above the enormous illuminated clock, he surveyed the city he ruled, feeling the juddering thud of each minute's passing in the mechanism beneath his feet.

For a time, he watched the docile Viennese plod about their business this brutally cold afternoon of the last day of January. The skies were clear, brittle blue, and afforded a view to the northwest of the Vienna Woods, flecked in snow.

Slowly, menacingly, he allowed his eyes to move to the far left middle distance. There stood the twin towers of the Votivkirche, which he regarded as an open insult to himself. This was the devotional church to the emperor, Franz Josef, built to commemorate the occasion when the young emperor survived an assassin's knife.

Doktor Karl Lueger, mayor of Vienna for three years, and something of a king himself, scowled as he gazed at the emperor's church. He and Franz Josef were old enemies; thrice had the Habsburg denied Lueger his place as mayor, even after the Viennese had resoundingly elected him. Three times Franz Josef had felt it his solemn duty to save the Viennese from themselves.

The old fool had the effrontery to call me a demagogue, Lueger thought. Me, a man of the people who simply takes to heart the plight of the little man and the true Christian in this mongrelized empire.

He made an audible snort.

'Is everything all right, sir?'

Kulowski, Lueger's beefy bodyguard, looked expectantly up at him from the bottom of the last flight of stairs.

Lueger shook his head dismissively at the man.

Of course everything is not all right, you dolt, he wanted to say. As long as there is a Habsburg left in Vienna, things will never be right.

Soon, however, very soon, things *would* be set right.

As he was accustomed to doing, he threw open the observation window on the tower, breathing in the crisp air. He could smell the scent of black pine and the sweetness of snow. Beneath, on the Ringstrasse, a solitary D streetcar, pulled by a dappled mare, was making its way to Schottentor. A new motorcar suddenly passed it, causing the horse a sudden fright, but the skilled tram driver soon brought the animal under control.

Another tradition: Lueger gathered a gob of saliva in his mouth and spat in the direction of the Votivkirche.

It would fall to earth as a snowflake, he thought.

Then he closed the observation window.

The world was changing. Here we are in the first year of the twentieth century. Motorcars will be the future of transport. The city is growing at an astounding rate; soon it will finger off into the hills of the sacrosanct Vienna Woods.

Now, as the day began to dim, electric street-lights along the Ringstrasse flickered on. Away with gas lighting and horse-drawn equipages – all remnants of an old and tired world. Even the holy shrine of the Vienna Woods could not stop the steady thrum of progress.

Lueger, at fifty-five, felt himself very much a part of the new century, not the old one. He did not wax nostalgic over that which might be lost with modernization, unlike the stodgy emperor who refused even to ride in a motorcar and intensely disliked the telephone.

'Your five o'clock appointment,' Kulowski called up the stairs to him.

Damn the man, Lueger thought. Still, it would not do to keep the ward boss of the Third District waiting too long.

'Coming,' he said.

He no longer carried himself with the same bounce as of old. Mentally he felt younger than ever, and his face was still as handsome as when he was a young man. Thanks to his good looks, he had mobilized the Gretl brigade, or the Amazons, as people called his ardent female supporters. Though these women did not have the vote, they idolized him and in turn enlisted their husbands and male relatives. They still remained his most ardent followers, dubbing him 'Handsome Karl'.

13

Physically, however, Lueger was beginning to suffer the outward signs of diabetes and nephritis. His illness was still a closely guarded secret, but he doubted it could remain so for long. Climbing the three hundred and thirty-one steps up to the top of the Rathaus was no longer an easy task for him; as a result, he restricted these visits to once weekly. It was worth the effort: to view the world beneath him like this, his personal fiefdom.

And before long he would not have to share it with his old nemesis, Franz Josef.

He was smiling so broadly when he reached Kulowski, that the bodyguard wondered what the mayor was up to. It was the grin of an imp, of a man scheming and damned pleased with himself.

'Nice view?' Kulowski said.

But Lueger ignored him, gripping the handrail as he continued descending.

Going down was worse than going up; perhaps he would have an electric lift installed? After all, he could put the expense down to advocating tourism. Not that he would allow the hoi polloi to ride his elevator, but it would make a fine excuse for funding from the City Council.

Lueger took his mind off the descent by going over the points he would need to cover in his upcoming meeting. His backers in the Third District were getting restless. And by 'backers' he did not mean the Marias and Josephs with their tiny corner *Lebensmittel* or *Bäckerei* who thought they were the mayor's special cause. No. His real backers were the landlords who had

14

put millions into his campaigns and were still waiting for some results for their money.

They had reached the bottom of the spire stairs, contiguous with the upper floor of offices, when they heard the shot. Not a military man, still Lueger knew for a certainty it was a gunshot.

So did his bodyguard. Kulowski attempted to grab him from behind and throw him to the parquet of the corridor to protect him.

Lueger resisted, however. 'Leave it, for Jesus' sake,' he bellowed. 'They're not firing at me.'

Kulowski looked at the mayor quizzically for a moment before he realized the shot was, in fact, nowhere near them. Footsteps were pounding along the corridors, followed by excited voices. They followed the throng of people to the southwest corner office.

They could now see that the crush of city workers and other councilmen had gathered at Councilman Reinhold Steinwitz's door; a hush such as at a funeral had fallen over them.

Lueger looked to the crowd of people and then beyond; Kulowski followed his gaze. When the bodyguard looked back to the mayor, Lueger wore a shrewd grin on his face.

The architect Otto Wagner, who had reached the office first and halted at the entrance, aghast at what he saw, now pushed his way back through the crowd. There was the harsh smell of cordite in the air, and Oberbaurat Wagner, despite being nattily attired in his frock coat, was not looking very professorial, Lueger thought. His eyes were wide and there was a nervous urgency about the man that the mayor, who had employed him on municipal projects from regulating the Danube Canal to building the metropolitan railway, the *Stadtbahn*, had never before seen.

Finally Wagner saw Lueger and rushed to his side.

'Mayor. It's your friend, Councilman Steinwitz. I think he's killed himself.'

Two

Despite snow flurries that kept most people indoors or on public transport, Advokat Karl Werthen walked to work the morning of February 5, 1900, a daily ritual he tried not to deviate from.

The Habsburgergasse in Vienna's First District was as void of human activity as if it had been a Sunday and not a Monday. As he approached his office at number four, Werthen could see the profiles of the supporting columns decorating the first-story façade. One of the naked Atlases bore an unfortunate protuberance of snow at just below waist level. These sculptures were a comfort to Werthen; a solid and reassuring presence in the midst of what some days felt to be pure chaos. He did not want to leave this particular Atlas in such disgrace.

Gazing up and down the street, he first made sure no one was about. Then, standing about knee-high to the figure, he took off his felt hat and jumped up, sweeping with the brim to rid the blotch of snow from the statue's penis. Chill flakes speckled his face, but he was pleased to see that the Atlas now stood in all its original and unadorned splendor.

'Grüss Gott.'

The greeting gave him a start. Behind him stood the building *Portier*. She was looking at him with a quizzical expression, but he felt in no mood to explain himself to this elderly woman, long the bane of his existence at Habsburgergasse 4.

He quickly put on his hat, then tipped it to her. 'Frau Ignatz.'

Bundled in numerous layers of woolen cardigans, most of them out at the elbows, she carried a rag and a bottle of polish.

'Surely you do not mean to polish the brass on such a day,' he said, attempting to be cordial, or at least to sound concerned.

Once again, his overtures were strongly rebuffed by the gruff old woman.

'Some of us have a living to be made.' She scowled as she spoke. 'Some snip of a girl is already in your office. Says she belongs there.'

'Yes,' Werthen replied. 'She does. She is my new assistant.'

He glanced for a moment at his own brass plaque outside the house door: *Advokat Karl Werthen: Wills and Trusts, Criminal Law, Private Inquiries*.

'And mind you get the edges of the plaque shiny, as well,' he said, trying to salvage some dignity from the exchange.

As Werthen climbed the flights of stairs to his office, hat in hand, his right knee began to hurt. Injured in a duel, that knee had not bothered him in months, but a chance meeting with Frau Ignatz could resurrect even long-dormant ailments.

The 'snip of a girl' was indeed at work when he entered the office. Erika Metzinger tried bravely to look the part of a secretary, wearing a prim white, high-necked blouse with full sleeves, her hair piled atop her head and affixed with several tortoiseshell combs. She'd even installed a typewriting machine and was busy clacking away at it with two forefingers. The little fingers on both her hands pointed quite elegantly upward, as if she were at a tea party.

Fräulein Metzinger, in fact, had the appearance of a Volkstheater actress attempting the role of secretary. Her obvious discomfort came from the fact that she was, in fact, much more than an office dogsbody. After the recent unfortunate loss of his former junior member of chambers, Werthen had been left in the lurch. He was attempting to build his new business as inquiry agent and thus needed a competent assistant.

'Morgen.' The young woman greeted him in the languid tones of the West Country, for she hailed from Salzburg. The accent, however, was the only thing Werthen had found to be relaxed about her. She was in fact a veritable dynamo; Werthen had never met someone her age so knowledgeable of the law.

However, because of Austria's outmoded customs vis-à-vis the education of women, she was denied entrance to the university. Indeed, it was only two years ago that the University of Vienna allowed entrance to its first female students, and those only in the philosophy faculty. There was talk recently of allowing women to study medicine in Vienna, but legal studies were still off limits to women in the Austrian capital and were likely to remain so for decades.

'Fräulein Metzinger,' Werthen said in reply to her greeting, nodding his head at her. 'Murderous weather.'

She looked startled at this comment. He had noticed a tendency toward literalism on her part.

'The snow,' he added, showing his snow-speckled hat, and she visibly relaxed.

The daughter and granddaughter of well-known jurists, Fräulein Metzinger might not possess a sense of fantasy or humor, but she had studied law privately and possessed as much legal knowledge as any licensed lawyer. The Austrian feminist Rosa Mayreder, good friends with Werthen's wife, Berthe, had introduced the young woman to him and vouched for her intelligence and character. Fräulein Metzinger had demonstrated both qualities during their brief interview, and Werthen decided immediately to hire her. Still, she was not a certified lawyer, and though she could do much of the paperwork at the office, Werthen had to be the one to check all her work, sign documents and meet with clients, a small price to pay for having one so capable – and yes, so willing and grateful – in the office.

'The Kleist file is waiting your signature, Advokat Werthen. It's on your desk.'

'Excellent,' he said. He could think of no higher praise, made almost speechless by her statement, for that file had languished for months, desperately needing reworking, rewording, adjustments, and disentanglements. Werthen himself had tackled it several times, only to

20

retreat with a headache after several hours of sifting through interminable memoranda and cancelled clauses. The Kleist clan, it seemed, had relatives on every continent, each of whom had numerous amendments to the wording of the family trust. Now Fräulein Metzinger, after only a few days on the project, had brought it to fruition.

'I mean, *very* excellent.'

You are a dithering fool, he told himself. Just get in your office and sign it.

With the office door closed behind him, Werthen took off his coat and hat, placing them on the mahogany rack, and settled into his chair. As promised, the Kleist file lay on his desk suppliantly.

Wonderful girl, he thought, even if she was deficient in a sense of humor.

He quickly browsed the documents and signed them. Then he settled back to peruse the morning papers, something that he had taken particular pleasure in of late.

For the last five days, Advokat Werthen had kept himself apprised of the Rathaus scandal surrounding the death of Councilman Steinwitz, for the man was a former client of his. He remembered the councilman quite well: a large, florid man who was a blend of Viennese bluff bonhomie and Czech fatalism. Had the Czech blood in the man gotten the upper hand? he wondered. Graft scandal or no, Steinwitz seemed to Werthen the last person in the world to take his own life.

The Viennese newspapers had made an event

of the councilman's suicide. Over the previous days the tragic tale had been featured in every newspaper in the land. The usually staid and conservative *Neue Freie Presse* was atwitter like a maiden aunt having taken too much elderberry wine. The day of the suicide, the headline of its evening edition attempted to balance itself between decorum and innuendo: 'Councilman Takes Life, Irregularities Noted.' Irregularities in the death or in his role as councilman? The eager reader must peruse the article and decide for himself. A feuilletonist for that paper felt called upon to go into great length in his meandering essay on the family history of said Steinwitz: married to Valerie Gutrum, youngest daughter of Colonel Gutrum, a veteran of the Battle of Königrätz during the Austro-Prussian War, and therefore an imperial icon; their two children, Joachim and Helene, 'distraught at the loss of their beloved *Vati*.' The less august *Neues Wiener Journal* did not bother with suggestion: 'Steinwitz Kills Self, Subject of Investigation.' Here the reporter posited a link between a recent City Hall graft investigation and the suicide of the center of that storm, Councilman Steinwitz.

The socialist *Arbeiter Zeitung*, which had first published the tale of City Hall corruption, also placed the story of Steinwitz's death on its front page, above the fold. 'Death of Councilman Laid to Graft Investigation,' read that paper's headline, though no such direct connection had, in fact, been made, for there was no suicide note. Facts, however, should never get in the way of a good lead. The anti-Semitic *Deutsches Volks-*

22

blatt put the entire matter – the story of City Hall graft and the subsequent suicide of Steinwitz – down to a Jewish plot to discredit Lueger and his associates. Even the gadfly journalist and social critic Karl Kraus used the councilman's death as an excuse for an exegesis on suicide, the Viennese sickness – one that, according to the journalist, claimed more lives per year in Vienna than did deaths from other killer diseases, such as tuberculosis and syphilis. Kraus pointed out in his *Die Fackel* article that between 1888 and 1896, 3,164 Viennese had taken their own lives, an average of about one a day. Men were in the majority, with a four-to-one advantage over female suicides. While hanging was the preferred method, gunshot came in a close second. And, Kraus added, December surprisingly (with all the expectations of the holiday season) proved to be the month with the lowest average number of suicides, while May, with its seemingly uplifting and invigorating weather, was the month with the most, over fifty on average.

Today, Werthen discovered as he glanced at the newspaper in front of him, the architect Otto Wagner had been turned into copy for the hungry dailies.

'I am a frequent visitor to the Rathaus,' Wagner told a journalist for the *Neue Freie Presse*. Werthen knew of and appreciated Wagner's role as artistic consultant to the municipality in numerous civic projects, including the newly opened *Stadtbahn* station at Karlsplatz in a Jugendstil design that infuriated many stodgy burghers. The elderly Wagner had also angered

23

many critics among the conservatives with his 1899 membership in Klimt's Secession. Though he did not necessarily agree with all of Wagner's theories of urban design, or with his concept of utilitarian design, or *Nutzstil*, Werthen thought Wagner was a national treasure. As was usual with Vienna, Wagner was more famous in the rest of Europe and even in the United States than he was at home; scores of his designs had been neglected and left unrealized because of politics and rivalries.

Wagner further noted to the journalist, 'I thought at first it was a motor car exhaust. I cannot imagine why, as it is very unlikely that one would hear such a sound three stories up the Rathaus.'

Equally unlikely that one would hear a gunshot there, either, Werthen thought.

Wagner had precious little to add to the tragic tale, but his name usually made good copy. His enemies, and they were legion, might even wonder if he had not pulled the trigger himself. The Viennese loved a scandal and delighted in mixing the names of the famous with such scandals, thereby reducing to their own paltry level whatever great man they selected for the honor.

As Werthen finished the article, he heard the door open to the outer office. There was a mumble of voices; he thought he recognized one. A tapping came at his door, and Fräulein Metzinger, a scarlet blush spreading into her scalp, looked in.

'Sorry to interrupt. There is a fellow here to see you. He says it is rather urgent.'

Not a 'gentleman,' but a 'fellow.' And someone who was able, within instants of meeting her, to embarrass Fräulein Metzinger with some wayward statement or glance. That could be only one person.

'Send Herr Klimt in,' Werthen said.

She looked at him with amazement, then backed out of the door, to be replaced momentarily by the bulky frame of the artist Gustav Klimt, attired in an Astrakhan wool coat and matching Cossack-style hat. He hardly looked the part of the *bête noire* of Viennese painters; rather if one saw him for the first time you might think him to be a jumped-up butcher or baker.

'My lord, Werthen, you have made improvements in this office. That girl's a wonder. Wherever did you find her?'

'It is nice to see you, too, Klimt.'

'Am I being too lax with my politesse once again? Sorry. I hate formalities. But, if you insist. "Greetings, dear Advokat. How hale you and your lovely wife, Frau Berthe?" Is that better?'

'And daughter,' Werthen added, going around the desk to shake hands with the artist. His first child, a daughter, had been born on January 19.

'Well, bravo for you, Werthen. A father. A wonderful institution.'

Klimt should know; for he had fathered numerous children in Vienna by various mistresses.

'Too kind,' Werthen said. 'Now what is it brings you here? It can't be the bill. I understand from Berthe that was finally settled.'

25

'A sore point, Werthen. Shall we move on to other, brighter topics? In fact, I come bearing blessings for you in the form of yet another commission. If this keeps up, I shall take a proper percentage for my troubles.'

Indeed Klimt had been responsible for starting Werthen on the road to inquiry agent when the artist himself was accused of murder two years earlier. And last year he had been good enough to send another client Werthen's way, the young beauty, Alma Schindler.

'Do tell, Klimt.'

But Klimt had seemingly lost interest in his errand. Instead he was busily surveying the room's décor: heavy mahogany furniture, green wallpaper, tasteful yet conservative prints of flowers and animals.

'Bit stodgy, don't you think?' Klimt said, nodding toward a print of a horse and jockey.

'It's a lawyer's office, not a salon,' Werthen replied.

'What you need are some paintings from our Secession. I could let you hang them here without a fee. Good for you, good for us. Expose your clientele to the new arts. Turn them into connoisseurs.'

'They come to me for reassurance, Klimt, not an introduction to aesthetics.'

'And some of our Werkstätte furniture would do wonders.'

'What commission, Klimt?'

'A Kolo Moser bookshelf, perhaps.'

'The *commission*, Klimt.'

'Fatherhood does not seem to be favoring you,

26

Werthen. You are damnably testy today. The little bugger keeping you up at night?'

Werthen shook his head. 'The "little bugger," as you so lovingly refer to our Frieda, is a sleeper.'

'Well, something is chewing at your nerves, then. If you were a dog, you'd be snarling.' Klimt divested himself of coat and hat, looking about for a place to throw them. Werthen took them, and placed them on a straight-back chair by the wall. He pointed Klimt to an upholstered chair near his desk and returned to the other side of it to his own chair. Sitting down, he let out a sigh.

'It's the parents, if you must know.'

'How do you mean?'

Too late, Werthen remembered Klimt's devotion to his own mother; she was faultless in his eyes. There would be no sympathy, let alone empathy, from Klimt regarding one's parents. The artist, despite his many affairs and entanglements, still lived with his aged mother, and his sisters. For many Viennese men, such a living arrangement was not a punishment, but a salvation.

Am I simply an ingrate, or are my parents more difficult than most? Werthen wondered. Estranged since his marriage to Berthe, whom they felt was socially beneath the Werthens, his parents had come back into his orbit once they learned of the advent of a grandchild. This was as it should be, and Werthen was initially happy for the reconciliation. They had taken a suite of rooms for the winter in the Hotel zur Josefstadt

27

in the Langegasse, close to his flat in the Josefstädterstrasse, and were often visitors to Werthen and Berthe.

But from his initial joy at having his parents back in his life, Werthen had begun to dread their visits.

'You'll put the wet nurses of the empire out of work, at this rate,' his father joked having learned that Berthe had decided to breastfeed her child herself. 'Simple division of labor.'

And his mother engaged in endless wrangling with Werthen's housekeeper and cook, Frau Blatschky, over the proper foods to prepare for a young mother. Frau Blatschky, happy that Berthe's interminable morning sickness was done with, relished the preparation of all the richest food in the Austrian culinary canon, for a feeding mother should be able to indulge herself.

'All that lovely mother's milk does not come from eating crusts,' Frau Blatschky intoned, as if Berthe had hitherto been subsisting on a convict's diet.

Werthen's mother, however, was worried lest her daughter-in-law lose her shapely figure. A mere week after the birth she said to Berthe with sweet insouciance, 'You don't want Karlchen to be harnessed to a dray horse, now do you, dear?'

Werthen hoped – he had long given up on praying – that his parents would finally pack their bags and go back to their estate in Upper Austria. Reconciliation be damned; he wanted his domestic peace once again.

'Werthen? Are you quite all right?'

Klimt's voice brought him out of his thoughts.

'Sorry, Klimt. Forget I mentioned the parents. As you say, put it down to lack of sleep.'

Klimt rubbed a thick hand through his short, disheveled hair. 'It's a case of missing persons. Well, one missing person.'

Werthen, accustomed to the painter's extreme egoism and narcissism, was not caught amiss by this seeming non sequitur.

'That's not really my line,' he said.

'Nonsense, Werthen,' Klimt spluttered. 'Anything is *your line* as long as it has to do with private inquiries. And this is very private, I assure you. My patron, Karl Wittgenstein—'

'He's gone missing?'

'His oldest son and heir.'

Werthen nodded judiciously at this information. Karl Wittgenstein, the powerful industrialist, dubbed the Carnegie of Austria, was indeed a commission of worth. The man was one of the wealthiest in the empire if not in all of Europe, and had recently retired, turning his interests to art. Among his other projects, he had helped fund Klimt's exhibition hall, the Secession.

'I thought you might be interested,' Klimt went on. 'The young man's name is Hans. Just turned twenty-three. He's been missing for the better part of a week.'

'What do the police say?'

Klimt leaned back in his chair. 'I don't suppose that wonderful young woman out there might find a cup of coffee for me?'

'No, I don't suppose she will. I can offer you a slivowitz, though.'

Klimt grinned like a fellow conspirator. 'The

29

cold, you know. One could do with a bit of lubrication.'

Werthen kept a bottle of ten-year-old plum brandy in a massive sideboard that took up one wall of his office. Moving to the sideboard, he secured the bottle and two glasses. To be polite, he poured himself one, too, though it was far too early for such indulgences.

'Your good health,' he said, handing one of the shot-size crystal glasses to Klimt, who did not bother with preliminary sniffs or appreciation. Remaining seated, he downed the fiery liquor in one swift gulp.

Klimt handed back the empty glass. 'No police involved. Herr Wittgenstein is rather prickly about publicity, you see. He has had a bellyful of it lately regarding his monopolies in steel and iron. Besides, he tells me he believes the boy is simply off on a lark. It's the wife, you see, who is worried.'

'A week is a longish lark,' Werthen said, resuming his seat. 'I assume there has been no note, no communication asking for ransom.'

'None.'

'A family of such wealth, kidnapping cannot be ruled out.'

'But a week and no note...'

'Yes, to be sure.' Werthen did not mention other possibilities swirling in his mind. Not only were the Wittgensteins one of the wealthiest in the empire, but they were also the most prominent Jewish family, assimilated or not. Perhaps some anti-Semite had a hand in the disappearance. There was any number of possibilities.

Interesting, however, that the father should think the son had simply run off for a final fling.

'Has the son gone missing before?'

'That, my friend,' said Klimt as he rose from the chair, 'is something you must ask Herr Wittgenstein. He has reserved a ten o'clock appointment for you. Meanwhile, I have a lady waiting for me at my studio.'

Werthen raised an eyebrow.

Klimt shook his head at this. 'She's fat and fifty, but the family is well endowed.' Klimt laughed. 'I shall make her look like a sylph. No one will recognize her. And please don't be late. Herr Wittgenstein keeps the wurst on my table. The Alleegasse, just behind Karlskirche.'

Redundant information, as everyone in Vienna knew the location of the Palais Wittgenstein.

Three

Werthen let Fräulein Metzinger know he would be out most of the morning and perhaps the rest of the day. He had no scheduled appointments at the office today; Klimt's timing could not have been more perfect.

The snow had let up now, but the world was muffled in its whiteness. Soon enough it would melt and be a filthy nuisance, but for now Vienna was transformed into a winter wonderland. A number of truant children were out in the Volksgarten, sledding along the pathways on discarded planks of wood to the great disapproval of older pedestrians. Werthen did not bother trying to find a *Fiaker*, but instead cut through the park on foot on his way around the Ringstrasse to the Alleegasse. As he walked, he tried to sort out his questions for Herr Wittgenstein. He knew the importance of confronting a man of such power with his own assured plan of attack.

Along with most other Viennese, Werthen was well aware of the importance of Karl Wittgenstein. Born in 1847, the industrialist was, like Werthen, just two generations removed from the land and from his Jewish roots. His father had run a successful dry goods business and converted to Protestantism. Instead of following the family route into business, Karl Wittgenstein became a draughtsman and an engineer and went to work for the Teplitz steel-rolling mill in Bohemia. By a mixture of hard work, overweening ambition, and a willingness to take huge risks, Wittgenstein built an empire from this humble beginning. Five years after starting work as a lowly draughtsman for the Teplitz Rolling Mill, Wittgenstein was running that business. He sold train rails to the Russians during the Russo-Turkish War of 1878, making a huge war profit for his company, and staged another coup by gaining sole European rights to a revolutionary steel manufacturing process. With these rights in hand, he leveraged other businesses, acquiring the Bohemian Mining Company and then the Prague Iron Company, creating a vertical monopoly in steel production in the Czech regions of the Austrian Empire. He repeated this success in the German regions with purchase of the Alpine Mining Company, and at the same time established the first rail cartel in Austria. It seemed to many that Wittgenstein had a finger in every economic pie in the empire, with seats on the boards of powerful corporations, including the Creditanstalt, the most powerful bank in the monarchy.

Then, in 1898, amid a firestorm of criticism over his shoddy treatment of workers, his monopolistic practices, and his attempts to artificially drive up the price of his steel stocks, Wittgenstein stepped down from the directorship. He became a patron of the arts, but knowledgeable observers knew that he still had a strong hand in the day-to-day operations of his far-flung industrial empire. His home at Alleegasse 16 had become one of the foremost salons in Vienna. Johannes Brahms premiered his late clarinet quintets here; Klimt and other members of the Secession first presented their work to the public in the immense rooms of that city palace. Through marriage, the Wittgensteins were connected with lawyers, doctors, industrialists, and ministers. Herr Wittgenstein could obtain a visa, an introduction to a general, medical advice, or an inside tip on investments with a simple telephone call.

At the same time, because of his cut-throat business practices, there were plenty of people who might want to harm Wittgenstein in some way. There were other businessmen whom he had driven into bankruptcy: angry shareholders of those competing businesses; workers seeking redress for long hours, low wages, and dangerous working conditions; socialist-anarchists who wanted to make an example of this ruthless American-style capitalist; consumers incensed at his monopoly pricing. All these in addition to a garden-variety kidnapper after money or a crazed anti-Semite. The list was long, Werthen knew.

By the time he reached the Karlsplatz, the sun had come out and the temperature had suddenly risen at least five degrees. Werthen was almost too warm in his heavy coat as he made his way to the back of the immense Karlskirche and on to the Alleegasse, home to many of the nouveaux riches of the empire. The last generation had seen construction of immense and ponderous city mansions throughout this neighborhood, not just in the Alleegasse, but in the intersecting Schwindgasse, all in the various historicist styles of the Ringstrasse. Here was an aggregation of wealth eager to show itself off. Neo-baroque mingled with neo-classic and renaissance styles. Amidst this milieu of ennobled industrialists was a smattering of town houses belonging to lower princes and even an archduke – though it was said the archduke in question was in attendance there far less frequently than was his mistress.

As Werthen turned into the Alleegasse he could see, beneath the now melting snow on the cobblestone street, that straw had earlier been spread. As he progressed up the street, he saw that the dried stalks extended for several blocks. It was a Viennese custom to spread straw to muffle the traffic noise for those of wealth, power, and/or prominence who had been taken ill.

The Palais Wittgenstein was an impressive, if dour town house of two floors, its banks of second-story windows seeming to frown down on the Alleegasse while the bottom floor presented a fortress-like appearance. The façade was at least fifty paces in length. Werthen entered through a pair of heavy oak doors, behind which a *Portier* was stationed and directed him via a forecourt with an impressive fountain and ample grillwork to an entrance hall huge and imposing. The floor was done in mosaic, the walls in carved paneling. Frescoes also adorned the space as did a statue, which Werthen thought might be the work of the French sculptor August Rodin. He passed through stone arches and went up six marble stairs to glass double doors. There he was met by a liveried servant who led him up the central red-carpeted marble stairway to the second floor and ultimately into Karl Wittgenstein's study, appointed in the most opulent gilt furnishing Werthen had seen outside a museum. Incongruously, modern paintings hung on the red plush walls, artists from Vienna and Munich, with Klimt prominent among them. On an immense carved walnut desk in the middle of the room were several small sculptures, obviously the work of Rodin. A fire pulsed in an open porcelain fireplace.

Wittgenstein sat at the desk, a bear of a man, who seemed even larger once he stood to greet Werthen, offering a crushing handshake. The man's dark hair was cut short (and perhaps dyed at the temples) and he wore a thick black moustache. He appeared much younger than his fifty-two years, wearing a frock coat, striped silk vest, maroon paisley bow tie under a fresh collar, and sporting spats – the newest fad from America. Werthen could not stop his eyes from traveling to these white canvas shoe coverings; for him they were too similar to the splatterdashes he had worn as a youth to protect his riding boots from mud to be considered high fashion. But fancy young men from Manhattan to Paris were wearing them this season, and it seemed Karl Wittgenstein or his tailor had decided to join the throng. It was hardly a fashion statement Werthen would have credited the man of business with.

'Your good friend Klimt sings your praises,' Wittgenstein said as he finally released Werthen's pummeled hand. The man's voice was deep and booming.

'He is too kind,' Werthen said, sitting in the pale-blue Louis Quinze chair Wittgenstein waved him toward. The industrialist sat in a matching chair, facing him, and crossed his legs by placing his right ankle over his left knee, American style.

'I suppose he's filled you in on the commission?'

'He mentioned a missing son.'

'*Mein Gott.* Hardly missing in the strictest sense. But he hasn't shown up for work in a week. He's the manager of mining interests at my Vienna offices on Kolowatring. Lord knows what the boy's thinking of. Always did have his head in the clouds. Wanted to be a musician of all things.'

Werthen registered this, but was not yet ready to follow the path of inquiry that comment might lead to.

Instead, he said, 'Perhaps we could review the facts. When was it first noticed that your son was missing?'

'Well,' the big man re-crossed his legs, 'Poldi, my wife, remarked last Tuesday, I believe it was, that Hans had not taken his dinner with us as is our custom. He is single, you see, and has a suite of rooms here. Then I found out from Prohaska, the second in command at the mining division, that Hans was not there on the Monday, either. No message. Nothing.' Wittgenstein shook his head. 'No sense of responsibility.'

The age-old complaint, Werthen thought: The younger generation is going to the dogs. Parents had been complaining of it since ancient Greece.

'Perhaps I might speak with your wife after we are finished here?'

Wittgenstein shook his head so violently that jowls, until now undetectable, shook.

'Afraid she is indisposed. Worry over her son has brought on migraine.'

Which, Werthen now understood, explains the straw in the street outside.

'I must be blunt, Advokat Werthen. It is because of Poldi that I have summoned you. She needs the reassurance.'

'And you, sir?'

'It's obvious, isn't it? The boy's taken himself off for a fling. I did the same thing myself when my father insisted I go into his property management. Ran off to New York and played guitar in a saloon for a year before I came back home, tail partly between my legs. I hardly credit Hans with the temerity to run off to the New World, though. He's probably holed up with some sweet young thing in the Inner City. Just trying to show his independence. But he'll be back. In the end, he's a Wittgenstein. We know our duty.'

Werthen marveled at the man's self-assurance. He could only imagine his own emotions were a child of his to go missing for a week.

'Has your son been missing before?'

'Skipped the odd lesson, I should say. My children are educated at home. The best instructors. Hans would hide out from Latin lessons to play his piano. Poldi, you see. She is a great one for the music. All the children play instruments. Other than that, no...'

The statement had the tone of uncertainty.

'Nothing?' Werthen pursued.

'The blasted Theresianum. I blame that school.'

The Theresianum was the most prestigious *Gymnasium* or preparatory school in Vienna. It was called the 'knights' academy,' for Empress Maria Theresa had established it in the eighteenth century to educate the young aristocrats of the realm to become administrators and political leaders. The nobles were still the only ones admitted as boarding students; the bourgeoisie had been permitted admittance as day students for the last half-century. Jews, assimilated or not, rarely gained entrance. Werthen knew this only too well; he himself had been denied admission. In any case it had not been *his* wish to attend the snobbish Theresianum, but rather his parents'. He had felt great relief being forced to attend the more liberal and secularized Akademische Gymnasium leading up to his entrance to the University of Vienna.

Werthen figured that Wittgenstein must have paid very dearly indeed to get his child into the exclusive school. He most likely pulled in debts of all sorts from influential colleagues and far-flung relations to win that coup.

'You said your children were educated at

home.'

'Yes, well, Hans did mope about so that I relented in his case. Allowed him to study at the Theresianum for two years. He fell into bad company there. It was then he began digging in his heels about going into the family business.'

Just as you had earlier, Werthen wanted to remind the man, but knew it was not his place to do so.

Herr Wittgenstein paused for a moment, then said, 'Ultimately, they chucked him out. Missed his lessons, forever playing the piano.'

'Anyone in particular?' Werthen asked.

Wittgenstein shot him an uncomprehending look.

'The bad company Hans fell into.'

'How should I know?' Herr Wittgenstein said with sudden impatience. 'I was engaged in business at the time. But it was then he started his campaign to become a composer. I told him to leave the composing for Sundays, but he became even more sullen than before. You would think the masters at the Theresianum would have knocked some sense into the boy. After all, one paid enough for the education.'

There followed a momentary pause. 'I don't want to take up more of your valuable time, Advokat Werthen.' Wittgenstein stood, smoothing down his trousers as he did so. 'I'll let you get on with it. I can pay a retainer now, or—'

'That won't be necessary, Herr Wittgenstein. We will talk about fees after I find your son. I *will*, however, need to speak to other members of the family and domestic staff.'

'Certainly. Meier will direct you. The servant who showed you in. Knows his way about the house, does Meier. Been with us since we moved here from the Schwarzenbergplatz in ninety-one.'

Wittgenstein moved to the door and pressed a small ringer. The door soon opened, revealing the same liveried servant who had shown Werthen to the study.

'Meier, please take our guest to Fräulein Mining. She should be in the conservatory now.'

Then to Werthen: 'That is my oldest child, Hermine. She is the family brick, the one to go to in times of crisis. She can give you the lay of the land here. Tell you who's who and what's what, if that is any help. She can show you Hans's room and all that. There's Kurt as well. A year younger than Hans and of a more sensible nature. Then Rudi, a younger brother. But he's a dreamer, like Hans. Wants to be an actor. He'll be a fine director one day. And I do not mean of the theatrical sort. I don't know if they can help you in your inquiries. They tell their mother they know nothing of Hans's whereabouts.'

'Thank you, Herr Wittgenstein.' Werthen was about to follow Meier out of the room, but decided on one final attempt to get through to the man.

'You'll pardon me for saying so, but you do not seem troubled by this disappearance,' he said.

Wittgenstein, about to sit again at his desk, seemed surprised by the statement, then irritated.

'Troubled? Why ever should I be? Young

scoundrel's probably off with a pretty girl, like I said.'

'There have been no ransom demands? No communication?'

Wittgenstein's face reddened. 'Why should there be?' He was like a patient diagnosed with cancer yet unwilling to take it seriously.

'You keep mentioning some pretty young thing. Was Hans having an affair?'

'I have no idea. That is Hans's business. He is, after all, a young man. And please do not ask Mining such a question.'

'This may not be the appropriate time for decorum, sir. Your son's been missing for over a week.'

'I really must attend to certain matters, Advokat. If you will excuse me. Meier, Advokat Werthen wishes to see my daughter now.'

Four

Meier led Werthen on an abbreviated tour of the house as they made their way back downstairs and past the famed Musiksaal, where the Wittgensteins held their fabled musical evenings, with everyone from Brahms to Mahler performing for the family and guests. Werthen caught a glimpse of it as they passed, the walls covered in hunting tapestries, the floor an intricate parquet pattern, two Bösendorfer grand pianos situated with keyboard facing keyboard in the center of the room, a large bust of Beethoven standing at one end. But Meier cleared his throat at Werthen playing tourist, and they continued via a large sitting room, its walls covered in paintings from Rudolf von Alt, Segantini, and more from Klimt.

By the time they reached the conservatory, Werthen felt overwhelmed by material wealth. Meier remained quiet throughout their perambulation, and once they arrived at the door to the conservatory, he was obviously prepared to leave Werthen to his business.

'You are well acquainted with young Hans Wittgenstein, I assume?' Werthen asked as the servant was about to leave.

Meier cast Werthen a questioning look. 'I have been with the family for quite some time.' He was a lean, slight man whose thin calves looked faintly ridiculous in the sheer white stockings he wore.

'That is not what I asked,' Werthen said.

'Yes, I have known Herr Hans since he was a boy.' But he offered no more.

'Let us understand one another,' Werthen said. 'I have been employed by Herr Wittgenstein to find his oldest son. You can confide in me. The more information I have, the more effective I will be.'

Still the servant remained silent.

'Is he a happy young man?' Werthen asked.

A slight trace of amusement passed over Meier's wax-like face.

'You find the question somehow humorous?'

'Happiness is not the primary goal of the Wittgensteins,' Meier responded in a monotone. 'But if you are wondering if the young man has been exceedingly despondent of late, I am clearly not the one to ask. I am a servant here, not a familiar. Decorum is exercised. Fräulein Hermine can, I am sure, better aid you in your inquiries.'

With that, Meier abruptly turned and left Werthen to make his own way into the conservatory.

Which he did, meandering through rows of potted palms and giant banana and elephant ear plants, making his way toward brighter light. Eventually he saw a young woman standing at a table under an atrium light well, the stained glass above her an elegant Jugendstil design of geometric shapes and swirls. The table was covered in cut flowers, and the young lady was busy making arrangements of them. She was dressed in a white blouse with a high neck, and a green tweed skirt that reached to the floor. Her brown hair was worn on top of her head.

'Fräulein Wittgenstein?' Werthen nodded at her as he approached.

She looked up from the red and white carnations she was arranging and smiled with quiet grace.

'You'll be the detective Klimt sent.'

'Private inquiries agent,' he said.

'Comes to the same thing, doesn't it?' Another winning smile, but with an edge. Her greenish-blue eyes were flecked with gold.

Werthen did not feel like quibbling. It seemed that even when the Wittgensteins were being friendly, they were difficult.

'What do you think happened to Hans?'

This abrupt shift did not throw her. She continued clipping flower stems with a pair of ivory-handled secateurs.

'I think he just needs a little vacation.'

'He couldn't wait for August?'

She shook her head, as if gently reprimanding his levity. 'Hans is a sensitive young man.'

'Your father mentioned his dreams of a musical career. Might that figure in his disappearance?'

'He has not disappeared. He is *somewhere*, we just do not know where.'

'He said nothing to his other siblings?'

She shook her head, more adamantly this time, and resumed clipping stems.

'Do you know any of his friends?' Werthen

45

asked finally.

'I can't say I do, Advokat Werthen. If you must know, Hans and I are not all that close. In age, yes, but not in temperament.' Another shake of the head. 'I am, in fact, closer to the second group.'

'How do you mean?'

'Sorry. Family nomenclature. Six of us children were born between 1874 and 1882. Myself, then Hans – actually, Dora next, but she died at birth – Kurt, Lenka – that's Helene – Rudi, and Gretl. Six years later Pauli was born, and then the next year, Luki – little Ludwig, the baby of the family. The little ones and I are very close.'

'I see.' But he did not at all. Or if it had any bearing on the whereabouts of Hans Wittgenstein. No nickname for him, Werthen noted. Or for brother Kurt.

'Is Hans close with his brothers? Perhaps he mentioned something, anything, that might give us a lead?'

'You're free to ask them, of course. We all live at home still. None of us has taken the dreaded marital step. But I doubt it will do you any good. No one seems to know where he is.'

She finished the arrangement of red and white carnations, laid down the secateurs, and took off her white gardening gloves.

'I expect you will want to see his rooms.'

'If I may.'

'It's back up the stairs again, then. We are a family that believes in exercise.'

She moved off briskly and Werthen trailed behind as she led him on another route, avoiding the main staircase and instead taking a narrow circular flight of stairs to the second floor. He saw the door to Herr Wittgenstein's study, but they turned the opposite direction, into a maze of hallways that totally disoriented Werthen. Fräulein Hermine finally opened the door to a corner room that was expansive and bright. A grand piano, yet another Bösendorf, sat in one corner. The room was simply appointed with oak furniture, but the walls were almost totally covered with framed posters announcing musical performances.

She waited as Werthen went through the drawers of a writing desk, looking for loose papers, a journal, any clue as to where Hans might have gone. He inspected the books in a glass-fronted bookcase: Schopenhauer, Marx, even the disturbing German Nietzsche was there. Also bound volumes of the plays of Arthur Schnitzler, and surprisingly, several of the red-covered volumes of Karl Kraus's review of popular culture, *Die Fackel*. Surprising, because Kraus had pilloried Karl Wittgenstein as a grubbing capitalist on more than one occasion in his review. Or perhaps it was not so unexpected if Hans and his father had little love for one another.

Werthen thought momentarily of his own brother Max, six years Werthen's junior. He was sensitive, unstable, and despairing of the fact that his parents demanded that he study law at the university rather than attend the Academy of Fine Arts, his fondest wish. Max had written to Werthen, then just beginning his criminal law practice in Graz and less than sympathetic with his younger brother's dreams of becoming a painter. After all, he himself had entertained dreams of becoming a writer, but ultimately found time for scribbling before and after his day of legal work. Surely Max could balance his dreams with practicality, too.

Early one autumn morning in 1888, while in Vienna with his parents for the university inscription, Max made off from their hotel near the Habsburg summer palace of Schönbrunn, climbed the slope of Maxingstrasse past the home of the Waltz King, Johann Strauss, and soon reached the Hietzing Cemetery. Before leaving Hohelände, the family estate in Upper Austria, Max had taken a revolver out of the gun cabinet. Now, in Vienna, he found the grave of the Austrian playwright Franz Grillparzer. Lying on the damp marble slab, he inserted the cold metal of the gun barrel into his mouth and pulled the trigger.

Had Hans sought the same way out? Werthen would need to check with the city morgue for recent corpses. Not something, however, that he would discuss with the family just yet.

After a full half-hour, he was satisfied that there was nothing in the room to provide him with a clue as to the whereabouts of its occupant.

'You really did not answer my earlier question, Fräulein Wittgenstein.'

'No? What was that?'

'About your own theory. A vacation. But any idea where? I assume your family has more than one abode?'

'Yes. We have a villa on the Neuwaldegger-gasse here in Vienna and a summer home at Hochreit, in Bohemia. We of course have inquired at both. The caretakers assure us that Hans has been at neither residence in months.'

'Very good. And the siblings, are they at home now?'

'Kurt is surely at the office. I can give you his address and telephone number. But I believe Rudi has come down with a slight grippe. You can find him in his room. Lenka and Gretl are at dance class this morning.'

'And the second group?'

'Oh, I hardly see how they can help.'

'Perhaps you will let me decide that.'

This comment set a muscle twitching spasmodically in her left jaw. Underneath her studied air of calm *noblesse oblige*, Hermine Wittgenstein seemed to be made of the same hard stuff as her father.

'Shall we begin with Rudi, then?' she offered.

The brother's room was removed by one hallway. She tapped at the door, but did not bother waiting for a response before she opened it to reveal a young man in a black and red silk Chinese robe lounging on a day bed, reading what looked to be the script of a play. The youth peered over the edges of the script and frowned to see his sister and a visitor. The expression made the wispy moustache he sported wrinkle like a troublesome caterpillar.

'A fellow does like a bit of privacy,' he said in a rather high voice.

As they drew nearer, Werthen could see a title

49

on the script: *Reigen.*

He had heard about this privately printed play by Schnitzler. Supposed to be extremely racy, all about the sexual goings on of ten different characters, five men and five women. The pairings go round and round from one character to another like a circle dance. His wife Berthe had been trying to find a pirated copy of the play, but with no luck. Hermine Wittgenstein was clearly oblivious of such things, and Rudi, for his part, seemed to count on this ignorance, for he did not bother to hide the script or its title.

'You had better not let Father catch you reading such things,' she said, as if she had read Werthen's mind and wished to prove him wrong. 'This gentleman is here to inquire after Hans.'

She made introductions, and Rudi rose from his couch long enough to shake hands limply, exchange names, and then resume his sickbed.

'Must forgive me, Advokat. It's bronchitis.' He coughed theatrically.

'I thought you told Meier it was grippe,' Hermine said in a brittle voice.

He waved a delicate hand at the objection. 'An illness of some sort. You may not want to get too close.' Then to Werthen, 'How do you propose to track your man, counselor?'

'I was hoping you could be of assistance in that.'

'Me?' Rudi took great delight in this, cackling until an actual coughing fit overcame him. His sister went to his side, pounding him on the back with enough force to make the young man wince.

'Jesus, Mining. Never go into nursing. I am not a lump of dough to be pummeled.'

'Do you have any information that might help Advokat Werthen?' She said this with not the slightest trace of humor or goodwill.

'I am afraid I am not my brother's keeper, Herr Werthen,' he said, his voice trailing away in a languishing tone.

Thereafter Werthen quickly ascertained that there was little information to be gotten from Rudi. He was much too immersed in his own human drama to notice what was happening with his older brother.

'I told you so,' Fräulein Wittgenstein said as she closed the door behind them. 'Hans kept to himself.' A beat. 'Keeps to himself,' she corrected.

Of the younger brothers, Werthen was only able to speak with Ludwig, for Paul was at a piano lesson with the well-known blind composer and pianist, Joseph Labor. Ludwig, or Luki, was in his room on the same floor – all the children had their own rooms, spacious enough for sleeping and work space. The somewhat chubby youngster was dressed in a navy suit and short pants and was busy at a woodworking table when Werthen and Hermine entered.

'About finished?' she asked.

'Oh yes,' the ten-year-old bubbled. 'And it is going to work, you'll see.'

'I am sure it will.' His older sister beamed at him. Then to Werthen, 'He's making an exact copy of a Singer sewing machine. In wood.'

'A *working* copy,' the boy emphasized.

51

There was a tapping at the door. Meier was standing outside the room when Hermine opened the door.

'There you are, Fräulein,' the servant said, sounding relieved. 'It's your mother. She's been asking for you. I think she needs more drops.'

Hermine Wittgenstein seemed upset by this at first, but quickly covered her irritation.

'I will be back shortly, Advokat. And Luki, see if you can help this gentleman track down your wandering brother Hans.'

'I'll do what I can,' Ludwig said earnestly to her retreating back.

'You're an engineer, then,' Werthen said once the sister was gone.

'Like my father,' the boy said. 'The others play music. I build. Well, that's not exactly true. Gretl is quite pitiful at the piano. Mother is always telling her how she has no sense of rhythm at all.'

'No instruments for you, then?' Werthen took a liking to the boy, obviously intelligent but not obnoxiously precocious.

'I play around with the violin, but no, not really. Not like Hans or Paul. They have real talent. Hans could play the violin and piano when he was still a toddler. By four he was composing. Me, I could still barely speak when I was four.'

He stated this astounding fact with a real sense of pride.

'Maybe you did not have anything to say.'

Ludwig smiled brightly. 'That's exactly what Mining says. Father calls her a brick. What do

52

you think, Advokat?'

'Solid as the Parthenon.'

'Yes.' The boy affixed one last piece of wood to his model, and then wound up a spring. Soon the contraption was humming along like an actual sewing machine.

'See. I told you. A *working* model.'

'Can you help me at all about your brother?'

Ludwig looked up from his masterpiece and shook his head. 'I wish I could. I miss him.' The spring wore down and the machine stopped.

'Did he ever mention having a room somewhere?'

'His room is here,' the young boy said. 'He was a child prodigy, you know. Another Mozart. All the teachers said so. But Father wants him to go into the business. Father usually gets his way.'

Suddenly the young boy looked intently at Werthen: 'I do not think Vati will demand my assistance in the company, do you, Advokat Werthen?' And then, without waiting for an answer, 'You really must find him. Hans is the best of us. He is special. And different. In *many* ways.'

Hermine Wittgenstein returned at that moment, reminding Luki it was time for his Latin lesson. The boy rolled his eyes, demonstrated his model for her, and then was off to the schoolroom.

Leaving the boy's room, Werthen had Fräulein Wittgenstein give him the business address and phone number of brother Kurt, as well as a description of the missing man: about five foot

53

ten inches and one hundred and fifty pounds. Dark hair, brown eyes, clean shaven and close-cropped hair, which had recently become the mode for the artistic types. They descended the main staircase and after much prodding, Hermine went to a sitting room and removed a framed photograph from an end table. It was a recent photograph of Hans, decked out in summer white linen, from a family portrait taken the previous August at their Neuwaldeggergasse villa. Back row, third from the right.

Hans was most definitely not a carbon copy of his bullish father; instead, he had the ascetic look of a monk on his face. He was staring off into the distance as the other members of the family were saying *'bitte'* into the camera.

'I would like the photograph returned when you are finished,' Fräulein Wittgenstein said without emotion. Then, as Werthen was about to leave, 'I suppose you will need it at the city morgue. For identification purposes.'

'It hasn't come to that yet,' he said. A half-lie. 'It helps to have visual identification when interviewing people. A name means little to people, a face much more.'

Then, after a quick salutation from Fräulein Hermine and an admonition to please find her brother 'for mother's sake,' Werthen was on his way.

Out on the street, it had warmed even more and the snow had almost completely melted, making for a slushy and quite miserable walk. As he picked his way along the sidewalk he thought of the youngest brother, Ludwig, and his final comment about his brother Hans being different in *many* ways.

It was a strange comment, Werthen thought, and piqued his curiosity about the missing Wittgenstein. After not speaking for the first four years of his life, young Ludwig obviously picked his words carefully.

So Hans was not simply different because of his musical skill and dreams, his desire to be an artist in a family of business people. Different how?

Five

Werthen was unsure of his next move. There were several avenues of investigation open to him. As Fräulein Wittgenstein suggested, he would need to check at the city morgue in the cellar of the Allgemeines Krankenhaus, Vienna's General Hospital, to find a likely candidate for the corpse of Hans Wittgenstein, possible victim of an accident, suicide, or homicide. Or he could pay a visit to the Wittgenstein office on Kolowatring to speak with brother Kurt. A third possibility was a meeting with the director of the Theresianum.

According to Herr Wittgenstein, Hans had fallen into bad company at that exclusive school. If he had made friendships, they would carry on throughout his life, for that was the way of the exclusive Theresianum. Its alumni continued to use the familiar *du* form with one another, even if one had become a minor bureaucrat and the other a Finance Minister. Though Hans had not graduated, he *had* spent two years at the place, long enough to forge friendships that lasted. Long enough perhaps to have a friend who might give Hans Wittgenstein a refuge, a home away from home.

As he was only a block or two away from the

Theresianum, Werthen decided to start there. He headed down the Alleegasse, away from the center of the city for one block, and then turned on to Taubstummengasse to its intersection with the busy Favoritenstrasse, where he turned right. He walked about a hundred meters along the immense three-story classicist front of the old Favorita to its main entrance. The Favorita was a former imperial summer palace converted in 1746 into a school. Werthen knew that the Jesuits were at first put in charge of the pedagogy, later to be replaced by the other Catholic teaching order, the Piaristen, the Pious Ones. Reforms in the 1850s put the educational system under state control and for the most part replaced clerics with professors, each trained in an area of specialization.

As he entered the portals of the school, a priest in black cassock with a cincture or sash around the waist scurried through the entrance past him, books hugged to his chest. Werthen had not seen him on the street; it was as if the priest had appeared out of nowhere and was headed like the rabbit in Alice's tale to some mysterious destination. The black cassock always gave Werthen a faint chill, just as did the long *payot* or side locks of the Hasidic Jews one saw in the Second District. Both so strange to the secular Werthen, bespeaking a life not just foreign, but other-worldly.

Obviously not all the priests had been replaced at the Theresianum.

The weather may have warmed up, but still it was chill enough to necessitate a coat. This priest seemed, however, in too much of a hurry to bother with such earthly necessities as winter apparel. Even his head was bare, his long hair ruffled in the morning breeze.

A sudden sweet smell of water was carried on the breeze, and made Werthen involuntarily smile as he proceeded through the gateway to the inevitable *Portier*'s booth. Through the other end of the arched entryway, Werthen saw rolling lawns under a mantle of melting snow and more ochre buildings, all part of the former summer estate. A flagpole in the central lawn bore a flag with a Habsburg eagle hanging at half-mast.

'You have an appointment, sir?' the aged *Portier* asked Werthen, bringing him out of his momentary reverie.

Werthen turned toward the old man, looking at a face covered with age spots, at eyes rheumy and squinting.

'I would like to speak with the director.'

The old man squinted even harder. He was wearing a blue uniform with red piping and brass buttons with a high rough collar. A patch of eczema showed under his Adam's apple.

'No appointment?'

'No,' Werthen said, quickly improvising. 'But I was hoping to make an endowment to the school. You do take endowments, no?'

This got the fellow hopping. He peered out of his glass cage and saw a young apple-cheeked student hurrying to class.

'You there, Trautman,' he called out to the blue-uniformed student through his window.

The boy stopped and turned reluctantly toward

the *Portier.*

'Yes, sir,' he said.

'Go see the headmaster. Tell him we have a visitor who wishes to make an endowment.'

'But I have Greek seminar now.'

'Do as I say, Trautman. Time for Greek later. An endowment, remember.'

The boy turned on his heels and headed to a staircase just past the old man's lodge.

It took the youth only a few minutes to deliver the message and return in a clatter of footsteps down the stone stairs and over the cobbled entryway.

'Master says to send the gentleman up,' he said through gasps of breath.

The *Portier* nodded at the boy, who did not move for a moment.

'Well, what are you waiting for, boy? Off with you. You've got lessons. And don't be late again.'

The old man was such an exact replica of the *Portier* at Werthen's *Gymnasium* that it took him back to his own school days. Koller was that man's name, and as he always reeked of garlic from his favored type of wurst, everyone called him *Knoblauch.*

'Herr Doktor von Dohani is waiting, sir.'

'Yes,' Werthen said, shaking off the memory. 'The staircase here, I assume?'

He indicated the one that the boy Trautman had used.

'Top of the stairs, to your left,' the *Portier* said.

'Tell me,' Werthen said on sudden impulse. 'Do they have a *Spitzname* for you?'

'This is the Theresianum, sir. Nicknames are for the other academies.'

'To be sure,' Werthen said, trying to conjure what the students here might be calling him. 'Old Spotty' came to mind, or 'Weepy,' perhaps.

On his way up the stairs Werthen tried to determine how he was going to explain his ruse to the disappointed Herr Doktor von Dohani. In the event, it was not necessary, for the director, a portly man with a halo of ginger hair and nose as purple as a plum, seemed to mistake Werthen for one of his students' fathers.

Werthen courteously explained as he sat in a leather club chair rather out of place with the rococo decoration of the office. Von Dohani sat opposite him, a slice of shiny ivory skin showing beneath his gray serge trousers. Werthen introduced himself and his legal profession. 'It's about the Wittgenstein boy.'

'Wittgenstein,' the director repeated, peering up at the gilt work on the white ceiling in an attempt at recollection. 'I know the name, of course, but I am not aware we have one of the children as a student here.'

'Had,' Werthen said. 'I was hoping you might be able to direct me to a prefect who knew him when he was here, about three years ago. Hans Wittgenstein is the name.'

'Well, I am not quite sure I recall that name. I was here three years ago, of course. But we have so many boys.'

'He was a day student.'

Von Dohani's lips mouthed a silent 'Oh,' as if that explained it all. He nodded his head in understanding. Not a noble student, then.

'That will fall under the purview of Mickelsburg. He makes a special project of the day boys. Not exactly a prefect, mind you, as the day students have no need of one. An advisor of sorts.'

'Might one speak with Herr Mickelsburg?'

'Is there some difficulty? I mean, you are an *Advokat* after all.'

Werthen smiled reassuringly. 'No. No difficulty. Just checking references.'

Another understanding nod of the head from von Dohani. The director rose from the chair, crossed to his desk and checked a large chart that occupied one corner.

'You're in luck,' he said brightly. 'You'll find him in the masters' lounge for his tea.'

Werthen took the directions to the lounge. As he was leaving, he overheard von Dohani speaking to his male secretary:

'You can send up that chap about the endowment now.'

Werthen went back down the stairs and out into the central yard quickly, hoping to avoid notice by the *Portier.* He crossed the yard to a somber little building tucked under a copse of bare horse chestnut trees. This looked to be a former carriage house converted into a lounge for the professors. The door entered directly into one large salon, part library and part dining hall, whose walls were covered in floor-to-ceiling oak bookcases stocked with uniform titles bound in leather. By the tidy looks of the volumes – everything from the works of Herodotus to Kant

– none of the tomes had been recently excavated from their positions on the shelves.

An elderly man sat at a table near the door, professorial-looking if ever Werthen had seen a professor: thickly bearded, rimless glasses, rumpled suit, his concentration fixed upon the print of the thick book spread out before him on the table.

Werthen approached silently, standing in front of the man for a moment before clearing his throat.

'Herr Professor Mickelsburg?' he asked in a near whisper.

The man did not look up immediately, so immersed was he in his reading. Then he suddenly noticed Werthen standing in front of him and put body and question together.

'Mickelsburg? No, heavens no. That's him over there. And it is Father Mickelsburg, not Professor. Teaches mumbo-jumbo.'

He was indicating a youngish man seated at a table in the far corner of the room. Werthen was surprised to note it was the priest who had hustled past him at the entryway.

He thanked the nameless pedant, but the man was already back to his book, and merely grunted in reply. The professor had lifted the book as if to cover his face. It was a copy of Darwin's *The Origin of Species*.

This time Werthen was less timid as he addressed the young man in the corner.

'Sorry to bother you during your tea, Father Mickelsburg.' The priest had a half-eaten piece of *Apfelstrudel* in front of him next to a large glass of buttermilk. 'Herr Doktor von Dohani suggested I speak with you.'

The priest looked up with large, curious eyes. 'About?'

'May I sit down?'

'Please. Forgive my bad manners. I was just eviscerating this bit of pastry.'

Werthen introduced himself and asked, 'What can you tell me about Hans Wittgenstein?'

This seemed to amuse Mickelsburg. 'The abbreviated or long version?'

'Whatever you can tell me.'

'Has he got himself into trouble then?'

'Not trouble. I am just doing some reference checking.'

'For employment? I assumed he was going – kicking and screaming mind you – into his father's business.'

'It is complicated,' Werthen said.

'I have the feeling, Advokat, that you are not being quite honest with me. I am young, but I have developed a sixth sense for artifice. Priests and lawyers. We both deal with the lies of men.'

Werthen took a liking to the priest and felt that he could trust him.

'You're right. I was hired by Herr Karl Wittgenstein to find his son. I came here hoping to find out if Hans formed any friendships while a student here, someone with whom he might still be friends.'

'Ergo, someplace that he might be hiding now?'

'Exactly.'

'I didn't think he would be able to last long as

a man of business.' Mickelsburg drank his buttermilk off in one long swallow, and came up for air with a yellowish moustache. Werthen tapped his own upper lip, and the priest dabbed the residue with a napkin.

'Was there such a friend?'

'Hans was a unique young man even when a student here. He can play the piano with extreme felicity. Did Herr Wittgenstein tell you that?'

'I have become aware of the fact. There seems to be a bit of competition for his soul.'

Father Mickelsburg smiled at this. 'For his earthly ambitions, perhaps. I am not so sure about his soul. I was an advisor to him here, especially when he began to run into trouble academically. He did not take Greek and Latin quite as seriously as his instructors would have wanted. But he could make you weep with his interpretation of the "Emperor" Concerto. He was a most unique young man.'

'You have said that twice. What exactly do you mean?'

'You will discover that for yourself when you find him.'

'So you do not believe he has done himself harm?'

'Is he capable of suicide, do you mean?' The priest sniffed at the word as if it were a nasty smell. 'One never knows, does one? You see our flag outside, I assume.'

'Yes. I was wondering...'

'In memory of one of our illustrious alumni. He took his own life rather than face public scandal. One would hardly credit him with such a sense of drama as to end his own life.'

'Are you referring to Councilman Steinwitz?'

Mickelsburg nodded his head solemnly. 'Yes. A great tragedy. I of course was not part of the staff at the time, but the councilman was in the original classes of day students, along with our mayor. In fact, I understand from the old-timers that the two were great friends here. Such a friendship continued beyond these walls, as it often does. You yourself pointed that out.'

It was difficult to get away from the Steinwitz affair. It seemed to follow one everywhere, Werthen thought.

'But that was not your question,' Mickelsburg continued. 'I am not sure I can tell you what the young Wittgenstein is or is not capable of. He had a certain high sensitivity and temperament.'

The priest seemed to blush as he said this.

'Did he have a close friend?' Werthen again asked.

'Oh, yes. That he did. Another special young man, I should think.'

'Unique?' Werthen ventured.

'Yes, quite. Very close the two were. His name is Henricus Praetor.'

'Any relation to the surgeon?' Werthen asked.

A quick nod. 'Yes. The son. The only son, I believe. Another day student. I heard the young man became a journalist. Yes, they were very special friends.'

Werthen had made arrangements to eat lunch at home today. By the time he finished speaking with Father Mickelsburg, it was twenty past eleven, not enough time to follow any other leads this morning but quite enough for a leisurely walk to the Josefstadt.

He let his mind roam free as he walked, not concentrating on the missing Wittgenstein, but taking in the sights and sounds of this city he loved so. He found that dwelling over-hard on a case produced the same results as when one concentrated too hard on a word that escaped the memory: nothing. Rather, simply take your mind off the problem at hand for a moment, and new avenues open, solutions beckon. Thus by the time he reached his apartment house, Werthen had built up a fine appetite and a real eagerness to see his wife and child again, and more importantly had put the Wittgenstein matter completely out of his mind for a time.

He was full of expectancy as he put the key in the lock to his flat. The door opened from within at this very moment, and Frau Blatschky was there to greet him, a sour look on her face.

'*Mahlzeit*,' he said by way of greeting, but she did not look in the mood for either food or greetings.

He sighed, came inside, and closed the door behind him.

'What is it?'

His housekeeper suddenly broke into tears. He had seen her near to tears only once before, the morning before he fought a duel, and to see her openly weeping was disturbing, as if the emperor himself were breaking down in front of him.

'What?' he said again, and gingerly patted the

66

round little woman on her trembling shoulders.

'Your mother,' she sobbed. 'She said she was going to see that you replace me. Called me incompetent.' Further sobs. 'Me. Incompetent.'

'What in the world?'

At that moment Werthen's mother appeared in the doorway to the dining room.

'You are making rather a fuss out of nothing, Frau Blatky,' his mother said. He knew she had purposely mispronounced the woman's name.

'Blatschky, *Maman*. Frau Blatschky. And what have you been saying to her?'

He felt himself get hot with anger, and tried to regain control.

'Oh, she should be at the Burgtheater.' His mother attempted a light tone. 'Such a thespian.'

He was growing tired of repeating himself. 'What did you say?'

His father came into the hallway. 'That's not the tone of voice a young man should be using with his mother.'

Werthen let out a long sigh. Things had been so much nicer when they were all estranged.

'I merely said that your servant needs to run a tighter household,' Frau von Werthen said.

'Servant!' Frau Blatschky all but shrieked.

'My housekeeper, *Maman*,' Werthen said, anger seething beneath the surface like a lidded pot on boil.

'Servant, housekeeper, it comes to the same thing. I simply informed the woman that the table linen is not properly folded. At Hohelände we—'

'This is not your house, *Maman*. This is my

67

apartment and Frau Blatschky works for me.'

Now his mother began to sob and his father wrapped a consoling arm around her.

'Look what you've done now. My lord, is this the manners they teach you at the university?'

His father was so cut off from reality that it was as if he thought Werthen were still a student. He saw the complete futility of talking to them like rational beings. Instead, he patted Frau Blatschky on the back once more and sent her to the kitchen.

Then turning to his parents he calmly said, 'I am sorry for talking sharply. It has been a hectic morning for me. I was looking forward to lunch, not domestic drama.'

But that merely set both his parents off again, aggrieved that he accused them of being dramatic. The upshot of it was that they left in a huff.

His father said as he gathered coat and gloves, 'This is the thanks we get for wanting to be good grandparents. When you can keep a civil tongue in your head, you know where we are staying.'

He felt a small twinge of guilt as they left, but he could live with that. Of course later he would have to pay for these moments of freedom; would have to go to their hotel with flowers and chocolates and beg pardon for being rude. But for now, peace and bliss, and from the smells emitting from the kitchen, the promised special *Gulasch* of Frau Blatschky.

Entering the dining room, he saw that Berthe and her father, Herr Meisner, were already there. It was naptime for Frieda and so a pleasant lunch together was in the offing.

'Hello,' Werthen said as he came to his wife to peck her cheek. Only when she stiffened at his kiss did he recognize that the climate in the dining room was no better than it had been in the foyer.

'Your wife is as stubborn as a donkey,' Herr Meisner grumbled. With that, he got up and stormed out of the room. Herr Meisner, however, would not be going back to his hotel, for he was staying with them. In the past, such visits had been enjoyable. Now, however, it was one more added strain on their domestic calm.

Herr Meisner and his parents were like oil and water. At first meeting a few days ago, the von Werthens had taken one look at Herr Meisner's long, almost rabbinical beard, and another at his birth gift – a pair of silver rattles shaped like miniature dreidels – and it was as if they were sea turtles, pulling their necks back into their carapaces.

Herr Meisner, a successful shoe manufacturer from Linz, was also one of the foremost Talmudic scholars in Austria, while Werthen's parents, offspring, the both of them, of Jewish merchants and bankers, had hidden their Jewish ancestry away in a tightly locked pantry of family secrets. Baptized Protestants, they even had a 'von' to their name, earned in 1876, and which Werthen himself refused to use. He and Berthe both despised the hypocrisies of the Austrian social system and its so-called *Dienstadeln*, or service nobility, and were also quite indifferent to religious matters.

At tea the day of Herr Meisner's arrival, with

Berthe holding the gurgling Frieda in her lap, Werthen's parents queried, almost in a chorus, 'When is the baptism to be?'

It was as if somebody had broken wind in the august Musikvereinsaal. Silence reigned for a full minute, and then Werthen's mother began bubbling on about the guest list.

'We have no such plans,' Werthen said, hoping to head off what he sensed might quickly become a domestic crisis.

'No plans?' his father blustered. 'Why, boy, you can't raise the little darling as a heathen. Nor can you deny us the great fun of mounting a celebration. That is the prerogative of grandparents.'

Herr Meisner had cleared his throat at that moment. Werthen hoped for words of wisdom from this wise man who had become a true friend, but the adults just were not doing their job.

Looking at Berthe, Herr Meisner said, 'I was rather hoping you might decide to raise Frieda in the faith of your fathers.'

Berthe rolled her eyes and was about to comment with the biting sarcasm Werthen knew so well, when Herr Meisner, the scholar, the man of rectitude, common sense, and affability, added further oil.

'I know it is what your mother would have wished.'

Her mother had died when Berthe was ten. She never spoke of it, nor had Werthen ever heard Herr Meisner mention his deceased wife before.

Lines had been drawn after that. Tension ruled

the household.

Now Werthen sat gingerly as if there were a bomb under his chair. He unfolded his napkin and placed it in his lap.

'Aren't you going to ask?' Berthe said.

'I imagine you will tell me when you want to. Besides, I have already had my own domestic crisis.'

'He still insists on an *Aliya* for Frieda.'

Werthen looked at her blankly.

'A formal naming ceremony and blessing at a temple. He wants her to have a Jewish name, too.'

'Like you,' Werthen joked.

'But I actually do,' she said. 'I just never use it.'

'What is it?' Werthen asked, wondering for a moment what other things he did not know about his wife.

'Rachel.'

'A nice name. I suppose we could add Sara to Frieda's name. Or Ruth.'

'It is not the name, darling...'

He nodded. 'I know. Why can't our parents behave like adults?'

Frau Blatschky, her eyes still red, came with the *Gulasch* and they settled in to the meal, forgetting their troublesome parents for the time. Finally, Werthen mentioned the new case.

'Wittgenstein,' she said. 'Impressive clients.'

'One could get lost in their town house.' He went on to explain how far he had gotten in the investigation.

'So what do you think happened to the young

71

man?'

'I think this Herr Praetor may be able to clarify matters.'

'That name sounds familiar to me. Other than his surgeon father, I mean.'

'The priest at the Theresianum thought he may have gone into journalism.'

'Yes,' she said, putting her spoon down. 'That's where I've heard the name. He writes for the *Arbeiter Zeitung*.'

'An interesting place for a former student of the Theresianum to publish his articles.'

'Perhaps he is a displaced socialist, like your wife.'

Finally, Werthen was beginning to feel they had their life back. It was moments like this with Berthe that he longed for: the small teases, the familiarity, the communal understanding.

Six

After lunch, and after finding a few moments to dandle the just-awakened Frieda on his knee, Werthen returned to the Wittgenstein affair. He placed a telephone call to the Vienna city morgue and ascertained that there was one un-identified body that might fit the description as well as the time period that Werthen supplied. There was nothing for it but to go there in person and make a preliminary identification. If the body in question looked closely enough like Hans Wittgenstein, then he would have to get a family member to make a conclusive identification. He hoped it would not be so.

This afternoon he decided he had already had enough exercise and took an *Einspänner*, a cab drawn by one horse, to the General Hospital, in whose basement the city morgue was located. The snow was gone now, but the temperature was once again dropping. February could be a quarrelsome, unsettled month in Vienna with sudden and unaccountable changes in weather. Werthen enjoyed the three-four time the horse's hooves kept as he was rattled along the Ringstrasse to Alsergrund.

Since first coming to the morgue with his colleague and sometime collaborator, Doktor

Hanns Gross, in 1898, he had made his own personal connections with the director, the unfortunately named Doktor Starb. Tall and jovial, Starb, whose surname came from the past tense of *sterben*, to die, hardly looked the part of director of a morgue, dressed as he was nattily in a checked morning coat and butter-yellow tie, but when it came to death, he was all business. He took Werthen personally to the drawers of unclaimed bodies.

'This one was found at the harness racing track at Freudenau,' Starb explained as they entered the chill of the basement rooms. 'Poor chap seems to have been despondent about something. Though the track is closed down now for the winter, it could be a symbolic act. Perhaps he'd lost money on the races last fall.'

Werthen had neglected to ask about the means of death earlier and thus did not know it was a suicide. He hoped it was not a messy one; his stomach for gore was not the strongest.

Sensing Werthen's thoughts, Starb added, 'Shot himself. We'll examine the good side of the head. Who is it you're looking for?'

Werthen shrugged. 'The family does not wish to make it public.'

'Ahh,' Starb said. 'Important, then?'

'Prominent,' Werthen allowed.

He took the family photograph out of his pocket as Starb found the proper drawer and pulled it out. The corpse came out feet first, and Werthen saw that the body was about the proper height. He caught a flash of dark hair as the head, turned to one side, came into view. A slight moustache, as well. This was not how he had expected this to end.

He moved around the body, getting closer to the head and making sure he kept the photograph concealed from Starb, who would surely recognize Karl Wittgenstein in the family grouping.

Werthen bent over the head, looking closely at the face in profile. But having never met Hans Wittgenstein, he was not sure. The photograph he had was of a full face, but obviously the other side of this man's head had been shattered by the self-inflicted wound.

Still, he needed to ask. 'Is there a frontal view?'

Starb shook his head. 'Not so you would notice.'

'I'll need to make a telephone call.'

'Upstairs. I assume you never met the young man.'

'No,' Werthen said, watching the affable Herr Direktor carefully close drawer number sixty-three, and the corpse, covered in white, slide into the cooler once again. A strong aroma of ammonia accompanied the opening and closing, from the gas the morgue used in its refrigerating vapor compressor.

Starb discreetly left Werthen alone as the Advokat placed a call to Kurt Wittgenstein at the Kolowatring office. The decision seemed a simple one: he could not ask the father to come for the identification for fear he would be recognized. The other members of the family he had met, brothers Rudi and Ludwig, were not appropriate: Rudi was sick and Ludwig too young. And though the sister, Hermine, was termed a 'brick', Werthen did not want to bring a woman for such a job. Kurt Wittgenstein, however, was seemingly a man of business, a man who might be expected to have his wits about him.

Calling the number he was quickly connected with Kurt, who happily had been apprised of Werthen's commission by sister Hermine. There was a momentary pause when Werthen explained his request.

Then, his voice breaking on the first word, Kurt said, 'I'll be there in twenty-five minutes.'

In the event it took twenty. Kurt Wittgenstein looked ashen as he followed Werthen and a white-coated worker – for Starb had maintained his discretion – to drawer sixty-three. White coat looked at Werthen as if asking for permission to begin, but it was Kurt Wittgenstein who answered the silent request with a sharp nod of the head.

The drawer came out slowly, accompanied again by the burning smell of ammonia.

Werthen kept his eyes on Kurt Wittgenstein, looking for any sign of recognition as the corpse's head cleared the drawer frame.

Kurt looked at the dead man for several seconds, then took a deep breath.

'No,' he said finally. 'That is not my brother. Poor man.'

'I didn't think it would be Hans,' the brother said as they breathed in the fresh, crisp air outside the hospital. 'We Wittgensteins are not the type to take the easy way out.'

'Out of what?' Werthen asked.

'Well, just an expression, you know.'

'Do you have any idea where your brother might be, Herr Wittgenstein?'

'I would look for the nearest piano, if I were you. But no, seriously, I do not. Like my father, I am sanguine that Hans will come home soon. I assume dear Hermine has informed you of the family dynamics. Hans and I may only be a year apart in age, but we are vastly different people. For me, taking part in Father's business is far from onerous.'

'And for Hans? I gather he has musical aspirations.'

'Yes. He can tickle the ivories quite flamboyantly.' He paused momentarily. Then: 'You must forgive me, Advokat. I am not quite myself. I must confess your call and then seeing that unfortunate young dead man ... well, it has all rather unnerved me. I do not usually talk such piffle. We Wittgensteins pride ourselves on being music lovers. Brahms, Mahler – many have found our house welcoming.'

'It is understandable, Herr Wittgenstein. Any information you can give me would help. Do you know any of Hans's friends?'

'I wasn't aware he had any.'

Werthen waited for an ironic laugh, but Kurt Wittgenstein was being absolutely serious; no more piffle.

'Ever hear of a fellow named Praetor? Henricus Praetor? He and Hans were supposedly fast friends at the Theresianum.'

'Sorry, can't say I do. Is he in Vienna, this Herr Praetor?'

'I believe so.'

'Well, then. There you are.'

'Where?'

'Well, Hans has probably bivouacked in his old school friend's cramped accommodations. Praetor? Name does sound familiar now I think of it.'

'His father is the surgeon.'

'No, I had newspapers in mind. Something to do with the hapless councilman who killed himself.'

'Steinwitz?'

'Yes, that one.'

Again, the Steinwitz connection.

'I believe a fellow named Praetor was the journalist who first wrote about Rathaus shenanigans. We in the business community follow such things. Especially when they reach Mayor Lueger's confidants.'

Werthen nodded at this, knowing that he still had one more question for the brother, and was not sure how to broach it.

'I gather Hans was a very sensitive sort.'

Kurt Wittgenstein shrugged at this. 'Hardly against the law. Especially in Vienna. Nerves and the waltz. City specialties.'

'Those I have interviewed seemed to make a special emphasis of this sensitivity,' Werthen said, pushing the point.

Kurt chewed on his cheek for a moment, squinting at Werthen.

'I suppose if Father employed you, you are a

78

man to be trusted with family skeletons, Advokat.'

'Is that a question?'

Wittgenstein rubbed his chin. 'I believe my
brother is, as some put it, inverted, sexually
speaking.'

'Shy, you mean?' Werthen said. He knew the
phrase, but wanted to make sure.

'Undoubtedly. But more than that. Inclined to
one's own gender.'

Which explained the priest's embarrassment at
recalling Hans Wittgenstein's personality and
character.

'You're sure of this?'

Kurt Wittgenstein shrugged. 'We are not
terribly close as siblings, Hans and I.'

'Meaning he did not confide in you?'

A sharp nod of the head from Wittgenstein.
'But one has a sense about such things.'

It was a very worldly comment for a man like
Kurt Wittgenstein, who, frankly, appeared quite
unworldly to Werthen.

'I thank you for your candor, Herr Wittgenstein.'

'At least Hans picked someone near to his own
class.' Seeing Werthen's puzzlement, he added,
'This Praetor fellow. One assumes...'

A quick consultation of the current year's tele-
phone directory told Werthen that 'Praetor,
Henricus, Journalist' lived at Zeltgasse 8. The
Turks had set up camp on the site of this small
street, not far from Werthen's own home in the
Josefstadt, two hundred years earlier when

79

laying siege to the city for the second time. And for the second time, Vienna had proven the bulwark of Europe, turning the Muslim hordes back. The flowing tents of the enemy, however, gave the street its name – they were that close to the city walls.

Late afternoon and there was an off chance that Herr Praetor would be home this time of day. Herr Praetor was what was called a free-lance journalist. Werthen found this a rather inspired usage from the real meaning of the term, denoting a medieval mercenary. The irony in Praetor's case was that the original meaning was, in a way, apposite: the pen being mightier than the sword. At any rate, there was the possibility that Praetor, with no office to go to, might work at home rather than in his favorite café.

Werthen knocked once at flat fifteen. After a decent interval he administered a second series of raps. He heard footsteps approaching, felt rather than saw an eye being applied to the viewing lens built into the door, and then heard a bolt being freed. The man on the other side of the door as it opened was tall, thin, and aesthetic-looking, dressed something like a Turk himself, in a long silk smoking jacket with a fez on his head.

'Herr Praetor?' Werthen said.

'Do I know you?'

Werthen quickly dug out one of his cards from the inside pocket of his overcoat.

'Werthen,' he said. 'Advokat Karl Werthen. I have been employed by the Wittgenstein family.'

'How fortunate for you.' Said with an acid dryness and a slight sibilance.

This was clearly not going to be easy, Werthen realized.

'I wonder if I might come in?'

'Please yourself.' The young man turned and moved with elegant grace from the foyer to a sitting room that was a jumble of furniture of every style from a pine table in Alpine rustic to the heavy black bookcases of Alt Deutsch. Obviously young Praetor was not didactic when it came to furnishing. The same sort of happy serendipity seemed to inform the choice of reading matter stacked in piles and littering the room. Grillparzer mingled with Spengler, while Rilke rubbed shoulders with Stifter. Ernst Mach's *The Analysis of Sensations* found a place with Sigmund Freud's recently published *Interpretation of Dreams*. In one corner a large Regency desk in cherry wood was scattered with papers and a mammoth Regina typewriting machine.

Praetor cleared a scattering of books and journals from a sagging daybed.

'Do please have a seat.'

Werthen ignored the arch tone and, unbuttoning his overcoat, sat. The young man preferred to stand.

'I was employed to find Hans Wittgenstein.'

Praetor did not change his expression: one of somewhat bemused curiosity.

'Poor Hans. Gone missing, has he?'

'Then you do know him?'

'Would you be here if you doubted that?'

'His family is worried. Nothing has been heard from him or of him in over a week.'

Werthen ducked as he sensed a sudden movement toward his head. There was a flapping of wings close to his nose and when he looked back at Praetor, the young man held a golden parakeet in the cup of his right hand.

'Now Athena, that is no way to treat guests.' He set the bird on his shoulder. 'Birds are famously good judges of character. Seems she doesn't care much for you.'

Werthen was taken aback momentarily. 'You let the bird out of her cage from time to time?'

'This apartment is her cage, Advokat.'

Werthen looked around quickly for signs of bird occupancy.

'Not to worry. Athena is a most tidy bird. Now, I could offer you coffee. But then I do not think you will be staying that long.'

Werthen found Praetor tiresome rather than irritating. But he suddenly did not want to spar with him. Perhaps it was the pressure at home from both sets of in-laws; perhaps it was the solemnity of the visit to the morgue; perhaps it was the cheekiness of that damned parakeet lodged on his shoulder. Whatever the cause, Werthen suddenly lashed out at Praetor in the way he knew was sure to injure and frighten the young man.

'I assume you know that an antipathic sexual instinct, if indulged in, is still a criminal offense? No matter if it is between consenting adults or not.'

It was as if he had struck Praetor across the

82

face. The young man visibly winced, and pinched his eyes at Werthen in an expression of intense dread and hatred. The parakeet flew from his shoulder in a graceful arc into a room leading off the sitting room.

'What you and your friends do is no concern of mine,' Werthen pressed on. 'But I want to know about Hans Wittgenstein.'

Werthen heard his own voice, and was ashamed of himself. He had never before stooped to such moral blackmail. For blackmail it was: any whiff of such sexual impropriety in Vienna could find Praetor, if not behind bars, then definitely ostracized from the journalistic fraternity and from society in general. Men might keep mistresses, they might frequent the seediest brothels, they might even beat their wives regularly, but let it be said that a man had carnal lust for another man and his career was ended, his public reputation in shreds. The emperor himself had banished his younger brother, Archduke Ludwig Viktor, better known as 'Luzi Wuzi,' from Vienna for his affair with a masseur and peccadilloes at the Centralbad. Were Praetor's father to hear of his son's sexual predilections, he would in all likelihood disown the young man. Werthen was about to apologize, when Praetor suddenly found his voice.

'He was not my lover, if that is what you are saying. Hans Wittgenstein was not, regardless of what you may have heard from his family, a homosexual. I should know. I tried my utmost to convert him. He is, if anything, asexual. In love with his music. There's no room in his heart for mere mortals.'

As he spoke, Praetor seemed to find his courage again.

'The sanctimonious bourgeoisie such as yourself have labeled my sexual preferences a crime. I, however, do not. And it gives me great pleasure to tell you and that grasping father of his that Hans is now well out of the reach of his family.' A momentary pause. 'No, not as you imagine it, Advokat. He is too full of life and art to kill himself. Instead, he has set off to create a new life. He stayed here for two days last week, borrowed some money, and then caught the overnight train to Hamburg.'

'He has taken a liner?'

'Very good,' Praetor said with his arch tone once again firmly in place. 'You should be a private detective and not a mere inquiries agent. A liner for New York and a new world. He wanted me to come with him, his dearest friend. But you see, in the end I am a coward. Hans's life is music. He can make that anywhere. But mine is journalism. My language is not international. No. I settled for Vienna and a life lived in the shadows. Is that sufficient for you, Advokat?'

'I really must apologize, Herr Praetor. I would never divulge such information—'

'Do save the platitudes for your wife, if you have one.'

Praetor was a young man difficult to like, Werthen decided. Difficult even to empathize with.

'I thank you for your information. I shall

84

notify his family of his whereabouts.'

'He sailed four days ago. I greatly doubt the steamship company will allow their vessel to be diverted in mid-sailing, no matter how powerful Herr Karl Wittgenstein is.'

'He is of legal age and can go where he will,' Werthen said. 'The family was merely concerned for his safety.'

'I am sure they are. He's safer away from them.'

In the end, Werthen did not attempt again to put Praetor at ease vis-à-vis the possibility of scandal. It was obvious that any such overtures would only be met with derision. Neither did Werthen bother to thank him again.

Outside, it had darkened almost to twilight. Evening was upon the city, and a chill gripped Werthen as he walked along the cobbled sidewalk.

Not a bad day of work, he told himself.

A call to Herr Wittgenstein was not enough for the industrialist: he insisted on seeing Werthen in person in the morning.

'But please tell your wife tonight,' Werthen said. 'It seems rather sure that Hans is aboard the SS *Wertheim*.' For he had checked shipping schedules after leaving Herr Praetor's flat. 'The passenger manifest is not available yet, I'm afraid.'

'Manifest be damned,' Herr Wittgenstein thundered down the line. 'The boy's absconded. We shall speak tomorrow. Nine in the morning. Please be punctual.'

He hung up before Werthen had a chance to respond. Vexing, but not enough so as to put him off Frau Blatschky's fluffy *Germknödel*, steamed yeast dumpling, filled with plum jam and topped with poppy seeds, butter, and powdered sugar. He was thankful his mother was not in attendance for dinner, as she would surely raise an eyebrow at such rich fare for the new mother. Which reminded him that he would have to make amends to his parents soon.

Berthe ate like a prize racehorse, even indulging in a glass of white Gumpoldskirchen wine. Herr Meisner was also at table, but still awfully silent as a result of the ongoing tiff over the naming ceremony for Frieda, who was happily sleeping in the nursery.

In the end, Werthen and Berthe simply ignored the grumpy older gentleman and he told his wife about the outcome of this first case of the year – withholding the fact of what he could only term his cruelty toward Praetor. It was not something he was proud of, this tacit bit of extortion using the implied threat of revealing to the world Praetor's homosexuality. Still, the young man was a considerable irritant and he was happy to put the Wittgenstein family at ease regarding the oldest son.

Dinner ended not long before cries from the nursery let Berthe know her daughter was once again hungry.

Next morning, Werthen appeared at the Palais Wittgenstein at nine precisely, and was ushered up to the study by the servant, Meier.

Herr Wittgenstein was engrossed in paperwork

at his large desk as Werthen entered, though the man was supposed to be retired. He waved away the servant, and then nodded to a chair for Werthen.

'Fast work, Advokat.'

Werthen took this as a compliment and nodded, placing the photograph he had borrowed from Fräulein Hermine on the desk.

'I understand you gave Kurt a bit of a shock at the morgue.'

'I felt he would be the best to consult,' Werthen said tactfully.

'You were wrong, Advokat. I do not need to be handled like an over-sensitive child. You really should have mentioned your deeper concerns.'

'After a week with no word, it was a possibility. Also, I assumed you preferred a degree of anonymity.'

Wittgenstein let out a low grunt at this. Werthen did not know what it was supposed to signify.

'So he's taken himself off to New York. Just like his father.' Herr Wittgenstein seemed almost proud of Hans for the deed. Then, 'Are you absolutely sure?'

'A school friend loaned him money. He seemed awfully certain. We'll know for sure when the passenger manifest is released.'

'Is it this Praetor chap Kurt tells me of?'

'Henricus Praetor,' Werthen said. 'A journalist.' He wondered if the father shared Kurt's misbegotten assumptions about Hans Wittgenstein's sexual orientation. He did not want to have to deal with that question again. Happily, the elder

Wittgenstein was more interested in Praetor's journalism than his choice in partners.

'The man's a cad, if you ask me. Irresponsible yellow journalism that cost a fine man his life.'

Werthen was surprised by this sudden outburst, unaware that Wittgenstein was a friend of any sort to those in power in City Hall. It was not just Lueger and company's anti-Semitism, but also their scapegoating of big businessmen such as Wittgenstein that would seem to make them natural enemies.

'He'll be back,' Herr Wittgenstein said at length. 'I was full of myself and searching for "freedom" just like young Hans. I came back. So will he.'

Werthen was not so sure of this, but it was not his place to offer such opinions. Instead, he indicated that he had pressing business and rose to leave.

'A payment will be posted.'

Werthen nodded at this, even though there had been no discussion of fees. He was sure Wittgenstein would know what was appropriate.

He was led downstairs by Meier and in the entrance hall met with young Ludwig Wittgenstein again, just returning home it seemed, for he was dressed in quite a sporty loden coat with a fur collar and his cheeks were brilliant red from the cold air.

'Advokat Werthen. It is nice to see you again.'

'And you, as well, Master Wittgenstein.'

'Have you found our Hans for us?'

So the patriarch had not eased family minds the night before.

'He is on his way to America.'

Ludwig smiled brightly at this. 'Good for him. And for you for being so clever as to solve the mystery in one day.'

'Thank you. It has been a pleasure.'

Werthen was about to step out the door when Ludwig added, 'I hope to meet you again, sir. Under more favorable circumstances. It is now time for my Greek lesson, or I would show you another project I am embarked upon. A working model of Herr Daimler's motorcycle.'

A week later Klimt came to the office at eleven forty-five with a smile on his face and a money order in hand.

'Quite generous,' Werthen said, looking at the amount and happy he had not stated his fees.

'Herr Wittgenstein was most pleased. The family received a telegram from New York yesterday. It seems Hans is safe.'

'All's well, et cetera, et cetera. It's awfully good of you to hand-carry this for Herr Wittgenstein.'

'None of that,' Klimt blustered. 'I've come for my reward. A fine lunch at the Café Frauenhuber.'

Seven

It was an auspicious date, Werthen thought, the forty-sixth day of the new century. According to his *Brockhaus* encyclopedia there had been a number of important events that occurred on February 15. Socrates was sentenced to death on this day in 399 BC; Ferdinand III became Holy Roman Emperor in 1637; the Spanish-American War started two years ago. And now, February 15, 1900, he, Advokat Karl Werthen, was about to become a landowner.

To attempt to do so, at any rate.

It happened this way.

He and Berthe were avid walkers, and the Vienna Woods afforded them a myriad of favorite hikes. One in particular would take them by the village of Laab im Walde, a pleasant little crossroads with a *Gasthaus* that served some of the best *Reh* or venison Werthen had ever eaten. Across the road from this inn was an old four-square: a farmstead from the seventeenth century built in a square like a fort around a *Hof* or courtyard. The walls of the farm were painted a delicate shade of ochre, reminiscent of the faded golden yellow one saw at the Habsburg summer palace of Schönbrunn. On their last hike, before Berthe grew too close to her delivery date, Werthen had seen a sign posted at the gate to this old farmstead. It was a notice of public sale of the farmhouse and some of the adjoining land. Werthen had just the previous weekend taken another hike to Laab im Walde and discovered that the sign was still there.

I am a family man now, Werthen had reasoned. How fine to have a place nearby for weekends and summers. He could even imagine the Christmas holidays that could be spent in such an environment, a candle-lit spruce tree giving off flickering shadows in the low rooms of the old farmhouse. He had peeked in a number of windows and could see that the interior of the farm needed a good deal of work, but also that several of the rooms bore exposed beams and one still had a blue ceramic *Kachelofen* in a corner for heating. He could well imagine fixing up that old farmhouse, and watching his daughter grow into adolescence and adulthood there. There would be other children, too, perhaps a boy with whom he would roughhouse in the yard. There was a stable attached to the house; a pair of horses could be kept and his children could learn to ride as he had. An idyllic picture.

Werthen had duly gotten in touch with an estate agent and was now in the process – with Berthe's blessing – of proposing an offer for the place.

The payment from Karl Wittgenstein had finally prodded him into action. Feeling adequately solvent, he decided it was time to make a bid on the farm in Laab im Walde, time to take the first step toward establishing a country house. Grundman, his agent, had spoken with the owners and ascertained that they were eager and ready to sell. All that remained was for Werthen to make a serious bid, a number from which subsequent negotiations could begin. Per Grundman, a serious offer would come in somewhere around sixteen thousand florins. The land agent told Werthen a similar property had sold in nearby Hinterbrühl for that price. Renovations would take another ten thousand, easily. The Wittgenstein payment would be coupled with the belated wedding present of twenty-five thousand florins his parents had presented him and Berthe with.

The extreme generosity was in part due to the guilt they felt at not recognizing the union at first. Guilt, of course, was a two-way street. Werthen's own sense of it had in part sent him to his parents' hotel last week to repair the damage done by his speaking plainly. He would love to have let it go for a time, to buy a portion of peace for his family for just a few more days. Berthe's father, Herr Meisner, had taken himself off in a huff, back to his home in Linz. The flat was once again theirs and they could enjoy their new baby unimpeded. But in the end, it had been guilt and Berthe – who had shoved his hat in his hand – that had sent Werthen with roses and chocolates to the Hotel zur Josefstadt to beg pardon of his mother and father.

But to the matter at hand: he would offer fifteen thousand.

He sighed contentedly after making this decision, luxuriating in the warmth of his office. The room actually felt cozy today, for the talented Fräulein Metzinger had seen to it that the office stove was supplied with just the right amount of coke, so the rooms were warm, but not stifling. She of course did not herself personally shovel in the fuel; rather she had taken it on her own authority to pay *Trinkgeld* to the *Portier*'s younger brother, who lived with Frau Ignatz in the building. This modest tip insured that Oskar – no one in the building knew him by any other name – made several trips each working day during the cold months to keep the fire humming along. Fräulein Metzinger had even begun to charm grumpy Frau Ignatz. What could the young woman not do?

He filled out and signed the document of offer and the next instant Fräulein Metzinger tapped lightly on his office door.

'Sorry to bother you, Advokat. Do you have a moment?'

She wore a look of pinched concern on her face that surely meant that no good news was forthcoming. He could only hope that she was not going to leave the firm. Fräulein Metzinger had already proved herself an invaluable and able assistant.

'Please,' he said, rising from his desk and gesturing to a chair. She sat primly, almost defensively, like a witness steeling herself against a potentially badgering counsel.

'I need your help, Advokat.'

Such a statement would normally be met with considered restraint from Werthen. 'Help' from an attorney usually meant unpaid legal advice.

But coming from Fräulein Metzinger the words were like a Mozart theme, soft and playful. He was relieved, nay overjoyed that she was not asking to be relieved of her duties, was not here to complain of overwork and a boss whose head was more attuned to inquiries than it was to legal matters.

'What is it, Fräulein Metzinger?'

'I have a certain friend.'

Oh, God no, Werthen inwardly groaned. Perhaps this was not better after all. He was hardly the one to be giving romantic advice.

'A "friend" is not really what I intended. But I just do not know how else to refer to him. He is a young boy, actually.' She paused.

Werthen leaned back in his chair. 'Yes.'

'His name is Heidrich. Heidrich Beer. His friends call him "Heidl."' She smiled at this thought. 'Well, you can see why I call him Huck, then. After Mark Twain's Huckleberry Finn.'

Werthen allowed that he did not.

'"Heidlbeer," you know, is the equivalent of the American blueberry or huckleberry. I went to Mr Twain's lectures when he was visiting our city a couple of years ago.'

'I did not know you were a literary lady, Fräulein Metzinger,' Werthen said feebly. But he found himself rather confused, wondering exactly what sort of help the woman needed with said Huck.

'He is a child of the streets so far as I can tell,' she said suddenly. 'I would see him by my tram station, offering to carry packages for people, to fetch coal. Any small task to earn a few *Kreuzer*.

94

I let him carry my shopping one day, and he chattered on and on as if he did not want me to leave.'

'He has no fixed address?' Werthen asked.

She shook her head. 'I believe he lives in the *Zwingburg* under the Schwarzenbergplatz.'

Werthen knew of this location through Berthe and a friend at the *Arbeiter Zeitung* who was working on stories about Vienna's homeless. Hundreds if not thousands lived in the sewers like rats, for there were walkways along the open channels of waste; nooks and crannies where one could get out of the elements at night. The *Zwingburg*, or stronghold, was part of the Vienna sewer system, the so-called 'cholera sewer,' because the expansion of the original Inner City sewers had begun in earnest only after a deadly cholera outbreak in 1830, which killed two thousand. These included places like the high arched nether regions beneath the fashionable Schwarzenbergplatz, reachable via the manhole covers in the square above and then down long spiral stairs. The *Zwingburg* was an underground warren of living spaces along the sewers. It was reachable only when a wooden plank was laid across an intersecting channel of the sewer. If the police came to raid the place, the residents simply lifted the plank, like a moat-encircled fortress raising its drawbridge. There were also numerous side channels along which those same residents could flee if need be, an intricate maze that only those who lived there could navigate.

'He goes there when it's wet or too cold at

night. Otherwise, he says he would rather sleep in the Prater. He has no family. His mother died when he was five, and his father is a *Strotter*, a rag and bone man who ekes out a living in the sewers using a net to catch scraps of fish and fish bone that he sells to the soap manufacturers. Or if he is lucky he might land a piece of jewelry someone has inadvertently flushed down the toilet. Huck has no connections with him.'

'It sounds a hard life for a boy. How old is he?'

She shook her head, a show of disgust rather than lack of knowledge.

'He cannot be more than twelve, thirteen. But in ways he is an old man already.'

She paused long enough for Werthen to wonder again where all this was headed.

'I want to adopt him, you see.'

He was shocked, quite speechless for a moment.

'Yes,' she said. 'Adopt him.'

'Fräulein Metzinger—'

The tone of his voice prompted her to interrupt.

'I do not want advice regarding the wisdom of my decision, Advokat. I am only asking you about the proper way to go about such a legal adoption.'

It was Werthen's turn to shake his head now. 'I do not see a court in the land allowing it. You, a single woman. No. It is an impossibility.'

'Please do not give me false hope, Advokat.'

Her irony broke the tension; he felt himself smiling.

'I am not judging you,' Werthen said. 'I may

96

think such a move would be a disastrous mistake, but that plays no part in my assessment. Legally, I can see no way that an Austrian court would allow such a thing. Number one, the boy appears to have a parent already—'

'He wants no part of the boy,' she interjected.

He held a hand up to ask for patience. 'A parent, delinquent in his paternal duties, but a parent nonetheless. The court will move to fine said parent for allowing his son to go homeless.'

'As if that helps Huck.'

'Please, Fräulein Metzinger. Allow me. Number two, you are, as I commented, a single woman. Employed, yes, but with the means to care for an adolescent? With the skills required to make a home for such a youth?'

'So it is better that he sleeps in the sewers? That he carries coal for strangers to make enough each day to buy a stale *Semmel*? That he risks bodily harm living on the streets? The boy has been abused, beaten. His left arm was broken so badly by another homeless person stealing a crust of bread from him that it never healed properly. To this day Huck's forearm has a crook in it.'

'I am merely telling you what the legal and societal arguments would be.'

'I am sorry, Advokat. I understand you are only trying to explain the legalities. But it is all so frustrating.'

Their discussion was interrupted by the sound of the outer office door opening and closing.

Fräulein Metzinger quickly glanced at the clock on the wall.

'He is early.'

She got up and moved quickly back to the outer office. Werthen heard her voice and that of another. Then a rapping at his doorframe.

'This is Heidrich Beer,' Fräulein Metzinger said as she re-entered Werthen's office. She had in tow a pathetic-looking youth of about twelve dressed in patched clothing and bearing with him a distinct smell of decay. The frayed cuffs of his pants reached well above the tops of the worn lace-up boots he had on; his upper body was covered in a hodgepodge of layers of over-sized vest, woolen jacket and knee-length pressed felt coat rolled up at the sleeves and obviously the property once of someone much larger than he. On his head he wore a shiny derby cut at a jaunty angle. Despite the angle of the hat, his face appeared weary, concerned, and almost defeated. As Fräulein Metzinger had said, he looked much older than his age; for this boy there had been few enough happy, carefree moments of childhood, Werthen knew. He stooped slightly to the left, perhaps the result of the broken left arm, as if he were still protecting the injury.

Werthen rose from his desk, approaching the boy with outstretched hand. The child flinched for a moment at the sight of the hand, then understood, putting his own frail hand out to shake with Werthen.

'Pleased to meet you, Heidrich.'

His face brightened at this.

'My friends call me Heidl,' he said.

'Yes,' Werthen said. 'And I understand Fräulein Metzinger has dubbed you Huck.'

A smile formed on the boy's face now. It was as if he were purring at such attention. Werthen began to see how Fräulein Metzinger could become attached to the young fellow.

Then the boy as quickly changed his expression, unsure if he were being teased.

'I delivered those things,' he said to Fräulein Metzinger in a thick Viennese street accent.

'Wonderful,' she replied. Then to Werthen, 'I thought I might use Huck for our personal delivery service. If that is all right with you, Advokat. We always have documents to be hand-delivered to other firms or clients.'

Werthen paused, feeling his eyebrows rise in spite of himself.

'Not to worry,' Fräulein Metzinger said. 'I have a new suit of clothes in the works at Loden Plankl. Huck here will cut quite the figure.' She so obviously wanted to pat the boy's cheek, but restrained herself.

Werthen finally managed to pull himself out of his officious mood.

'I think that is a fine idea, Fräulein Metzinger.' He thrust his hand out to Heidrich Beer once again. 'Welcome to the firm, Huck.'

'I am proud of you, Karl,' Berthe said to him as they sat down for lunch.

'Why do I have the feeling that Fräulein Metzinger spoke to you about this before she did me?' Werthen asked.

'Because you are a fine judge of character as well as the possessor of an acutely analytical mind. Oh no, darling Frieda. Not on your nice new pinafore.'

The baby looked quite content at having spread cream all over her top. Though she was in Berthe's arms, Frieda still managed to make a swipe at anything in sight.

'And you will try to help her with this adoption?'

Werthen put his cup down on the Biedermeier dining table. 'You're sure it's wise? I hate to act the sagacious paterfamilias, but what really does she know of the boy?'

'She has a good heart.' Berthe was partly distracted by trying to wipe the cream from Frieda's front.

'She does, to be sure. It is Heidrich Beer I was wondering about.'

'Fräulein Metzinger is of age. She is not some febrile young mimosa who has led a sheltered life. You yourself said what a fine legal mind she has.'

'Yes, a legal mind.' Werthen said it as almost a sigh.

Berthe ignored this. 'She clearly finds the boy special and wants to make a difference in his life. Is that so wrong? Unconventional, perhaps, but wrong?'

'Not at all,' Werthen said, reaching out now to hold Frieda. He loved the feel of her snug little body in the crook of his arm; did not even mind the occasional bit of spit upon his jacket or waistcoat. 'It is an exemplary thing to do, in fact. It is good she has brought him into the firm, so to speak.'

'So that you can vet him more easily.'

'Yes. I am not ashamed to say so. I admit, at first meeting he seems a nice enough fellow. A bath and a suit of new clothes will do him a world of good.'

'And how is he to keep that suit of new clothes tidy living in the sewers while you go about investigating his bona fides?' Freed of her daughter for the time, Berthe tucked into Frau Blatschky's *Beuschel*, cutting herself a healthy portion of the bread dumpling in ragout with strips of calf's lung.

'I believe Fräulein Metzinger has seen to that,' Werthen said. 'Really, the young woman should go into politics; she can charm anyone. She spoke with Frau Ignatz of all people, and secured accommodations for Huck under the eaves at Habsburgergasse. He will be rooming with the *Portier*'s brother Oskar, in point of fact.'

Berthe almost choked on a bite of dumpling. She coughed, her eyes filled with water, and then she managed to say, 'How in the world did she ever achieve that?'

Werthen merely raised his eyebrows and shook his head.

'It buys us time, however,' he said. 'There is no need to rush into things now, as it would seem the boy is safe enough as is.'

They were silent for a moment, and then Berthe sighed. 'That seems an easily resolved crisis compared to ours.'

'They aren't still talking about the baptism?' Werthen said.

She nodded. 'And Father wrote today that he

101

has decided to remain in Linz until we make
some decision about the naming ceremony.'

'Jesus, Mary, and Joseph.'

'That about sums it up,' she said.

Werthen had a guilty conscience. The young
chap Praetor was a pompous ass, but Werthen
could not stop feeling shame at having coerced
him with the threat of exposing his homosexuality. The deed hung like a metaphorical
albatross around his neck.

All that afternoon at the office it stood in the
way of his concentrating on Herr Eckhof's
newest will.

He worked late at the office and walked home
in the gathering darkness, up the gentle slope of
Josefstädterstrasse leading from the Ring out of
the Inner City. Werthen suddenly decided he
would do something about the heavy feeling in
the pit of his stomach. He would pay one more
visit to Praetor. And he would do it this very
evening before returning home for dinner.

Werthen turned left off the Josefstädterstrasse
at Piaristengasse and followed that street to the
corner of Zeltgasse. The little lane extended for
only one city block. The house door at Zeltgasse
8 was already closed for the evening, unlike at
his last visit to Praetor when he had been able to
simply walk up the stairs to the man's flat.
Werthen looked up at the windows of the apartments, seeing the lights on in Praetor's flat on
the third floor. A shadow passed in front of the
curtained window. So the young journalist was
at home. Sometimes a *Portier* would close the

house door early in hopes of earning tips from those caught outside.

Surprisingly, the building, though old, actually had one of the new house intercoms for visitors to ring the tenants when the house door was locked. But Werthen did not want to take chances on Praetor simply hanging up on him. Just then, a young couple stopped at the door to Praetor's building, the man ringing an apartment and getting an immediate answer. The house door clicked open. On impulse, Werthen decided to follow them in. The couple looked surprised as he did so, but he tried to reassure them.

'Sorry. I'm newly moved in. I left my change purse in the apartment and cannot very well bother the *Portier* without tip in hand.'

The woman smiled at this, but her husband, a thin and wary man, simply stared at Werthen as he headed to the stairs and they made their way to a street-level apartment.

Reaching the third-floor landing, Werthen knocked lightly on Praetor's door, trying to gather his thoughts, wondering just how he would approach the young man. There was no answer and he knocked again, a bit louder. Another half-minute passed and this time he used the zinc twist knob of the manual doorbell. Still no response.

He put his ear to the door and thought he heard movement from within.

'Herr Praetor,' he said to the blankness of the door, feeling rather silly as he did so. 'It is I. Advokat Werthen. I have come to apologize. Please let me in.'

He tried knocking once more, raising his voice a notch in volume this time. 'Herr Praetor?'

A door opened down the dimly lit corridor and the figure of a woman appeared in a backlit silhouette in the doorway.

'What is it you want, young man?'

'Sorry. Just trying to rouse my friend. We were to meet. He must have fallen asleep.'

'I suggest you take that as an official rejection then and cease with the everlasting clamor.' She peered more closely at him as if trying to recognize this visitor. 'And how did you get in if your friend is sleeping?'

Werthen did not wait for the woman to gather steam; she was sure to start making a grand fuss, summoning the *Portier* and who knows what all. He did not attempt further explanations. Instead, he sensibly turned on his heels and beat a hasty retreat.

At home, Werthen made no mention of this abortive visit to Praetor. He enjoyed a quiet dinner with wife and child, and an early night in bed.

The next morning at the office Werthen sat back in his chair to peruse the morning edition of the *Neue Freie Presse*. Since the birth of Frieda, his newspaper reading had been confined to the Habsburgergasse. When at home, he liked to be able to give full attention to his beautiful daughter.

He let out a contented sigh as he began with the front page of the newspaper. His contentment was short-lived, however, for prominent on that page was a report on the mysterious death of a young journalist, whose body had been found in his apartment in the Josefstadt.

Henricus Praetor – friend to Hans Wittgenstein and the journalist who had first written about financial wrongdoings at City Hall pointing to Councilman Steinwitz – had been found with a bullet through his head, an apparent suicide.

Eight

'I am not necessarily saying it was murder. But there appears to be something decidedly strange about it.'

The man speaking, Victor Adler – head of the socialist party in the empire and publisher of the *Arbeiter Zeitung* – sat at the Werthens' dinner table on Saturday evening. He was diminutive with a bushy head of hair and wire-framed glasses over bulging eyes. A thick moustache drooped over his lips and extended to the sides of his mouth, giving him a scowling appearance even when smiling. Next to Adler sat his wife Emma, who was a friend of Berthe's, and who, Werthen decided, was far more appealing physically than her husband. Though in her forties, she still had a glow to her skin and a softness of features that drew one in. Her husband, on the other hand, was above all earnest in demeanor, like a family doctor. Indeed, Adler had been trained, Werthen knew, as a doctor and a psychiatrist.

As Werthen listened to the man speak, he felt his stomach sinking. When Berthe had mentioned that the Adlers were coming to dinner, he feared that there might be this connection to the death of Henricus Praetor. After all, Praetor had

106

freelanced for Adler's newspaper.

'I am not at all sure the verdict of suicide is warranted,' Adler added.

'Suicide is a strange business,' Herr von Werthen said. Werthen's parents were in attendance tonight, much to their obvious discomfort.

Werthen quickly glanced at his father. It was hardly like him to address this taboo topic, given the history of his own dead son, Max.

'Yes,' Adler allowed. 'But it is more than that. More than the mere shock of death. More than one wishing to discount the possibility of suicide in one so vital. After all, suicide in one both young and healthy, with all of life stretching before him, is one of those actions that seems an affront to all of us. A challenge to our own predications of the value of this life we lead. It is, in that sense, an assault against the very fabric of society.'

Emma Adler placed a hand over her husband's now, as if to restrain him. Did she know of Werthen's dead brother?

'Not a very pleasant topic, darling,' she said to her publisher husband.

Frau von Werthen muttered assent to this.

However, Adler smiled at his wife as if he had not heard.

'At any rate,' he continued, 'the strangeness comes not so much from the deed, but from its context. As you might know, young Praetor was engaged in a series of articles for us on various dealings at the Rathaus.'

'There was the Steinwitz article,' Werthen said. 'Perhaps he felt remorse at having possibly brought about Steinwitz's death through his disclosures.'

Since learning of Praetor's death, Werthen had been wrestling with competing and distressing feelings. On the one hand, he was anxious that the newspapers were correct about the cause of death. After all, he, Werthen, had been at Praetor's flat Thursday evening, and several people in the apartment building had seen him. In effect, he might become a suspect in the event that Praetor's death was not suicide. But at the same time, if Praetor had committed suicide, was it because of Werthen's visit? Had he pushed the young man over the edge of reason? Had Praetor thought Werthen had come to further threaten him?

Werthen had not told Berthe on Thursday night about the attempted visit, not wanting to bring up the whole matter again because of the residual guilt he bore about his first interview with Praetor. And now he was trapped in this unspoken lie. The death of Henricus Praetor was the last topic he wanted to discuss tonight.

'There were other articles, as well, weren't there?' Frau Adler said. After attempting unsuccessfully to redirect the conversation, she apparently decided to join in.

Victor Adler quickly nodded at this. 'Yes. Praetor was looking into the 1873 Vienna Woods preservation act at the time of his death. Our editor-in-chief told me yesterday that the young man felt he was on to something quite important. Herr Praetor was, however, rather secretive. No one at the newspaper knows the direction his investigation was headed.'

'He kept no notes?' Berthe asked.

Adler shook his head. 'Not at his desk at the newspaper.'

'I thought he was freelance,' Werthen said.

'The roast beef is delicious,' Frau von Werthen interjected, another implicit plea for a change of conversation.

'There are several desks set aside for those people,' Berthe explained, and then, to her mother-in-law, she replied, 'Yes, Frau Blatschky has quite outdone herself tonight.'

For the next half-hour the talk was of a more domestic variety: extolling the charms of young Frieda, who was approaching one month of age; describing a recent letter the Adlers had received from their son, Friedrich, studying physics in Zürich and how he had made the acquaintance of a terribly talented young student at the Federal Polytechnic, one Albert Einstein; and of the possibility of Werthen and Berthe buying a country home in the Vienna Woods, though there had been as yet no response to Werthen's offer. The last topic in particular brought out emotion in Herr von Werthen, who pronounced how glad he was to see his son taking part in the world in such a way.

It was a typical remark, and Werthen did not take it wrongly. The sole worldly participation his father thought valid was the accumulation of property.

His parents left soon after dessert was served, his father confiding to him at the door, 'That Adler chap is not half so bad as one would expect. A family man and a businessman. Not the dreadful Marxist one hears of.'

'Yes, Father,' Werthen said. 'He seems a very regular sort.'

'Not a bad looking bride he has, either.' Followed by a lascivious wink, which took Werthen aback. It seemed that now they were two conspiring males together in his father's eyes.

'Quite attractive,' Werthen agreed.

'Rather too much unsavory talk at table, Karlchen,' his mother chided on her way out. Then she gave him a peck on the cheek.

After his parents left, the four of them settled in for a brandy in the sitting room, and Werthen hoped they would not resume the discussion of young Praetor's death.

'Now,' Berthe said to Adler, 'you were saying about Praetor's investigations...'

Werthen let out a barely audible sigh that caught Berthe's attention.

'Yes,' Adler said, warming the snifter of brandy in his hand. 'About his research notebooks. Clearly he kept such notebooks, for his fellow colleagues witnessed him scribbling notes in them.'

'Perhaps at his flat?' Emma Adler suggested.

'Yes, they must be at his flat,' Berthe said, a note of excitement in her voice. 'But why are you so concerned about these notebooks, Victor? Do you want to continue with his articles?'

Werthen had a very strong premonition of where all this was leading. If he were not so distressed about his own presence outside Praetor's flat the night of the man's death, he would take the conversation to that end point at once. Instead, he sat back observing as it unfolded before him.

'Praetor's father came to me late yesterday,' Adler said. 'He thinks his son was murdered.'

Once this was said, Werthen felt a sudden release; no longer was there any internal conflict. He realized that fear of being implicated in Praetor's death was far outweighed by the possibility that his visit had tipped the scales and made the journalist commit suicide. Thus, he knew what he had to do. Prove the death was a homicide.

'Why does the father think that?' he asked.

Adler turned his attention to Werthen, seemingly relieved that the lawyer was finally taking interest.

'Herr Doktor Praetor knew his son. I am not absolutely certain he was aware of his son's sexual inclinations, but they were best of friends. The two of them were planning a trip to Ravenna just next week. His son gave him no indications that he was troubled, let alone feeling suicidal. I trust the good doctor's judgment in this matter. It is more than the self-delusion of a grieving parent. And then there is the matter of the missing notebooks.'

'I understand what you are implying, Herr Adler,' Werthen said. 'You feel that these notebooks might supply some motive for Praetor's murder. But we can hardly say they are missing. Has the father examined his son's flat?'

Adler shook his head. 'The police have secured it until a coroner's verdict of suicide is given.'

'Then, as suggested, these notebooks could very well be in the flat. I remember seeing a writing desk when I visited Praetor.'

'You mentioned sexual inclinations, Victor,' Berthe said. 'What exactly do you mean?'

'Well...' He brushed his walrus moustache and glanced at Werthen for assistance.

'Come now, Victor,' his wife said. 'We are all adults here.'

'He is ... he was homosexual,' Werthen said.

'You never mentioned that,' Berthe said to Werthen. 'Not that it matters, I suppose.'

Werthen nodded. 'Yes, it matters. You see, I thought he and Hans Wittgenstein—'

'Were lovers?' Berthe finished for him.

Another nod. This was the time to make a clean breast of things. Now. And not let this secret fester a second longer.

'And I cruelly used his secret to force information from him. Not something I am proud of. As it turns out, Hans Wittgenstein was not his lover, merely his old school chum. But I felt miserable stooping to such tactics. That is why I did not mention that I stopped by Praetor's flat Thursday evening.'

All eyes were on him now.

'You see,' he said to Berthe, 'I was just so embarrassed at my earlier actions that I did not want to mention the name. I decided to stop and apologize again for my brutish behavior. But he would not answer his door. Praetor was in there. I saw a shadow behind a curtain from the street. And then I read the notice of his death the next day in the newspaper. I wondered if my presence had driven him to it.'

'Dear Karl,' Berthe said, kissing him on the cheek. 'You can be boorish at times, but not to the point of making one suicidal.'

This levity from Berthe released the tension in the room, for the Adlers had clearly begun to feel uncomfortable at Werthen's extended confession. Their laughter at Berthe's remark was louder than her bon mot justified.

'Well then,' Adler said in a jocular tone, 'it would seem you have good reason for looking into this case. After all, you may have been the last person to attempt to visit Praetor. You could be a suspect if there actually were foul play.'

There was more laughter, but Werthen knew only too well that Adler's off-hand comment might prove very accurate indeed.

A telephone call from Doktor Praetor the next day sealed the bargain. The doctor was adamant that Werthen aid in finding the killer of his son. Thus it was that Werthen took on the commission, to be paid for jointly by Adler and Doktor Praetor, to investigate the death of Henricus Praetor.

Werthen lost no time the following Monday getting in touch with Detective Inspector Bernhard Drechsler of the Vienna police. He spoke to Drechsler by telephone from the Habsburgergasse. Drechsler, at his office in the Police Praesidium on Schottenring, was obviously just getting over a cold, for his voice was scratchy and still nasal in tone.

'I appreciate you letting me know of this,' the

inspector said after Werthen fully explained the contacts he had had with Praetor. 'And you were home by what, seven, seven fifteen, seven thirty last Thursday evening?'

'Rather closer to seven fifteen, I suppose. I remember my housekeeper, Frau Blatschky, greeted me at the door, happy she did not have to hold dinner.' He was about to ask the reason for such questions when Drechsler ploughed on.

'Good. I think you can rest assured that you were not responsible for the young man's death. People like Praetor lead a complex emotional life. It is far more probable that the fellow was despondent over a love affair. These people become fixated on such things.'

These people. Werthen did not respond to this, however. Instead, he asked, 'You are sure it was suicide?'

A momentary pause. 'No. Though we thought it best to tell the father so. No use causing the man further pain.'

'I'm not following you,' Werthen said.

'There was no gun at the scene, only a shell casing and a bullet lodged in the wall in back of the body. No suicide note. Thus, the alternate version is that his death was the result of a tryst gone wrong. Perhaps even male rage at an unwanted advance. No telling what such people get up to, is there?'

'Now see here, Drechsler,' Werthen began, but then thought better of it. After all, he had been guilty of a similar offense regarding Praetor.

'You sound rather agitated, Counselor. No need to be. I am merely explaining why we are

114

giving this death a somewhat lower priority than others.'

Werthen made no reply at first. Then, 'Is there any indication when death occurred?'

'At seven thirty-one that evening.'

So that explained Drechsler's questions about the time he arrived home: it eliminated him from further suspicion.

'Someone heard the shot?'

'Very good, Advokat. Now I know why our mutual friend, Herr Gross, has such faith in your powers of deduction. A neighbor on the same floor, Frau Czerny. A very acute witness to events in her house. She heard a loud noise and looked immediately to the pendulum clock on the wall. She says she knew the sound was that of a gun going off. Lived through the events of 1848, did Frau Czerny, and seems to have had an intimate relationship with such sounds ever since. She saw you outside Praetor's flat, as well.'

The woman who came out when he was knocking at Praetor's door, Werthen figured.

'Quite good ears for an elderly woman,' Drechsler went on. 'Said she heard some crazy person addressing Herr Praetor's closed door. She recalled quite well that name: "It is I, Advokat Werthen." The very words she heard. So you see, it is a good thing we had this little discussion. I was going to contact you today at any rate.'

Werthen felt doubly pleased with himself for calling Drechsler so promptly.

'We would like permission to enter the apartment,' he said.

'We?'

'Herr Doktor Praetor and myself.'

'Sounds like you have taken on another case, Advokat. Trust me, though, this is a dead end, for you and the father. Nothing but grief will come from stirring things up.'

'Still,' Werthen said, leaving the rest unsaid.

'Yes, yes. You'll get your permission. I'll notify the men on guard duty to let you in. But remember, this is a possible crime scene.'

'Just as Doktor Gross would counsel,' Werthen said, getting in the last dig, for it was the criminologist Gross who preached the sanctity of the crime scene and the police who had reluctantly and at long last come to accept that principle. 'The father simply wants to gather some mementos.'

It must be my imagination, Werthen thought.

There was the smell of decay about Praetor's apartment. The father did not seem to be disturbed by the odor, but instead went about searching his son's wardrobe and drawers for any sign of notebooks. Afternoon sun poured through the windows.

While the father busied himself in the bedroom, Werthen inspected the Regency desk. As he did so, he tried to form a mental picture of that same desk the time he visited Praetor. What he saw in front of him hardly tallied with that picture, for the desk, once a jumble of papers, now was clean and tidy. Paper was neatly stacked in one corner, an oilcloth cover was draped over the typewriting machine, pencils were stored with their freshly sharpened tips up in a ceramic jug, reference books lined the back edge of the desk, held up between two large jade dragon bookends.

And there was no sign of any notebooks, neither on top of the desk nor in any of the tidy compartments and drawers. He got down on hands and knees underneath the desk to make a careful search of the carpentry so as to assure himself that there were no hidden or secret drawers.

Getting up, he asked himself a simple question: Who would leave a desk so tidy just before killing himself?

And why no final message to anyone? No explanation of why he was killing himself? And most damning of all, where was the gun? After all, if Praetor had shot himself, the gun would, perforce, have to be next to his body. Unless, that is, one of the policemen on the scene decided to pocket it to use as an illicit and unregistered weapon. Werthen had heard of such things occurring.

Werthen now noticed the patch in the wall near the desk where the bullet must have lodged after tearing through Praetor's brain. The police had obviously dug the projectile out. A dark stain in the wood of the floor below must be blood. So the body was found near the desk. But could Praetor have been seated when he died? Not probable, for in that case, the desk itself would have been splattered with blood. So Praetor was standing, pacing, perhaps. Who shoots them-

117

selves standing up?

Again the powerful scent of decay reached Werthen's nostrils. He wanted to throw open a window, but remembered Drechsler's admonition. He had earlier advised the father to leave things as he found them.

He tried to make himself believe that the smell was caused by an over-active imagination. After all, Praetor's body had not lain in the flat long enough for any such smell to originate, let alone linger. According to Drechsler, the vigilant Frau Czerny had waited fifteen to twenty minutes before investigating the sound of the gunshot. After repeated attempts at rousing Herr Praetor, she had alerted the local constable. Praetor's body was thus discovered before nine o'clock on Thursday night.

Still, Werthen was sure the stench was real. Looking behind the cushions on the daybed upon which he had sat on his previous visit to the flat, he quickly found the source. It was the golden parakeet Werthen had earlier seen flitting about the apartment. Its neck was broken, one wing was torn completely off, and its body was beginning to bloat with gas. This fact alone convinced Werthen that Praetor had been killed. He would never have committed such a barbarous act upon his pet. Killing the bird had been a final deed of spite, of revenge.

Whoever it was killed Praetor, he had done so out of an anger and spite so great that it could not be vented by simply pulling a trigger.

'Have you found anything, Advokat Werthen?' Praetor's diminutive father came out of the bedroom, and began sniffing. He, too, finally smelled the decay. Perhaps, being a surgeon, his nostrils were inured to such odors.

Werthen showed him the dead bird and explained his theory.

The doctor's shoulders slumped as if all the energy had been sucked out of him by this discovery.

'You are right,' he sighed. 'Ricus would never hurt Athena. She was his prized possession.'

The father took no delight in being right about the cause of his son's death. There was no vindication in this discovery. The realization brought only misery to the man. It was as if he visibly aged while gazing at the mangled parakeet. Perhaps Drechsler was right? Maybe there was only grief to be gained by this investigation.

'This seems to be the act of some deranged individual. My son did not associate with such violent people.'

Werthen did, and knew that you can never predict the behavior of someone. Outwardly proper and well-mannered, the best of persons could turn homicidal if pushed to extremes. As a criminal lawyer in Graz, he had made a living from good people doing bad things.

No parents tonight. Berthe and Werthen had a quiet dinner together. Even Frieda cooperated, going to sleep early. They sat at the table amid a clutter of dirty dishes, enjoying the glow of candlelight, sipping the last of a Bordeaux Werthen had picked up on his way home. They spoke of small domestic things – Frieda's new

119

smile when she passed gas, the delivery of coke fuel that was overdue, Frau Blatschky's recently discovered recipe for potted kidneys.

After the housekeeper had cleared the dishes and delivered the coffee, Werthen began a discussion of his new investigation. Berthe listened with rapt attention, eager it seemed for communication of a non-domestic variety. Werthen could understand; Berthe was a wonderful mother, but she also had a mind that needed to be fed.

'Why do you discount what the father says?' Berthe asked once Werthen finished his description of the investigation thus far.

'You mean as regards the sorts of people his son would or would not associate with?'

She nodded, stirring a silver spoonful of sugar into her coffee.

'I suppose it is because I suspect fatherly pride trumping reality.'

'But he was right about his son not being suicidal,' Berthe said. 'Perhaps he knows his son better than you think.'

'I have not discounted his opinion, but merely set it against opposing theories.'

'Drechsler's "these people" theory, you mean. What a horrid man.'

Werthen made no reply to this and Berthe took a sip of coffee, then set the cup aside with a sigh. She was being a good nursing mother; of the wine she had drunk only half a glass, as well.

'You didn't mention Drechsler's response to your discovery,' she said.

Werthen shook his head. 'No. For the very

good reason that I did not inform him of the parakeet.'

'Is that wise?'

'Telling Drechsler of it would not necessarily make him change his opinion of the case. In fact, I think it would convince him even more of his "berserk lover" scenario. Someone so deranged he would tear a harmless bird apart. There's nothing to be gained then by telling him of the mangled bird, and doing so would, pardon the metaphor, very likely ruffle Drechsler's feathers. After all, he warned about interfering with the crime scene, and then there is also the not insignificant matter that he and his fellows completely missed this vital clue.'

'My, but I have a competent husband. Not only an investigator, but a diplomat.'

'This is Vienna, remember?' he teased. 'I do not want to get on the wrong side of Drechsler. We may need him before this case is over.'

'Theories?' she asked.

Werthen took a sip of his coffee, unadulterated with sugar.

'Discounting the homosexual angle—' he began.

'Thank you...'

'I ask myself who might have a reason to kill a young journalist. These missing notebooks come to mind. His colleagues said he kept research notebooks, but there is no trace of them at the offices of the *Arbeiter Zeitung* or at his flat. The desk there had, I am sure, been tampered with. Someone had tidied it.'

'Isn't it possible that Praetor himself had just

121

done a little housecleaning? After all, we are now virtually certain that he did not kill himself, so such an act would not be out of the ordinary.'

Werthen did not fail to notice the 'we' in Berthe's sentence. It made him smile slightly.

'Agreed. But he hardly seemed the house-keeping sort.'

'Perhaps you should check with the building *Portier* on Zeltgasse to see if he employed a cleaning lady.'

'Excellent,' Werthen agreed, taking his small leather notebook from the breast pocket of his jacket to make a list.

After scratching a few lines, he looked up. 'That is one direction of investigation. The whole idea of the notebooks and the story he was working on. Adler says it had to do with the 1873 Vienna Woods preservation act. Though it is difficult to believe someone would kill him over that. Hardly sounds inflammatory enough.'

'What about Steinwitz?' Berthe said.

Werthen leaned over and kissed her full on the lips, holding her face in both hands as he moved back.

'You see? That's why we are married. Exactly my thoughts.' He let go of her face. 'Say that Praetor's article about the graft investigation in the Rathaus caused Steinwitz to take his own life. Then it could be that a friend, a colleague...'

'A relative,' Berthe added.

'Yes, or a relative – any one of those close to Steinwitz who might have a motive to kill Praetor. Simple revenge.'

'Or to silence him,' Berthe offered. 'Perhaps

there were other revelations coming. Maybe Steinwitz was not the end of the investigation, but instead the beginning. I only wish I could be of more help to you with this. But with Frieda...'

Werthen scribbled some more in his leather notebook. Then, 'I propose a simple division of labor. You know the journalists at the *Arbeiter Zeitung*. Without leaving this apartment, you could interview them by telephone, try to ascertain more closely the parameters of the story Praetor was working on. What might be in those missing notebooks. Meanwhile, I will investigate the Steinwitz angle and the Rathaus.'

It was Berthe's turn now to lean over and give her husband a generous kiss.

Nine

Werthen's right knee was acting up the next morning. Sometimes it felt as if the bullet from the duel was still lodged in there. He did not let it stop him, however, from walking to work as usual. He merely took his mahogany walking stick with him. Berthe had bought it for him last Christmas; a handsome piece of work with a brass grip in the shape of a globe that fit perfectly into the palm of his hand. Berthe knew him so well: Werthen's vanity would not allow him to use a mere cane, but this walking stick had a distinguished feel to it. He felt a bit of the dandy as he strolled to the Inner City, high clouds scudding in the sky ahead of a chill north wind.

No sooner had Werthen arrived at the Habsburgergasse and settled in at his desk, than he received a visit from an old friend.

'My God. Gross,' he said, pumping the man's hand after he was shown into the office by Fräulein Metzinger. 'How wonderful to see you.'

Doktor Hanns Gross, a tall, somewhat portly man in his early fifties, returned the handshake with equal vigor. His lips seemed to quiver under his salt and pepper moustache, which, Werthen noticed, had lately been transformed from a pencil-thin sprig of foliage to a bristling and slightly confused snail-like growth, curving up cavalierly at its right terminus yet dipping down into the doldrums on the left. Gross's pate, ringed with a fringe of gray hair, gleamed from a fresh application of bay rum, which he used every morning.

'Did you just arrive?' Werthen asked.

'We've been here since Friday, actually.'

'Where have you been hiding? And who is "we"? Don't tell me that you actually brought Adele with you this time.'

Gross grimaced as if in sudden pain. 'Yes, dearest Adele is with me. Or, more accurately, I am accompanying her.' He sat in a chair with a slight sigh. *'Fasching*, you see.' Another grimace.

'You're not?'

'Afraid so. After years of politely requesting, my dear lady wife finally made an ultimatum: we would attend the Vienna ball season or else. I was too devastated to inquire about the nature of "else." Thus, here I am in your pre-Lenten city.'

Werthen sat down in one of the client chairs next to Gross instead of sitting behind his desk. 'So you are actually going to attend a ball?'

Werthen did not think he had ever seen the criminologist looking so miserable, not even when faced with hemorrhoid surgery in Graz. Gross made a quick nod of the head.

'Have done already, in point of fact. Last Saturday night's *Gartenbau* Ball. Would it were otherwise. I am not as graceful on my feet as I

125

once was, Werthen.'

'Well, I for one think it is damn fine of you, Gross. Poor Adele has been pining to attend the Vienna ball season ever since I first met her in Graz.'

'Oh, long before that, my dear friend.'

'And you finally consented.'

'Relented,' Gross corrected. 'And there was the plumiest band of dandies and swells in attendance at the ball. Insipid and bored lower aristocracy with too much drink taken. All they could think of doing to entertain themselves was wager thousands of crowns on snail races. My God, what an occupation.'

It was the latest rage in Viennese society, Werthen knew. Dissipated nobility purchased snails at exorbitant rates to see which could climb to the top of a meter stick first, wagering even more exorbitant sums in the process.

'It was an outrage,' Gross spluttered.

Inactivity of any sort was anathema to Gross.

'But come, tell me Werthen, what lovely case do you have in hand?'

Werthen quickly outlined the major points in the Praetor murder.

'One of those, eh?' was Gross's immediate reply.

'Not you, too,' Werthen all but groaned.

'I was referring to the young man's profession rather than his sexual inclinations. Journalists make prime targets for homicides, as they so often step on the toes of the powerful or merely the vengeful.'

'You've come close to the truth there,' Werthen allowed, and proceeded to relate Praetor's possible link to the death of Councilman Stein- witz as well as the missing notebooks, which may or may not contain damning information from Praetor's unfinished investigation.

Before Werthen had a chance to further elabor- ate on the direction of his investigations, as he and Berthe had determined last night, Gross interrupted.

'I assume you are investigating possible links between Herr Steinwitz's death and Praetor's?'

Werthen made to assent, but Gross barged on.

'And are making inquiries with fellow journal- ists regarding the possible whereabouts if not contents of said notebooks?'

Again Werthen attempted to say yes, and again was drowned out by Gross.

'And are tracking down any leads regarding Praetor's relations. His ... well, his lovers.'

Not wishing to respond to this, Werthen was now presented with silence from Gross, who peered at him like a slightly perverse owl.

Finally Werthen said, 'Yes to the first two, and no to the last. I do not discount the possibility of a tryst gone wrong, as your friend Drechsler surmises, but rather prefer to follow what seem to me to be more pressing leads.'

'Ah, Detective Inspector Drechsler is in charge of the case?' Gross asked.

'And dragging his heels. Willing to list it as a suicide in spite of the lack of either weapon or note simply to avoid complications.'

'And in light of this dismembered avian crea- ture?'

Werthen sat silent at this question.

'You haven't told him, have you? And bravo. Nor should you. The man and his minions were too incompetent to discover it. Well, that is their problem.'

How like Gross, Werthen thought, to make this a competition.

'I would very much like to help, if I may,' Gross said after a moment more of silence. 'There is much to do. Follow the leads to Steinwitz, other councilmen, the bereaved widow, *et al*. I assume your good wife is off to the offices of the *Arbeiter Zeitung*.'

He said the name of the socialist newspaper the way one might pronounce a distasteful disease.

'Actually, Berthe is pursuing such leads from the comfort of our apartment, using our telephone. You must not have received my card.'

'Which card, dear Werthen?'

'Telling you of the birth of our daughter Frieda, on the nineteenth of January this year.'

There followed several moments of well-wishing from Gross, who apparently had not received the communication. He had left Czernowitz, where he held the chair in criminology, almost a month ago, during the long semester break. First he and his wife had gone to their home in Graz, and then finally to Vienna, and had not had their mail forwarded.

'Marvelous news,' Gross concluded. 'Truly marvelous. Adele will be so happy to hear of it. All the more reason for me to help out in this investigation then. I suggest I follow the lead to

Praetor's father.'

'But there is no lead to the father,' Werthen protested.

'Oh, I imagine we will find one. If the man knew his son as well as you say, then he surely knew if his son were in love, or at least entangled.'

Werthen nodded at this. From his long acquaintanceship with Gross, he knew there was no way of dissuading the criminologist from joining an investigation that piqued his interest.

'I would take it as a personal favor,' Gross suddenly added. 'A respite from my *Fasching* requirements.'

'Agreed,' Werthen said. In fact, he rather relished joining forces with Gross once again.

'And it is just as well that you did not shame Drechsler with the discovery of the bird. We need him for another small favor. As Herr Praetor was a journalist, I assume he used a typewriting machine.'

Werthen nodded at this.

'Excellent,' Gross said. 'I have lately been making an investigation of deciphering the marks left on the platen of a typewriting machine as well as on the ink ribbons. Some of my students in Czernowitz have assisted me in my endeavors, setting up a separate mechanical decipherment department at the crime laboratory I instituted at the university. There I have begun to assemble a rather workable technology in recovering typed impressions. I would like to see what can be discovered from Herr Praetor's typewriting machine.'

'Excellent,' Werthen said, and then came a brief rapping at his office door.

He called out for Fräulein Metzinger to enter, and she did so, her young friend, Huck, in tow, looking awfully well-appointed in a new gray suit from Loden Plankl, his thin legs encased in green knee socks and woolen knickers.

'Sorry to interrupt, Advokat Werthen. But I was thinking of sending Huck to the *Bezirksamt.*'

This was her usual duty, carrying wills to be registered at the local district office in Naglergasse. To send Huck in her stead was an elevation in duties from mere delivery boy to official representative of the firm, for Huck would sign the ledger at the district office. Werthen knew that Fräulein Metzinger had been working on Huck's penmanship and clearly now thought that the youth was ready for this promotion. Huck stood up straight and proud in his new suit and Werthen did not have the heart to do other than consent.

'I am sure Huck will carry out his duties successfully,' Werthen said importantly, and was pleased to see the boy puff out his chest even more.

After Fräulein Metzinger and Huck left, Gross peered at Werthen, a slight smile on his lips.

'Doing good works are we now, Werthen?'

'I have no idea what you mean.'

'You can clothe him like a gentleman, but it is painfully obvious that young boy was lately living rough on the streets.'

'However can you know that?' Werthen said,

amazed.

'The color of his skin, for one. Far too ruddy for this time of year when sensible people stay indoors. Then there is the matter of the gray under his eyes, which suggests not just lack of proper sleep, but also a poor diet, something that cannot be reversed overnight. Additionally there was the very manner in which he held his body, so proud of himself as if this were the first good suit of clothes he has possessed.'

'That is quite impressive, Gross. From those scant clues you could conclude that he was once a street urchin?'

Gross waved off the compliment as if such deductions were nothing.

'From that, and from the bits of conversation I overheard between your new assistant and the boy when I arrived and was taking off my coat waiting to be announced. It is quite surprising what people will say around one they think is too old or perhaps too proper to attempt to overhear them. Your young secretary was giving the boy tips on how to enter and leave a room with grace rather than the manner in which one might "pull a scamper in the sewers," as I believe she put it in quite good street argot. Not something the young woman would know on her own. Ergo...'

In the end, they decided to take lunch together. Gross and his wife were staying at the Hotel Imperial. Before, when on his own, Gross would be Werthen's house guest, but that was now out of the question with the coming of Frieda and the fact that the criminologist was here with his wife. It spoke of the level of their intimacy that

131

Werthen made no insincere invitations, nor did Gross expect one.

Thus, they walked to the nearby Imperial for lunch. Adele was indeed pleased to see him, for Werthen had been a constant guest in the Gross household during his years in Graz as a young criminal lawyer. And though he had already twice collaborated with Gross on criminal investigations since leaving Graz, Werthen had not seen Adele in the intervening years.

She was a short, thin woman, and, like many smaller women, she was full of a bubbling strength and confidence that made you forget her stature. Hearing of the birth of his first child, Adele leaned across the table to kiss him on the cheek. As she did so, she whispered, 'Do not ruin *your* child.'

At least he thought she had said that. Implying that Gross had done his utmost to ruin their own child, Otto, a budding twenty-three-year-old psychologist by all accounts, but who, as a youth, had been at loggerheads with his authoritarian father.

Werthen merely smiled in return to Adele. It felt almost like a betrayal of Gross even to receive such advice. Still, Werthen would not have wanted to be the man's son. Hard enough being the offspring of Emile von Werthen.

They spoke of food for a time once the carp was served, and then Gross regaled them for a full half-hour about the discoveries he had made yesterday at the Kunsthistorisches Museum viewing his beloved Bruegel paintings. In particular, he had been inspecting *The Fight*

Between Carnival and Lent.

'A most propitious painting for this time of year,' Gross remarked.

Gross thought he had discovered the mystery behind the change in orthography for Bruegel's name. Prior to 1559, the Flemish painter spelled his name with an 'h': Brueghel. However, thereafter for the final decade of his life, he spelled it without the 'h,' even though his offspring – both painters as well – kept the 'h.' Many art historians credited such a spelling change to the influence of humanism on the painter, wanting to Latinize his name. However, in *The Fight Between Carnival and Lent*, from 1559, Gross felt that he had uncovered the secret reason for this change. Amid the bewildering myriad of characters populating the canvas, Gross had discerned a recurring pattern: in each group there appeared to be a hunched crone plying some occult trade. According to Gross, the 'h' thus represented to Bruegel the word *heks*, the Flemish for witch or sorceress.

'In effect,' Gross said with a satisfied smile, 'Bruegel underwent a form of self-exorcism of the witch within himself with this spelling change.'

Adele was quite obviously uninterested in such a discussion; she peeled a dessert apple and left it untasted, then proceeded to fold and refold her napkin. Werthen, too, felt a little impatient with this discourse, not because it was uninteresting to him, but rather because he had his own mystery to chew on and would have preferred Gross to confer with him on further details of that

133

business. However, it soon dawned on him – as Gross requested Werthen's company for an after-lunch visit to the museum – that the criminologist was using the Bruegel matter as a ruse. Adele had finally shamed Gross into making a round of the *Fasching* balls; she would obviously not want his attention diverted by a new criminal investigation.

'I would be pleased to join you,' Werthen responded to the invitation, which brought a wide and satisfied smile from Gross.

'Remember we have a dinner engagement tonight with the Hausmanns, Hanns,' Adele said as they were leaving the restaurant.

'Of course, my sweet. It is uppermost in my mind.'

'You are as sharp as always,' Gross said as they left the Imperial. 'I confess that in a moment of weakness I vowed to Adele that I would not become involved in a criminal investigation while in Vienna. But really, Werthen. *Snail races*. I'll be sold for a donkey before being exposed to such foolery again.'

They did not, of course, go to the Kunsthistorisches Museum. Instead, with Werthen's knee feeling better now that he had his walking stick, they took a leisurely stroll to the nearby Maximilianstrasse 13, one street in from the Ring and just across from the Hofoper. In a cramped and cluttered corner office they found Karl Kraus hard at work getting his latest edition of *Die Fackel* ready for the printer.

Kraus, whom Werthen had the occasion to

consult on an earlier investigation, was more than a mere journalist. He seemed to know where all the bodies were buried in Vienna, who was sleeping with whom, and even what the emperor had for dinner the night before. His network of colleagues and friends extended to every section of society. Kraus, a slight man with a curly head of hair and tiny oval wire-rim glasses, was happily surprised at their visit, even setting out three small glasses of rather too sweet apricot schnapps in honor of the occasion. Theirs was a symbiotic relationship: in exchange for quite accurate gossip, Kraus had been, in the past, provided by Werthen and Gross with material for his thrice-monthly journal that, as the Americans said, 'scooped' the dailies.

They made small talk for a time, Kraus encircled by uneven piles of Viennese newspapers which he scoured daily for signs of hypocrisy, pomposity, and, worst sin of all, poor grammar.

'So, gentlemen,' Kraus said after appropriate toasts to communal health had been made, 'I trust you have not paid a visit solely for a bit of free schnapps. What wonderful case are you currently engaged in and how can I be of service?'

Gross, who at first meeting had heartily complained of Kraus's affectedness, was now a convert and greeted the journalist's flair with a smile.

Werthen set his empty glass on to the small desk amid the clutter of newsprint. 'I am interested in the colleagues of Councilman Steinwitz. Any close friends he might have had at City Hall or elsewhere.'

Kraus leaned back in his chair, clasping his hands over his narrow chest.

'Ah, the dear departed Councilman Steinwitz. His name has been quite eclipsed in the press of late. We journalists are a fickle lot.' He squinted at Werthen. 'By friends, do you mean acquaintances?'

'Real friends,' Werthen said.

Kraus nodded. 'I assume you know that he and Lueger were school chums. Both at the Theresianum together.'

Werthen remembered now the flag at half-mast at the school when he was investigating the disappearance of Hans Wittgenstein. The words of Father Mickelsburg came back to him, for the Piarist priest had reported that Steinwitz and Lueger were among the first class of commoners to be allowed to attend the school, and that the two had remained close friends after graduation.

'Quite attached to one another, by all accounts,' Kraus continued. 'Lueger brought him into his government despite certain irreconcilables.'

'How do you mean?' Werthen quickly inquired.

'Well, the two were not of one mind about the Jewish question at all. Lueger has gone so far as to suggest the Jews all be loaded on a ship and sent off to Palestine.'

Werthen noted that Kraus, a converted Jew like Werthen himself, did not use the pronoun 'we' when speaking of Vienna's Jews.

'And Steinwitz?' But Werthen, having formerly represented the deceased councilman, felt he already knew the answer.

'Race and religion were never one of Herr Steinwitz's concerns,' Kraus said. 'But their differences went beyond that.'

He smiled at them rather enigmatically for a moment.

'Do you intend to share your knowledge, Herr Kraus?' Gross asked with a degree of irony.

Which brought a pinched smile to the journalist's face. 'Our esteemed mayor fashions himself the representative of the little man. He loves them so much, he tells us, that he wants to create parks and open spaces in their honor. Let the *Kleinbürgertum* enjoy nature along with the toffs, right? Every time a tree is planted or a new green space, no matter how small, is installed, then there is an accompanying plaque commending Mayor Lueger for this worthy deed. Why, it has got so bad that last month, after the birth of an elephant at Schönbrunn Zoo, one of our leading journalists, hardly before known for his waggish tongue, suggested a plaque be erected at the elephant house: "Born during the Mayoralty of Karl Lueger."'

'Yes,' Gross interrupted, 'but what does this have to do with Councilman Steinwitz?'

'Not to worry, Doktor Gross. I shall come full circle presently. From all this, one must conclude that Lueger is sincere in his connection with the lower middle classes. Correct?'

There was silence in the small office for a time. It took Werthen a moment to realize Kraus had actually posed a question.

'Well, it might appear so,' the lawyer answered

while Gross sat thin-lipped.

'Yes,' Kraus said. 'Appearances. They are so important to our mayor. In fact, however, the so-called little man hardly benefits from such beautification schemes. I could count on one hand the number of parks that Lueger has built in working-class districts. And those he built in the rest of Vienna have used up open space that could have been put to better use building affordable housing. But that would not please Lueger's real constituency, the landlords and the moneyed classes. Building more housing would tend to bring rents down, something the land-lords, and therefore Mayor Lueger, do not want. Our mayor is touted for building the new metro-politan railroad, but no one now mentions that he single-handedly vetoed extension of it into outlying suburbs where the workers and lower middle classes could find more affordable hous-ing. Instead, Lueger confines those classes to the city limits and thereby again helps to keep rents high. The countryside around Vienna, it seems, is fit only for those who can afford their own carriages.'

Gross let out a sound midway between clear-ing one's throat and retching. 'A rather cynical interpretation, wouldn't you say, Kraus?'

'Cynical,' the journalist allowed, 'but accurate. The two are not incompatible.'

'Then I am to assume,' Werthen said, 'that Steinwitz was opposed to such policies.'

Kraus swept his hand magnanimously in front of him. 'Assume away, Advokat. My minions inside the Rathaus tell me that of late there was no love lost between Steinwitz and Lueger. In fact, things were quite frosty between them. Steinwitz felt that Lueger had abandoned all his old principles in a mad rush for power. Old friendships turning sour. One never knows where that might lead.'

'And who were the man's supporters at City Hall?' Gross inquired.

'You mean who might have been close enough to seek revenge on the journalist who drove Steinwitz to suicide? I assume you are ultimately investigating the death of the unfortunate Henricus Praetor?'

Thus spoken, the theory seemed absurd even to Werthen, who had proposed it in the first place.

'Yes to both your queries,' responded Gross with conviction.

'Off hand, I can think of more colleagues who might have been happy to see Steinwitz dead. However, he had one quasi-supporter in the inner circle. Councilman Hermann Bielohlawek.'

The name was familiar to Werthen. A Christian Social city councilman, Bielohlawek was an urphilistine, infamous for his reaction to a Jewish Social Democrat member who wanted to introduce a book into evidence in debate. Werthen well remembered Bielohlawek's response: *Another book! I'll puke!*

Kraus nodded at the look of wonder on Werthen's face. 'Yes, *that* Bielohlawek. I strongly doubt, however, that he would avenge Steinwitz's death. Theirs was a profoundly political alliance. Friendship did not enter into it.

Bielohlawek likes to keep a foot in both camps. Other than that, rumor has it that Steinwitz had a wide circle of special friends.'

'Special?' Werthen said.

'Rumor only. I do not like to speculate further.'

But by the wry smile on Kraus's face, Werthen could see that he was pleased to have piqued their interest in this way.

'Any possible avenging angels among them?' Gross asked.

'Not the dueling sort. And now, gentlemen, if you will forgive me. I have an edition to prepare for the printers.'

Ten

'Well, what do you make of that?' Gross sputtered as they regained the sidewalk.

'Kraus enjoys his little games,' Werthen said. '"*Special*" could mean anything from a sweet young thing to a bookmaker. For now, though, that seems a moot point.'

'Agreed,' Gross said, picking up his pace. 'We need to get on with this or I won't have enough time to dress properly for dinner.'

Werthen made no comment, but was momentarily irritated by Gross's egocentricity.

'Yes, I know,' Gross said. 'I am a self-centered old beast, but there it is. I cannot change. Nor would you want me to, eh, Werthen?'

'Well...'

'Thought not. Where to first? The Rathaus or Herr Doktor Praetor?'

'There is also Frau Steinwitz, the widow, to consider. She should be aware of her husband's friends.'

'Even the *special* ones?' Gross asked.

'Point taken.'

'So, as we are close by, why not storm the battlements of City Hall?'

They both walked briskly now, not out of urgency, but out of a desire to keep warm. A biting wind had come up, bringing the smell of snow from the *Puszta*, the great flat plains of Hungary to the east. For no good reason, the words of the statesman, Prince Metternich, sounded in Werthen's mind: *Asia begins at the Landstrasse.*

And indeed, Vienna was infused with an undercurrent of Byzantine protocol and corruption. Werthen wondered just how high such corruption reached in the corridors of City Hall.

In the foyer of that august building they were greeted by a bulky fellow at the main information desk. He looked as if he might have been a staff sergeant earlier in his life. Gross and Werthen had decided on the direct approach, and informed the man that they were private inquiry agents looking into the death of Councilman Steinwitz. They desired an audience with Councilman Hermann Bielohlawek if possible.

The man at the desk looked at them gruffly for a moment, and Werthen thought he may not have heard him properly. Before Werthen could speak again, however, the ex-sergeant picked up the handset of a recently installed inter-office telephone, told the in-house operator who he wished to be connected with, and then, after the few moments it took to direct the call, repeated into the mouthpiece their request for an interview. Werthen could hear the hollow, tinny sound of the voice on the other end, but could not make out what was said.

'The councilman is happily available for a short meeting,' the man said, setting the handset back into its cradle.

So much for having to storm the battlements.

They were directed to the top floor of offices, and began climbing the broad stairway, their heels and Werthen's walking stick echoing in the vast space. Werthen had had many occasions to visit the City Hall as a lawyer in wills and trusts, but he was still awed by the sheer size of it, boasting over fifteen hundred rooms, two thousand windows, and a *Festsaal*, a festival or ceremonial hall, that was over seventy meters long and twenty wide, spanning two stories in height. Large enough for the royal Lipizzaner stallions to romp about in, performing a *levade* here, a *capriole* there.

Like other official buildings along the Ringstrasse, the Rathaus was a stone-hewed symbol. Built during the heyday of the liberals in the 1870s, the building was meant to stand for the rise of democratic, or at least quasi-representative government after centuries of absolutist rule by the Habsburgs. The competition for its design had been won by the German architect Friedrich von Schmidt, who created an imposing neo-Gothic edifice, reminiscent of the old Flemish and northern German town halls. Such a style was meant to symbolize the medieval roots of the city when Vienna was a free commune. Werthen doubted any of those old town halls were quite so extravagant as this modern embellishment on the style.

They reached Bielohlawek's office after ten minutes of fairly arduous stairs. Workmen were busy at the door as they approached the corner office. It seemed that it necessitated three of the workers to install a small bronze plaque over the lintel with Bielohlawek's name. Werthen glanced at the one recently removed and now lodged in a tin refuse pail. It bore the name of Councilman Steinwitz.

Bielohlawek, it appeared, was coming up in the world, not only taking over the coveted office of the deceased councilman, but also, most likely, Steinwitz's position as personal aide to Lueger.

Werthen and Gross made their way around these workmen, and Werthen used the brass globe of his walking stick to knock on the closed door. An instant later they received a *basso* command to enter. The workmen now doffed their hats at the gentleman as they entered through the door.

Bielohlawek, dressed in a dark three-piece suit and stand-up collar, was seated at the desk formerly occupied by Steinwitz. Or had they got rid of that piece of furniture? Werthen wondered. After all, the councilman had killed himself while seated at it. One did not have to be overly squeamish to wriggle at that thought, though Bielohlawek did not look the sort to be easily upset. He had a street fighter's face with deep-set eyes, brown hair cut short and bristling like a hedgehog, long, tapering sideburns, and a moustache curled up at the ends. His jaw line was camouflaged partly by premature jowls, but still Werthen could see that it was jutting and strong.

Much of the parquet floor beneath their feet was covered by what appeared to Werthen to be a Ushak medallion carpet of a delicate ochre hue.

'You'll be the two investigators, I suppose.'

Werthen had heard more enthusiasm in the greeting from a condemned man to his executioner. Everything about Bielohlawek was gruff and rough-edged, even the sound of his voice. There was a strong hint of Czech heritage in his accent, though Bielohlawek had been born in Vienna. A man of about forty, the newly elected city council member was, according to some accounts, the chief clown in Lueger's court, and to others, a shrewd political operative who used his street-thug façade to conceal his machinations. He was, at once, a man who could call the great Russian master Tolstoy an 'old dope' or ask for the deportation of all of Vienna's Jews to Devil's Island along with the Frenchman, Dreyfus, while at night studying French and Latin to better himself.

'I doubt I can be of help regarding our friend, Steinwitz. But Karl, Bürgermeister Lueger, that is, says our doors should always be open to our electorate. You vote, I assume?'

Werthen was about to make a polite response when Gross jumped in.

'That is hardly your concern, my good man. As a *Beamter* you have only to know that citizens, who pay your salary, have a query for your office.'

Bielohlawek visibly stiffened when called a civil servant.

'We appreciate you seeing us on such short notice,' Werthen began, attempting to smooth things over, but Gross was having none of it.

'Now, if we could get down to business. We are investigating the death of one Henricus Praetor.'

Bielohlawek scowled at the name. 'Papers say he shot himself.'

'Quite,' Gross said. 'One cannot, however, always believe what is reported in the press.'

'What's it to do with me?' the city councilman said. 'I'm a busy man. I thought you wanted to ask about Steinwitz.'

'You see—' Werthen began, but was once again cut off by Gross. He thereafter relinquished the interview to the criminologist, who appeared to have his own sense of how to handle the brusque Bielohlawek.

'You were a friend of the deceased councilman's?' Gross inquired.

'We knew one another. Colleagues more than friends. But what does all this have to do with that *Schwuchtel*?'

Werthen felt the hair bristle at the back of his head at this coarse usage of fairy for homosexual.

'I assume you are referring to Herr Praetor?' Gross calmly replied.

'I repeat, I'm a busy man. And a simple one. Just tell me what you want and no fancy stuff.'

'What we want is to know if Councilman Steinwitz had any friendships strong enough at City Hall that someone might want to seek redress for his victimization.'

Bielohlawek stared at Gross as if he had been speaking a foreign language.

'You mean kill the scrawny journalist because

he broke the scandal?'

'Precisely.'

Bielohlawek broke into sudden laughter. 'Oh, that's a rich one. I thought you told the deskman you were investigators, not comedians out of a *Hanswurst* show.'

'I fail to see the humor,' Gross said.

Bielohlawek stopped his laughter as abruptly as he had begun. 'This is the Rathaus, not some army corps with outdated ideas about honor. *Verstehst*? We're all big boys here, with thick skins.'

Werthen could keep quiet no longer. 'You mean to say that you doubt Steinwitz killed himself over the embezzlement scandal?'

'Bravo. That is exactly what I mean.'

'Then why kill himself?' Werthen wondered out loud.

'You're the investigator,' Bielohlawek chuckled. 'You tell me. And something else you can tell me. Who hired you?'

But they left then, without mentioning their employer. Victor Adler, Werthen supposed, would not be looked upon favorably in the hallowed halls of the Rathaus.

On the way out of the office they ran, quite literally, into a massive man in a tight-fitting suit, his hair cut so short it bristled like a hedgehog.

'Sorry,' Werthen said, as the three of them made contact, for the large man was just coming into Bielohlawek's office.

The beefy man said, in a surprisingly high voice, 'Yes.'

Which made no sense, but Werthen, who recognized the man as one Adalbert Kulowski, bodyguard to the mayor, knew that the man seldom made any sense. With that much brawn, it was hardly his brains for which Lueger employed him. Kulowski had been a fixture at the Rathaus ever since some madman had attempted to stab the mayor during his first year in office.

'A pompous ass,' Gross muttered once they were on the portico of the Rathaus.

Gross, Werthen understood, did not mean the bodyguard.

'Only one way to deal with that sort.'

'You *were* rather abrupt with him.'

'Civil servants.' Gross sneered as he said the words. 'A greater misnomer I have never heard. There is nothing civil about them, and as for being a good servant to the people? *Bitte.*' Said with heavy irony.

'Did you believe him?' Werthen asked, lifting the collar on his overcoat against the cold.

'I assume you mean the manner in which the councilman discounted our theory of revenge as a motive for Praetor's death.' A moment's pause. 'Yes. I do. You knew Steinwitz. Was he the thick-skinned sort?'

'A veritable hippopotamus.'

'Then again one ponders your earlier question. Why would the good councilman commit suicide?'

A chilling thought occurred to Werthen. 'Perhaps Steinwitz did not kill himself.'

'Well, the authorities were wrong about Praetor's death,' Gross allowed.

'I think we need to pay the widow a visit,' Werthen said.

'After which I must prepare for dinner.'

'I can visit the good lady on my own.'

'Nonsense,' Gross said. 'You'd be lost without me.'

Werthen made no response to this; it was useless to do so with Gross.

He knew the Steinwitz address from the time the deceased councilman was his client. The widow lived in the Reichsratstrasse in the fashionable Rathaus Viertel, or quarter, only minutes from where they were now standing. Steinwitz himself could never have afforded the location on his pay as a city councilman; his wife, the former Valerie Gutrum, came from an old family and old money. Werthen and Gross headed toward the house, midway between the City Hall and Parliament. It was a handsome street with its ground floor businesses elegantly concealed behind galleried arcades as in the Rue de Rivoli in the French capital.

Reaching the Steinwitz house, they took the master stairway up two floors to the so-called *Nobelstock*, the noble floor, above which were the less imposing apartments. A maid answered the door and, after delivering Werthen's card to her mistress, she ushered them down a long hall filled with glass cases containing museum-quality family heirlooms and a collection of weapons large enough to remind Werthen that the woman's father was Colonel Gutrum, a shibboleth of the Kaiserlich und Königlich, Imperial and Royal army.

They were finally shown into a sitting room with windows looking out to the Rathaus Park and, far to the right, to the back of the Parliament.

Werthen was appreciating the view when a rustle of silk skirts caught his attention and made him turn. Frau Steinwitz was dressed in emerald green, her thick blonde hair piled atop her head attractively. A good-looking woman in her thirties, she did not have the appearance of a grieving widow, but rather of someone preparing perhaps for a ball later that evening. Werthen withheld judgment on that, however. He knew people reacted in all sorts of ways to the death of a loved one.

'Advokat Werthen.' She extended her hand to him and he held it a discreet few inches from his lips as he bent over it.

'*Küss die Hand, gnädige Frau,*' he said in the timeworn greeting whose meaning was closer to 'Your servant, madam,' than to the literal 'I kiss your hand, dear lady.'

'How nice to see you again,' she said, sounding as if she meant it. 'And your colleague.'

'May I introduce Doktor Hanns Gross?' Werthen said.

'Dear lady,' Gross murmured as Frau Steinwitz nodded at him.

'I was not aware Reinhold had further business with you, Advokat.' She motioned toward a pair of damask-covered fauteuils, while she perched on a settee.

'No,' Werthen said, sinking into the armchair.

150

'He didn't. And may I extend my condolences for your loss. I was very sad to hear of his passing.'

She managed a small sniffle, but then shrugged it off as if such emotion were a failing on her part.

'We all miss him very much,' she said flatly. 'It was good of you to come in person to convey your commiseration.'

He felt Gross's reproving eyes on him.

'Not at all, Frau Steinwitz. Actually, I am also engaged in another inquiry. The death of a certain Henricus Praetor.'

Werthen noticed a sudden red at her cheeks with the mention of this name; already sitting with a straight back, she seemed to stiffen even more on the settee.

'You recognize the name?'

'Of course I do. He is the journalist Reinhold was working with.'

This comment took Werthen aback. 'Working with?'

'Yes, Advokat Werthen.'

'But Praetor was the one who implicated your husband in a financial scandal.'

She nodded. 'I think I can trust you. Reinhold always spoke well of you, even after he found other representation. It was nothing personal, you see, but when he became a city councilor, they demanded he avail himself of an older attorney.'

'No need to explain, Frau Steinwitz. I fully understand. I believe he found further representation with a member of the Christian Social

151

party.'

In other words, a non-Jew.

She nodded glumly.

'That party,' she hissed.

'You were mentioning trusting my esteemed colleague,' Gross said. 'Perhaps it were better if I afforded you some privacy.'

'Herr Gross is my valued associate,' Werthen quickly explained to the widow, 'as well as an internationally recognized criminalist.'

Only then did he notice that she was not listening. Rather her shoulders jerked forward several times spasmodically, and a flood of tears flowed down her cheeks.

Werthen went to her, putting a caring hand on her shoulder, but remaining silent. He knew words would not soothe at this point.

She took deep breaths, and her sobs diminished finally. 'You must pardon the outbreak. You see, I have been so frightened. I did not know to whom I should turn. My father has a poor heart, and I do not want to worry him.'

'Frightened,' Werthen said, realizing he had misunderstood her tears. 'Whatever of, madam?'

'As I said, my husband was working with young Praetor. After publication of the initial story implicating Reinhold, my husband contacted Praetor in an effort to clear his good name. He was giving the journalist all manner of information. Reinhold would not talk to me of it, but I am sure it was very serious indeed. Poor Reinhold could not sleep for weeks before he ... before his...'

'What manner of information, Frau Steinwitz?' Gross inquired.

'I did see one of the files my husband later gave to the journalist. It detailed missing funds from a public building project.'

'*One* of the files?' Gross said.

'They met several times at this flat. Perhaps they had other meetings as well. Each time, Reinhold had a thick file to hand over to the young man.'

Werthen withdrew his hand from her shoulder. 'And that is what is frightening you, these disclosures.'

'Don't you see? First my husband and then Praetor. Someone killed them both to silence them. Maybe the same person will come for me and my children. I do not know where to turn.'

'Never fear, madam,' Gross said with utter conviction. 'If such is the case, we shall find the culprits and bring them to justice.'

She nodded and sighed at Gross, then turned her attention to Werthen.

'And in the meantime?'

'Perhaps you should go to the police,' he offered.

She shook her head violently at this suggestion. 'The police are for criminals. And the scandal it would cause.'

Werthen was not surprised at the illogic of such a reaction. Here was a woman essentially saying she feared for her life, yet would not go to the police because tongues would wag about the Gutrum name. It was the Viennese thing to do.

'I repeat, madam,' Gross said, 'we shall find

justice. And meanwhile, Advokat Werthen will keep a protective eye on you.'

'Oh please,' she said with real emotion. 'That would be too good of you.'

Werthen shot Gross a disapproving look, angered that the criminologist offered up his services so lightly.

'I would be happy to retain you, Advokat,' she said.

'My pleasure, entirely,' Werthen said.

'Good of you to offer my services,' Werthen said once they were outside.

Gross shook his head. 'It won't do. Pretty young woman like that needs a knight around.'

'She's got the whole of the royal army to choose from,' Werthen protested.

'Remember her father's poor heart. Besides, I have a feeling that we may want to remain close to Frau Steinwitz.'

Gross took his leave of Werthen then, in a hurry lest Adele should become suspicious of his whereabouts and business.

'Clarity ensues,' Gross offered as a parting comment.

It *was* clear enough, Werthen thought as he made his way home through the late afternoon darkness. They had considered that a possible motive for killing Praetor might be to keep him from making even further allegations, from reaching ever higher in City Hall to uncover corruption. Now this theory had been extended to Councilman Steinwitz, as well.

Even though the councilman's death had been

determined a suicide, Werthen knew such a thing could easily be staged. Gross planned to examine police photographs of the crime scene in the morning. The revelations from Frau Steinwitz opened up an entirely new direction for their investigation.

Werthen crossed the Landesgerichtstrasse and began cutting through back lanes to reach his apartment via the shortest route. As the streets were all narrow and short, this was also the least chilly route, for the wind had come up now and whistled down the wider boulevards, reaching to the bone with its cold.

Walking up the Schmidgasse, he heard footsteps in back of him quickly approaching. He noticed that the street was empty but for him and whoever was in back of him. Turning, he caught a blow to his left cheekbone that sent him sprawling on to the cobbled street. A pair of legs straddled him, and then a boot to the kidneys made him curl like a fetus as other blows rained down upon him.

Suddenly he lashed out with his walking stick, catching his attacker in the knee with the brass globe. The man cried out in pain, and Werthen rolled away, getting to his feet.

His attacker, a hulking man in worker's clothes, now pulled out a knife from his waistband, and Werthen, his youthful fencing training returning to him automatically, assumed a fighting pose, his walking stick held high like a foil. The man lunged at him, and Werthen parried the thrust with a blow to the man's middle followed by another to his back as Werthen spun out of

155

knife range.

They squared off once again, the man panting and eyeing him savagely.

'What is it you want?' Werthen said to him. 'What are you after?' But he knew the man was no common thief.

The man said nothing, but once again lunged for him. This time Werthen brought the brass globe down satisfyingly on the man's head. It was fortunate for the villain that he was wearing a bowler hat, otherwise he would have been concussed. As it was, he stumbled to one knee for a moment, his hat going askew and showing a thick growth of coal-black hair. Then he righted the hat, let out a scream of rage and rushed at Werthen once again, catching the lawyer off guard, and slashing his overcoat with the knife. The knife tore through fabric with a swishing sound, and Werthen swirled away from his attacker, bringing the stick down upon the man's back, this time hitting his kidneys.

Voices from down the street caught the man's attention. Other strollers were approaching and now the hulking man snarled at him in a thick Ottakring worker's accent:

'You keep your nose in your own business if you know what's good for you.'

The man glared at him for a moment, and Werthen noticed that the bridge of his nose had a large lump, as if it had been broken and poorly mended. Then the man ran off with surprising speed for one his size. Werthen knew he would never be able to catch him, not with his bad knee.

The pedestrians, a man and what appeared to be his young son, spied Werthen and his unkempt appearance, took him for a drunk, and crossed the street away from him.

'I repeat, it is not a profession for a gentleman. Fisticuffs in the street!'

Herr von Werthen had not touched his *Fritattensuppe*, a light broth with thinly cut pieces of crepe in it. Werthen's mother, seated next to her husband at the Biedermeier dining table, cast her son a commiserating look as she had when he was a child with a bruised knee.

'I really think you should report it,' Berthe said.

Werthen's account of the attack had not put her off her appetite, he noted. She left not one bit of crepe in her soup bowl. Frau Blatschky brought in the main course, *Wiener Reisfleisch*, a savory concoction of veal, bacon and onion pan fried and blended into cooked rice with a light tomato and paprika sauce. Truth be told, Werthen's mouth started watering at the aroma of it as Frau Blatschky set it in the middle of the table. Nothing like a bit of a tussle to get the appetite up. Werthen felt as if he could eat the whole bowl of it.

'Just some drunk looking for trouble,' he said. There had been no way to conceal the welt on his cheek nor the rent in his coat, otherwise he would not have worried his family with a tale of physical attack on the streets of the capital. Nor did he really believe it was a random outrage.

Berthe helped him to a large serving of the

157

Reisfleisch.

'Not good for the family name,' his father continued to bluster. 'One would think Doktor Gross would have better sense.'

Werthen had informed them of Gross's appearance today and of his offer to help in his investigation.

'Doktor Gross was not there at the time of the attack,' Berthe reminded her father-in-law. 'And I think there are more serious consequences to worry about,' she added sharply. 'Karl could have been badly injured.'

Herr von Werthen reddened at this rebuke, and Werthen had to jump in quickly to avoid another family ruckus.

'I am sure no one recognized me,' he said with irony.

'Thank the Lord for small favors,' said Frau von Werthen.

Which remark made Berthe shake her head in despair of ever understanding her in-laws.

In bed later that night, Berthe put her fingertips to the bruise on his cheek.

'Does it hurt?'

'It's nothing, really.'

'Don't be so stoic. And please do not insult me in the privacy of our bedroom with that story about a drunk. What really happened?'

'It seems that Gross and I may have stirred a hornet's nest this afternoon.'

He quickly explained his earlier activities: the visit to Kraus and then to City Hall, and finally the revelations of Frau Steinwitz.

'Well, a hornet's nest it is,' she agreed. 'The only question is who at the Rathaus commissioned that ruffian to dissuade you from further investigations.'

'So sure it was City Hall?' But he needed no convincing, he just wanted confirmation of his own suspicions.

'A matter of timing, darling. Your mind is still reeling or you would see that for yourself. It could hardly be Frau Steinwitz, as you had just left her. There was no time – not to mention no reason – for her to set a mastiff on you. No, it had to come from the Rathaus. The only question is, from how high up?'

Eleven

He and Adele had a late night at the Hausmanns', and Gross had taken one too many
snifters of Pierre Ferrand '65. This morning – a
brutal and blustery day – he was nonetheless in
a buoyant mood as he made his way to the Ninth
District, the Alsergrund, for his meeting with
Doktor Siegismund Praetor, father of the murdered journalist.

As far as Adele knew, he was busy in the hallowed halls of the Kunsthistorisches Museum,
working on another monograph to be published
under his nom de plume, Marcellus Weintraub.
He had, to be sure, already published one such
article, dealing with stylistic irregularities in the
early career of Bruegel, or as the painter called
himself then, Brueghel. Gross would probably
have to write something about the missing 'h,' if
only to keep the deception alive with Adele.

Such a thought brought a wry smile to his lips.

He enjoyed this morning's brisk walk along
the Ring, turning off the broad boulevard at
Universitätsstrasse and then making his way to
Schwarzspanierstrasse, where the elder Praetor
had his office. As it turned out, the office was in
a building just next to the one – so a bronze
plaque at number thirteen told him – where Lud-

wig van Beethoven had died on Monday, March 26, 1827. Looking at that building with its gabled roofs and crumbling façade, Gross wondered how long before it was torn down to make room for a new block of flats. And good riddance. Gross's musical tastes had their upward limits with Haydn and Mozart; the excesses of Beethoven rang in his ears like the cacophony of a metal works.

On the other side of this Beethoven death house was a Protestant church which Gross, Catholic that he was, ruefully thought might also be torn down with no great loss.

Prejudices in order, Gross entered the door of house number fifteen, itself a baroque structure, but one kept in much better condition than its neighboring buildings. An odd place to have one's office, he thought, even if it were just consulting rooms. For surgeries, Doktor Praetor would employ the nearby General Hospital with its three thousand beds.

The doctor's rooms were on the top floor of the three-story edifice, and Gross climbed the circular stairs with ease. A highly polished brass plaque on a white-lacquered door identified the consulting rooms and told visitors to show themselves in. Gross did so, and the door opened on to a ballroom-sized waiting room filled with the fragrance of a bouquet of yellow and brick-red hothouse chrysanthemums atop a large, oval rosewood table in the middle of the room. Comfortable armchairs ringed the room, but none of them were occupied, for – as he had told Gross earlier on the telephone – Praetor did not have office hours today.

A small door at the far end of the room opened as Gross entered the waiting area, and out stepped a small, neatly dressed man with the reddest cheeks Gross had ever seen.

'Doktor Gross?' the man asked.

'Doktor Praetor,' Gross responded. 'Good of you to make time for me.'

The doctor merely nodded by way of reply, and then turned leading the way for Gross to the inner rooms.

Gross was surprised at the extent of Doktor Praetor's suite of rooms in the old baroque house. There had been some clever partitioning of space under the rafters. Praetor's office was in one corner of the building; paned windows gave off on to a quiet inner *Hof* with a large, though bare, linden tree spreading its branches almost to the height of the panes. It would afford, Gross decided, a pleasant green view in the spring, reminiscent of his own office in Czernowitz.

'Again, it was good of you to see me, Herr Doktor,' Gross said, taking an offered chair. They did not sit at Praetor's desk, but instead at an informal Biedermeier grouping nearer the window. Another display of yellow mums adorned the small table between them.

'Nonsense. It is I who thank you for taking interest in this. The police surely are not.'

'They have their own theories, of course.' Gross quickly sized up the man: tailor-cut three-piece suit in fawn brown, clean shaven, hair thinning on top and two silvery wings of hair on the side brushed neatly back. No-nonsense,

162

logical, pragmatic.

'By which you tactfully suggest they subscribe to homosexual jealousy gone berserk. No need to worry about sparing my feelings, Doktor Gross. I have lost my son. I have no need for platitudes, only vengeance. Measured vengeance, to be sure. Legal vengeance. But I want to see the person who killed my lovely Ricus brought to justice. That is my only concern now.'

There was a slight trembling in Praetor's voice as he said this, but his gray-blue eyes remained steely cold as they fixed on Gross.

'We will do everything we can to find the perpetrator,' Gross assured him. 'But to that end I need to ask you for more information.'

'Anything.'

'From what Advokat Werthen tells me, you and your son were close.'

'Yes. Very. He was, aside from my profession, my whole life. You see, my wife, God rest her soul, died not long after Ricus was born. I raised him, I watched him form as a young man. It is very hard to lose a child.'

Gross, momentarily thinking of his own son, Otto, and their eternally strained relationship, quickly moved on.

'Devastating, I am sure. Did he confide in you?'

'I believe he did. Though I have no way of knowing what he did *not* tell me.'

'He seemed to be happy, content?'

'Yes. Very. His work was progressing. Writing was extremely important for him. He took it seriously. He viewed himself as society's watchdog.'

'And his own social life?' Gross said.

'By which you mean possible lovers.'

Gross arched his eyebrows in assent.

'I only know that he had recently met someone whom he felt to be important in his life. Ricus did not share the intimate details of his life, nor did I inquire further. It was enough to know that my boy was happy. And, I believe, in love.'

He said this last without the least hint of irony, Gross noted. Doktor Praetor was, he decided, as much a critical scientist about his son as he might be in the diagnosis of a patient. He was, in short, exactly the sort of witness Gross respected.

'No talk of where the two might have met? Any indication at all about the man's identity?'

Doktor Praetor squinted at him. 'The *man's* identity? I do not recall saying that Ricus was in love with a man.'

'I simply assumed—'

'There was every possibility that Ricus may have met a young woman who finally put him on the right path. Who would make him settle down, start a family. Give me grandchildren.'

Gross internally sighed. It seemed the good doctor was no better than the usual unreliable witnesses: he confused his own needs with those of others. The farther into the recent past his dead son receded, the more Doktor Praetor would reshape him in the form he desired.

'And the notebooks,' Gross said, changing the subject. 'Have you found any trace of those?'

'None. Ricus lived on his own. He had very few possessions left at my flat. Mementoes of his youth only. Nothing recent.'

'Did he discuss his work with you? I ask because we have discovered that your son and Councilman Steinwitz appear to have been working together to uncover corruption at the Rathaus.'

'You mean the councilman who killed himself?'

Gross nodded at this; no reason to go into his suspicions about that death.

'This is the first I have heard of it.'

After another five minutes of questioning, Gross determined that Doktor Praetor was not as much an intimate of his son as he would like to have been. That too was being reshaped with time, however. But it was not Gross's job to point this out to his client.

Suddenly the man's clamoring need for justice outweighed his self-delusion.

'I want justice for my son,' he blurted out. 'One way or the other. Do you understand? Justice.'

Werthen had not expected to see her so soon.

'A pleasure,' he said, guiding Frau Steinwitz into his office.

She wore an anxious expression, but that was hardly uncommon for clients seeing their lawyer. Or for someone in fear of her life.

Once seated, she began fidgeting with her fox stole. 'I do not mean to make a pest of myself.'

'Not at all,' Werthen reassured her.

'I simply wanted to ascertain if what you said yesterday was more than merely conciliatory.'

'I am at your service, Frau Steinwitz.' Internally, Werthen cursed Gross for his high-handed generosity with other people's time.

'So you do not fear to take on such a responsibility?'

Suddenly she peered closer at his bruised face. 'Whatever did you do to your cheek, Advokat?'

He shrugged the question away. 'A collision with a door, I am afraid. Nothing heroic. But to answer your previous question, no, I have no fear in taking on a commission to protect you. I have men whom I can employ to keep a watch on you and your children.'

This suggestion seemed to alarm her more than the prospect of sudden death.

'That would hardly be *au fait*. After all, I do have a social life to conduct.'

'These men can be quite discreet,' he said, though truth be told, the fellows he was thinking of might stand out a bit at afternoon tea at the Sacher.

'I must consider it,' she said. 'I imagined that you personally...'

'Frau Steinwitz, I have a law office to run and an investigation under way.'

She straightened in her chair. 'I see. Investigating the murder of Herr Praetor takes precedence over protecting a defenseless widow.'

He tried to be reasonable. 'You must understand that in any circumstance I would have to hire assistants to maintain a watch around the clock.'

But she apparently was little concerned with reason. 'I only understand that you were my husband's trusted attorney and that you owe his widow similar allegiance.'

There were so many responses he could make to that absurd contention; instead, Werthen remained silent, steadily looking at her.

Finally she glanced away with a sigh. 'Forgive me, Advokat. I am under a great deal of strain. Let me consider your offer.'

She stood and he did so, as well. 'Of course. Take your time. But really I cannot believe that you or your children are in any real danger.'

She merely shook her head at this comment and adjusted the fox stole.

As he was escorting her out the outer office, the pink face of young Ludwig Wittgenstein peeked around the door.

'Oh, hello,' he said to them both as he might to old friends. 'I was just coming to see you, Advokat.' Wearing his distinctive loden coat with a fur collar, he cast a smile at Frau Steinwitz.

'Master Wittgenstein,' Werthen said with a smile. 'How good to see you. Just a moment while I show this good lady out.'

Frau Steinwitz looked from the Wittgenstein boy to Werthen, squared her shoulders and nodded an adieu.

'I shall consider your proposal,' she said once more before leaving.

Turning, Werthen noticed that Master Wittgenstein had already introduced himself to Fräulein Metzinger and in fact was aiding her in replacing the ribbon in her Underwood typewriting machine. Into this charming domestic scene entered Heidrich Beer, freshly back from delivering copies of a will to the Countess Isniack on the Stuben Ring. Like young Wittgenstein, the boy's cheeks were flushed red with the cold.

'Good day to you, Huck,' Werthen said, giving in to the use of the boy's nickname.

'Advokat Werthen,' Huck said importantly, struggling to make his voice deeper than it was.

'Huck,' said Fräulein Metzinger. 'Come and meet Master Wittgenstein.'

'They call me Luki,' he said turning his attention from the typing ribbon to the older boy.

'Pleased to meet you,' Huck said, extending his thin hand.

Fräulein Metzinger smiled to herself as the two boys shook hands with great seriousness.

That done, Huck promptly reported delivery of the documents.

'Do you work here?' Ludwig asked, his eyes growing large.

Huck breathed in deeply, expanding his chest. 'Yes.'

'That's wonderful. I mean, you go out into the town and all?'

'Every day.'

Ludwig simply shook his head in disbelief. 'That's the life,' he muttered.

'You've got a very handsome coat, if you do not mind my saying so.'

Huck had been taking lessons in polite small

168

talk from Fräulein Metzinger and was obviously trying his new skills out now.

'You think so?'

Huck nodded. 'Really. *Kein Mist.*'

He reddened when he realized he had slipped into his old street argot again, meaning 'no manure,' or, in this context, no nonsense.

'So, Herr Wittgenstein,' Werthen broke in. 'What brings you here, and...' he exaggerated a glance at the door, 'apparently on your own.'

'Luki,' he reminded. 'And I have to make this quick. I am supposed to be at the Fine Arts Museum with my tutor. We are studying Raphael today,' he said with a sigh. 'He left me there for a time to have his *gabel Frühstuck.*'

Werthen thought he could do with a mid-morning snack today, too, and led Ludwig into the inner office. 'And what was so important that you are playing truant?'

Werthen closed the door behind them, and Ludwig promptly pulled out a maroon-colored leather-bound diary from his coat pocket.

'I thought you would be interested in this. Hans left it with me.'

'But that is all settled. Hans is in New York.'

'Yes,' Ludwig said somewhat impatiently. 'But Hans told me I should give this to someone I really trust. Someone who could make use of it. I don't know many people and this has been nagging at me. Please take it.'

The boy handed the diary to Werthen. 'Anything to relieve you of the burden.'

'You make a joke about it, but it really has been bothering me. I feel badly about not giving

169

it to you earlier when you were investigating Hans's disappearance. But you see, at that time I did not know if I could trust you.'

Werthen smiled at the child's conundrum. 'And now you do?'

'Trust you? Well, as much as anyone, I guess. But this diary's been bothering me so much that I have made no progress at all on the model of Herr Daimler's motorcycle.'

'Well, I hope now you can concentrate on your work,' Werthen said kindly. 'What's in it that it is so important?'

Ludwig looked abashed. 'Gentlemen don't read other men's mail or diaries. Papa always says so.' Then he brightened. 'You were trying to trick me, right? To find out if I could be trusted. Very good. Now I know I have the right person.'

On the way out, Ludwig and Huck exchanged a few more words. Fräulein Metzinger had another envelope ready for delivery, and so Huck accompanied Ludwig on his way back to the museum.

When the boys were gone, she beamed at Werthen. 'I really think they hit it off.'

'And I do believe you would make a fine matchmaker. That letter you gave Huck already went out two days ago.'

She had the good grace to blush at being caught out.

'I was thinking of getting tickets for the Remington show in the Prater. What do you think, Advokat?'

What he thought was that Remington's Wild

West Show was the most tasteless performance event yet thought up by Americans, in many cases the kings of bad taste. He would never subject even his basest enemy to the supposed jollities of seeing fake Indians slaughtered or herds of buffalo decimated by sharpshooters. Remington himself was a crass businessman and showman whose Wild West Show had traveled several times around the world and was definitely the worse for wear. That's what Werthen thought.

'What an excellent idea, Fräulein Metzinger,' he said. 'I am sure Huck would love seeing it.'

'Really, Gross. Each time you come to town, you make everything topsy-turvy.'

Police Praesidium Inspector Meindl was a small, fastidious man who did not like his closed cases reopened. He was ensconced in a massive armchair behind his cherry wood desk at police headquarters and cast Gross a look of exasperation at his request for crime scene photographs from Steinwitz's office at the Rathaus and for permission to enter the Praetor apartment, which was still under seal, there to obtain the platen and ribbon from the dead man's typewriting machine.

'I do not live to complicate your life, I assure you, Meindl.'

Gross used a teasing tone; Meindl had been a former junior colleague of his in Graz before finding higher office in Vienna and well before Gross himself had been elevated to his current position in Czernowitz.

171

Detective Inspector Bernhard Drechsler, sitting beside Gross and looking more painfully gaunt than usual, followed these proceedings with a sardonic expression.

'I've no objections to Doktor Gross taking those items from Praetor's apartment,' he offered. But there was an unpleasant edge to his voice that Gross could not fail to notice.

Meindl, hands on his chest, formed a steeple with opposing fingers. 'I am delighted to hear that, Detective Inspector. But I thought you put the young man's death down to suicide.'

'Well,' Drechsler began with a Viennese drawl. 'There could be a loose end here and there.'

'Such as the absence of the death weapon?' Meindl peered down at the Praetor report on his desk. 'What did the gun do, simply walk off by itself?'

Now it was Gross's turn to watch events and smile inwardly.

Just as quickly Meindl turned his attention back to the criminologist, his former mentor.

'And what is this about photographs from the scene of Councilman Steinwitz's death? Are you suggesting his death was not a suicide as well?'

'It is one possible theory,' Gross said without offering more.

'You believe there is a connection between these two deaths?' Meindl's voice sounded peevish.

'Of course if you are unable to assist...' Gross began.

'Who said anything about not being able?' Meindl sat forward in his large chair now, hands on the edge of the desk. 'You'll get your photos and permit to enter the Praetor flat. But please, Gross, keep us posted, eh? I should like to know if we have a killer running loose in Vienna.'

Drechsler left with Gross, maintaining a stony silence as they took the newly installed elevator to street level. Outside the wind whipped up off the nearby Danube Canal; Gross tucked his hands more deeply into his woolen overcoat.

'A bit dour, Drechsler,' Gross said, thinking that perhaps the man was ill.

Instead Drechsler stuck his hawk-like face so close to Gross that the criminologist could see the pores in the man's nose.

'I do not appreciate being ambushed like that. By you or Werthen.'

Gross jerked away from him as one would from a leper displaying his sores.

'I assure you, Detective Inspector, that you were not *ambushed*, as you put it. Werthen and I are investigating a case. Clients are paying good money for us to get to the bottom of the death of young Praetor. You cannot blame us for your own oversight.'

'You've got the luxury to have fancy clients paying your way. Me, I'm stuck with grade G-4 in the Austrian bureaucracy. And I've got a full plate what with keeping track of Serbian anarchists and a crime gang that is operating out of the sewers and using runaway children as their proxies. You'll find that Praetor had a lover who got jealous or that he tried to solicit the wrong sort of gent. I've no time for that sort of thing, nor would you if you were in my place.'

The speech was so unlike Drechsler that Gross was momentarily stunned. No one ever accused the Vienna constabulary of being the most gifted lot, but Drechsler had, Gross always thought, stood out from the rest of the pack for whom *Schlamperei*, or lazily muddling through, was a way of life.

'What is it, Drechsler? This does not sound like you.'

The thin man's face contorted momentarily, then he let out an immense sigh for one so narrow in the chest.

'It's the wife, Gross. She's sick. Been so for weeks. Sorry. You're right. I am not myself lately.'

'What is it? She's been to the doctor, of course.'

Drechsler ran a hand over his bony chin. 'They say she needs an operation. But she's dead set against it. Had an uncle who was operated on and died.'

'But if the doctors say she needs it...?'

'Oh, she needs it all right. Women's trouble. But you can't budge her. Once Traude sets her mind on something, that's an end of it.'

Gross had a bright idea. 'You know Praetor's father is a well-respected surgeon.'

'There you go with Praetor again.' But he calmed himself quickly, and shook his head. 'No. I didn't know.'

'He is one of our clients in this affair.'

Drechsler did not reply to this.

'Perhaps he could talk to your wife. Reassure her. Maybe even perform the operation himself.'

Drechsler said nothing for a time, merely stared at Gross.

Finally, 'There's something you should know.'

'What is that, Inspector?'

'The gun found at Steinwitz's office. It was one of those fancy new Roth-Sauer automatic pistols. Fires a 7.65 mm.' Drechsler paused.

'Is there something I should glean from that?'

'We didn't find a gun at Praetor's, but we did find a casing.'

'A 7.65 mm?'

Drechsler nodded. 'Clearly can't be the same weapon, as Steinwitz died more than two weeks before Praetor. But it made me wonder at the time. Can't be too many of the Roth-Sauers around. They only went into production this year.'

Walking from Werthen's office in the Habsburgergasse, Gross regaled his friend about his morning's activities, including the forlorn Drechsler, the rather startling linkage provided by similar weapons in the death of Steinwitz and Praetor, and the possibility of securing the inspector's further cooperation in their investigations.

'But it is his job to investigate the death,' Werthen said. 'He should not need what is tantamount to a bribe.'

Gross shook his head pityingly at his colleague. 'How many years have you lived in Vienna, Werthen? Not enough, obviously, to let you know how things work here. Connections, connections, good friend. They make our tiny

175

empire go round.'

'And how can you be so sure that Doktor Praetor will agree to see Frau Drechsler?'

'Praetor may be an unreliable witness where his son is concerned, but I am absolutely certain of his commitment to see his son's killer brought to justice. I am sure I can put it to him in such a way that he sees the benefits of such altruism.'

'You can't be proposing that he operate without a fee?'

To which Gross merely hmm'ed a response.

When they finally reached their lunchtime destination, the Café Frauenhuber, the place was in a state of confusion, as much as such an orderly establishment can be. The *Herr Ober* standing by the door when Gross and Werthen entered did not give them a polite salutation; yesterday's *Neue Freie Presse* was still hanging in the wooden reading rack; and Herr Otto took a full three minutes to get to their table for their order.

For a noble coffeehouse such as the Frauenhuber, this was pandemonium approaching chaos.

'Unheard of,' Werthen muttered to Gross.

'Yes, it is,' Herr Otto, whose hearing was most acute, agreed as he sidled up to their table. Then, in a conspiratorial whisper, 'They want to get rid of number fourteen.' He pulled his pad of paper out of his jacket pocket, the tip of a stub of pencil poised to write. A look of bereavement etched his face.

'A blasphemy!' Gross sputtered, setting the bill of fare down resolutely on the marble-topped table.

Werthen did not understand at first, and then it dawned on him. Herr Otto was referring to the classic bentwood café chair produced by the Brothers Thonet. The firm, not to mention their famous number fourteen production line, was a Viennese fixture. The very chair he was seated on now had likely been around for several decades and would assuredly last several more. Thonet's design was simple yet both elegant and ingenious: a mere six pieces of wood bent by steam and assembled with ten screws and two nuts by anyone with access to a few tools. This ease of assembly had made the number fourteen one of the world's first mass-produced chairs, sold in pieces and put together in a matter of minutes. The chair had taken design prizes and was universally recognized as *the* café chair. Werthen often wished his father had been prescient enough to invest some money in the firm at its outset.

Herr Otto allowed his voice to rise a bit now, sensing a sympathetic audience. 'You can blame it all on Herr Loos, that's what I say. Him and that hospital ward he calls a café. Though I do not mean to speak ill of anyone.'

'I could not agree with you more,' Gross said, a finger impatiently edging the menu. 'The Café Museum is an abomination.'

'Herr Loos is an architectural pioneer,' Werthen said. Or at least that was what Berthe told him. Rosa Mayreder, close confidante of Berthe, was married to the architect Karl Mayreder, who had in fact employed said Loos in his architectural firm. Remembering this, Werthen also recalled that Karl Mayreder's brother, Rudolf, was a city councilor. Was there an inroad for him there?

Werthen did not, however, spend much time in the Café Museum, an establishment where ornament had been kept to a minimum.

'A pioneer he may be,' Herr Otto allowed, 'but whoever said we needed any re-inventing of the coffeehouse? A man goes to his coffeehouse for comfort, for a nice quiet and comfortable place to sip his *kleine Mocha*, not for an education in art.'

The comment made Werthen smile, for he'd made a similar argument to Klimt not that long ago about the decoration of his law office.

'The management cannot seriously be considering getting rid of this furniture,' Werthen said.

Herr Otto put pad and pencil down now and jerked his head toward the waiter at the door.

'Herr Bauer has now become lead *Ober*. Which means he speaks with Frau Enghart from time to time. The good Frau loves this establishment of course, but since the death of Herr Enghart it has not been easy for her. There are no children to counsel her in the operation of such a noble institution. But now Herr Bauer has gotten her ear. I'm told he takes night classes at the Museum of Art and Industry, even attends lectures on his days off. Oh, he's got ideas, he has.'

Though Werthen was all for self-improvement, he found it too much that a waiter at his favorite café should be the arbiter of taste for interior design.

'He's even mentioned getting rid of the potted palms.'

Gross huffed at this comment, again losing interest in the food at such a challenge.

'We must put a stop to this travesty.'

'We'll sign a petition,' Werthen said. 'Pass it around to all the customers and get their opinion on these proposed changes. Surely Frau Enghart would listen to reason then?'

'I wouldn't want to stir up any trouble,' Herr Otto said rather too meekly, again preparing to take their order.

Werthen felt that he had been played like a Stradivarius, but that was fine. Herr Otto, after all, had a job to protect, a family at home to support. It was the task of the clientele to preserve such a haven as the Frauenhuber.

'I'll make a note of it,' Werthen said.

This seemed to mollify even Gross's outrage, for he was already deep in a perusal of the dishes on offer today.

In the end, Gross opted for a *Kalbs Beuschel*, tender slices of calf lung and tongue in a light purée over *Semmelknödel*, bread dumplings of the softest consistency. Werthen chose the *Bauernschmaus*, a hearty heaping of sausages and pork with sauerkraut and a massive dumpling – the perfect food for such a bone-chilling day. They shared a bottle of Gumpoldskirchen Müller-Thurgau, a relatively new Riesling hybrid that was fast becoming a favorite of Werthen's.

During the meal Gross explained his further progress: he had secured the platen and ribbon from Praetor's typewriting machine and would send it express mail this afternoon to his eager students in Czernowitz. The photographs were to be delivered to Werthen's office this afternoon, courtesy of Inspector Meindl, who after all did owe his career to Gross's tutelage. Not a bad sort, Gross informed Werthen, but like so many small men, inclined to bark at the slightest excuse.

'I wish I had such progress to report,' Werthen said. And then detailed the visit of Frau Steinwitz and of Ludwig Wittgenstein's delivery of his brother Hans's diary.

'What is in the diary?' Gross asked.

'Afraid I haven't had the opportunity to look. Seemed like rather a dead end. I mean, that case has been solved.'

'Yes,' Gross said, but not very convincingly. He peered more closely at Werthen for the first time. 'I do not mean to pry, old friend, but isn't that a bruise you are sporting on your cheek?'

'How observant of you, Gross. Yes, it is. And I have a matching one on my back. You see, I was attacked on the street yesterday after leaving you.'

'But why have you waited so long to tell me? You should have telephoned the hotel, sent a pneumatic.'

'And have Adele discover that you are involved in another case when you promised her not to? Or spoil your evening out? To what end?'

'You play awfully fast and loose with violent crime, Werthen. And did you consider the possibility that someone might be dispatched to deal with me, as well?'

No conciliatory words from Gross, not that Werthen expected them. He did, however, feel badly about Gross's second comment. It was something he had not thought of, and he should.

'What did the scoundrel look like? Describe him.'

Werthen gave as close a description as he could, but realized that he could be giving the particulars of any number of toughs and rough-necks to be hired for a handful of *Kreutzer.* Truth be told, he had been too intent on merely pre-serving his life to take real notice of the man's features, other than that he was hulking and menacing and had at one time or several times in the past broken his nose.

'Bielohlawek?' Gross said, echoing Berthe's assumption. 'Would he have set someone upon you?'

They were momentarily interrupted by Herr Otto, who wished to know if they would com-plete their meal with a *Mehlspeisen.* There was a *Kaisertorte* today, fresh from Fiegl's bakery.

Werthen patted his abdomen. 'I think not, thank you, Herr Otto.'

Gross reluctantly shook his head, as well.

'I meant to tell you, Advokat,' Herr Otto said as he totted up their bill. 'There was a ... certain fellow inquiring after you the other day.'

Both Werthen and Gross pricked up their ears at this information.

'A large, bullish-looking fellow?' Werthen in-quired.

Herr Otto shook his head. 'Quite the opposite.

181

Short and thin and dressed in a manner to suggest he perhaps makes his living on the street.'

'What did he want with me?'

'To know if you were a frequent customer. I told him that was none of his business and to be off or I would fetch a constable. But obviously he did not take me seriously. He is there now, waiting at the corner of the street. I noticed him a few moments ago.'

Gross stood, tossing his damask napkin to the table and leaving Werthen to pick up the tab as usual.

'Well, let us see what this chap wants then,' he said.

Werthen signed the chit that Herr Otto produced, for he now ran an account with the café. Gross was halfway out the door by the time Werthen caught him up.

The man saw them coming, but did not budge from his spot on the corner. He wore a shabby derby hat and an overcoat a size too large with patches on the hem and at the wrists. There was something about the way the man stood, feet spread and hands on hips defiantly, that reminded Werthen of somebody. As they drew closer Werthen could see the man's face. Though the pallor of his cheeks was the sickly gray of the underside of a fish as if he seldom saw the sunlight, there was withal a somewhat robust nature to the man's face: round and full with a nose that could serve as a beacon. He was grizzled; obviously the fellow could do with a good shave. With a bath as well, Werthen discovered as he got within scent-range of him.

'You were looking for me, sir?' Werthen said, standing a meter from him and towering at least a head higher.

'If you would be Justice Werthen, I am.'

'Advokat,' Werthen corrected. 'What exactly is it you want, Herr...?'

'They tell me you have my son,' the man said in quite the thickest Viennese accent Werthen had ever heard. There were those who swore they could place a Viennese to their home district by their accent; all Werthen could tell by this man's was that he most definitely belonged to the vast underclass of the metropolis, homeless perhaps, assuredly out of work.

'Your son?' Werthen repeated.

'My name's Beer. Erdmann Beer. Friends tell me you have my son.'

'Beer?' Then it clicked. 'You mean Huck?'

The man stared at him as if Werthen were insane.

'Heidl?' Werthen corrected. He remembered now that Fräulein Metzinger had mentioned a ne'er-do-well father who practiced the trade of *Strotter*, a rag and bone man scooping out bits of fish detritus from the sewers to be sold for soap fat. Which explained the man's pallor.

Herr Beer nodded his head. 'That's my boy, all right. You do have him, you do not deny that?'

'Now just one moment,' Gross broke in. 'I do not like the sound of that question.'

'Not to worry, Herr Doktor, not to worry. I know what you aristocrats get up to, and it's no worse treatment than he might get on the street.

It's just that I thought...'

'We are not aristocrats nor profligates,' Werthen all but shouted at the man. 'And we do not prey on young boys. Heidl is, in fact, employed in my law office.'

A look of cunning swept over the man's face at this piece of information.

'He's earning an income, is he? That's more like it. In that case, I can rightfully ask for a small compensation. An apprentice fee sort of.'

Werthen felt his anger rise and knew his face was growing red.

'You silly man,' he said. *'You* pay the apprentice fee, or didn't you know that? I should have you taken to court for non-support of your son.'

'Now hold on,' Beer said, shaking his palms at Werthen to calm him. 'It was just a suggestion.'

'Or better yet, take your urchin back with you to the *Zwingburg* where he belongs. I will not be extorted by the likes of you. Yes, that is the very thing. Come with us this very moment and take the boy with you. It's about time you took on the responsibilities of a father.'

'Your Magistrate, please listen to reason,' the man all but wailed. 'I had no idea of the fine situation my wonderful boy had landed himself in. I'm not trying to pestulate things for him. No, none of that. I'm his dear loving father. Just give him my best and tell him to wash his hands. Little beast never did like washing up. We can just forget we ever had this meeting, right?'

'And you will not attempt to contact the boy again,' Werthen said.

'Never a thought of it,' Beer said.

'Then be off with you.'

Beer tipped his dented derby at Werthen then at Gross.

'And Beer,' Werthen said, digging into his vest pocket and extracting a crown. He flicked the coin in a gentle arc to the man, who caught it with alacrity.

'Get some good food in you,' Werthen told him.

Beer did everything but bite the coin, so excited was he by his good fortune.

'That's the first and last from me,' Werthen said with his courtroom voice.

'Yes, sir,' Beer replied. 'This is the last of Erdmann Beer you'll be seeing.'

He was gone and Gross looked askance at Werthen. 'He'll only spend it on liquor.'

'I suppose so. He's got little enough else.'

'Do I hear the quivering beginnings of a social conscience?'

Werthen shrugged away the question. A moment later he began laughing to himself.

'Might one inquire what is so humorous?' Gross asked.

'It just struck me,' Werthen said. 'His name. Erdmann Beer. A fruit, just like his son.'

'Are you quite all right, Werthen?'

'You see, we call the boy Huck because his name is Heidl Beer, which if put together means blueberry or huckleberry.'

Gross gazed at him, seemingly unimpressed.

'As in Mark Twain's Huckleberry Finn.'

'Ah, quite,' Gross said. 'And let me then finish your thought. Herr Erdmann Beer's Christian

185

name could be shortened to Erd. Say both names together quickly and you have – *Erdbeer*, a strawberry.'

Gross could not restrain himself. He now enjoyed a low chuckle at the absurdity of the names.

'But,' he quickly returned to his usual stern demeanor, 'this is not getting our case solved. First we must send off Praetor's evidence. Secondly, the crime scene photos from the Rathaus might have been delivered by now. Thirdly, your attacker adds a new dimension. I should think it is time we seek an interview with Mayor Lueger.'

Twelve

Lueger, however, would have to wait. A visit to the spa at Bad Ischl had taken the mayor out of town for several days.

There was a flurry of rumors surrounding this visit. The official Rathaus line was that Lueger was leading a Viennese trade delegation to the famous Austrian spa – Franz Josef himself summered in Bad Ischl – in hopes of securing contracts for a Viennese glassmaker who had perfected a new process to make the thick-walled, flask-shaped drinking glasses spa guests used. Such flat glasses were extremely handy as they could be easily carried in the patient's pocket as he strolled from fountain to fountain.

The Vienna rumor mills, such as *Neues Wiener Journal* and other 'tabloids' as they were recently dubbed, had it instead that Doktor Karl Lueger was taking the cure himself for an unnamed but very serious complaint. Journalists doubling as spa cognoscenti even attempted a diagnosis of the mayor's supposed complaints: Bad Ischl was known for high salt and sulfur content in the water and attracted those in search of relief from respiratory and cardiovascular problems. Other spas, such as Baden bei Wien, Marienbad, Karlsbad or Baden Baden, were noted for water with high carbon dioxide content or temperature, appropriate for nervous disorders and digestive complaints, or for their therapeutic mud baths that relieved joint pains, rheumatism, even eczema. Thus, these *knowledgeable* journalists opined in their tattler columns: Lueger most definitely had a heart problem.

But Werthen was not worried about the mayor's health this morning. He had a far more unnerving task than long-distance diagnosis. Indeed, in light of the attack he suffered two days ago this task bordered on the reckless, for he was once again in the company of Councilman Bielohlawek, the very man, Werthen assumed, who commissioned the attack upon him.

Gross, however, said the risk was worth it. Easy enough for Gross to say; he would not be playing decoy.

It was all because of the crime scene photographs. Gross, an expert in numerous unexpected fields, also seemed to be one on carpet patterns. In this case it was the Ushak medallion carpet that was in Bielohlawek's office and that had, according to the photographs received from Meindl, been there also at the time of Steinwitz's death. As Gross noted, this particular carpet specimen was almost certainly seventeenth century from West Anatolia, and though much of the design was in iodized browns and ochre, it was happily much lighter than some of the deeper maroon carpets of a later period. In the black and white photographs supplied by Meindl, Gross could detect, amid the fecundity of floral ornamentation, a darker patterning that was not part of the design. He would make no further comment on what he could see in the photographs other than that he had to get into Bielohlawek's office and inspect the carpet first-hand.

Thus Werthen was seated in the Café Landt-mann just across the Ring from the Rathaus attempting to make small talk.

'Let us just forget it, shall we?' Bielohlawek said. 'As you say, you cannot be held respon-sible for your colleague's speech.'

'I just wanted you to know, face to face, that I did not approve. Herr Doktor Gross can some-times be a bit ... well, exasperating. Calling you a civil servant.' Werthen shook his head in disapproval. 'It was not what I had expected. And I do so very much appreciate you meeting me like this.'

'*Aber, bitte.*' Bielohlawek shrugged the apol-ogy away.

'Allow me to treat you to a bit of strudel as a small sign of my regard. Never too early for a bit of fruit, eh, Councilman?'

'I really should not.' Then Bielohlawek glanc-ed at the confectionery cart that Werthen had beckoned over to their table. His greedy eyes fell on a *Nusstorte*, and it was love at first sight.

'Perhaps just a bite,' he said. 'It will be a long day for me.'

Gross did not know how long he had. He told Werthen to keep the gorilla occupied for half an hour. But there was no assurance he would be able to do so. Gross entered the Rathaus by the trade entrance in one of the interior courts. Unfortunately he wasted several minutes trying to then find his way to the second floor of the main staircase, yet he could not have simply entered the main doors, for the former staff sergeant would be seated there directing visitor traffic.

Finally he worked his way along the warren of hallways and stairs to the main staircase, and from there followed the route he knew to Bielohlawek's office. The hallway was clear. He quickly fetched his key pick out of his breast pocket. The lock on the door was a simple mortise variety with pin-and-tumbler mechanism. Inserting the pick, he expertly tripped the pins out of the cylinder as he'd had occasion to do dozens of times as an investigating magistrate in Graz. Truth be told, the experience still gave him a small frisson, a delighted shiver at this quasi-illicit behavior. In Graz, the deed would be done with warrant in hand. No such conveyances here, however. Though he might have been able to persuade Drechsler to get him entrée to the office officially, such a move would have given away his suspicions to the councilman. And Gross was very much beginning to look in Bielohlawek's direction for a connection to the deaths of Steinwitz and Praetor.

As the lock clicked open, he glanced quickly over both shoulders: still clear.

Inside, Gross lost no time in setting to work. Bielohlawek's office was well lit by a large window looking down on to the Ringstrasse.

Thus, no need to turn on a lamp and risk attracting attention. The primary tool he needed was in the large pocket of his overcoat: a folding magnifying glass made in Birmingham from sterling silver, a birthday gift from Adele. Gross loved the design with a single strip of silver doubled over itself as the handle. The lens could then be folded sideways into the thin cavity created between the two sides of the handle. The lens itself was six-power magnification; any stronger and it would have been too difficult to use by hand. In the same pocket he had a smaller folding lens at ten and twenty times magnification for use once he identified a particular spot for examination.

Gross had not been able to bring the crime scene photographs with him for Meindl had insisted they be returned by courier last evening. He had, however, a mental picture of them and knew exactly what he was looking for. But something was wrong. The pattern of the carpet suddenly seemed at variance with what he had seen in the photographs. Was this the same carpet after all? The poppy and duck motif in the lower left quadrant seemed simply to be missing. Or was his memory faulty?

Gross felt the time slipping away; how long could Werthen entertain the councilman? And where were the telltale poppies?

A sudden inspiration led him to examine the lower right quadrant of the carpet. Yes. That was it. Whoever had printed the crime scene photographs had accidentally reversed the image, easy enough to do from a negative. What he had seen in the left side of the photographs was actually then on the right side of the actual carpet.

This problem solved, Gross did not bother to divest himself of his overcoat or his derby hat. He got down to his knees and closely examined the carpet in the regions he had found suspicious in the photographs. It took less than a minute to find the first example. His heart was racing as he found a second and then a third and fourth similar smudge, each growing a trace darker nearer the desk. In all, Gross tallied six such smudges, each a small elliptical shape, the curves pointing toward the door. No need for the stronger magnifying glass; he knew what this was. He took out a roll of measuring tape from another pocket and stretched it between smudges. The first pair closest to the desk was one hundred and two centimeters apart; from the second to the third smudge was a distance of ninety-eight centimeters. The distances continued to decline, until the last pair spanned eighty-six centimeters.

Satisfied, Gross was just rolling his tape when he heard footsteps outside the door. They suddenly stopped at the door. He hadn't locked it. A stupid oversight. The handle began to turn. With no time for subtlety, Gross moved with the alacrity of a man half his age.

The door opened inward and the bullish-looking fellow from the other day, Kulowski, the one Werthen had said was Lueger's bodyguard, poked his large head into the room.

'Hermann? Time for *Wurstsemmel* and beer.'

Getting no response, the man stepped briefly into the office, breathed heavily, muttered

'*Scheisse*,' and left, closing the door behind him.

Gross, crouched under the desk and viewing the man through a crack in its front apron, let out a sigh of relief. He forced himself to wait another two minutes, and then crawled out of the cramped space and brushed off his knees. He'd made such a rush of getting under the desk that he had badly dented his new derby. That would take a bit of explaining to Adele.

Werthen could no longer keep Bielohlawek without making him suspicious. He walked with him partway back toward the Rathaus.

'We must do this again, Advokat. Perhaps we might even have some work for a smart young yid like you, eh? Scratch each other's back. You know Lueger's philosophy. He's the one to decide who's a Jew and who's not.'

Werthen was so astounded by the crassness of Bielohlawek's comments that he was speechless. He found himself smiling like a harlequin at the ignorant beast when a part of his brain wanted only to attack the fool with his walking stick and feel the satisfying crunch of skull under the brass knob. It was one thing to hear rumors of such outlandish behavior, quite another to experience such blatant prejudice first-hand.

Bielohlawek tipped his top hat and made off across the broad boulevard. Still speechless, Werthen could only watch the man leave, hoping that Gross had gotten out of the office by now.

'The man's more of a fool than I took him for initially.'

Werthen spun around at the voice. Gross was

grinning at him from one of the benches lining the Ring, huddled in his coat with derby drawn down over his eyes. There was, Werthen registered, a V-shaped dent in the hat.

'You may be a "yid," but I dare the man to say again that you are young.'

The comment made Werthen smile, losing some of the anger he felt.

'That was fast.'

Gross beamed up at him. 'Yes. And productive.'

They had taken a private carriage.

Over the objections of her mother-in-law, Berthe had brought Frieda with her. The baby had slept most of the way to Laab im Walde, lulled by the rocking motion of the vehicle and the rhythmic clopping of the four pairs of hooves. Meanwhile Herr von Werthen stuck his nose in a copy of the latest auction catalogue from the state-run Wiener Versatz und Fragamt, or Viennese Pawn and Query Bureau. Though its new headquarters in the Dorotheergasse were not yet finished, many Viennese were already calling the state-run pawnshop by a new name, the Dorotheum. Also in the carriage, Adele Gross and Frau von Werthen made small talk about country homes and the importance of roots.

Berthe liked Frau Gross; she was not the woman she had expected as the partner of the overbearing Doktor Gross. Adele Gross was no shrinking violet, but neither was she confrontational. Watching her and Gross at dinner last night – for she had insisted that they come after learning of their presence in Vienna – Berthe could see that theirs was a union, a relationship unique to themselves. It was not a caricature of the hen-pecked husband nor of the browbeaten, dominated wife. Werthen had told Berthe of the unhappy circumstances vis-à-vis their son. However, whatever their differences in that regard, the couple appeared to have a deep and abiding respect for each other, even if a degree of prevarication were still needed to maintain marital happiness.

Berthe had been sworn to secrecy by Werthen: there was to be no mention of their new case in front of Adele. But he had also suggested that she, Berthe, devise some entertainment for the woman, so that she did not grow suspicious of Gross's absences.

The primary topic of conversation last night had been the reply to Werthen's offer for the farmhouse in Laab im Walde. Grundman, the land agent, had, after almost a week of waiting, just received a counter offer from the owners: they wanted seventeen thousand florins.

'Which means sixteen as a compromise,' Werthen had allowed at table. 'Exactly what Grundman recommended in the first place.'

'Will we pay it?' Berthe asked.

Die Katze im Sack kaufen,' Herr von Werthen said sternly.

He was somewhat nettled that he had not been asked to inspect the place and seemed to take real pleasure in warning against buying a cat in a sack. Suddenly Berthe realized that she was

195

also relying on her husband's glowing descriptions of the place. She only knew it from the outside.

Thus was born the idea for today's outing.

The carriage deposited them at the inn, where they would later take their lunch. Berthe was happy to see that venison was on the menu, and before she set out, she had the *Ober* set aside four orders of that delicious meal. Their carriage driver would remain at the inn while the party of five inspected the place. Grundman had been contacted, but was unable to supply a key on such short notice. He nevertheless assured Berthe they could see the various rooms from the windows.

The weather was a little less inclement today, though the wind was blowing across the empty fields, ploughed under for the winter, as they made their way down the single-track road to the house that could be theirs soon. Berthe had Frieda wrapped tightly in a blanket and held her close to her bosom inside the bulky *Wetterflecke*, the loden cape she wore. Only the baby's small, smiling face stuck out of the top buttons of the cloak. She wore a white cap with embroidered buttercups that Berthe herself had knit out of fine lambswool. Seeing the ochre-colored four-square in front of her on the narrow road, Berthe's heart began to swell with sweet expectation. A place to raise a brood of children.

'It looks lovely,' said Adele Gross.

'Why, it's just a farmhouse,' Herr von Werthen said as they drew nearer.

'Of course it's a farmhouse,' Berthe said. 'A

beautiful old fortress of a farmhouse.'

She noticed Frau von Werthen take her husband's hand and give it a squeeze. It did not appear to be an act of affection, rather of reproof.

'Well, yes,' Herr von Werthen said. 'Farmhouses *can* have their own sort of charm, one supposes.'

They entered the courtyard created by the sides of the farmhouse and Berthe noticed that the For Sale signs had been taken down. Obviously the owners were confident that they would meet their revised offer.

There would be a good deal of renovation, Berthe saw immediately, even from an exterior view. She must have seen the building first in bright sunlight, which disguised some of its faults. But now she could see tiles off the roof, a drainpipe hanging loose from the side of the building, patches of white undercoating showing through the paint, cracks in several of the windows and in one of the walls. But these did not deter her; she was still in love with the place, in love with the idea of a country home for her children to grow up in.

They all went to the windows, looking in the various rooms.

'What a lovely *Kachelofen*,' Frau Gross said.

'And this would make a fine nursery,' Frau von Werthen added, peering in another window.

'Quite,' her husband said.

'Say, what are you lot doing in here?'

The voice was gruff and commanding.

Berthe spun around from the window. Three men stood at the entrance to the court.

'Are you the owners?' Berthe asked. 'We checked with Herr Grundman before coming.'

The name obviously meant nothing to these three. Two of them were dressed in heavy coats and leggings as if working in the fields.

'This is private property,' said the one in the middle, a large man who appeared almost to burst out of his clothes. Unlike the other two, this one had a suit on under his heavy overcoat and wore no hat; his hair was cropped short like a criminal's. 'I'm telling you to get out of here.'

'My good man—' Herr von Werthen began.

'Now!' the big man spat out.

'We are here to view the property,' Berthe said. 'We've made an offer on it and are here legitimately. And that is no way to speak to people.'

'You're trespassing,' the same man said, now with an edge of menace to his voice.

The three men began approaching.

'If I were you, I would take that baby out of here before someone gets hurt.'

'This is really too much,' Herr von Werthen said, moving protectively in front of Berthe and the baby.

'Look, old one. You take these ladies along home now. And don't come back.'

'The police will hear of this,' Adele Gross intoned.

This remark got the attention of the one doing all the talking. The other two men looked at him quizzically.

'Lady, you are the trespasser. Who do you think the police are going to arrest?'

This brought rough laughter from the other

198

two men.

'Now, out of here.' He came closer to Herr von Werthen, who stood his ground. The man gave him a sudden shove, and Herr von Werthen landed on his backside in a spot of mud.

'You brutes,' Frau von Werthen yelped, hesitating as if deciding whether to slap the ruffian or help her husband up. She finally opted for the latter.

'I don't know who's been talking to you, but this place is not for sale. Understand? Now leave.' The man made a fake bowing motion and swept his hand toward the road.

'See here,' Herr von Werthen said, struggling to his feet.

But Berthe stopped him. 'We should go now,' she said to the others. Frieda had begun to cry, frightened by the gruff voices. This was hardly the joyful outing they had planned.

'That lady's got some sense,' the stranger said.

Before they left, however, Berthe made a close observation of each. She would be able to identify them later if need be.

'Why, that is assault,' Gross fumed. They were gathered at Werthen's flat later in the day, and Berthe had informed them of their misadventure at Laab im Walde.

Werthen returned from the foyer where he had been on the telephone to Grundman.

'They've taken it off the market,' he said.

'But they can't do that,' Berthe said. 'Can they?'

'Afraid they can,' Werthen said, taking her

hand. 'No reasons. Grundman just says the owners have reconsidered.'

'Draughty old farmhouse, anyway,' Herr von
Werthen said.

'These men,' Gross asked, 'did they identify
themselves as the owners?'

Adele Gross answered the question: 'No.
Though Frau Werthen asked directly.'

Gross had Berthe and the others describe, once
again, their assailants. Werthen listened closely
as she described the leader of the three, but the
description – other than of a large man – did not
tally with that of the man who had attacked him.
That man wore an old bowler and had a thick
head of hair. Neither could he see any connection between his attack and his wife's visit to a
property for sale.

'Shouldn't we contact the owners?' Berthe
suggested. 'Try and trace these men? It seems
awfully odd that last night the farmhouse was for
sale and suddenly today it is off the market.'

'I suppose we could,' Werthen allowed. 'I
don't quite see the point, though, unless we want
to prefer charges.' He looked at his father. 'What
do you say, Papa? After all, you were the one
pushed to the ground.'

'It was hardly a fair fight,' Herr von Werthen
said. 'The blackguard gave me no warning.'

'That is not the point, Emile,' his wife coun-
seled. 'Karl wants to know if you would like a
legal solution.'

'Police, you mean? I don't think so. Not for
me, at any rate.'

Werthen imagined his father would not be over

fond of having his name in the newspapers in connection with such a sordid little affair.

'But surely you will not let those ruffians get away with their bullying,' Adele Gross interjected. 'They scared poor little Frieda.'

'I think she will survive,' Berthe said, for she too was losing her sense of outrage now.

'I'll have a word with Grundman,' Werthen said, by way of addressing Frau Gross's concern. But Berthe sensed his disappointment at losing their dream house. Perhaps it was better just to put the whole thing in back of them.

Adele Gross looked squarely at her husband. 'Does this have anything to do with the case you and Werthen are occupied with?'

This statement brought absolute silence for a moment to the sitting room. Gross glanced at Werthen as if to accuse him.

'Nobody told me,' Frau Gross said. 'So do not go bullying Werthen or his lovely wife. You do realize, Hanns, that you are far too happy lately. That cannot simply be the result of esoteric studies of a dead Flemish painter. And most definitely not the result of your attendance at Viennese balls or dinner parties. Ergo, you must be involved with a case. Every time you visit Vienna you do so.'

'My dear Adele,' Gross said. 'I had no idea. You are quite the detective yourself.'

'No. Just an observant wife.'

'It would have been a fine place for our children,' Berthe said when they lay together in bed that night. 'But it's not to be.'

'We'll find another place,' he told her, wrapping an arm around her warm body.

'With all the to-do, you never mentioned what happened with Gross's visit to the Rathaus today.'

'It was as he thought. There were blood traces leading from the desk to the door.'

Gross had explained that the thickness of the smudges nearer the desk meant that someone had stepped in the blood and then tracked it out with them, the smudges getting fainter as the person continued to walk.

'Which proves...?' Berthe asked.

'Fairly conclusively that Steinwitz was murdered. And by the same type of weapon used to kill Praetor.'

'Perhaps the police fouled the scene?'

'No. Gross checked with Drechsler. The police were there immediately following the shooting. They were careful to stay to the edges of the room, just as he has been advocating for them to do in order to avoid contaminating the scene. Drechsler guarantees that none of his men could have stepped in the blood.'

'So it was murder,' she said with a shiver. 'You've got to be careful. Both you and Doktor Gross. These men...'

'There is one other possibility,' he said, trying to steer her away from these fears. 'The architect Otto Wagner was the first to discover the body. We do not think he entered the room, but Gross wants to interview him to make absolutely sure.'

Which reminded him that he wanted Berthe to contact her friend Rosa Mayreder and see if she could arrange a meeting for Werthen with her brother-in-law, Councilman Rudolf Mayreder. He might be able to provide further inside knowledge from the Rathaus.

'I am sure she would be happy to help out,' Berthe said when asked, and then yawned.

'Are you a tired mother?'

She nodded. But before sleep, she also had information to impart: her contacts at the *Arbeiter Zeitung* had come up with nothing more than what Adler himself had stated the other night at dinner: that Praetor was supposedly involved with the 1873 Vienna Woods preservation act.

'Nothing there, then,' Werthen said. Or was there? Was it mere coincidence that their own plans about the Vienna Woods had been thwarted? He and Gross suspected that whatever Steinwitz and Praetor were working together to expose got them killed. Did it, in fact, have something to do with the Vienna Woods?

Thirteen

Werthen's late-night ruminations were vindicated the next morning. He was reading the *Neue Freie Presse* at his desk at the law office when he noticed the leather-bound diary Ludwig Wittgenstein had delivered. Werthen had left it on top of the desk amid what was becoming a hillock of documents. It was most unlike him to allow such a mess on his desk; he put it down to his attention being focused on this troublesome case that seemed to grow daily in complexity.

He should store the diary away with the report on the missing Hans, he figured. Idly flipping through it as he pulled out the file drawer for inquiry cases, he stopped cold at the sight of a familiar name: Steinwitz.

He read the entry from January 17 of this year:

Ricus tells me of the secret meetings he is having with Councilman Steinwitz. Personally, I have warned him against such collaboration. The man is in Lueger's back pocket. Can he be trusted? Ricus insists that Steinwitz is one of the old boys. But to me shared attendance at the Theresianum is hardly grounds for trust. Those were miserable times for me and for Ricus. How quickly he forgets. Outsiders then, outsiders always. According to Ricus, though, Steinwitz has this same sense of being an outsider. He was after all a middle-class scholar, the first from that class to attend the Theresianum. But then so was Lueger, I reminded Ricus. Might just as well trust Handsome Karl, too. Ricus made no comment to that.

Then another entry from January 22:

Ricus has finally confided the nature of his investigations. They are planning on secretly selling off great swaths of the Vienna Woods. By 'they' he means Lueger and his crew at the Rathaus. To subvert the 1873 act protecting the Woods. Ricus says that he will publish and stop them, but I warn that this can be a dangerous game. Lueger does not take kindly to being confronted. Ricus assures me that he cannot publish immediately anyway. He needs more documentation from Steinwitz, and now the councilman is beginning to have second thoughts. Where will this all end? I do fear for Ricus.

The final entry was made on January 30:

All is lost. Best to leave, go right away from here and this pernicious influence.

The very next day Councilman Steinwitz was – as Gross had now partially proved – murdered in his Rathaus office.

Werthen could feel the excitement building in him. Was that what was behind all of this: a

205

secret plan to sell off much of the Vienna Woods? But why? For what gain? And, what lengths would Lueger or his henchmen like Bielohlawek go to in order to stop publication of this intended sale? And what did Hans's final cryptic message mean? What was lost? It could not refer to the death of Steinwitz, for that happened the next day, January 31. Or did Hans learn something about the murder beforehand? Is that what sent him off to America? And then a further thought: Could this scheme to sell off the Vienna Woods also be associated with the incidents in Laab im Walde yesterday?

Unfortunately, there was no way to ask these questions of Hans Wittgenstein, for he had given his family no return address when contacting them from New York.

Still, this truly was explosive information. If Hans Wittgenstein were accurate in the reporting in his journal, two deaths might very well be laid at the door of Mayor Lueger.

Herr Pokorny, it turned out, was almost a neighbor of Werthen's in the Habsburgergasse. He ran a small pharmacy, was thick in the waist and small in the head, and nicely outraged at Werthen's visit.

'I cannot assist you. I do not know why Grundman gave you my name.'

'You are on the deed. You are the one who listed the property. You are the one who countered my offer. Those are just a few of the reasons.'

Werthen had to resort to threats of a lawsuit claiming professional incompetence against

Grundman to get the name out of him.

Pokorny lifted from the counter a large ceramic jar with *Kamillentee*, chamomile tea, written in blue glaze against a cream background. This he placed on a shelf about shoulder height behind the counter. The interior of the pharmacy was traditional in design, with elegantly tiled floor, an abundance of mahogany and brass, and overall the smell of respectability and *Protektion*, the connections with which businesses such as Pokorny's Löwenherz pharmacy needed to open and stay in business. The issuance of new operating licenses was strictly controlled by the pharmacists' guild and the city in order to control competition. Pokorny, oddly enough, did not look the sort to have such connections, nor did he, despite the white laboratory coat he wore, seem to have any scientific or professional inclinations.

He listened coolly to Werthen's list of reasons for visiting him. 'That proves nothing,' he maintained.

Werthen lost what little patience he had with the man.

'Understand this. My wife and child, along with my parents and close family friend, were threatened and abused on your property yesterday.'

'That's no matter for me. What were they doing there anyway?'

'You know perfectly well what they were doing. Inspecting the property we were proposing to buy.'

'That property is no longer on the market.'

207

'It is still yours and you can be held responsible. In a court of law.'

This last statement got his attention. 'Jesus, Mary and Joseph. That farm's been a cross ever since my wife's parents died and left it to her. A burden and a headache. Money to repair this, money to repair that. Money for taxes, money for land rehabilitation. I just want to be rid of it.'

'You need to give me an explanation.' Werthen looked at the man steadily.

'They said not to mention it.'

'Who?'

'The fellows who came around yesterday. Doing a survey they were for the city, so they said. And they suddenly find that my wife's property is sitting smack in the middle of other open and protected land in the woods. Well, what's that to me?'

'What was it to you?'

'They made it clear, these men, that my property was no longer for sale. I would be hearing from important people who would give me a price for it. But I should take it off the market or else.'

'Herr Pokorny, you are making no sense. Or else what?'

'They take my business license away from me. That would be an end to it all. No license. How could we survive?'

Werthen turned to leave. He did not wait to hear any more complaints from Pokorny.

'You're so interested, where are you running off to?'

But Werthen did not bother to reply.

Only one entity could single-handedly revoke a business license: the Rathaus.

It was fitting that they take the *Stadtbahn*, Vienna's metropolitan railway, for it was designed by Otto Wagner himself. Construction had begun in 1894 and was scheduled for completion next year. Wagner had done literally thousands of drawings for the massive urban rail system, employing a workshop of dozens of engineers and architects.

They were taking the River Wien Line from Karlsplatz in the center of the city all the way out to the Fourteenth District where Wagner lived. Until eight years ago this area had been merely green suburbs; now they were part of Vienna proper, the Rudolfsheim District.

On the way, Werthen was pleased to be the one regaling Gross with the startling news from Hans Wittgenstein's diary and of his visit to the owner of the property in Laab im Walde.

Gross listened carefully, looking straight ahead at the granite walls surrounding their train as they sped westward along the trench-like carriageway. They were sitting in the first-class car of the railway; the other classes were not heated.

Gross continued to mull over what Werthen said for a few moments after he finished.

Finally he muttered, 'As I suspected.'

'I beg your pardon?' Werthen was damned if he was going to let the criminologist get away with such a preposterous claim.

Gross turned to look at him now. 'Or perhaps I should have said as *we* suspected.'

'Thank you, Gross.'

Werthen noticed a man sharing the first-class carriage with them – the only other passenger at this time of the day, for sensible people would be finding a cozy *Gasthaus* or inn where they might delight in a warm meal on this frigidly cold day. Werthen's attention was caught at first by a resemblance in this man to someone else he was familiar with. It teased him, this similarity. The man, perhaps in his thirties, wore his curly, golden-brown hair short, a thin moustache graced his lip. It was the eyes, however, that held him. Deep-set, they looked out at the world with curiosity and a faint hint of disdain. Like a scent that recalls former times, these looks reminded Werthen of another man, perhaps older now, but with similar sensitive looks as a younger man.

The other thing that caught Werthen's attention about this young man was that he was quite obviously trying to overhear their conversation. Well, perhaps not obvious to one unschooled in tricks of observation, but to Werthen it was plain to see the man was either a chronic eaves-dropper, or that he wished to follow the course of their discussion.

Seated to the right across the aisle from Werthen and Gross and two rows forward, the man found ample excuse to turn back toward them, as if righting his muffler or brushing at lint on the left shoulder of his coat. He had taken up position on the aisle seat and was positioned at an angle so that he could attempt to see their reflection in the glass on his side of the car.

They were speaking in low tones, so Werthen

did not believe that the man could hear him. Still it bothered him. Had someone put a spy on their trail?

Gross, seemingly oblivious to the man's attentions, prattled on about Adele's discovery last night and how angry she still was at the events in Laab im Walde. So angry in fact that she was now determined to aid in their investigations.

Suddenly he stopped, smiling at Werthen's discomfort.

'Not to worry, dear friend,' he said. 'Were he a professional, we would not be aware of his presence. Nor would he have chosen to ride in the same car as us, the only other passenger and thus so ridiculously obvious in his curiosity.'

They rode in silence the rest of the way to the penultimate stop, Hütteldorf-Hacking, right out in the greenery of the Vienna Woods itself.

They rose to exit the car, but their curious co-passenger remained on the train as it pulled out of the small station toward the terminus at Hütteldorf-Bad.

'Typical Viennese,' Gross said, dismissing the traveler as merely congenitally nosey, as most Viennese tended to be.

Out of the station, the two made their way to the nearby Hüttelbergstrasse where Wagner had his villa. They walked in silence, each deep in his own thoughts. The narrow street climbed steeply up into the woods with large villas on both sides surrounded by park-like settings.

A brief visit to Karl Kraus earlier had brought Werthen quite up to date on the private life of Oberbaurat Otto Wagner. Werthen knew that

Wagner had built his villa here in 1888, to be used as a summerhouse for his growing family. All told, Wagner had seven children by three different relationships. Kraus was careful to term them relationships rather than marriages because the first of these was not consecrated. Wagner had two sons, Otto junior and Robert, by Sofie Anna Paupie, daughter of a well-to-do building contractor. Wagner's domineering mother, however, would not approve marriage to this woman despite the fact that her father had earned an honorary 'von' to his name. Their ménage was ultimately torn apart by Madame Wagner.

'A pliable sort of chap, our Oberbaurat Wagner, when it comes to certain women,' was Kraus's trenchant comment on this state of affairs.

Wagner's first wife, Josephine Domhart, who was his mother's choice rather than his own, was the mother of two daughters, Susanna and Margarete, the second of whom had died in adolescence. With the death of Wagner's mother, the architect finally determined to leave the unhappy marriage with Josephine, and in 1884 he shocked much of Vienna by his marriage to the much younger Louise Stiffel, governess to his daughter Susanne. Theirs appeared to be a true love marriage according to Kraus, and three children resulted from the union: Stefan, Louise, and Christine.

It was for this third 'family' that Wagner had built the villa, and they were just approaching it now at Hüttelbergstrasse 26. Sitting stately on a hillock above road level, the building was a graceful Palladian structure, with a central portion reached by an impressive range of steps leading to a magnificent portal entrance. Four large pillars decorated the balustrade, each covered in vertical bands of colored porcelain. Statues of Greek gods were fitted into niches on each side of the entrance. This central rectangular living section was further elongated by a pergola at each end. These had latterly been converted into a spacious living room at one end and into Wagner's home studio at the other, its windows done in stained glass. This summerhouse had now become Wagner's year-round abode.

The spacious and dignified villa was made utterly bourgeois by a white picket fence surrounding the grounds at street level; Werthen had to check a laugh as he and Gross went through the main gate and made their way up the wide flight of marble stairs to the front entrance. Painted wrought iron in a riot of design served as a balustrade for the entrance porch; plaster relief work of cupids at play filled three friezes over the door. Similar relief work decorated the overhanging sections of the slightly peaked roof.

How much must such a home cost? Werthen wondered. And how could Wagner, who was essentially a university professor, afford such a place? After all, everyone knew that his building designs were more often discussed than built. His work on the metropolitan railway and the regulation of the River Wien and the Danube Canal was in no way remunerated in accord with the countless hours he had put into these projects, the thousands of sketches he had made in their planning. During the hectic years of the *Stadtbahn* construction, Wagner's studio employed a staff of seventy architects, engineers, and draftsmen. Other city buildings by Wagner had been constructed on speculation; he would occupy them for a time, but then always sell them. This villa, however, was his family seat and substantial enough for an archduke. In fact, rumor had it that it was initially intended for Crown Prince Rudolf, but that Wagner's wife had so fallen in love with it that the architect withdrew his commission to the Hofburg. Which might account for difficulties Wagner had in winning commissions from the emperor.

Meanwhile, Gross had begun rapping on the large front door. After a second round of knocks, they heard footsteps echoing on floor tiles from inside and then the door opened.

Much to Werthen's surprise, it was the same fellow from the *Stadtbahn* who opened the door, coat still in hand as if about to hang it up.

'Oh ... Hello,' he said in recognition. 'You must be the detective fellows Father was mentioning.'

'That is quite all right, Otto Emmerich.' These words came from a small, round woman who looked rather like a defiant pigeon. She bustled to the door. 'I shall welcome our guests.'

She seemed put out that Otto junior should have answered the door and not she. The man was clearly Wagner's illegitimate oldest son, whom he had in fact adopted and given his surname, and who, Kraus had told Werthen, had trained as an architect and sometimes worked with his father. The female pigeon must be Frau Wagner, Werthen surmised. Clearly no mere housekeeper could be as curt as she was to young Wagner.

Otto junior ignored her. 'I was just arriving myself. Had I known you were the ones Father invited, I would have told you to stay on till the last stop. There's a shortcut.'

'And I am sure the von Adrassys do not take kindly to your traipsing through their grounds.'

Nothing Frau Wagner said, however, seemed to get through to Wagner's illegitimate son.

'Leave your coats and follow me,' he said. 'I'll take you to the studio.'

Gross was having none of this. 'Doktor Gross,' he said, with a head nod to Frau Wagner. 'And my colleague, Advokat Werthen. Do we have the pleasure of addressing Frau Wagner?'

She puffed up her chest at this. 'Yes, you do. And it is a delight to make your acquaintance.' She hesitated for a moment as if about to offer her hand, but thought better of it.

'This way, gentlemen,' called Otto junior as he strode across the marble floor of the foyer.

'You must excuse Otto Emmerich,' she said, shaking her head.

'May we?' Gross asked, motioning his hand at the retreating figure of Otto Emmerich Wagner.

'Yes, but of course. Hurry or you shall be completely lost.'

They did not bother divesting themselves of coats, but did doff their hats as they entered the high-ceilinged vestibule. Wagner led them something of a chase through suites of rooms at the back of the central portion of the villa, all nicely appointed. Werthen noticed that there was not one piece of Jugendstil furnishing or any Secession paintings hanging on the walls of the main house, not even by their mutual friend Klimt. This seemed odd to the lawyer, considering Wagner's recent defection to the Secession from the more conservative Künstlerhaus and its slavish devotion to historicism.

Finally they came to the south wing of the villa, and entered the converted pergola. A rainbow of light filled the room, as a sudden break in the clouds outside allowed the sun to shine through the stained glass windows of the eastern side of the studio. Here, then, was their first discovery of Secession work, for the swirling trees in a riot of shades was clearly Jugendstil in design.

'You like it?' Otto Wagner stood at the door to greet them.

'Yes, I do,' Werthen said, looking again at the windows.

Under his open white work coat Wagner wore a gray, vested, wool suit and a black tie loosely knotted under wing collars. His Van Dyke beard was more salt than pepper, the moustaches rather dramatically twisted and curled upwards at the ends. Thinning gray hair was swept back off his forehead. His most prominent features, his eyes, were lightly cloaked, as if the eyelids had extra folds. However, their piercing glance gave one the sense that this man saw everything and

216

through everything. Eyebrows that arched upward added to a general air of knowing and almost condescension.

'The series is called "Vienna Woods in the Autumn,"' Wagner said. 'Gives the studio a bit of warmth in the winter, too.'

Introductions were made all around, and Werthen shook the architect's hand, noting that Wagner used only his forefinger and thumb for a grip. Another detail Kraus supplied came to mind: Wagner lost the use of the middle finger on his right hand as a result of a hunting accident in his youth. That did not stop the architect from becoming one of the best draftsmen in the world.

'You've met my son, of course.' Wagner clapped Otto Emmerich on the back. 'Boy's taking after his father. Make a fine architect one day.'

Otto junior smiled like a schoolboy at the praise.

Wagner quickly lost his affability, however, turning to the matter at hand.

'Now what is this nonsense about Steinwitz?'

'We do not find it nonsense, Oberbaurat,' Gross said.

A drawing on one of the drafting tables caught Werthen's attention. It appeared to be the sketch of a large domed church standing alone like a beacon on a hillside. Another building project that would go unbuilt?

'Well, I was there just moments after the shot. I can assure you that I saw no one leaving the room.'

'I understand there was some confusion in the hallway,' Gross said.

'Yes, of course. One does not expect to hear a gunshot go off in the Rathaus.'

'Where were you when you heard the shot?'

'In my special office. It is on the same floor. I was on my own and looked up immediately from the drafting table when I heard this crack sound. Unmistakably a shot.'

Werthen was pulled out of his observation of the schematic of the church by this remark.

'Excuse me, Herr Wagner, but did you not tell the *Neue Freie Presse* in an interview that you thought it might be an automobile backfiring?'

'Well, one could hardly hear such a thing several floors up in the Rathaus.'

'But it was your first reaction?'

'Yes. Silly of course.'

'Nonetheless,' Werthen went on, 'it would not have alarmed you as the sound of a shot would have. You would not have been spurred into immediate action.'

Wagner sighed. 'Yes, I quite see what you mean. Perhaps there was a moment or two before I went to investigate matters.'

Werthen left it there. No use in antagonizing the man by driving home the point that there may indeed have been time for someone to leave the office before he, Wagner, arrived first on the scene.

Gross picked up the interview again. 'And what brought you to the door of Steinwitz's office? How could you know that was the origin of the noise?'

'The smell. Cordite. That I recognized immediately. I followed the odor.'

218

'Did you touch the body?' Gross asked. 'I mean, in order to ascertain if he were dead or not.'

'Absolutely not,' Wagner replied. 'I did not enter the room. One look from the doorway was enough for me. Half the man's head had been shot off.'

'And you are sure you saw nothing suspicious? Someone, for example, in the vicinity of the office who did not belong there?'

'I was rather more concentrating on Stein-witz.'

'Yes,' Gross allowed. 'Quite understandable.' A pause. 'One other thing. Perhaps you could indicate how far you were from the door to the office. Would it be possible to measure the distance by one of your strides?'

'But I was standing in the doorway itself.'

'Actually inside?'

'No. Well. Let me see ... How might this be important?'

The Oberbaurat was obviously losing his patience.

'Please indulge me,' Gross said. 'I am something of a perfectionist in my approach to a crime scene, much as you are in your preparation for building. Let us say this is the door.'

Gross marked a rectangle in the space in front of him.

'Now perhaps you could indicate exactly where you were in relation to that door.'

Wagner sighed. 'If you insist. But I really—'

'It would aid in knowing your field of vision,' Gross assured him.

'Go on, Father. The sooner you answer their questions, the sooner we get back to the Steinhof drawings.'

Wagner said nothing, but took a stride forward, positioning himself just at the outer extension of Gross's imaginary door.

'Excellent,' Gross said. 'Now perhaps again, just to be sure. Could you take two normal strides backward, and then approach once more, just to be sure?'

Again Gross sketched the imaginary door in the air.

Wagner did as he was bid, eager to be rid of his intruders now. Werthen noticed that Gross was careful to observe the stride.

'That should do it, then,' Gross said as Wagner approached the air door at approximately the same point as before. 'We will leave you to your work.'

'A new commission?' Werthen said, gesturing toward the sketch of the church.

'A competition,' Wagner said. 'For the church and sanatorium on Steinhof. Why I bother, though, I don't know. They will surely give it to someone with better connections than I have.'

'But one assumes your work for the municipality—' Werthen began.

'Indeed,' Wagner interrupted. 'The municipality, not the state. I have no friends in the higher corridors of power. That is why I am relegated to building my castles in the air.'

'It's hardly as bad as that, Father.'

Wagner gave his adopted son a withering glance. 'Tell me that in twenty years when none of your prized plans have been built. We can have a philosophical discussion about Vienna and connections at that time. For now, please show our visitors out.'

Wagner turned to his drawing, not bothering with goodbyes. Werthen and Gross followed the son out of the studio.

'You must forgive my father,' he said once they were out of earshot of the elder Wagner. 'It has been difficult for him. Dozens of first-class projects – for an art colony, for an imperial museum, for a new war ministry building – and the contracts have been awarded to far less able men.'

'Still,' Werthen said, 'he is a university professor, the head of the architecture department at the Academy of Fine Arts.'

'A sinecure. But yes, as a teacher Father has great influence. He is cultivating a new generation of architects, people who will take his dictums of form following function around the world. Yet, it does not compensate. He often feels that he is Vienna's neglected genius.'

'Is that how you see your father?' Gross asked as they approached the foyer once again.

'How is that?' Frau Wagner said, coming out of the shadows as if lingering in ambush. 'You see your father in what way?' she insisted.

'A genius,' Otto Emmerich said, smiling at Gross and Werthen.

'And rightly so,' she said. 'And a compassionate man. After all, he has so many of his own children, and he still adopts you and your brother.'

221

A squeal of girlish laughter from deeper in the house reminded Werthen that the children born to Wagner by his present wife would range from only eleven to sixteen years in age.

'As I said,' young Wagner noted, 'a genius and a saint.'

Back out in the blustery day, Gross and Werthen headed down the Hüttelbergstrasse toward the *Stadtbahn* station.

'A bitter man,' Gross said as they set a brisk pace.

'Father or son?'

'The elder, of course. The son is a puppy looking for love.'

Werthen sensed that Gross had formed one of his instant dislikes. Werthen always found this odd for a man such as Gross who professed to use the methods of deduction rather than pure intuition; who championed reason over emotion.

'Nothing wrong with instant dislikes,' Gross had once told him. 'I find it saves so much time.'

'Do the strides match those found on the carpet?' Werthen asked.

'Bravo for you, Werthen. I hope it was not that obvious to everybody.'

Werthen made no response to this.

'I could think of no subtler way to view his stride length. Doors made of air. What idiots brilliant people can be.'

'Do they?'

Gross puffed his lips. 'Difficult to ascertain. Well within the range of possibility, and the man's boot is on the smallish side.'

'Do you think he knows of the Vienna Woods sell-off? Rather ironic if so.'

Gross looked perplexed. 'My dear Werthen, whatever could irony have to do with this case?'

'I simply meant that Wagner has his family seat in the Vienna Woods. A full fifty percent of this very district is part of the Vienna Woods. The irony is in his stained glass windows. Leave it to the mayor and his cronies and those windows will soon be all that is left of the woods to see.'

'No need for melodrama, Werthen. As yet we have only the diary of Hans Wittgenstein to attest to such a scheme.'

'I see no reason for him to lie,' Werthen retorted.

Gross merely shrugged at this and quickened his pace toward the station.

'Brutal weather,' he muttered. 'Goes right to the bone.'

'Could he have done it?' Werthen asked suddenly.

They were now nearing the station, done in the Jugendstil mode that was so sparsely represented in Wagner's home.

Gross stopped mid-stride.

'Yes, I suppose he could have. He has no alibi. After all he told us himself that he was on his own in his office. And as for motive, let us say that Herr Wagner is party to this scheme to sell off the woods...'

'He has written widely about the modern city,' Werthen interrupted. 'That progress and business should regulate such a city. Its growth should not be restricted by natural impediments or boundaries.'

'Quite,' Gross said, taking small umbrage at being interrupted. 'As I was saying, let us assume there was or is a scheme to sell the Vienna Woods and that Wagner was somehow involved with it. Perhaps he is offered the monumental job of planning the building of it. Such an offer would mean much to him, that is clear.'

'And then he somehow gets word that Steinwitz and his journalist friend Praetor are set to spoil the deal,' Werthen added.

'Ergo, a man *in extremis*,' Gross said. 'He clearly knows his way around firearms. He tells us he is familiar with the smell of cordite.'

Werthen offered the information Kraus had earlier given him regarding the hunting accident Wagner had suffered as a youth.

'All in all, I should say yes. Oberbaurat Wagner surely is a suspect. And not simply because of instant dislike,' Gross added. 'In fact, I rather liked the man. He is devoted to his work, that much is clear. And he is talented. Qualities I admire.'

'Pity if he were a murderer, too,' Werthen said.

Fourteen

Later that afternoon, Werthen was in attendance for the free weekly public lecture at the Museum of Art and Industry on the Stubenring. Today's guest speaker was the director of the State Trade School, the architect and city planner, Regierungsrat Camillo Sitte. The title of his lecture: 'Uncontained Urban Growth: Progress or Abomination?'

Werthen was no fan of such rhetoric; the very phrasing of the question presumed the answer. But he was here with a purpose, for Adele Gross – commissioned to the task by Berthe – had met with Rosa Mayreder's brother, Councilman Rudolf Mayreder. The city council member had little to relate about the deceased Steinwitz in terms of friendships and allegiances. However, he had presented one piece of interesting information: Councilman Steinwitz was latterly in consultation with Regierungsrat Camillo Sitte.

Werthen intended to find out what sort of consultations the two had.

Sitte soon made his way on to the stage of the small auditorium, a short, stocky man, with a frosted beard grown long in front, and wire-rim glasses framing a cherubic face. He wore a morning coat and floppy, bohemian-style beret.

Sitte seemed an odd figure upon the stage, approaching the lectern rather reluctantly, adjusting a sheaf of notes, his head lowered, so that all the audience could see of him now was his incongruous beret.

A man of about Otto Wagner's age, he was also a theoretician of urban planning. His *City Planning According to Artistic Principles* appeared in 1889 and caused something of a stir. In fact, Sitte and Wagner were polar opposites in their view of city development. For Wagner, a city had to be utilitarian, built in grids for the easy flow of commerce and traffic. Its architecture should be functional, unadorned; its vistas unbroken. For Sitte, however, the baroque square or plaza was the apex of urban design. He favored such intimate squares and meandering lanes. Not for him the Haussmann-like boulevards of Paris.

The audience this Friday afternoon consisted of a jumbled assortment of students in rumpled suits and short-haired, earnest-looking types who were most likely architects or architectural critics, as well as a flock of older women, as out of place here as Sitte's beret, who seemed to have thought they had come to a lecture on flower arrangement. One young man, ruddy-faced with a dapper moustache and well-tailored suit, sat apart from the others, as did Werthen. The Advokat thought he had seen this man before, but would not swear to it. Werthen had no idea if this was a large or a small number for such public lectures.

His attention now went back to the stage. A

tall, gaunt-looking fellow in a charcoal suit came on to the stage after Sitte, looking as concerned as a mother duck. He turned out to be the director of lectures at the Museum of Art and Industry and quickly made an introduction of the architect and urban planner. Thereafter he left the stage to Sitte, who suddenly remembered he was wearing the beret, and took it off, stuffing it into one of the pockets of his jacket. He cleared his throat and immediately boomed out in a resonant bass voice, without preamble, 'Modern systems! Yes, indeed. To approach everything in a strictly methodical manner and not to waver a hair's breadth from preconceived patterns, until genius has been strangled to death and *joie de vivre* stifled by the system – that is the sign of our time.'

Sitte at once caught the attention of those thirty people and for the next three-quarters of an hour ploughed on through his topic, here extolling the virtues of crooked streets and an organic tangle of lanes and alleys that promoted human discourse and interaction, there deprecating the inhumanity of the eternal, infernal right angle in city streets – the geometrization of the urban. He touched on topics from the importance of the enclosed medieval square in creating a cityscape of human dimensions to the prevalence of the newly diagnosed neurosis, *Platzscheu*, or agoraphobia, a fear of crossing vast urban spaces, such as those the architects of the Ringstrasse had necklaced Vienna's Inner City with.

'A square should be seen as a room,' he intoned. 'It should form an enclosed space.'

The great enemy to urban development was the grid system, he declared, whereby planners, such as Otto Wagner, took utilitarianism to the extreme.

'A city is not only about the smooth flow of traffic, nor is it solely to do with commerce. A city should also touch the deepest sense of the aesthetic in each of us. It should be, as another much better known Wagner, the master of Bayreuth, has stated, a *Gesamtkunstwerk*, a total work of art.'

Werthen's ears pricked up at these mentions of Otto Wagner, but he soon found himself focusing on other considerations as Sitte went on to praise the importance of parks and areas of greenery in and around a city:

'The large open areas in metropolises, especially when laid out as parks and perhaps supplied with expanses of water and with waterworks, form the air pockets essential for breathing in the city. They have appropriately enough been called its lungs.'

For Sitte the city, and Vienna in particular, had limits. The green belt of the Vienna Woods was, for him, a means for the city to renew itself not only physically, but also spiritually.

'One has only to stand in the midst of one of our city streets and gaze upon the nearby gently undulating folds of the Woods to feel a certain spiritual weight lifted from one's shoulders. Beware, for the despoilers are busy at work even now, the speculators, the propagandists for growth and the increase of commerce at any cost. You must all take this message with you tonight: Demand city leaders to go beyond blind obeisance to the impudent drumbeat of progress, progress. Beware those who declare, "Necessity is art's only mistress."'

The last bit was a specific dig at Wagner, Werthen knew, for that was the Oberbaurat's artistic creed.

The audience broke into spirited applause as Sitte moved away from the lectern. Werthen found himself standing and applauding with the others. He only now realized that Sitte had not once consulted the papers lying before him.

The tall, gaunt director of lectures returned and announced a period of questions and answers. There were the usual few students, probably from the State Trade School itself, who played the sycophant, asking questions that were in essence abject flattery tagged with a question mark. There was also a pair of questions from one of the fellows whom Werthen had falsely assumed to be architects or critics. The man in fact turned out to be a stockbroker from the Börse, or stock exchange, accusing Sitte of being out of touch with the times, of hampering progress and the growth of industry. Sitte brought a hoot from the student section when he replied:

'No, sir. It is you who is out of touch with your soul.'

And the women Werthen suspected of having got into the wrong lecture were actually members of a committee of concerned citizens who hoped to preserve the Vienna Woods from any development. Their leader, a heavily powdered matron, wanted to know what Sitte thought of rumors going about City Hall regarding a proposed sell-off of the Woods.

Sitte answered: 'I shall have more to say of this rumor in the very near future, my good madam.'

A small group gathered near the stage to exchange final pleasantries with the urban planner, and Werthen joined it, hat in hand. He waited patiently until the others had their say and drifted away in ones and twos. Sitte's eyes occasionally focused on him, as if wondering what this stranger might want. Finally left alone, Sitte nodded at him.

'A wonderful lecture, Herr Regierungsrat,' Werthen said. 'It has given me much to think on.'

'You are no fan of the modern city, sir?'

'To be honest,' Werthen said, 'I no longer know. There is much to be said in favor of your arguments. But can we actually go back in time to the medieval city?'

'Ah, you misconstrue my argument, Herr...?'

'Werthen.'

Sitte looked rather surprised at this.

'Advokat Werthen?'

Now it was Werthen's turn for surprise. 'Yes. You have heard of me?'

'We have a friend in common, I believe. The conductor, Hans Richter. He mentioned you as regards a case involving our esteemed Court Opera Director, Herr Mahler.'

Werthen had indeed made the acquaintance of Richter while working on a case involving

Mahler. He was surprised that the man should remember him, however, for their intercourse had been brief enough in that instance.

'We were schoolmates at the Piaristen Gymnasium,' Sitte explained. 'Herr Richter is sadly missed, however, living as he now does in London. But he did speak highly of you and the manner in which you deported yourself in the Mahler affair.'

One more proof, if any were needed, that Vienna was an overgrown village where everyone was connected to everyone else in some manner or another.

Werthen made no immediate reply to the compliment, and Sitte filled the silence.

'Does official business bring you to my lecture or are you actually a concerned citizen?'

'A little of both,' he replied honestly, for he could see that subterfuge was not the appropriate tack to take with this man.

'And you must know Olbrich,' Sitte said, looking over Werthen's shoulder. Turning, Werthen saw the ruddy-faced young man he had earlier noticed.

'Olbrich,' Sitte said, catching his attention. 'Meet Advokat Werthen.'

Olbrich approached and extended his hand. 'Herr Werthen.'

Werthen was pleased by the man's grip; neither too limp nor bone-crushing. Josef Maria Olbrich was the architect of the Secession gallery. They had briefly met when Werthen was employed on his first case involving Klimt, leader of the Secession.

'We have been introduced before,' Werthen said. 'Though you may not remember me.'

'Why of course he does,' Sitte said.

Olbrich smiled at Werthen. 'Of course I do. Klimt still speaks most kindly of you. Though I see little of him these days. I shall have to return to Germany tomorrow.'

Werthen now remembered that Olbrich had recently been wooed away from Vienna by Grand Duke Ernst Ludwig of Hesse-Darmstadt, where he had been commissioned to build an artists' colony for the duke. Before that, the young architect had been allied with Otto Wagner in the building of the *Stadtbahn*. Olbrich had, in fact, been responsible for many of the design flourishes of the stations of the railway which those not in the know credited Wagner with.

'I am rather surprised *you* two know one another,' Werthen now said, meaning Sitte and Olbrich, for they would seemingly be on opposite sides of the great artistic-architectural divide in Vienna.

'Easily explained,' Sitte said. 'Olbrich here was my student not long after I assumed the directorship of the school. A most promising young boy he was. I believe I gave you an "excellent" for your final grade.' He clapped Olbrich on the back. 'I do not hold it against you that you later studied under the esteemed Otto Wagner at the Academy of Fine Arts, nor that you went to work for that urban despoiler.'

'Hardly a despoiler, Herr Sitte,' Olbrich protested. 'Let us not go down that cul-de-sac again.'

Werthen smiled at Olbrich's witticism, for it was Sitte who actually coined the phrase and developed the concept of a cul-de-sac or dead end street.

'Herr Sitte,' Werthen interrupted, 'you mentioned in your talk rumors of the Vienna Woods being in danger.'

Olbrich rolled his eyes at this, and Werthen assumed that he had once again stumbled into controversial territory.

'Most dire,' Sitte said, sounding like a doctor at a deathbed.

'Do you actually know of plans under way to sell the Woods?' Werthen asked.

'Herr Sitte sees conspirators behind every door at City Hall,' Olbrich said archly. 'But if you will both forgive me,' he said, 'I really must be going. Splendid lecture, Camillo.'

'Many thanks for coming to hear this old man prattle on.'

Olbrich smiled at this, again shaking Werthen's hand. 'A pleasure to meet you once again.'

After he departed, Werthen asked Sitte about Councilman Steinwitz and their meetings.

'Why the curiosity? Do you suspect foul play?'

The man's eyes lit up at the use of this dramatic term.

Werthen sidestepped the question. 'What were you consulting him about?'

'A most stubborn *Advokat* you are. Very well, your question first. Councilman Steinwitz had me in to offer a different view to the Rathaus on urban development. The councilman had been swayed, it seems, by my little book about city planning. We met three times in all. Not an overly intelligent man, I must confess, but one, once he had a bit of leather between his teeth, not to let it go. Steinwitz felt that our mayor, Herr Lueger, was rather too much under the artistic sway of Otto Wagner. He wished to change that situation.'

'Did he tell you of a scheme to sell off the Vienna Woods?'

'Yes.'

'What I don't understand is the legality of it. I thought that was all settled decades ago.'

'With Josef Schöffel, you mean? One would have hoped so. That man almost single-handedly took on a Salzburg consortium ready to buy the woods. You may remember that our great empire was in dire straits in the early 1870s. We had lost wars to the Italians in 1859 and to the Prussians in 1866. The economy was at breaking point. And then a group of corrupt officials decided they would sell off the lovely forest and mea-dowland of the Vienna Woods to speculators, men who would cut down the magnificent beech trees for mere lucre. Schöffel, a retired military man, banded together with the journalist Ferdi-nand Kurnberger to expose those knaves. Yes, they saved the woods. But that was almost thirty years ago. A motion was propagated, not an ordnance. There is no official law protecting the Vienna Woods.'

'What did Steinwitz have to say about it?'

'He mentioned that he was considering making

public the fact that members of City Hall were planning to sell off a vast tract of land in the midst of the Vienna Woods.'

'Did you know he was talking with a journalist about the Woods scheme?'

'No. I rather thought he was looking for arguments initially to present to our most noble mayor to make the man change his mind.'

'Did he mention Lueger directly?'

Sitte thought about this. 'No. I do not believe he did. The implication, however, was clear.'

'The journalist was later murdered.'

'Come now,' Sitte said. 'We are all civilized people here. We do not go about murdering those who disagree with us.'

Werthen wondered if he should inform Sitte of the obvious. Indeed people did kill those they disagreed with and who could ruin a lucrative business deal. Sitte was in fact lucky to still be alive.

But the town planner was no naïf.

'In other words, I could be next.'

'Doubtful now. Too many know of the scheme.'

Sitte considered for a moment. Then, 'You should speak with Taylor Remington.'

'The American impresario?' Werthen remembered that Fräulein Metzinger had mentioned interest in seeing the man's Wild West Show with Huck. 'Whatever for?'

'Steinwitz was convinced Remington was the one buying the Woods parcel. I assume he would have the most to lose if the deal collapsed for some reason.'

They were dining together, the better to review the day's happenings. Doktor and Frau Gross sat on one side of the Biedermeier table, the von Werthens on the other, and Berthe and Werthen at either end.

There were no complaints from Frau Blatschky, despite the extra work these added guests at table made for her. In fact, she seemed in absolute bliss, bustling about 'her' kitchen with real delight. Tonight she had outdone herself, bringing compliments even from Frau von Werthen. It had begun with a *Wiener Suppentopf* with bits of beef, sausage, noodles, and turnips in a clear bouillon. This was followed by a *Lungenbraten*, a tenderloin filet floured and cooked in butter with onions, mushrooms, and parsley, accompanied by a green bean salad in oil and vinegar with just the right amount of dill and diced onion. Now they were lingering at the table over coffee and *Kaiserschmarren*, a sugared crêpe with raisins.

Over the soup daily pleasantries were passed – Frieda had missed one of her naps, suffering from an acute case of hiccoughs; Frau and Herr von Werthen had spent much of the day at the Imperial Natural History Museum indulging one of Emile von Werthen's few hobbies: lepidoptera. In particular, they had examined a new addition to the collection, a birdwing, or *Ornithoptera alexandrae*, the largest known butterfly. Discussion of this specimen took them on into the meat course, by which time Werthen had begun to detail their interviews with Wagner and later with Sitte.

'Sounds like an odd duck to me,' Herr von Werthen said following his son's description of Camillo Sitte.

'Happily so,' Berthe said, for it turned out she had read his *City Planning According to Artistic Principles*, and was a believer in his theories of urban growth.

Emile von Werthen eyed his daughter-in-law as if demanding an explanation of her comment.

She obliged.

'Just because we are in a new century does not mean we are bound to the idea of progress at any cost. Unbounded urban growth as some call for will create miserable lives for the vast majority. Now in Vienna half the area is taken up by the Woods and by parks and gardens. I for one would like that to continue so that Frieda and other children can grow up in a city that is habitable.'

'I second that,' Frau Gross said.

'But surely you would not let a tree stand in the way of a new business,' Herr von Werthen said, aghast at the idea. 'Think of the work created. You have sympathies for the workers, as I understand. Would you pit their welfare against the life of one tree?'

Werthen chuckled at the analogy. 'Papa, I do not think we are talking about one tree here.'

Werthen glanced at Gross, who nodded his assent. They had not yet shared the most volatile nugget of information gleaned today: the scheme to sell off a vast tract of the Vienna Woods, as detailed in Hans Wittgenstein's diary. After

237

Werthen divulged this plan, there was a pro-
longed silence.

Finally Emile von Werthen exploded: 'The
blackguards!'

'Calm yourself, Emile.'

His wife attempted to pat the back of his hand,
but he jerked it away.

'But what of the 1873 ordinance?' Berthe asked quite sensibly.

'Sitte says they have found a way around that,'
Werthen answered. 'That it is not a legally bind-
ing ordinance at all.'

'Let me get this straight,' Emile von Werthen
said, facing his son now. 'You and Doktor Gross
contend that this councilman and also a
journalist were murdered to silence them.'

'Correct,' Werthen said.

'And that it was this secret scheme to sell off
the Vienna Woods that is the reason for their
deaths?'

'That would appear to be the case,' Gross
answered.

'Unbelievable,' Herr von Werthen said.

Werthen was glad to see that his father's sense
of justice was finally aroused; for once he was
not focusing on mere self-interest.

'That means,' Herr von Werthen continued,
'that you have put us in danger by sharing this
information. I warned you that this investigating
business of yours would bring ruin to us all.'

'Now Emile. Calm yourself,' cooed Frau von
Werthen.

Werthen could only groan.

* * *

After his parents left, Werthen brought out the Wittgenstein diary he had taken from the office so that his wife and the Grosses could see it personally. When it came his turn to examine the journal, Doktor Gross examined entries closely preceding the final ones. He also inspected the empty pages to make sure there truly were no more entries, turning all the way to the end pages.

'What's this?' he said, finding a sleeve glued on to the inside of the back cover. From this he carefully extracted a folded piece of paper. By the looks of it, this paper had once been crumpled, perhaps balled up and thrown away and then later retrieved by Hans Wittgenstein.

Gross slowly unfolded the paper, which with closer examination was revealed to be a piece of fine linen stationery. The others now left their chairs and gathered around him. Once the paper was laid out flat on the table, two things were immediately apparent. The letterhead indicated it was from the desk of Karl Wittgenstein, father of the runaway Hans. Secondly, the letter, or protocol as it turned out, was titled 'Opening and Development of the Outer Ring of Vienna.'

'Meaning the Vienna Woods,' Berthe said.

'I believe so,' Gross said, quickly scanning the letter. The others were doing the same and it quickly became apparent to them that this was a draft of a letter by Karl Wittgenstein, representing other unnamed investors, to offer bids on purchasing a large tract of the Woods for an estate development: large villas surrounded by immense grounds.

Gross thumped his forefinger on the letter. 'This may explain why the son took leave of the family house.'

'The final straw,' Werthen agreed, returning to his seat along with Berthe and Frau Gross. 'That his own father was involved in the scheme.'

So that was what the youth meant by the last entry, 'All is lost,' thought Werthen.

'But what of this Remington person you mentioned?' Adele Gross asked. 'Isn't he the one Herr Sitte said was the prospective buyer?'

'It looks from this,' Gross said, 'that Lueger was going to sell the land off to the highest bidder.'

'Auction off the Woods,' Berthe said. 'It's ridiculous.'

'But,' Werthen said, 'apparently not illegal.'

'What could he hope to achieve by it?' Frau Gross said. 'It would be the ruin of him politically.'

Fair question, Werthen thought. If the sale could be done in private, the development of the Woods surely could not. Public outrage and outcry would follow. Or was Lueger wily enough to deflect his critics? After all, if he could turn anti-Semitism into a winning campaign plank, perhaps Lueger could make the sale of the Vienna Woods appear to be in the interests of the little people, too. But what was it all for? Why this grand risk?

'We now have a template to follow,' Gross said, interrupting Werthen's thoughts. 'Our theory is that Councilman Steinwitz and the journalist Henricus Praetor were both murdered and that there is a direct connection between the two crimes. We lack direct evidence, such as any sign of the various files Steinwitz shared with Praetor or of the journals that Herr Praetor is said to have kept. However, we have ample indirect evidence from Hans Wittgenstein's diary entries that the two were linked by their involvement in making public the plot to sell off large parts of the Vienna Woods.'

'Indirect evidence substantiated by Sitte,' Werthen added, 'and confirmed by this letter from Karl Wittgenstein.'

'Thus...?' Gross said, his voice rising at the end as if asking for conclusions.

'There are at least four persons or groups of persons that would benefit from the deaths of Steinwitz and Praetor,' Werthen said. 'First, the sellers. Those involved at the Rathaus.'

'You are assuming that Mayor Lueger himself was directly involved in this?' asked Berthe.

Gross nodded again. 'You have a valid point, Frau Werthen. As yet we have no direct proof that Lueger authorized such a sale. His name is not actually mentioned in this letter. However, it would be a strong inference. Who else could authorize such an action?'

'That is something I would like to pursue,' Frau Gross said. 'And I believe I have a direction to follow. Perhaps his legion of female supporters could tell us something. Far better for a woman to talk to a woman, don't you think so, dear?'

They paused for a moment. Gross was not the sort to appreciate having one of his investigations become co-opted. However, issues of domestic harmony appeared to outweigh other considerations.

'I think that would be a fine contribution to our inquiries,' he said.

Werthen cast a smile at Berthe, who raised eyebrows at this suddenly domesticated Gross. Werthen suspected that there had to be other motivation for Gross. Surely if he kept his wife occupied interviewing the Amazons who supported Lueger, they would hardly have time to attend more balls. Clever man, Gross.

'So,' Werthen continued where he had left off. 'The Rathaus is surely one avenue of investigation. I believe it is high time that we spoke with Lueger face to face.'

'When he returns from the spa,' Gross said.

'That should be this Monday,' Werthen said. Then, 'Karl Wittgenstein and his investors are another group to investigate, for they would benefit if their bid won and lose out if the newspapers broadcast the scheme. And finally, Taylor Remington, another prospective buyer, would have the same motivation.'

'Kill two people because of a business deal?' Berthe sounded skeptical.

'Lesser motives have resulted in larger death tolls,' Gross pronounced.

But Werthen thought she seemed unconvinced.

'You mentioned four,' she said to him.

'Sorry?'

'Four persons or groups that stood to benefit. You only talked about three.'

'Right. It is not likely, but Otto Wagner should

be on the list. He had opportunity. He was the first on the scene. Gross estimates his stride and footprint could be consistent with the stains left on Steinwitz's carpet.'

'But whatever for?' Adele Gross asked.

Werthen detailed his theory that perhaps Wagner, a close professional associate at the Rathaus and acknowledged friend of Lueger's, had been offered some sort of commission to build and develop the land sold. After all, he appeared bitter that the majority of his designs had never been built. And after a little digging, Werthen had also discovered that the man was over his head in debt, having built two apartment and commercial buildings on speculation and now having difficulty selling them. The buildings were located on the Magdalenenstrasse on the River Wien, and one of them, in particular, the Majolika Haus, named so after the pink, blue, and green floral faience design on the façade, was termed by Wagner's detractors as ugly beyond description. Thus far, according to Kraus, two separate purchases had fallen through, the prospective buyers put off at the last minute by the bad press the projects were receiving.

'In short,' Werthen said, 'Wagner is badly in need of an infusion of funds.'

'Aren't we all,' said Frau Gross. But both she and Berthe seemed unconvinced with this theory.

'I said it was not likely, but we cannot rule out any suspects at this stage. Right, Gross?'

He looked to his old colleague for support.

'I rather liked the fellow,' was Gross's sole response.

Fifteen

The Prater was powdered in a light snowfall. A sky gray and threatening hung overhead, but all around could be heard the delighted shouts and squeals of children. It was Saturday half-day at school and it seemed that most of the children of the city had thronged to Remington's Wild West Show.

A tent city had popped up overnight on the grounds of the Prater like a cluster of gigantic mushrooms. Giant hoardings all around proclaimed the delights of the show: 'Custer's Last Stand,' 'The Buffalo Hunt,' 'The Greatest Shot in the World.' It took several trains to deliver the four hundred white and Indian actors and stagehands, two hundred and fifty horses, twenty buffalo, fifteen elk, a dozen long-horned Texas steers, and all the paraphernalia needed to outfit the show – including an electrical generating plant to illuminate the night shows.

Gross puffed vapor bubbles into the chill air as they walked on to the grounds.

'What would impel people to hold an outdoor attraction at this inclement time of year.'

It was not a question, but Werthen offered an answer anyway. 'The feuilleton writers say Remington thought he was going to Australia.

It's summer there.'

Gross gave Werthen a look of utter disbelief.

'It is possible,' Werthen added. 'After all, there have been numerous American tourists to arrive in Vienna only to be disappointed at its lack of canals.'

'They'll be searching for kangaroos next,' Gross muttered.

Whether by accident or design, the arrival of Remington's Wild West Show surely did not lack for enthusiastic customers. Schoolchildren, still in their uniforms and with school bags on their shoulders, roamed the grounds like hungry Indians on the prowl. Many of them carried paper sacks full of small puffy white balls. Werthen noticed that these bags came from a number of stands that looked much like a traditional Austrian *Wurstel* stand. Large signs advertised 'Popcorn.' It was something Werthen had read of, this toasted or popped corn, in relation to the early Spanish explorers in the New World. The indigenous people had attempted to sell the exotic food to these explorers, but the Spanish were having none of it. Werthen vowed to try some of this strange confection before he left the grounds. Of course this desire was not something he wanted to share with Gross.

'Go ahead, Werthen. Buy a bag,' the criminologist said. 'You look as eager as a schoolchild yourself.'

Werthen sheepishly queued up at one of the stands, paid his twenty *Kreutzer*, and took a bite of the puffed corn. He liked the somewhat crunchy texture and the salty taste. Following the example of schoolchildren all around him, he took a handful of the stuff and plopped it in his mouth. Immediate pain erupted as he bit down wrong on an unpopped kernel.

'*Verdammt*,' he said, spitting the unchewed mess on to the ground and then threw the remainder of the bag into a nearby receptacle.

'An acquired taste, one assumes,' Gross said, a smile on his face.

'I believe in future I shall content myself with roast chestnuts in winter.'

They had arrived ninety minutes early – the first show did not begin until three in the afternoon – but the crowds were already so thick that they had difficulty in maneuvering their way to the tent marked 'Management.' They were greeted there by an Indian so large and terrifying-looking that Gross halted in the entryway.

Werthen, whose sense of adventure was a little more pronounced, entered. He dug out his schoolroom English and dusted it off:

'We would to speak with Herr ... Mr Remington.'

The Indian, dressed in beaded rawhide top and pants, a full-feathered headdress on, scowled down at Werthen, his massive arms folded across his chest.

'Excuse, please,' Werthen continued hopelessly.

'Yes, I heard,' the Indian said in German with a northern accent. 'And please do not bother with your "Me want speak" English. I'm from Hamburg.'

'Well, for the sake of Holy Maria,' Gross said,

246

approaching now that he knew it was safe. 'Why didn't you say so?'

The German-Indian continued to scowl at them. 'I did.'

'And what are you doing dressed up in that costume?' Gross asked as if it was his concern. 'I suppose that is red paint on your face.'

The man frowned at Gross then finally said, 'You ever heard of theatricals?'

This was not going at all well, Werthen realized, changing the tone of the encounter.

'How did you come to be with the show?' he asked.

The German now let his arms hang at his sides. 'I once worked on the docks in Hamburg. Hard work, heavy lifting. Not much future there. Then one day, about five years ago, Remington and his show arrived by boat from America. I helped unload it, and when they left, I was with them. Simple as that.'

'But how did you get the job? After all, you spoke no English, I assume,' Werthen said.

The man merely shook his head at the question, amused. 'You think his name is really Taylor Remington?'

Neither Werthen nor Gross responded.

The German looked over each of his broad shoulders, then spoke to them as if confiding a state secret.

'Thomas Remminghaus. Straight from Bavaria.'

'No,' Werthen said. After all, Remington was an American almost as famous as Mark Twain. He had fought alongside Custer, it was reported;

had built an entertainment empire out of his shows depicting scenes from the Old West.

'Too true,' the German assured them. 'Went to America when he was twenty.'

'And fighting with Custer?'

The man put a thick finger to his right eye and pulled down on the lower lid: the gesture for 'believe that and you'll believe anything.'

'Why are you telling us this?' Gross said. 'After all, we could be the press come to interview your employer.'

'You aren't the press?' he said, a look of disappointment sweeping across his rugged features.

They shook their heads.

'And he is not my employer. Not any longer. He just gave me the sack. Says I've been at the schnapps again.'

Werthen was now aware of the powerful scent of alcohol in the air.

'Feininger,' a voice boomed out from the depths of the tent, its owner then saying in German, 'I thought I told you to get out of here. Now. Pack up or I'll have the police pack you off. And leave the buckskins, you worthless bastard.'

Remington, a short, stocky man in tall leather boots, long flowing hair and a Van Dyke beard, came out of the shadows.

'Sorry,' he said, reverting immediately to English the moment he saw Gross and Werthen. 'I did not know we had visitors.'

'They know you're German,' the man called Feininger said with apparent enjoyment.

248

Remington froze in place.

'We are not from the newspapers,' Werthen quickly said. 'We just need a few moments of your time to ask some questions.'

Remington was so relieved to hear they were not journalists that he did not seem to register the rest of Werthen's comment. The impresario turned on his former employee.

'Look, you. If I find out you've been talking with reporters, this continent won't be big enough for you. Understand? I have friends, powerful friends, everywhere. Now you take your rotten carcass back to Hamburg where I found you.'

Werthen expected that he would have to intervene. Surely the much larger and stronger Feininger could squash Remington with one of his granite fists. Instead, the man snuffled once, made a feeble attempt at an apology, which Remington waved off, and meekly left the tent.

'And remember. The buckskins stay here.' Then to Werthen: 'But who they will fit, I don't know.' He took a long breath. 'You folks know how to keep a secret, I suppose.'

'Absolutely,' Werthen said.

'Of course,' Gross added.

'So what brings you here? I mean, other than the show?'

'As I said, we have just a few questions.'

'Are you from the police? My licenses are all in order, I can tell you that.'

'We are private inquiry agents,' Werthen said.

'You mean like Pinkertons?'

'Somewhat,' Werthen said, not enjoying the

comparison to that agency known for hiring out as a private army for American industrialists to keep their workers in line. He made quick introductions, but Remington had obviously never heard of Gross, nor of his criminalistic studies.

Gross jumped in as the man appeared to be ready to end the conversation.

'We will trade favors. Our silence about your nationality in return for a short interview. I assume that would be amenable to you.'

'I have a show to put on,' Remington said.

'Very brief questions,' Gross said.

Remington sighed. 'Follow me.'

They did so, leaving the reception area in the front of the tent for Remington's private dressing room in the shadowy depths. He would, of course, be billeted at the Sacher Hotel or some such establishment in the city, but here he kept his trunk of costumes, for he took part in the show as the master of ceremonies, announcing each act.

They took seats at a deal table in his dressing area.

'Now, what is it?'

Gross led the way. 'We understand you are interested in purchasing a tract of the Vienna Woods.'

The statement took Remington by surprise. 'Who says?'

'It has been reported,' Gross replied.

'Damn,' he said in English. Then once again in German: 'What is it to you?'

'We want to know if in fact this is true. And remember, we are trading favors here,' Gross added.

'One word of this to the press—' Remington wagged a stubby finger at Gross.

'We are investigating two murders, Herr Remminghaus. I can make no such assurances to you regarding this illicit sale.'

'There's nothing illegal about it.' The deal table shook under his pounding fist.

'Then you should feel no constraints in assisting us in our inquiries. I repeat, is it true you have been involved in negotiations for sale of acreage in the Vienna Woods?'

'Yes, yes. Not just acreage, but nearly half of it.'

This made Werthen exhale with almost a whistle.

'Yes, monumental, eh? We Americans do not do things by half measures.'

Spoken like a true transplanted German, Werthen thought.

'And with whom were you in negotiations?'

'That's obvious now, isn't it?'

Gross looked sternly at him. 'If it were, I would not be asking. I am not here to waste your time or my own.'

'With Mayor Lueger, of course. He's the only one could authorize a sale of this magnitude. A forward-looking man, Karl Lueger.'

'The asking price?'

'Now that is going too far. How do I know you aren't representing the other bidders?'

Gross straightened in his chair. 'Then you know that there are others involved?'

'What's an auction without bidders?' Remington seemed vastly entertained at the idea of a bidding war. 'So you'll understand my reluctance to make the amount of my bid public. Enough to say it's in the millions.'

'Crowns or florins?' Werthen interjected.

Remington looked pityingly at him. 'Dollars. Greenbacks. Real money.'

'When are the bids to be tallied?' Gross asked.

'You mean when do I know if I won? That would be next Wednesday.'

My god, thought Werthen. They had only a handful of days to prevent this travesty from happening.

'Very well,' Gross concluded. 'I must thank you for your time, Herr Remminghaus.'

'It is Remington now. All legally changed. I like to do things on the up and up.'

They rose to leave, but Werthen could not restrain himself.

'If you do not mind telling me, what plans do you have for the Woods?'

'No, I do not mind at all talking about my Tales from the Vienna Woods.'

'Pardon?'

'That's the name I've selected for the park.'

'You're making a park out of the Vienna Woods?' Werthen asked. 'But it is already a park, a wild park.'

'Mine will be unique, a very particular sort of park, I can tell you that. One that will bring visitors from all over the world. You see, I have been at this entertainment job nigh on to three decades now. And I tell you, entertainment is the industry of the future. Travel and tourism, those are the growth industries of the twentieth century. Great times ahead.'

'And in what way is your park going to be "particular," as you say?' Werthen queried.

'Well, Tales of the Vienna Woods will be in the vanguard of tourist destinations for a new century. Your average visitor to Europe, he doesn't know a whole lot about cultural things. Doesn't really know where to go and what to see. I intend to simplify travel. Concentrate the experience. I've learned a bit with my Wild West Show. So there will be re-enactments. Great moments in Austrian history, from the Habsburg coronation to Mozart at the piano and Strauss leading a waltz. Imagine a re-creation of the siege of Vienna with hordes of bloody Turks at the city gates. Or a fortress like in Salzburg so the tourist can focus his travel. Or the Gross Glockner right here in Vienna's backyard. Well, a smaller model. Alps with manufactured snow year-round.'

'But Austria has these things for real,' Werthen said.

'Not in one place and in one time. That's the genius of my travel itineraries. Simplification. Concentration. We are in negotiations for a bit of land near Milan now. It'll have models of the Roman Colosseum, St Peter's, the Forum. Put in a leaning tower, the Venetian canals.'

'That sounds dreadful,' Gross suddenly said.

'What's so dreadful about it? After all, you have the "Venice in Vienna" park right here in the Prater. I'm only expanding on the idea. We'll have medieval lanes with men in livery, sedan chairs at the ready. I can see it, almost smell it.'

'And it smells, sir, of offal,' Gross blurted out. 'Good day to you.'

Gross stomped off leaving Werthen to attempt a quasi-polite farewell.

'Your friend has a definite problem,' Remington said. 'He should get out of the classroom more. Into the real world of ideas and progress.'

'I will suggest it to him, Mr Remington.'

'You're not staying for the shows?'

'Maybe another day.'

'You just tell them at the front ticket window you're a friend of Taylor Remington. You'll get a day pass.'

'Very generous. And thank you for your co-operation.'

'Remember,' the man shouted as Werthen was leaving. 'Thomas Remminghaus exists no longer. It is Taylor Remington. Done all legal in New York City.'

Werthen caught up with Gross just outside the tent.

'We know now,' the criminologist said.

'Yes,' Werthen agreed. 'If that is the future, I am not sure I want to know.'

'That is not the future, I guarantee you. Not if I have anything to do with it.'

'One thing seems clear,' Werthen said.

Gross waited for him to continue.

'It would seem Remington is not responsible for the deaths of Steinwitz and Praetor.'

'What leads you to deduce that, dear friend?'

'Well, we are still alive and able to discuss our interview with the man. If those two posed such a dire threat to Remington that he or his lackeys killed them, then would we not also be seen as a comparable threat that needs eliminating?'

'Good. And the second reason?'

Werthen shook his head. 'I did not mention a second reason.'

'Then I shall for you. Remington and his show only arrived in Vienna last Sunday. *After* the deaths of both men.'

'How long have you known this?'

'I ascertained it last night from the clerk at my hotel. It seems Mr Remington is a guest there as well. He must have already been in communication with Lueger before his arrival. But his physical presence here began last Sunday, that is certain. I placed a call to Drechsler this morning to make sure. The foreign registration office shows Remington's entrance at Braunau am Inn on February 18, along with his menagerie.'

'Advokat Werthen!'

Werthen turned at the sound of his name and saw Fräulein Metzinger with young Heidl Beer and, of all people, young Ludwig Wittgenstein.

'I had no idea you were an enthusiast of the Old West,' his assistant said.

'Actually we are here on business. But it looks like you are prepared for a good time.'

Both young boys had large bags of popcorn in their hands.

'And how were you able to effect an escape this time, Master Wittgenstein?'

The boy blushed. 'Well, I practiced a bit of

255

magic.'

He nudged Heidl as he spoke, for the other boy was obviously in on the scheme.

'Yes?' Werthen said. 'Don't worry. I am no longer representing your father.'

'Saturday afternoon is my piano lesson. I go to Madame du Pauly in the First District for my torture and am not expected back until teatime. So—'

'Allow me a conjecture,' Gross said. 'You had your young friend here, Herr Heidl Beer, appear in all his finery at Madame du Pauly's with a message.'

Young Wittgenstein's eyes grew large at Gross's speculation.

'Ah, I see I am close to the truth. Perhaps the message would be from your parents, stating that you needed to return home. A sensitive young lad like you would not use illness as an excuse; that could have an unfortunate resonance.'

'You said you wouldn't tell anybody,' Ludwig said, turning on Heidl.

'I didn't.' The other boy sounded outraged at the suggestion.

'Thus, barring medical emergency, I would suggest the unexpected arrival of a favorite relative. An aunt, perhaps. Or an uncle, latterly traveling in South America.'

'You're a wizard,' Wittgenstein said.

Gross shrugged. 'No. Merely a reader of the "Notables" column in the daily paper. I see your uncle did return from Paraguay this very week.'

Wittgenstein now looked disappointed, and

huddled himself into his fur-collared coat.

'Explanation ruins magic,' he said.

He sat back in the first-class coach of the Alpine Express and watched the snow-blanketed landscape race by outside his window. The time away from Vienna had done him good; no longer was his left foot so swollen and painful. Gout, the doctors said, but he knew better. It was only a matter of time. He could try to control his disease, but he knew that eventually it would get the better of him.

He lit a Gross Glockner cigar, only his third of the day, and exhaled a wreath of blue smoke into the compartment where he sat alone. He had taken the entire car; his aides were scattered in the other compartments.

The train whistled through the station at St Pölten. Its platforms were empty except for a mother and her small daughter standing at her side, thumb in her mouth, staring wide-eyed at the express flying past her, ruffling her long mauve skirts.

How long did he have? No one was saying, but he tried to live each day as fully as possible. Keep your mind in the present; the future will take care of itself.

But events in the present were now intruding on his future. His vendetta against the Habsburgs was so near to coming to successful closure, all his careful machinations about to come to fruition.

Yet at the same time everything was beginning to unravel. He understood from Bielohlawek that investigators were snooping about, picking at the ashes of Steinwitz's death, nosing around the affairs of the Rathaus. If so, it was only a matter of time until they would make associations, put the pieces together. The press had not come into it yet, but that, too, was only a matter of time.

He had to contain this, at least until Wednesday. Then let the critics wail and gnash their teeth. He would weather it. The Christian Democrats would weather it. He could always count on the small people of Vienna who loved him like a saint. He could always blame it on the Jews. After all, the Jew Wittgenstein represented one group of bidders; Remington, or whatever he chose to call himself, the other. And he, Mayor Lueger, had done his homework on Taylor Remington, formerly Thomas Remminghaus. The man was a chameleon. Not only had he re-created himself as a frontier American, a character out of the pages of Karl May, but before that he had already reinvented himself as a German. For, Lueger and his aides had discovered, the impresario and his family had originally hailed from Galicia, where his name as a young boy was Tomas Remstein. The Jewish Remstein.

Lueger looked at his bearded handsome reflection in the window of his train compartment and smiled contentedly.

Once again, the Jews did it. The despoilers of the country.

And once the money was collected there were a thousand and one ways to conceal its uses.

Through years of redirecting 'gifts' from industrialists and municipal funds toward campaign expenditures, Lueger and his team had devised a Byzantine structure of funding channels and money redirection and 'cleaning' that not even a Swiss bank director could follow. Just get him the money from the sale, and it would be safe.

Lueger looked at the stub of cigar wedged between his forefinger and middle finger. Those fingers were stained almost as dark as the cigar itself. He had long ago given up on trying to eradicate that nicotine stain.

But this stain of disclosure was another matter. Only a few more days of containing this affair.

Was it time to enlist Kulowski's aid in the matter?

Karl Lueger was a tidy man in his personal habits; he liked to have his desk neatly arranged, his affairs in order. Hildegard, his older sister, looked after domestic arrangements at his simple apartment in the Rathaus. Lunch was always on the table promptly at twelve ten. Clean suits and freshly polished gold cufflinks awaited him every morning after his bath. His life was untroubled by marriage. Like a priest to the church, he felt he was married to politics, to his duties as mayor of the finest city in Europe. He found release with Marianne, but that, like the state of his health, was a closely guarded secret.

Now, his orderly plans were at risk of becoming messy in the extreme. And all because his old school chum Steinwitz had suddenly found a conscience. That was a deep betrayal. Middle-class boys, the both of them. And the Theresianum had been the making of them. They were the bright boys, the day boys, the first of their generation to claw their way into the lair of privilege and nobility. And Lueger had not forgotten his friend Steinwitz. He had taken him with him on his meteoric rise in Vienna politics. He had made the man. And to be paid back in such a pitiless manner. It was really too much. Where was the man's sense of loyalty? The killing paid him back, though. He could almost understand—

His thoughts were interrupted when the door to his compartment opened unexpectedly, letting in the noise of the rushing train. Kulowski stood there, looking uncomfortable as usual in a suit that appeared at least one size too small.

'Just to let you know we will be there in ten minutes, chief.'

'I am quite aware of that,' Lueger said, irritated at having been torn out of his thoughts.

'You told me to remind you.'

'And now you have.' Lueger waved his cigar dismissively at the man.

After the door closed, Lueger leaned back against the linen-covered headrest, closed his eyes and said quietly out loud, 'Buffalo.'

But at least Kulowski was loyal.

Sixteen

Sunday morning Werthen awoke to a nearly silent world. It was not just that Sundays were usually more quiet than other days, with less traffic and fewer pedestrians on the street. He knew this Sunday was special.

His robe on, he looked out the front windows of the sitting room and saw a swirling mass of snow coming from the skies. A childish glee filled him.

All morning long it snowed with an intensity that he had not known since his youth. The green ceramic oven in the sitting room hummed with heat and outside the snow fell silently. A white, mute presence. They did not even attempt their usual Sunday stroll around the Ringstrasse.

He determined to take his mind off the case for at least one day. Really, he had no choice. The Viennese were sticklers for Sunday-day-of-rest. There were no interviews he could conduct, no leads to follow on the hallowed Sunday.

So, he and Berthe sat reading in the sitting room while Frieda gurgled and lolled about on a large blanket between them on the leather sofa. Werthen held his little daughter through her morning nap, marveling, as millennia of doting parents have, at the absolute perfection of their

261

progeny. Today he was focusing on her ears, miracles of precision and sweetness. The pinkness of the lobes, the almost translucent quality of the skin filled him with a sudden awe. Were he a religious man he would have put it down to God's doing.

This thought spurred others: he would have to come to terms with his battling parents and father-in-law sometime. Herr Meisner should be here; should be enjoying his granddaughter. He felt guilt at this, but it was as much his father-in-law's fault as theirs. He was a stubborn goat. At least he had gotten his parents to remain quiet about a possible baptism, yet he knew it was only a matter of time before they began clamoring again for a proper church ceremony. The old hypocrites, he thought, not without a certain degree of fondness.

Werthen managed to put these thoughts out of his mind and enjoy the morning and the unexpected snowfall. They were just about to sit down to their Sunday lunch of *Backhendl*, fried chicken served with parsley potatoes and a fresh kraut salad, when the ringer on their apartment door sounded. He and Berthe exchanged quick glances, for no one was expected today. Perhaps his parents, he thought, bored with nothing to do on a wintry day. It was Frau Blatschky's day off, so he got up to answer the door.

Standing on the threshold was Detective Inspector Drechsler looking rather glum.

'Detective,' Werthen said, attempting to hide his surprise. 'Please come in and warm yourself.'

Drechsler shook his head at the invitation. 'Sorry to bother you on a Sunday, Advokat. We have a problem.'

'Please, come in. What is it?'

'I don't want to disturb you.'

'You already have,' Werthen said with a smile, but he was not feeling very jolly. Drechsler's expression was worrying. 'We can't talk out here.' He took the man by the arm and guided him in.

Berthe had come to the foyer by now, Frieda in arms, and smiled as the policeman came in.

'You remember my wife,' Werthen said.

Drechsler tipped his snow-dusted derby at her. 'Good day, madam,' he said. 'Apologies for the intrusion.'

'You must be frozen,' she said. 'Can I offer you anything? Tea?'

'No, not now. Too kind of you. I just need a quick word with your husband.'

Berthe nodded at this implicit request for privacy, and returned to the dining room.

'What is it, Drechsler? You look done in.'

'I wouldn't bother you except that I know you have a certain relationship with Herr Wittgenstein.'

'Well, yes. He was, as you know, a client. But what has Herr Wittgenstein got to do with anything?'

Drechsler pulled out an envelope from his coat pocket and retrieved a small card kept in the envelope. It looked to be something official, for he caught a glimpse of the Austrian eagle stamp. It was also smudged with what appeared to be

263

dried blood. Drechsler was careful to handle the card so as not to get his fingers on the stains.

'This was found earlier today on the body of a ... a person who fell to his death under the *Stadtbahn* at the Karlsplatz station. Not a large person.'

'You mean a child?' Werthen began to feel his heart race.

'Yes,' Drechsler said, his head bowed. 'A child. He was killed immediately and his head...' He let out a long sigh. 'Well, he could not be identified. They think he must have slipped. All this snow, you know, and the platforms were wet from people's shoes. Irony is, the trains just started running again before he fell. They had to clear the tracks and there was quite a crowd at the station waiting. No one saw it happen, just that he suddenly fell as the train was pulling into Karlsplatz.'

'And this card was on the body?'

'Yes.'

'Does it have a name?' But Werthen knew already. Knew with a sickening feeling in his heart.

'It is a yearly pass to the Imperial Natural History Museum. All that could be found on the body. It was in the boy's overcoat.'

'Young Ludwig Wittgenstein?'

A curt nod of the head from Drechsler.

'You're sure?' Werthen asked.

'Like I say, physical identification is impossible. But with this card and the proximity to the Wittgenstein palais ... I thought perhaps it would be better coming from someone who at least knows him. I don't mean to avoid responsibility.'

'You were quite right to come, Detective Inspector. Just let me tell my wife. I'll be with you presently.'

Drechsler had secured a *Fiaker* from the Police Praesidium; it was still waiting in the street at Werthen's apartment.

They spoke little on the way to the Palais Wittgenstein, but at one point Drechsler did grow expansive.

'I wanted to thank you and Doktor Gross. That surgeon fellow, Praetor, we had a consultation with him and he says he can make the wife fit as a French horn in no time. She goes in for surgery the end of the week.'

'Splendid news, Drechsler. I am happy for you.'

The policeman seemed to want to add something, but thought better of it, as if this was hardly the time to express feelings about his good luck.

The *Fiaker* pulled up to the Wittgenstein mansion finally and Werthen still did not know what he was going to say to Karl Wittgenstein.

Drechsler accompanied him, but it was clearly on Werthen to break the news to the industrialist. He had thought of approaching the daughter, Fräulein Mining, first, but then remembered how Wittgenstein had chastised him before for not summoning him to the morgue. No. He would go straight to the father.

Meier, the servant, opened the door.

'Yes, sir?'

'I would like to speak to Herr Wittgenstein,' Werthen said.

'Which one would that be, sir? We have several in residence.'

Werthen wanted to throttle the supercilious servant, pretending he did not recognize him, and acting as if he did not know exactly to whom he wanted to speak.

He was about to give the man a piece of his mind when he heard the chatter of excited children approaching the forecourt from within the house. Fräulein Mining herself came into view behind Meier, accompanied by two younger boys bundled for the cold and carrying sleds.

One of them was Ludwig Wittgenstein, who stopped dead in his tracks when he saw Werthen at the door.

'Advokat,' he said. 'What are you doing here?'

Werthen could hardly believe his eyes. 'Master Ludwig.' He turned to Drechsler, who could only shrug in disbelief.

The young Wittgenstein came up quickly to Werthen, sled in hand. He inserted himself in front of Werthen.

'That will do, Meier,' he said, dismissing the servant. Then to Werthen, 'You aren't going to tell Father about yesterday, are you?'

Werthen let out a nervous laugh. He felt tears build in the front of his eyes. 'No, of course not. We thought...' Again he looked to Drechsler, but there was no help coming from that quarter.

'May I have the envelope, Detective Inspector?'

By this time the older sister, and the brother Paul Wittgenstein, had also approached.

'What is it, Advokat?' Fräulein Mining asked.

He took the card out of the envelope and showed it to Ludwig, ignoring for the time being the young woman's question.

'Is this yours?'

Ludwig looked at it, and suddenly his face turned beet red.

'I must have forgotten to take it out of my coat.'

'What do you mean?' Werthen said.

'Before I traded it. But what happened to it? Why is it all stained? Is that ... is that blood?'

'Before you traded it?' Werthen said. 'For what? With whom?'

Ludwig now had the trapped look of a guilty child.

'I repeat, Advokat,' Fräulein Mining said. 'What is this all about? Why are you pestering my brother about his coat?'

Werthen could no longer restrain himself. The relief he had felt at seeing Ludwig Wittgenstein alive was quickly being replaced with another emotion, a numbing dread and fear.

'This is about a dead child, Fräulein Mining. He fell under an engine of the *Stadtbahn* this morning.'

'Heidl.'

It came out of Ludwig like a groan, as if he had been struck.

* * *

He and Drechsler wasted no time in getting to the Habsburgergasse and ascertaining from Frau Ignatz that young Heidrich Beer had in fact gone out earlier in the day and had not yet returned.

'We had a fine midday meal planned and all,' the *Portier* said. 'What can that rascal be thinking?'

But she said it almost fondly.

It was now clear to Werthen what had happened. The two boys had formed a friendship. Heidl had, Werthen remembered, made mention of Ludwig's coat with the fur collar, and finally Ludwig decided to make him a present of it. As Ludwig earlier told him, they had both snuck away this morning to make the exchange. But what was Heidl doing at the Karlsplatz station? Where would he be going? The fastest way home was to walk back into the First District.

Werthen let his mind occupy itself with such thoughts to take the pain away. But this time they had to be sure. He must see the body, look for any distinguishing characteristics before he informed Fräulein Metzinger.

At the morgue in the Ninth District, Doktor Starb, director of the facility, was in charge. The highest levels of authority had been called in on the sacred Sunday when it was thought a Wittgenstein had met an accidental death. The man was dressed in a black suit today, nothing flashy or colorful. He seemed highly relieved when Werthen explained the contretemps of the exchanged coat.

'I am not sure how you plan to identify the body,' Starb said after Werthen told him of his mission. 'It is badly mangled. We have done our best here for a viewing, but...'

Werthen understood. However, he knew what he was looking for. Fräulein Metzinger had told Werthen of the boy's broken left arm that had never healed properly. Werthen had witnessed on several occasions how the boy favored the arm.

'I need to look at the left forearm. It was broken and I believe is still disfigured.'

They reached the drawer containing the body of the youth and Starb signaled to an assistant.

'If you would rather...' Starb said.

Werthen had been dreading this. 'Yes, perhaps.' He did not have the stomach for viewing the body. Instead he looked away while he heard Starb and the assistant conferring and heard the rustle of linen behind him.

'You may want to see this for yourself, Advokat,' Starb said.

Werthen turned. The body was covered in a sheet; only a thin arm stuck out. There, on the forearm, was an unmistakable crook or bend.

'It has been badly broken,' Starb confirmed. 'The left arm.'

'How old would you say the boy is?' Werthen asked.

'Surely no more than twelve, perhaps thirteen. The Wittgenstein boy is younger, but we assumed as the museum card was in the overcoat that it belonged to the deceased.'

Starb nodded to the assistant again and the drawer was closed.

* * *

It was early afternoon by the time Werthen arrived at Fräulein Metzinger's flat in the Third District just off the Landstrasse near Stadtpark. He was accompanied by Rosa Mayreder, friend to both his wife and to his young assistant, whom she, Mayreder, had introduced to Werthen.

Berthe, after her unfortunate experience at Laab im Walde, did not want to expose Frieda to any more stressful situations and at the same time did not yet feel comfortable leaving the baby with others. Thus, Frau Mayreder had agreed to accompany Werthen to break the news of the death of Heidl Beer to Fräulein Metzinger.

Mayreder, writer, painter, musician, and feminist, carried herself with quiet dignity. She had earlier aided Werthen in one of his cases via her connection to the composer Hugo Wolf. Mayreder had in fact written the libretto to Wolf's opera, *Der Corregidor.*

The *Fiaker* let them off mid-block. The snow had begun again after an interval of a few hours. It was falling in dense tufts, turning daylight into murky twilight. The snow settled on Werthen's hat as they approached Fräulein Metzinger's building, drifted on to the curls around Frau Mayreder's forehead. A regal-looking woman though slightly plump, Mayreder had a way of gazing at a person with eyebrows slightly arched that exhibited, Werthen thought, a slight degree of derision. But not today. Her face was drawn and concerned. She did not look forward to this anymore than Werthen did.

The house door was open, and they announced

themselves at the *Portier*'s lodge in the foyer before they mounted the stairs. Fräulein Metzinger's flat was on the fourth floor, and Werthen found himself taking his time on the stairs, delaying the arrival and the inevitable emotional scene.

'It's not good to delay,' Frau Mayreder said, as if understanding his intent. 'Short and sharp is the best. The kindest.'

He knew she was right, still he could barely bring himself to carry such news to his young assistant. Fräulein Metzinger truly loved the young boy.

Rosa Mayreder lost no time in climbing the stairs and rapped assertively on the apartment door. Cowardly, Werthen hoped that Fräulein Metzinger was out. They had not called in advance to see if she was home on this Sunday. Perhaps she was meeting friends somewhere; perhaps out for a skate on the Stadtpark pond.

The door opened abruptly and Werthen felt sudden amazement.

'Herr Beer. What are you doing here?'

Heidrich's father looked as grizzled as he had the first time Werthen met him. His face, however, did not have any of the robust quality he had seen in it before. The eyes were red-rimmed; his mouth was sullen.

'They've gone and killed my only son.'

'It's all right, Herr Beer.' Fräulein Metzinger came up behind the grieving man. Her own eyes showed no sign of tears. She took the man's arm to lead him back to her sitting room. 'Please, come in,' she said to Werthen and Frau Mayreder.

They took off their coats and hats and followed her into a sitting room furnished in nothing but huge overstuffed pillows on the parquet. She settled Beer on to one of the pillows covered in Turkish carpet and motioned for her other guests to do likewise. Werthen had a certain amount of trouble doing so, his right leg refusing to bend properly. But finally he seated himself, his leg sticking straight in front of him.

'I thank you for coming,' Fräulein Metzinger said to them, 'but Herr Beer has already informed me of the tragedy.'

At this word the man let out a small sniffle. Werthen eyed him with real disdain. It was possible Beer felt honest sadness for the death of his son, but it was even more possible that he was trying to somehow turn this to his advantage.

'How did you know of the accident?' Werthen asked.

Herr Beer shrugged, lounging back on the pillow now, and his patched trousers rucked up to reveal glaringly white shins. 'I have my informants. We stick together on the streets. News came to me fast. The boy was coming to meet me.'

Now he broke down completely, and Fräulein Metzinger put a consoling arm around him.

Equally amazing as the presence of Herr Beer was his assistant's seeming lack of emotion. Not a tear in her eye, no hysterics. Obviously, she had been too busy taking care of the father to mourn the son.

'You were planning to see your son?' Werthen said.

Beer looked out warily between gnarled fingers covering his weeping eyes.

'I know what you told me, Advokat. But he is my flesh and blood. I needed to see him, to give him a fatherly embrace.'

Fräulein Metzinger looked alarmed at this statement. 'You have met before?' She looked from Beer to Werthen.

'We have, to be sure,' Beer said before Werthen could respond. 'Told me to stay away from my own flesh and blood.' He cast a cringing smile Werthen's way.

'I don't understand,' she said.

But Frau Mayreder had no difficulty in assessing the situation.

'A pecuniary motive, one suspects.'

'What's so peculiar? He's my own son. I have a right to see him.'

But Fräulein Metzinger was not about to have the blinders taken from her eyes.

'He is ... was the boy's father, after all,' she said. Fixing Werthen with a steely look, she asked, 'Did you actually tell him to stay away from Huck?'

'I am not sure this is the proper time to be going into all this,' Werthen said. Then, seeing the determined look on Fräulein Metzinger's face, he decided otherwise.

'Well, Herr Beer and I did make our acquaintance. He was waiting for me at my favorite coffeehouse.' Then to Beer, 'Another example of information from your friends?' But Beer was not responding. 'At any rate, there was a discussion of recompense for his son. I believe, at first, he assumed that we had spirited young Heidl off for purposes—'

'All right, all right,' Herr Beer suddenly interjected. 'I admit it. I thought there might be a little something in it for me. And why not? I raised the boy. Taught him all he knew. But I did love the little tyke. I assure you of that. Loved him as much as life itself.'

And indeed the man looked so miserable that even Werthen's heart was tugged by his words.

'Please, Herr Beer,' Fräulein Metzinger said, holding his shoulders even more tightly. 'No one doubts your love. I was not trying to take him away from you. I simply wanted to give him a home.'

Now, at long last, she broke down. Tears flooded down her cheeks, and the two clasped to each other on the huge pillow like tempest-tossed survivors of a shipwreck.

Finally Beer looked again at Werthen and Mayreder. 'I'll do the person who killed my son. I swear. I'll track him down and do him the same he did to Heidrich.'

'It was an accident, Herr Beer,' Werthen said. 'There's no one to blame. No one at fault.' Yet now, for the first time, Werthen began to wonder at that simple description of Huck's death. Was it a mere matter of coincidence that one close to him, close to his firm, should die in the midst of this investigation? Werthen ran a hand through his hair as if to clear his mind. Death happens, he reminded himself. Sometimes it simply means

274

nothing. It really is an accident. Yet someone at the station must have seen something.

Beer's reaction, however, refocused Werthen's attention. The man shook his head slowly. 'Took Heidrich away from me and the young lady here. Snuffed him out like a bedbug. I'll see that person gets what he deserves.'

In the end, Werthen left Frau Mayreder at the apartment. There was nothing more he could do there, and Rosa Mayreder seemed genuinely interested in, if not intrigued by, Beer.

'The perfect example of a sort of cunning intelligence,' she said to Werthen as he retrieved hat and coat in the foyer. 'One cannot really tell if he loved his son or not. If not, then we have just witnessed acting of a quality much better than one sees at the Burg.'

Meaning the Burgtheater, stage of the best actors and actresses in the empire. Werthen felt no such fascination with the man; to him Beer was simply a conniving rotter. However, it was not his job to persuade otherwise.

Outside the snow was still falling, but less frenetically now, and he decided to walk home to clear his head. He cut through Stadtpark and stopped for a time at the ice pond to watch the skaters. They were out in force today, spinning and circling in eddies and flows. Many of the women were dressed *à la Esquimaux*, wearing cap, coat, tight-fitting breeches, and leggings all made of fur, their hands tucked into muffs as they sailed over the ice. It was a fashion made popular after the near disastrous Austrian Arctic expedition of 1874, when sailors aboard the sailing ship *Tegetthoff* discovered and claimed the two hundred ice-covered islands of Franz Joseph Land in the Arctic Ocean. Later their ship became icebound attempting to break through polar icebergs. The trapped ship served as a virtual prison for two years for the crew of twenty-four. Finally the men had to abandon their ship and head southward on foot. Ninety days they journeyed through blizzards and with dwindling supplies until Russian fishing boats saved them. News of their safe return spread around the world by telegraph; in Vienna their exploits were celebrated by this fashion statement, still popular after a quarter of a century.

Werthen watched the skaters for a few more moments, smiling inwardly at this display of a simple pleasure. It took his mind – for the moment – off more tragic and pressing matters at hand.

Seventeen

Werthen was met by Meier the next morning at the glass doors to the entrance hall of the Palais Wittgenstein.

'I cannot say as you will be welcome,' the servant said as he led the way up the sweep of marble steps.

'How do you mean?'

But Meier had said all he intended to. Reaching the second floor, he rapped gently on the door to his master's study. He entered, bidding Werthen wait on the landing, and returned a moment later.

'Herr Wittgenstein is otherwise disposed.'

'Tell him I've had a communication from his son, Hans.'

Meier hesitated, obviously not wanting to displease his employer.

'Vital information,' Werthen added. 'I am sure Herr Wittgenstein would want to hear of it.'

With a long-suffering sigh the liveried servant rapped again on the door to the office. This time when he came out, he nodded at Werthen to enter, holding the door for him.

Werthen had barely got in the door when Herr Wittgenstein, seated behind his desk, said crossly, 'What do you mean by exposing my son to this street scum?'

The word struck Werthen like a fist. 'I beg your pardon?'

'The urchin Luki gave his coat to. He says he met him at your office. And why didn't you tell me the scoundrel had snuck off from his tutor?'

Werthen was still reeling from the foul description of the hapless Heidrich Beer.

'Speak up, man. What is it you've got from Hans?'

Werthen finally found his voice. 'You'll be pilloried.'

This comment stilled Herr Wittgenstein for the moment.

Then, 'What are you talking about?'

'The Vienna Woods scheme.'

Another short silence from Herr Wittgenstein. His face turned scarlet.

'How did you hear of it?'

Werthen handed him a copy of his own letter; the crumpled original was at his office.

Wittgenstein quickly perused it, then looked up at Werthen, who had not been offered a chair.

'So?'

'You don't refute this?'

'Why should I? My only question is how you came into possession of this information. If one of my house staff has been digging about in my dustbin—'

'It was not one of your domestics, I assure you. But more importantly, can you not see the disservice a sale of a huge swath of the Vienna Woods would do to the citizens of this city?'

'It is a business dealing, pure and simple.'

The man's complete nonchalance flummoxed Werthen. He had expected at least a trace of embarrassment, but Herr Wittgenstein evinced none.

'Then don't you see that you are just being used by Lueger and his cronies? They'll get the money and blame the sale on you, on the "money-grubbing Jews."'

Wittgenstein sat in stunned silence for a moment. Suddenly he crashed his fist down on the desktop.

'The Wittgensteins are not Jews! We are as Christian as anyone in the empire. Now I believe our interview is finished, Advokat. Do what you wish about this, but business is business. The sale will go forward. Good day to you.'

'The man is blinded by ambition,' Gross pronounced later that morning when they met at Werthen's office. His wife, Adele, was accompanying him, and nodded in assent.

'There was no reasoning with him,' Werthen said. 'Wittgenstein and his group are not going to pull out of the sale.'

Gross, sitting across the desk from him, rubbed his hands together. His eyes sparkled as he said, 'We shall have to find another way then.'

'What is it, Gross? You seem oddly pleased with yourself.'

The criminologist shook his head firmly. 'Not with myself, but with my good lady wife.' He nodded at Adele, who seemed almost to blush. They sat shoulder to shoulder as giddy as newly weds.

'Please tell,' Werthen said encouragingly to Frau Gross.

'Well, as I indicated on Saturday I have been talking with the female supporters of Lueger. As a woman, I hesitate to use the pejorative name—'

'Nothing so damning about calling them Lueger's Amazons,' interrupted her husband, 'nor in Lueger's Gretls.'

'Quite,' Frau Gross said. 'But their official title is the Christian Viennese Women's League, and they have proved a decisive factor in getting the men out to vote for Handsome Karl. I spoke with one of the deputies of the league, Frau Dagmar Platner.'

'That name sounds familiar,' Werthen said, and then it came to him. 'That's it. The lady was in charge of an outing of the League. On their way to the Semmering, I believe. This was two, perhaps three years ago.'

Gross slapped his knee most uncharacteristically. 'You're right, Werthen. I remember now, as well.'

'I assure you,' Frau Gross said, 'none of this has anything to do with—'

'And a train of Socialists on a similar outing pulls up on the platform next to theirs,' Doktor Gross continued. He began chuckling to himself. 'When the Socialists saw the bunting on the League's train, they began shouting and taunting the ladies about what a miserable person Lueger is. And then these very respectable women, these very Christian ladies, simply raised their skirts and showed their pantalooned backsides to the

Socialists.'

'Really, Hanns,' Frau Gross said.

Werthen had to still Gross, worried lest his laughter carry to the outside office. Fräulein Metzinger had insisted on coming in today, and Werthen did not want to show disrespect to her mourning.

Gross wiped a tear of joy from his right eye, sniffed once, and then resumed his usual professional demeanor.

'Please continue, *Schatzi*,' he said.

Werthen nearly fell out of his chair at the sound of this endearment coming from Gross's lips.

'At any rate, Frau Platner was most helpful. Of course I did not bring up the matter of a sale of part of the Vienna Woods nor the investigation of Steinwitz or Praetor. I simply told her I was a journalist working on an article about Lueger for a German newspaper. She was only too eager to supply me with names of women who have worked closely with the mayor. One of these was a certain Frau Gréy. It seems this woman gave lessons to Lueger in rhetoric and later became a trusted *advisor.*'

The way she raised her eyebrows let Werthen know the woman was far more than an advisor.

'Did Frau Platner know of this relationship?' he asked.

'No, of course not. For her, Mayor Lueger is as cloistered as a priest. A rather silly woman. Frau Gréy, on the other hand, is a sophisticated woman of the world. An actress and a theater director at one time. And, I believe, a Jew. Not that it matters, but with Mayor Lueger's political stance, it does seem ironic.'

'Remember, dear,' Gross said, 'Lueger's favorite dictum: "I'll decide who is a Jew."'

His wife continued, 'Most helpful, Frau Gréy. I believe she really loved the man. She claimed that he even asked her to marry him, but that she refused, telling him he was too much married to politics to have a wife. They went their separate ways about four years ago.'

She stopped and smiled at both men.

'And?' Werthen asked.

Another slight smile. 'She had no current first-hand information about Herr Lueger, but did provide another name of someone we should see. Marianne Beskiba. Fräulein Beskiba was a chapter secretary for the Women's League and a rabid organizer for Lueger. She also, it appears, is a painter.'

'Herr Lueger seems to appreciate the bohemian type,' Gross said.

'Have you spoken with her?'

'No, not yet,' Frau Gross said. 'That is why Hanns, Doktor Gross, is so pleased with himself today. It seems the lady requests that we visit her.'

She fetched a letter out of the silken purse she carried, and handed it across the desk to Werthen, who quickly perused it.

'So she heard you were asking questions about Lueger and about her?' he said looking up from the letter.

'Yes, apparently,' Frau Gross said. 'I left an address for the Hotel Imperial with Frau Platner.

It seems that Fräulein Beskiba believes my story of a newspaper article about Lueger.'

'And what are these "important revelations" that she wishes to share?' Werthen asked.

'Ahh,' said Gross. 'That is what we are going to discover. You will join us, won't you, Werthen?'

He wanted nothing more, yet, a lawyer, he continually saw beyond immediate desires.

'Would our presence not be a hindrance?' he said. 'After all, Fräulein Beskiba might unburden herself more fully in the presence of another woman.'

'Nonsense,' spluttered Gross.

'I actually would appreciate the assistance, Advokat,' Frau Gross said. 'Duplicity is not my strong suit. I am not sure, after all, that I am made for an investigative life.'

'You've done wonders, dear.' Gross patted his wife's hand with real affection. Then to Werthen, 'So, what about it. Game for a visit to the lady's atelier?'

On the way out they stopped for a moment at Fräulein Metzinger's desk and Doktor and Frau Gross gave their condolences. Werthen stayed behind for a moment as the others headed for the stairs. He and Fräulein Metzinger had not yet had a chance to talk.

'Might I once again say how awfully sorry I am about Heidl.'

She looked up from her typewriting machine, her eyes red-rimmed. A peculiar sour odor rose from her; he had never known Fräulein Metzinger to be lax in matters of hygiene before.

'Thank you, Advokat. And about yesterday. I am sorry for going at you like that. It was the shock.'

'Please do not think of it,' he said. 'It is a great loss. Have you made arrangements, or shall I—'

'No, no. Herr Beer is seeing to all that.'

He tried to hide his disapproval, but failed.

'He really does mean the best, Advokat Werthen. You shouldn't be too hard on the man. His life has not been easy.'

'As you say, Fräulein Metzinger.'

'Nor am I being a typical needy female. I am not blind to Herr Beer's faults. I am sure he intends to get something for himself out of this. But I need him at the moment. Someone else who loved the boy.'

He noted that she could not yet bring herself to use Heidl's name.

'Of course,' he said and gently patted her shoulder. 'If there is anything I can do...'

'Thank you, Advokat. Now you had better hurry up or Doktor Gross will leave you behind.'

As it turned out, Fräulein Beskiba was a near neighbor of Werthen's in the Seventh District, the Neubau. Her studio and living quarters were on Siebensterngasse, on the top floor of a rather nondescript apartment block. There was no lift in the house and thus the three of them plodded up the four flights of stairs. There was a dampness to the place that made the wooden handrail sticky to the touch.

Finally they reached her flat, and Gross did the honors of rapping on the door. It was duly opened by a rather wispy woman in a Murano wool shawl.

'Good day, Fräulein Beskiba—' Frau Gross began.

'I see you've brought friends,' the woman said in a commanding voice that in no way fitted her diminutive frame. 'That's fine by me. Come in, come in. Don't let the damp in.'

The light was bad in the foyer and it was not until they entered the studio itself with its wall of north-facing atelier windows that Werthen could see how attractive she was. She had sparkling green eyes and fine, high cheekbones. Her nose was longish, but on her it was quite perfect.

'I appreciate your asking to see me,' Frau Gross said.

'Please, sit.' Fräulein Beskiba indicated an elegant sitting arrangement by one of the windows. Now that Werthen had a chance to survey the surroundings, he noted that everywhere were signs of good taste and of wealth. The parquet floors were covered in the best of carpets, rosewood and mahogany furniture graced the room. He doubted if such fittings could be afforded on the money provided by a portrait painter's commissions. On an easel deeper in the studio he noticed a work in progress: undoubtedly Mayor Lueger, dressed in a gray suit with a Styrian hunting hat atop his salt and pepper hair. His beard was combed to perfection and he looked quite at home in the heavy Alt Deutsch chair, the original of which sat near the easel.

Noticing the focus of his attention, Fräulein Beskiba said, 'He makes a wonderful model.

285

Always so aware of his public presence. A handsome man, indeed. But you know, up close you can see the wrinkles and the weather-beaten nature of his face. It has taken a toll on him.'

He assumed she was referring to the hectic life of a politician.

Once seated, the painter lost no time.

'I have summoned you for one reason and one reason only. I heard of your interviews with members of the Women's League, of course. But, Frau Gross, you really should use another name when pretending to be a journalist. And, I might add, what kind of journalist can afford the Hotel Imperial?'

Gross now squinted at his wife in approbation.

'Do not be hard on her, Doktor Gross.' Then turning to Werthen, 'Nor should you blame her, Advokat. You see, I know all about your investigations from Karl. From Mayor Lueger. I mean to help you.'

The three of them were speechless for a moment at this pronouncement.

'Yes, you heard me right,' she said.

'I assure you, Fräulein Beskiba—' Gross began.

'Please do not insult my intelligence, Doktor Gross. It's all about this sale of the Vienna Woods, isn't it?'

Again her blunt statement made them mute for an instant.

'Yes,' said Werthen, the first one to recover. 'Yes it is.'

'I suppose you don't like it much. You think the Woods should be left for the people.'

'Something like that.'

She shrugged. 'It's all the same to me. Nature.' She actually shivered as she said the word.

Looking outside the massive windows, Werthen could see that the snow had begun again.

'But I am on your side in this. I want the sale stopped, too. And I might have the ammunition to help you.'

'Why would you do that, Fräulein Beskiba?' asked Doktor Gross. 'It would seem an act of disloyalty.'

'Do not misunderstand my motives,' she responded. 'I am not seeking some twisted revenge on the mayor. In point of fact, I am quite in love with him.' She looked at each in turn after she announced this. 'And it is because I love him that I want this sale to be stopped. Do you know why he wants to sell off the Woods?'

'No,' Werthen answered. 'That is the part of all this that makes no sense.'

'He needs money. Karl is a most ambitious man. He needs money to mount a political campaign that will make him prime minister. Once in that position, he intends to get the small people in back of him and establish a republic, to get rid of the Habsburgs once and for all.'

'Preposterous,' Gross said.

But Werthen thought otherwise. The elected government of the empire was disastrously rent by divisions in Parliament. No laws had been passed by that body since 1897 when the emperor took over what little democratic power he had relinquished, ruling by decree according to paragraph fourteen of the constitution. Discontent was everywhere. Were Lueger to mount an empire-wide campaign, his fabulous popularity could bring him victory, Werthen was sure of it. Lueger knew how to talk to the little people, to sway them with rhetoric and emotion. And once he became prime minister Lueger could always turn to the people if the emperor attempted to curb his power. He and he alone could bring disparate groups out on to the streets, perhaps even foment a revolution. And once Lueger had the money in hand from the sale of the Woods, he could use it freely, Werthen knew, for the financial machinations of the Christian Socialists in City Hall were legendary. The money would be hidden in a myriad of ways and Lueger would manage to make the Jews at the center of the sale the villains; like a magician, he would keep the public's eye off the money and on the supposed perfidy of those who had bought the Woods.

'He hates them so,' Fräulein Beskiba continued. 'Blames the Habsburgs for all the faults in society. It was the emperor himself, after all, who refused to accept the voice of the people, declining several times to allow Karl to become mayor. He will do anything to destroy the Habsburgs.'

'And to mount a campaign across the length and breadth of the empire he needs large cash reserves,' Werthen said.

She nodded.

'And you do not want him to do this,' he added.

'No.' She said it firmly, unequivocally. 'It

would kill him. You may not know it, but Karl suffers from diabetes. The stress of being mayor is bad enough, were he to become prime minister...' She did not voice her concluding thought.

'Besides,' said Gross, 'if he became prime minister, there would hardly be time for you, would there?'

'Hanns,' his wife said, shaking her head at him.

'Yes. That, too, I suppose. One never has pure motives, does one? But now you know. Now you have ammunition. I only ask that you never let him know where you learned these secrets.'

'Agreed,' Werthen said.

She rose. 'I must get back to my portrait now. I imagine you have preparations to make, as well.'

Werthen was impressed by her absolute self-control and self-assurance. He wondered if she would ever manage to get Lueger to herself as she wished.

Leading them out, she turned abruptly. 'And one thing more. You really cannot believe Karl is somehow responsible for the death of Councilman Steinwitz, can you? Or of this journalist fellow?'

'I see that very little gets past the mayor,' Werthen said, but he did not answer her question.

They had a busy afternoon.

Adele left the men to their work, deciding instead to attend to her attire for the upcoming Lawyers' Ball this Saturday. It was to be the crowning jewel in her ball season and not even a murder investigation or the imminent sale of an enormous section of the Vienna Woods was going to interrupt it.

For the second time in one day Werthen marveled at female strengths. Frau Gross's ability to compartmentalize her activities so thoroughly was quite amazing. It was obvious to Werthen that her husband did not share her childlike eagerness for the gala evening. For Gross, a ball was clearly the last thing on his mind now that they were getting so close to the heart of the matter with their investigations.

As Adele left them after the interview with Fräulein Beskiba she said blithely, 'I am sure you men will have things completed by the weekend.'

Werthen could not understand her optimism; though they had gotten to the crux of the Vienna Woods sale, he was not sure that it brought them much closer to finding the killer of Steinwitz and Praetor. Clearly the fact that the two men were planning to disrupt the sale with their reporting provided motive to someone involved in the business proposition, but to whom? Could it be the huckster-like Remington with his dreams of a 'Tales from the Vienna Woods' park? Perhaps the commission for the killings came from Wittgenstein and his shadowy band of investors, who stood to lose millions if their proposed estate development fell through? Or had orders for the killings come from Lueger himself, so intent on his dreams of power that he would let no one stand in his way, even an old schoolmate?

After all, it was now apparent, according to the testimony of his lover, that Lueger had eyes and ears everywhere. Surely he would know of Steinwitz's defection, of his meetings with young Praetor.

Increasingly Werthen was coming to believe that their main suspect was indeed the mayor himself. Yet how to prove it?

This afternoon, however, they concentrated on stopping the sale of the Vienna Woods; finding the murderer of Steinwitz and Praetor would have to wait for another day.

To that end they paid a call on Victor Adler at the offices of the *Arbeiter Zeitung*.

It was dinnertime when Werthen returned to his flat; Gross and his wife would be dining with friends of Adele tonight. Werthen knew his parents were also staying in this evening, as his mother had caught a touch of the grippe and did not want to spread the illness to baby Frieda. He was looking forward to a quiet evening alone with his wife and child. He needed it, a sort of psychic recharging.

As he fitted the key into his apartment door and began turning it he realized, however, that this intimate evening was not to be. Instead he heard voices from inside, and as he opened the door, they grew clearer. In the foyer he saw a leather valise by the coat rack. His disappointment at not being alone with Berthe and Frieda was supplanted by a more positive emotion.

He burst into the sitting room, from which issued the voices, and was well pleased to see his

291

father-in-law seated on the leather couch. Frieda sat astride his thigh bouncing gently to the nursery song, *so reiten die Damen* ... 'this is the way the ladies ride.'

'Herr Meisner! How wonderful to see you.'

The older man looked up from the child, evident glee in his eyes.

'And you, son.'

They said nothing of this miraculous reconciliation during dinner. Instead, Werthen regaled them with the course his investigation had taken, and Herr Meisner seemed to take it all in as a youth would the adventures of Old Shatterhand from a Karl May novel of the West.

It was not until later, with Herr Meisner off to the guest room, Frieda happily asleep in her crib, and Werthen curled around his wife, that he discovered Berthe understood her father's return no better than did he.

'You mean he gave no explanation?' Werthen asked.

He felt her shrug.

'And you didn't ask?'

She looked over her shoulder at him, eyebrows raised. 'I did not witness you jumping into the fray, either, Karl.'

'But does he still insist on the naming ceremony?'

She sighed. 'I don't know. I just know it is good to have him here again. To see him with our baby.' And they left it at that.

Eighteen

He had time for a brief visit to Frau Steinwitz the next morning before he was to meet Gross at the Rathaus.

I'll be in the quarter, anyway, Werthen told himself, feeling guilty that he had not yet contacted the woman. Of course, they had left it that she would get in touch with Werthen if she needed help, but he knew she was a proud woman; perhaps too proud to ask for help.

So he was out early to make this call before confronting Lueger. Ushered into the Steinwitz flat by the same maid, he was led down the hallway once again past the glass cases full of family heirlooms and weapons to the sitting room where they had talked before. The curtains, however, were still drawn and the room sat in a melancholy gloom.

It was ten minutes before Frau Steinwitz entered, dressed in riding clothes: a sapphire-blue satin skirt surmounted by a waist-length jacket in moss-green suede. The maid bustled in beside her and finally opened the curtains, casting off the noxious pall.

'Advokat, I was just on my way to the Prater for my morning ride.'

'Sorry to interrupt, dear lady,' he said, kissing

the air just above her proffered hand. 'But I realize I have been remiss in my duties.'

'How so?' she asked brightly. 'I believe we left it that I would contact you if I felt the need.'

'Yes, but then I have also felt a good deal of guilt about that meeting. Though I continue to have no time personally to conduct protective services for you, I wanted to ensure that you ... well, that you—'

'Were still alive?' She smiled condescendingly. 'I greatly appreciate the consideration, Advokat, but I believe my earlier fears were completely unfounded. A simple case of nerves. In fact I hope you do not take seriously my contention that someone killed my poor husband and this journalist fellow. I was still in shock. No, worse. I was being a silly female. I believe I shall be quite safe without a *bodyguard*.'

'I am glad to hear that your fears have been allayed,' he said. 'I won't keep you from your ride any longer.'

Frau Steinwitz nodded, and then asked as an afterthought, 'And how is your investigation proceeding? Will you continue now? I mean, I hope my earlier misinformation did not put you on completely the wrong path.'

'Not at all,' Werthen said. 'Gross and I are approaching the truth.' Hardly, but he felt suddenly defensive that Frau Steinwitz should think he had been basing his entire investigation on her tales and fears. Frau Steinwitz was the sort of coddled Viennese woman who felt the world revolved around her.

'If that is the case,' she said with a cold edge to

her voice, 'then I will not detain you either.'

She rang for the maid and Werthen found himself on the landing, given short shrift.

What was that about? he wondered. Had somebody from the Rathaus gotten to her, either paid her off or made further threats? Why so eager to distance herself from her earlier comments?

In the event, of course, it was Werthen who had to wait in the bitter cold for ten minutes. Gross made no apologies when he finally arrived, merely asking Werthen if he had got the sheets from Adler.

'In my coat pocket,' Werthen answered.

They mounted the steps to the vestibule, and inside the same hefty ex-military fellow was on duty at the information desk.

'We would like to see Mayor Lueger,' Gross said to the man.

This request was greeted by a plosive sound in the man's nostrils: half snort and half snigger.

'I'm sure you would. So would half of Vienna. Do you have an appointment?'

They had purposely not tried for an appointment, ensuring that the element of surprise would be on their side.

Gross nodded to Werthen, who pulled a folded front-page dummy of a newspaper out of his coat pocket.

'Perhaps you could show him this. I believe he will see us.'

The guard took the newspaper and tossed it on to his desk along with other mail.

'Now,' Gross said with an authority to his voice that made the man sit ramrod straight.

'I can't very well leave my desk,' he protested.

'We will keep watch over it, right, Advokat?' he said to Werthen.

'Absolutely,' Werthen agreed. Then to the guard: 'You really should hurry. That is this afternoon's edition and I believe Mayor Lueger might have something to say about it.'

'Or should we tell Mayor Lueger later that his own vestibule guard was responsible for the end of his career?' added Gross.

The man rose, suspicion written on his face. 'This better not be some damn trick. When I come back, I expect to see you two waiting here.'

Gross saluted him. 'We won't budge from this spot.'

They waited several minutes as other well-dressed men entered and departed the vestibule. Each time steps descended the wide marble staircase they looked expectantly for the returning guard, only to be disappointed.

Suddenly the inter-office telephone on the guard's desk rang. The abrupt jingle of it startled them at first, but then they returned their attention to the stairs. The telephone continued to ring. A most persistent caller, Werthen thought. And then the realization struck.

He picked up the receiver. 'Hello,' he said.

'I am waiting,' came the voice on the other end of the line. 'Bielohlawek's office.'

Werthen knew that high, resonant tone. It was Mayor Lueger himself.

They wasted no time in getting to the council-man's office, not knowing what to expect there, wondering if they had over-played their hand. At least they had come armed, for at Gross's insistence each was carrying one of the Steyr automatic pistols the criminologist always traveled with.

Reaching Bielohlawek's corner office, however, they were met by the mayor's bodyguard, Kulowski, who demanded to search them.

'I assure you,' Gross protested, 'we have not come to assassinate your mayor.'

'That's as may be,' the man growled.

Suddenly Werthen made a connection that had until this moment eluded him. It all added up now that it was clear that Lueger was in back of the Vienna Woods sale. Adalbert Kulowski was in fact the large beefy man Berthe had described, the man who had assaulted his father and chased the party away from the farmhouse in Laab im Walde.

'Do you enjoy terrorizing women and children?' Werthen looked the man straight in the eye.

'What are you talking about?' The man glared back at him.

'About a little farmhouse at Laab im Walde. Sound familiar?'

Kulowski cut his eyes from Werthen for a fraction of a second.

'The courts might have something to say about your tactics, Herr Kulowski.'

'What's keeping them, Kulowski?' Lueger's voice boomed from inside the office.

'Indeed,' Gross said with heavy indignation.

'What *is* keeping us? Let us leave this bully to easier pickings. Come, Werthen.'

They brushed past the bodyguard, who by now was too confused to bother with his search.

Inside the room, Lueger sat behind Bielohlawek's desk, and the councilman was seated in a smaller chair at his side. On the desk in front of them both was the mock-up of the front page of this afternoon's *Arbeiter Zeitung*, which Adler had kindly supplied them with. The banner headline was upside down to Werthen, but he knew very well what it said, for he had written it:

Lueger to Sell Woods in Bid for Higher Office

A smaller headline underneath got the point across for any who could not interpret the main headline:

Man of the People Steals the People's Woods
for Private Gain

Under the two headlines was an article detailing the sale and naming those interested parties who were putting in bids, as well as their plans for development. It ended by elucidating Lueger's own plans for the position of prime minister. The whole sordid business was laid out in plain, but sometimes breathless prose. Also written by Werthen.

'I'll sue if you print this,' Lueger said, not bothering with introductions.

'You will have to speak to Herr Adler about

that,' Werthen said. 'I believe Herr Kraus will also be carrying a similar story in the next edition of *Die Fackel*. You might want to speak with him, too.'

Werthen wanted to make sure that Lueger understood that others were involved in this, as well. That others knew of their interview at the Rathaus today.

'The censors would never allow it.'

Gross was impolitic enough to laugh at this. 'I am afraid it is the Habsburgs who do the censoring around here. And they will be only too happy to have such news broadcast.'

'You'll regret this,' Lueger snarled at them. 'For as long as you both live.'

Neither responded to this threat, but rather stood in silence and let Lueger make the next move. Werthen's hand slipped into his coat pocket and was comforted by the cold touch of the Steyr pistol.

'Why are you doing this to me?'

'You are not the victim, Mayor,' Gross said. 'This is only what Councilman Steinwitz and Herr Praetor were attempting, before they were killed.'

'Killed!' Lueger stood as if an electric current had been shot through him. 'Councilman Steinwitz shot himself in this very office. And of this journalist, I can only assume that a man with his predilections might meet with some very bad company.'

Werthen and Gross refused to be drawn into diversions from the issue at hand: stopping tomorrow's sale of the Vienna Woods. They stood silently across the desk from Lueger as the mayor looked from one to the other.

Finally, 'What is it you want?'

'I should think that would be very clear,' Werthen said. 'Call off the sale. Neither Remington nor Wittgenstein would be very interested, I assume, with such adverse publicity,' he said, pointing at the paper on the desk. 'And your hopes for higher office, let alone another term as mayor, will be null if this is published.'

'In your opinion,' the mayor shot back.

Werthen shrugged. 'Take your chances, then. The afternoon editions will be on the streets in three hours. Which gives you plenty of time to call this off and instead appear to be a heroic mayor who uncovered a despicable cabal out to privatize the Vienna Woods and foiled it.'

Lueger glanced at the front-page dummy in front of him. 'Where does it say that?'

'It doesn't,' Werthen said. 'But it will, in this afternoon's edition. A carrot for you and an assurance that you really will call off the sale.'

Lueger, despite his obvious anger, nodded in appreciation at the gambit. 'You have given this some thought.'

'We try,' Werthen said. 'Do we have your word?'

Lueger clenched his jaws violently.

'Mayor?' Werthen prodded him.

'Yes, yes. My word.'

'And you might tell Herr Kulowski that next time he decides to play rough with women and children there will be consequences.'

'I have no idea whatsoever of what you are

speaking,' Lueger replied.

Bielohlawek, who until now had remained quiet, suddenly found his voice.

'I for one do not know what motivates men such as you to destroy a brilliant political future—'

But Gross cut him off. 'On the contrary, we are ensuring your mayor's political future ... in Vienna.'

They could not believe how easy it had been. After leaving the Rathaus, Werthen placed a call to Victor Adler to let him know he should run the positive story about Lueger foiling a plot to sell the Vienna Woods to an unnamed American developer.

'Neatly handled,' Gross pronounced after Werthen came out of the telephone cubicle of the telegraph and exchange office near the Rathaus.

'Too neatly, I fear,' Werthen said.

'Do not despair, my friend. We have yet to catch the killer of Steinwitz and Praetor.'

'Do you still think Lueger was responsible?'

Going back out on to the chill of the street, Gross pulled the collar of his coat up.

'I believe that was your theory,' he replied. 'I have not yet made a determination. There is still much evidence to be gathered. We should hear from my researchers in Czernowitz this week about the ribbon from Herr Praetor's typewriting machine. With any luck that might give us a new direction to pursue or confirm old suspicions. I admit I expected more direct threats from Mayor Lueger.'

'He could not very well make us disappear. Not after I made it clear that Adler, Kraus and who knows what others were aware of our presence there today.'

'That is true. But still, a man who has killed twice, one of the victims his old friend ... Well, one expects a bit more fight.'

'He knew he had lost,' Werthen said. 'Perhaps he did not want to raise our suspicions about his culpability for the deaths, did not want us focusing too hard on him as a suspect. His financial scheme was foiled this time, but he will have other opportunities. However, if homicide is traced to him, that is quite another matter.'

'Hmm.' Gross did not seem convinced. 'That is one theory. I suggest, however, that we watch our backs.'

They reached the Josefstädterstrasse in time for lunch. Frau Blatschky had promised stuffed kidneys.

They found pandemonium instead.

'It's Father,' Berthe said to him as they entered the apartment. 'He's been badly injured. The doctor fears for his life.'

The immediate thought came into Werthen's mind: Another attack from the Rathaus. But he had no time for other rumination.

They quickly followed Berthe to the guest room. There Herr Meisner was laid out on the bed, a nasty gash over his right eye. Doktor Weisman, a local physician, was leaning over the man. Berthe began sobbing now that Werthen had finally arrived. It was as if she had been holding herself together as surrogate head of the household, but now that Werthen was here, she could finally let her emotions out.

'It was horrible, Karl. This brute of a man came to the door. Frau Blatschky answered it, and he came storming in, demanding to see you. I screamed when I saw him coming in and Father came out of the reading room, newspaper in hand and demanded the man leave. At that the thug struck him in the face. I am sure he was carrying something heavy in his hand. And Father fell back with such force that he knocked his head against the base of the telephone table.'

'Easy,' said Werthen, putting an arm around her shoulder.

'I was frantic. There was Father flat on his back, not moving. Frieda was screaming. Thank heavens for Frau Blatschky. By this time she had retrieved one of your shotguns from the study. I am sure it was not loaded ... but she aimed it straight at his chest. The coward ran without a word.'

Gross meanwhile was conferring with the doctor, who was shaking his head. Herr Meisner's breathing was labored, ragged.

'We've got to get him to the General Hospital,' Werthen said, instinct telling him that if they left him here the man could easily die. Weisman was a good general practitioner, but surely he knew nothing of head wounds.

'I would advise against moving him,' the doctor said. His voice was high, almost a falsetto.

'I'll take that risk,' Werthen said.

'Karl,' Berthe said, holding him tight.

'He may just as easily die here,' Werthen said to Weisman. 'Am I right, Doktor?'

The elderly medical man began to protest, checked himself, and made a curt nod of his head.

'Then let us waste no more time,' Werthen said. He went to the phone and dialed the number for the city ambulance corps. The dispatcher took the information and promised to have an ambulance there in half an hour.

'But he could be dead by then,' he said.

'There was a fire in Hietzing this morning,' the lady replied, her voice taking on an icy edge. 'Do you still wish to have an ambulance sent?'

Werthen did not bother replying, but simply hung up the apparatus.

'I'll be back in a moment,' he called to whomever was listening. Racing down the stairs, he reached the street and hurried to the nearest *Fiaker* queue. He was in luck, for his favorite driver, Bachmann, was there whistling his usual tune from Strauss. Werthen had once done the man a service regarding his challenged birth status, and Bachmann had since been grateful and cooperative.

He doffed a battered derby as Werthen approached. His thick frame was covered chin to boot top in an ancient and somewhat moth-eaten woolen coat that could have been a hand-me-down from one of Napoleon's generals.

'A wonderful day, Advokat. Can I be of service?'

Werthen quickly explained the situation and Bachmann lost no time in leaping to his seat.

'Get in,' he ordered. He wheeled the *Fiaker* to Werthen's door, tied the horses to the reins pole on the sidewalk, and hurried up the stairs with Werthen.

'You can't mean to move him by cab,' the doctor said when they entered the guest bedroom. 'His pulse is weakening.'

'All the more reason to move him now. Will you accompany us, Doktor?'

With Bachmann carrying Herr Meisner's upper body, and Werthen and Gross grabbing a leg apiece, they gently lifted the injured man from the bed. Werthen could now see a large lump at the back of his father-in-law's head. There was no blood.

As they made their way down the hall of the apartment, Gross told Berthe, 'Try to contact Doktor Praetor. As I recall, he has office hours now. See if he can arrange for a specialist to meet us.'

Frau Blatschky was at the door, her wits about her. 'We will see to it,' she promised.

'And get the police over here,' Werthen said over his shoulder. 'Call Drechsler. That lunatic may come again.'

'I'll have shells in the gun next time,' Frau Blatschky said.

The trip to the General Hospital passed in a blur for Werthen, with Herr Meisner splayed across the knees of the three men inside. Bachmann used his quirt liberally and the *Fiaker* rattled over the cobblestone streets in and out of traffic, at one point perilously overtaking a streetcar.

But Werthen was focused on one thing: the identity of the burly man who had attacked his family. His first thought had been an attack sponsored by the Rathaus. But now he attempted to evaluate things more methodically. Clearly it was not the same man as at Laab im Walde, otherwise Berthe would have immediately mentioned that. Not the bodyguard, Kulowski, then. Could it be the same thug who had attacked him in the street? He would not know for sure until he was able to speak with his wife again. Who had sent the man? But that was patently clear. On both instances Werthen had just been to see someone at the Rathaus.

He would avenge this outrage, he promised himself.

Herr Meisner's labored breathing seemed to echo in the narrow confines of the carriage.

'His pulse grows weaker and weaker,' Doktor Weisman said.

Finally they arrived at the hospital and miraculously Doktor Praetor himself was there, with another doctor whom he introduced as Doktor Sulzman. 'Foremost man in brain surgery,' Praetor said as two strong assistants guided Herr Meisner off their laps and on to a stretcher.

Following closely behind he heard Doktor Sulzman say, 'By the looks of that lump there could be internal hemorrhaging.'

They followed the stretcher carrying Herr Meisner as far as they could, finally forced to stop at a door marked 'No Admittance.'

They stood there dumbly for a few minutes. Doktor Praetor came out to speak to them.

'No use staying on here,' he told them. 'There is a waiting room on the second floor. I will look for you there when there is anything to report.'

'Will he live?' Werthen asked.

'I will not give you false promises. The gentleman is badly injured. But he will have the best care available, I can assure you of that. Did he fall?'

Obviously Berthe had not given him all the information. 'No. He was attacked.'

Doktor Praetor took a breath. 'Was it in association with your investigations?'

'I believe so,' Werthen said. 'I think the same assailant may have earlier attacked me in an effort to stop the investigation.'

'That it should lead to your family...' Doktor Praetor was clearly shaken. 'I do apologize. Perhaps we should stop.'

'Nonsense,' said Gross. 'We will not be cowed by such savage actions.'

'No,' Doktor Praetor said. 'Nor will I.'

They were silent for a moment and then Doktor Weisman, who Werthen had almost forgotten, offered, 'I was the physician who attended him in the first instance. If I may be of any assistance...?'

'A pleasure,' Praetor said, shaking the man's hand. 'I believe you have already been of immense help. Most wise to bring him here posthaste. Head injuries can be notoriously deceptive.'

Doktor Weisman bowed his head at this, not offering a correction or explanation.

Praetor hurried back to assist Sulzman, and

307

Doktor Weisman pleaded other obligations and departed. Gross and Werthen found their way to the second-floor waiting room, already filled with several groups, their faces wearing similar expressions of pinched expectancy.

'Perhaps in the hall,' Werthen said, going outside where there was a bench. If Praetor came to find them he would have to pass in this direction, and Werthen could not see spending hours in the company of others so filled with tension and anxiety.

'We are close, very close,' Gross said. 'Our killer grows frantic. This was obviously a most desperate act.'

'Agreed,' Werthen said, sitting and leaning forward, elbows on his thighs.

'Where to from here?' Gross asked.

'Not now, Gross.' For now another thought filled him with fear and anxiety.

'Sorry. I thought it might take your mind off—'

'He could just as easily have injured Berthe or Frieda. Killed them.'

He could hardly bear to think of that. His wife, his baby girl. That some demented stranger could force his way into his home...

'I can stay here,' Gross offered. 'You should be with them.'

But at that very moment Detective Inspector Drechsler approached, two uniformed men along with him.

'Bad business,' he said, shaking their hands in turn. 'I've stationed two officers at your flat, Advokat. Not to worry.'

'Berthe?'

'She is holding up. Your cook seems to be solid as a rock. She gave us a description.'

'A large, unkempt man in worker's clothes,' Werthen said. 'Wearing a bowler with a thick growth of coal-black hair underneath. A thickened lump at the bridge of his nose as if it had been broken several times. Spoke in an Ottrakring accent.'

'She told you then,' Drechsler said.

Werthen shook his head. He explained to Drechsler about being attacked himself, apparently by the same man.

Drechsler rubbed his chin. 'You seem to have turned over a rock someone wants left in place. Care to explain?'

Werthen glanced at Gross.

'Well, Detective,' Gross began, 'I think we have fairly well proved a connection between the death of Steinwitz and that of Praetor.'

'On the widow's say-so?' Drechsler shook his head. 'She came to us and mentioned how she had great nerve stress after her husband's unfortunate death. That she had even thought for a time that both he and the journalist Praetor were murdered because of some silly newspaper article they were working on.'

'Hardly *silly*,' Werthen interjected. 'Nothing more than revelations about a scheme by Lueger to sell off an enormous section of the Vienna Woods.'

Drechsler rubbed his chin again at this news, clearly impressed.

'Be that as it may,' the inspector continued,

'she said she was recanting any suspicions she had about her husband's death. She said she could just not stand the shame of knowing he was a suicide, so she let her imagination run away with her.'

'Why would Frau Steinwitz bother coming to the police with this story?' Gross asked. 'When we spoke to her earlier, she would not go to you even though she feared for her life.'

'Makes sense then, doesn't it,' Drechsler said. 'She wasn't really in fear of her life.'

'I repeat my question,' Gross said. 'Why come to you at all with this explanation?'

Drechsler looked somewhat sheepish.

'Out with it, Inspector,' Gross thundered.

'She said she had spoken to a couple of private inquiry agents who had been very pushy about wanting information. She did not want to be bothered by those men again.' He turned to Werthen. 'In point of fact, my man told me you went to pay her a visit early this morning.'

Gross turned to him. 'Is that so, Werthen?'

Werthen explained his visit and also his surprise at the change in Frau Steinwitz's story. But as events had thereafter overtaken him, he'd had no time to inform Gross of the interview.

'It was quite cordial, I assure you, Inspector. As was our former visit. I had been her husband's *Advokat* before he became a council member.'

'Any other evidence except what the widow said and then later recanted?'

'You gave me the first bit of connection yourself, Inspector,' Gross said, reminding him of the

310

use of the same type of weapon in each case, a 7.65 mm Roth-Sauer automatic.

'Correct. Not the same weapon, though.'

'No, of course not.' Gross peered at Drechsler. 'Has someone talked to you, Inspector?'

Drechsler did not look at either man when he spoke. 'Frau Steinwitz spoke with Inspector Meindl directly. He was furious, of course.'

'He always is,' Werthen said.

But Drechsler was not to be humored. 'I feel awful about this, after what you are doing for my wife with her upcoming surgery and all. But after the drama of last Sunday with the Wittgensteins, Meindl told me to warn you two off. Now, with this latest incident—'

'Warn us off?' Gross said. 'Off what? That infernal little toad.'

'He was quite serious this time,' Drechsler continued. 'Lueger's office also spoke with Meindl earlier today. After that call he made it very clear to me that there's a posting in Carinthia where I will end up tracing cattle thieves if I don't convince you two to call it quits with the investigation of Steinwitz.'

'I quite understand,' Gross said.

The statement shocked both Werthen and Drechsler.

'You do?' Drechsler said.

'And you may tell Inspector Meindl that as of today we will curtail our investigation of Councilman Steinwitz.'

Drechsler's face broke into a wide grin. It was the first time Werthen had ever seen the man smile.

'Thank you, Doktor Gross. And you too, Advokat. I won't forget this, you can be sure of it. I'll have every available man looking for the thug that did this to your father-in-law.'

'Much appreciated, Inspector,' Werthen said.

Once Drechsler and his two policemen left, Werthen wheeled on Gross.

'Whatever got into you to make that promise?'

'The man's obviously distressed,' Gross said. 'Do you wish him to end up in the cow patties of Carinthia?'

'No, but—'

'I am sure you will notice that I made no such promise about curtailing the investigation of Henricus Praetor's death.'

It felt good to smile. 'You cunning old dog,' Werthen said.

'And now tell me, Werthen, just what enticement did you offer that *Fiaker* driver to take a badly wounded man in his carriage? How much did it cost?'

'Nothing.'

'*Und bitte*,' Gross said with utter disbelief.

'Truth is I helped Bachmann with some family difficulties last summer. He was very grateful for the support.'

'Legal problems?'

'A strange situation. You see it turns out that Bachmann is actually the son of a certain count, distant cousin to the Habsburgs themselves.'

'Werthen, if you are having me on—'

'I assure you, this is only too real. I do not know if you noticed, but Bachmann moves with a distinct limp.'

312

'No, I must admit I was too concerned with other matters at the time. Quite unlike me to miss something like that, though.'

'He compensates well, but he was born with a club foot. His parents – well, the count in particular – were most adamant about not having a cripple for a son and heir. So they sought out a fine healthy specimen from the lower classes, a cabby's son, as a matter of fact.'

Werthen found himself rather enjoying the recounting of this curious history; it was a distraction from the harsher realities at hand.

'You don't mean to say they traded sons?' Gross was indignant at the idea.

'Actually, they purchased the new one and gave their deformed baby in return. All quite legal, I assure you.'

'The aristocracy.' Gross almost spat the word out.

'Well, the count's true son thus grew up with the cabby's family and later began to drive a *Fiaker* himself, while the cabby's son grew up in the count's family and later went into the military, where, I am sorry to say, he was killed on maneuvers in the Balkans last year. And since the count too had already died, the countess wanted her real son back. She petitioned the courts, and when Bachmann received word of how matters stood, he contacted me. He had heard from other *Fiaker* drivers that I was an honest man – how they determine that, I do not know other than that I tip well. At any rate, Bachmann wanted no part of any nobility. "A cabman I am and will always be," he told me. He hired me to write up an official renunciation of the title of count, which would pass to him. Instead a distant cousin in Voralberg is now the count and inherits millions.'

'What a curious story.'

'Bachmann is happy as he is. His adoptive father is long dead, but his mother still cares for him and his wife and small family. He told me he would never renounce that woman, not for all the gold in Budapest.'

They were interrupted by the approach of Doktor Praetor, who was walking briskly toward them along the hallway.

Werthen could not read his face.

'Doktor?' he said.

Praetor said nothing until he was within arm's length of Werthen.

'They are still operating. But I think he will survive. There was leakage in the brain from the contusion. The surgeon has now allowed the blood to drain and released the pressure on the brain.'

He did not sound optimistic, however.

'What else?' Werthen said.

'We cannot know how much damage was done to the brain until later. There could be lasting effects, with speech, perhaps with movement. We will only know these things in the next days and weeks.'

'The man must be on Lueger's payroll,' Werthen said.

Both Gross and his wife were at dinner, as well as the von Werthens.

314

'Do you think it is completely safe here?' Herr von Werthen said. 'I mean if that animal struck twice, why not again?'

Werthen attempted a jocular tone: 'Do you need assurances beyond the fact that there is a police watch and that Frau Blatschky assures me next time the shotgun will be loaded?'

The cook was just taking away the dinner plates as Werthen said this, and blushed down to the starched white band of her collar.

Berthe sat silently, Frieda on her lap now, for the child's naptime had been turned topsy-turvy. Berthe had gotten back from the hospital not long before with good news. Her father was out of surgery, and seemed to be recovering well. Still, the doubt about long-term damage lingered.

Werthen and Gross had had little time to discuss all these alarming new developments, and so used the dinner hour for that purpose.

'As I was saying at the hospital,' Gross said, 'we must be very close now to provoke such a desperate act.'

He nodded to Berthe as if to apologize for speaking so clinically about her father's injuries, and she quickly shook her head, moving Frieda to her shoulder to burp her.

'No, please go on,' she insisted. 'I want this monster behind bars in the Liesel.'

Werthen put a hand on her shoulder reassuringly, and Frieda suddenly gripped his forefinger with rather extraordinary firmness.

'It's about time at that,' Herr von Werthen said. 'I don't see how you fellows can make a living

315

of this investigating business if you can't solve cases.'

No one, not even Frau von Werthen, responded to this. Nor, seemingly, even paid the man any attention.

'As you noted to Detective Inspector Drechsler today,' Gross continued, 'each time we have paid an official visit to the Rathaus, there has been an attack. Of course I discount my little inspection tour of Councilman Bielohlawek's office, as no one was aware of that. Is this a mere matter of coincidence? It would seem unlikely.'

'Right,' agreed Werthen. 'There was nothing Lueger could do to us directly while we were at the Rathaus this morning, for I made it painfully obvious that others knew our whereabouts. So later he dispatches this creature of his to put a further scare into me.'

'What do you think he would have done if you had been home?' Berthe wondered aloud. But as with Herr von Werthen's comment, this one drew no response.

'It has to be Lueger,' Werthen said.

'Guilty of corruption, but of murder?' Gross said.

'Find the attacker and we will know,' Frau Gross said, joining the discussion.

But Werthen knew this would not be easy. Such a man could easily hide away among the criminals and other lowlifes of Vienna; there was nothing distinctive about his features except for the broken nose. And how many toughs in Vienna's Second District bore such battle scars? Perhaps they could attempt to trace him back to

Lueger's known employees?

'If I had only been here,' Herr von Werthen said, puffing out his chest.

Werthen dearly wanted to remind his father of his 'protective' presence at Laab im Walde, but thought better of it.

'Emile,' Frau von Werthen said. 'Perhaps you would care for an after-dinner cognac?'

'Of course, *Maman*,' Werthen said, getting to his feet and fetching bottle and snifters from a sideboard. He passed glasses all around, grateful for the diversion.

After they had all had a sip, Herr von Werthen cleared his throat. Werthen sighed internally. He, like his mother, was hoping that the cognac would change his father's focus.

'I believe,' he said importantly, 'it is time that I and Frau von Werthen return to Hohelände. I had word today from young Stein that the stables were in frightful disarray. High winds tore off one of the roofs. I really should be there to over-see things.'

Werthen checked his initial impulse to dis-suade his parents from leaving.

'If you think it best, Papa,' he said.

Nineteen

Wednesday was clear and so cold Werthen wondered that anyone could break through the snow and frost to dig a grave. But they had, and the mound of dirt was covered in a black drop cloth, the narrow coffin dangling from wooden supports over the hole.

Technically speaking, it was neither the best nor the worst plot in the Zentralfriedhof, the Central Cemetery of Vienna. Fräulein Metzinger had used family relations to secure a plot belonging to the descendants of a great-aunt. This lady had been a great supporter of hers, a champion of her attending university. Of course, for the burial to be allowed in this section of the cemetery, Fräulein Metzinger had to invent the fiction of Herr Heidrich von Beer, legal assistant. Otherwise the child would have ended up in a pauper's grave.

Fräulein Metzinger, all in black, stood at the head of the coffin, her cheeks reddened by the chill air. She was flanked by the boy's father, who had somehow managed to find a black suit for the occasion, and by the *Portier*, Frau Ignatz, and her brother, Oskar, from the Habsburgergasse. Rosa Mayreder was also in attendance, bundled in a black fur coat. Werthen had remembered at the last minute amid yesterday's chaotic events to order the funeral wreath; it now lay atop the coffin, its hothouse lilies beginning to shrivel in the extreme cold.

Heidl had not, as it turned out, been baptized. Thus, Fräulein Metzinger, a Protestant, had asked her minister to conduct the brief funeral ceremony. The man was surprisingly young and went without the benefit of a hat on this cold day.

The minister began promptly at eleven, as scheduled, reciting the Twenty-third Psalm.

'The Lord is my shepherd, I shall not want,' he intoned in a pleasantly calming voice. Werthen found himself lulled by the familiar words, comforted almost.

'He maketh me to lie down in green pastures, he leadeth me beside the still waters.'

Taking succor from these ancient words, Werthen suddenly wondered at his and Berthe's obstinate refusal to let the von Werthens schedule a baptism for Frieda or to allow Herr Meisner even to have a naming ceremony for his grandchild. What did it matter, anyway? Frieda would be her own person; she would be the one to decide personal matters such as whether or not to follow a religion and if so, which one. Meanwhile, it would give pleasure to the grandparents. And now perhaps Herr Meisner would never have the opportunity to perform the naming ceremony of his own granddaughter.

'Surely goodness and mercy shall follow me all the days of my life, and I will dwell in the House of the Lord forever,' the minister concluded and the subsequent moment of silence brought Werthen out of his thoughts.

The minister began again. 'My friends, we are brought together on this day for the passing of a brother, Heidrich Beer, a young boy whose life was cut tragically short.'

Werthen was relieved that the fiction of Heidrich's name did not have to be continued in the service.

'This young man, who had experienced so many adversities in his short life, was on the cusp of momentous changes. But the good Lord had other plans for him, and brought him home to His eternal favor and bliss.'

At this point, both Fräulein Metzinger and Herr Beer began crying. The entire scene – shabby little coffin, mound of earth ready to spread, shriveling lilies, the few shivering mourners gathered at graveside – was incredibly tragic. Yet suddenly Werthen had the irrepressible desire to laugh. He had never reacted so to sadness, but the laughter welled up inside of him, a hiccough that could not be repressed. He quickly pulled a handkerchief from the inside pocket of his suit and pretended to be blowing his nose; all the while laughing uncontrollably into the cotton as if sobbing. Finally he had to remove himself from the proceedings to walk up and down rows of graves before returning as the minister was delivering the final prayer.

'Grant, O Lord, rest to your servant Heidrich Beer in a place where there is neither sorrow nor sighing nor pain.'

Both Fräulein Metzinger and the boy's father

had recovered their composure, watching closely as the coffin was slowly lowered into the grave. Once the ropes were removed, Fräulein Metzinger was the first to throw a fistful of dirt. It landed with a hollow plonking sound on the top of the wooden coffin.

Only now did Werthen notice other spectators watching the proceedings from a distance. Two of these were Ludwig Wittgenstein and his sister Hermine. Seeing him looking his way, Ludwig waved, but then allowed himself to be dragged off by his sister without exchanging a word.

The other observer was Kulowski, bodyguard to Mayor Lueger. He stood his ground as Werthen approached.

'What brings you here, Herr Kulowski?'

'Same as everybody,' the man responded. 'Death.'

'I wasn't aware you were acquainted with young Heidl Beer. Or is this a subtle form of threat, perhaps? If so, I warn you—'

'You're a suspicious sort, aren't you,' Kulowski interrupted, his voice a low growl like a gravel machine.

They stared at one another for a moment.

'The mayor sent me,' Kulowski said. 'He wanted to thank you for the story in the *Arbeiter Zeitung*. Said it was good you kept your end of the bargain.'

'I assume *he* did, as well?'

Kulowski nodded. 'Can't say as I am sorry about it.' He stepped closer to Werthen and spoke confidingly. 'Between you and me, I like the Vienna Woods just the way it is. After all,

321

what's Vienna without its woods?'

'A loyal Viennese at heart.' Werthen said it with a twist of irony.

Kulowski understood. 'Nothing funny about that, is there? I suppose you're not from Vienna at all?'

'No, not originally.'

'Then why bother?' Kulowski asked. 'I mean why risk anything trying to stop the sale? Mayor Lueger is not a man you want as an enemy, I can tell you that for a certainty.'

'It's a matter of honor, actually. Two men gave their lives to stop the sale. And you can tell the mayor that his thug beat a harmless old man. That attack has only served to make me more committed than ever to seeking justice.'

Kulowski appeared honestly confused. 'Look, I've got no idea what you mean about this thug, but I assume the two lives you're talking about are the councilman and that journalist?'

'Yes.'

Kulowski blew dry air through his lips. 'Steinwitz. Now that was a surprise to the mayor. We were there when he shot himself. Well, not there, but coming down the stairs. Poor bastard. That's a thing I can never understand, killing yourself. And with her there, too.'

Werthen wanted to leave the man's company; he'd often found it the case that former enemies became unfortunately loquacious after a crisis such as they had had yesterday.

'Well, Herr Kulowski, it was good of you to bring the message...' Then something registered in his brain.

322

'What was it you just said?'

'About Steinwitz killing himself? Suicide's not my game.'

'No. After that. With *her* there. Who was there?'

'The wife, of course. Don't know that others noticed her. They were too busy taking cover once they heard the shot. But when we got closer to the office, I saw her just going off down the stairway. Must have been on her way to see him just when he killed himself. Horrible thing for the woman. Of course, I don't think she saw her husband. That builder fellow, Wagner, he was at the door of the office. Say, where you off to in such a hurry?'

But Werthen did not bother to answer. He had to meet Gross. This changed everything.

Gross knocked on the door. There was no answer.

He was at the Zeltgasse apartment building where Henricus Praetor had lived, attempting to discover anything he could from the watchful Frau Czerny, the old woman who had seen Werthen the night of Praetor's death. Perhaps she had seen something else, heard something else that could aid in their investigations, something that she had not told the police. Gross was sure he could ferret it out of her if that were the case.

He knocked again, but still there was no response.

He would try to speak with other occupants and perhaps also find out whether young Praetor had a cleaning lady who might shed some light on the dead journalist's freshly cleaned apartment and the possible location of the missing notebooks. Not that such notebooks mattered now, but Gross liked to tie up loose ends in such matters.

Still standing at the old woman's door, he checked his watch. Eleven thirty already. He had arranged to meet with Werthen following the funeral of the unfortunate office boy. Just a slip of a youth. Tragic, really, but not an unexpected outcome for a life lived so carelessly. Gross could not understand the younger generation. All of them, including his own son, were thoughtless and irresponsible in his book. They refused to take seriously the old values of respect and hard work. What invidious societal deformations would take place in this new century Gross did not want to contemplate.

He let out a grunt of disapproval at these thoughts just as the door to Frau Czerny's flat opened.

'What are you doing making rude noises outside my door?' The woman was of a certain age, to be sure, but hardly the meek little sparrow one might think of as elderly; rather she was large and florid of complexion, wearing a white housecoat and brandishing a feather duster like a saber directed at Gross's head.

'Frau Czerny?'

'Who wants to know?'

He extracted a professional card from the leather case he carried and handed it to her. She held the card out at arm's length, squinting at it.

'Criminalist. What's that supposed to mean?'

'I am assisting the police in the investigation of Herr Praetor's death,' Gross said, enlarging somewhat on the truth.

'Then you know what I told them.' She made to close the door.

'Dear lady,' Gross quickly added. 'From long years of study, I understand that sometimes it is not what one remembers, but rather what one is asked that matters.'

'No. What matters now is that I have an apartment to clean. Wednesdays are cleaning day.'

'Admirable that you do your own house-cleaning, dear lady.'

This faint compliment made her pause. 'Not always so, I can assure you. Frau Novatny is my cleaning lady. But she has been sick lately. Comes from working nights, I suppose.'

Gross was about to let this remark go, but instinct made him pursue it, for there was an ironic edge to the comment that intrigued him.

'A cleaning lady working at night? For offices?'

She shook her head, obviously disgusted at what she took to be his complete lack of understanding.

'How should I know that? No, not offices. Here, in this apartment house. All very well for her to work nights, but the days she is supposed to come to me she is suddenly sick.'

Gross was no longer intrigued. So much for his instincts. He was about to throw a question at her regarding any persons, known or unknown, who might have been at the apartment house the night of Praetor's death. Not a visitor but a person.

The distinction mattered, for witnesses often overlooked the obvious: a mail delivery, the gas man come to check the meters, someone's personal help. But suddenly she squinted hard at him.

'Well, I'll be... I see what you mean.'

'Madam?'

'I mean about it mattering what one is asked. Aren't you a clever one? Let us hope your wife thinks so at least.' A lascivious wink from the old woman made him almost blush.

Gross was completely at sea. 'I cannot see what my wife has to do with anything,' he protested.

'Don't you? Well, it's Frau Novatny, isn't it? I heard her the very night of Herr Praetor's death. Said she was too sick to come to me on the Wednesday and then here she was the next night.'

'You did not report this to the police, did you?'

She shook her head. 'I hardly thought of it. Herr Praetor used her services from time to time.'

'You are sure it was Frau Novatny here that night? You saw her?'

'No, of course not. But I heard voices from Herr Praetor's apartment when I passed it that evening.'

She did not mention it, but it was clear Frau Czerny passed the other apartment on a trip to the *Clo*, or communal toilet. Like most apartments in Vienna, major plumbing was reserved for common areas in the hallway of each floor.

'And you recognized her voice?'

326

'It had to be her,' Frau Czerny said. 'After all, Herr Praetor was not the sort of man to have female guests, that I know.'

'So it was a woman's voice you heard and you simply assumed it was Frau Novatny?'

'Yes. I suppose so.'

'Frau Czerny, I thank you. You have been more helpful than you can imagine. This voice you heard. How close was it in time to when you heard the shot?'

'How am I to know that?'

'It is important, dear lady. No one will blame you for not recalling this vital fact before.'

'Blame? I should hope not. Now I am finished with talking. I have cleaning to do.'

This time she shut the door before Gross had a chance to offer further flattery.

Werthen was at the Ritterhof at twelve thirty as scheduled, eager to share his new information with Gross, but in the event he had to wait another fifteen minutes before his colleague arrived. Time enough, despite his excitement, to dispose of a bowl of *Leberknödel* soup, one of the specialties of the house, and to figure out the motives of Herr Kulowski – and ultimately Mayor Lueger – in supplying the information regarding Frau Steinwitz. It was clear Kulowski had not made a simple slip of the tongue, but had, in fact, attended the funeral in order to impart this very piece of information. But why?

By the time he had finished the nicely warm bowl of soup, Werthen had come up with several plausible reasons. First, it was obvious that his and Gross's interest in the Vienna Woods scheme and in the deaths of Steinwitz and Praetor had rattled Lueger. He was eager, as Gross had pointed out yesterday, to deflect suspicion from himself for these murders. That much was patently clear. So, perhaps Lueger simply invented the presence of Frau Steinwitz at the scene of the crime to divert Werthen and Gross in their investigation. Or perhaps she really had been at the Rathaus that day. But why (if indeed Kulowski had actually seen the lady leaving the scene of her husband's death) had Lueger protected her in the first place? To that, one could answer that Steinwitz's death was put down to suicide initially and Frau Steinwitz's presence would then be in no way unusual. However, once he, Werthen, and Gross had begun to investigate, why protect her? Two reasons presented themselves to Werthen. First was simple gratitude. If Lueger believed the woman had killed her husband, would he not be happy to simply have this nettlesome problem – a councilman with a conscience – taken care of for him? Or perhaps Lueger had thought to cash in this favor later with Frau Steinwitz's powerful father. After all, if Lueger really did have imperial pretensions, then he would need the army in back of him in a standoff with Franz Josef. In this scenario, knowing what he knew about Frau Steinwitz provided Lueger with powerful political capital. Now, however, with a net closing around the killer of Steinwitz and Praetor, Lueger simply cut her loose to keep prying eyes off his business.

One thing supported this last theory. Kulowski's absolute befuddlement at the mention of the attack yesterday. Werthen did not think the man was acting. So if Kulowski's tale could be trusted, if Frau Steinwitz had been to see her husband the day of his death, did that make Frau Steinwitz the killer? Perhaps she merely found him dead and left in a panic. But why never mention that fact to the police?

Werthen knew there were many things people did not want to offer up to the police, who were paid to be suspicious. Yet she never mentioned it to him either when she was supposedly attempting to hire him for protection. Did that make her guilty of murdering her own husband?

And then another and much more unnerving thought: If she killed her husband, did she also kill Praetor? But why?

No. He was running much too far ahead of himself. This made no sense. The only ones who stood to gain from Steinwitz's death would be those involved in the Vienna Woods plan.

At this moment in his ruminations, Gross arrived at the restaurant. Red-faced and somewhat out of breath.

'We must be off, Werthen. Things draw to a close.'

Werthen barely had time to leave the proper change for his slight repast before Gross was out the doors of the restaurant.

'Gross, I have startling news,' he said, finally catching him up.

'I too, Werthen. But you first, please.'

As they kept up a brisk pace, Werthen explained his meeting with Kulowski and the man's mention of having seen Frau Steinwitz at the scene of the crime at the Rathaus. He also voiced his concerns about the veracity of such a claim.

'There is something in favor of the Kulowski story, though,' Werthen added. 'Now that I think of it, both times the thug struck followed close upon a visit not only to the Rathaus, but also to Frau Steinwitz. Berthe and I postulated that Frau Steinwitz would have had no time to organize the first attack. But there was something we neglected. What if this thug works for her and was thus already at her apartment the day I was attacked? And then there is the fact of her visit to my law office the day after that initial attack. It was as if she was checking to see if her warning salvo had put me off the investigation.'

'Bravo, Werthen. Exactly so. I received partial confirmation of these new suspicions this morning from Frau Czerny at Zeltgasse.'

Gross now shared his newly-won information, as well.

'I was late for our meeting as I stopped off at the telephone exchange to place two calls. The *Portier* at the Zeltgasse was good enough to supply me with the telephone number of the domestics firm that employs Frau Novatny. They confirm that the lady has been seriously ill for the last two weeks and in hospital. Thus, hers could not have been the voice Frau Czerny heard at Herr Praetor's flat that night.'

He looked rather pleased with himself.

'You mentioned two calls,' Werthen reminded him.

'Yes. I was just getting to that. The second was a trunk call to my laboratory assistants in Czernowitz. The long-distance lines only opened this year via Budapest. I can assure you I do not wish to spend more time in the confinement of a telephone cubicle. After a half-hour of attempts, I was finally put through to my chief assistant, Nagl. Bright young lad.'

A twinkle in the man's eye made Werthen expectant. 'And what did you learn?'

'I put a simple question to the lad, for I know they have not yet had time to analyze the entire ribbon from Henricus Praetor's typewriting machine. One name only I was seeking.'

'Frau Steinwitz?'

A nod from the criminologist. 'Nagl supplied me with the desired outcome. Happily, the ribbon was quite new and Nagl and his team did not have to analyze the entire length of it. They had, in fact, already come upon the name of Frau Steinwitz. They are attempting to put together the message accompanying this name, but one other bit of information has already been culled. A date was clearly typed in close proximity to the name. February fifteenth.'

The date was not lost on Werthen. 'The night Praetor was shot,' he said.

They were shown into the parlor, and the maid told them the mistress was still at table.

Werthen took a seat on the settee, but Gross wandered about the room, picking up silver-framed photos off a cherry wood side table, examining a vase of hothouse tulips, and then meandered off to the hall. In search of the facilities? Werthen dared not ask.

After a few more moments, Gross came back into the sitting room, smiling to himself. Werthen had no chance to ask about his discoveries, for at that instant Frau Steinwitz breezed into the room, dressed in a no-frills house dress.

Werthen stood as she entered; Gross was already standing.

'I thought I told you, Advokat, that I no longer have need of your services.'

'Yes, Frau Steinwitz. You made that very clear.'

She tilted her head an inch or two to the left as if to say, 'Well, then?'

'We have come about a related matter, Frau Steinwitz,' Gross said. 'To wit, what brought you to Herr Praetor's apartment the night of February fifteenth?'

Werthen had to hand it to her. She did not flinch. Not even so much as a blink. It was as if she were expecting this visit. Had Lueger let her know he could no longer protect her?

'Is that any of your business?' she asked, still cool and in control.

'I notice that you have a fine collection of pistols,' Gross said, suddenly changing the subject.

'What are you prattling on about?'

'Among them is a very nice piece. A sample of one of the new Roth-Sauer automatics, in point of fact. And the space next to it looks to have once contained another weapon but is now empty. A matching automatic perhaps?'

Still she did not respond, but no longer did she

wear such a haughty countenance.

'I observe also a bevy of ribbons in those same glass cases,' Gross said. 'Forgive the *prattling*, but I notice they were won by you, Frau Steinwitz. You are no stranger to guns?'

'I come from a military family,' she said in a voice much subdued in tone.

'Tell me, Frau Steinwitz,' Gross pushed on, 'why did you kill your husband and Herr Praetor?'

The question shocked Werthen; Frau Steinwitz seemed to crumble once it was put to her.

'I didn't want to,' she said, tears beginning to form. She cupped her hands around her mouth and slumped down on to the settee recently vacated by Werthen.

'You admit it, then,' Gross said.

She waved a dismissive hand at the question. 'They shamed me. Shamed the Gutrum name.'

'Because they were ready to tell the public about the Vienna Woods plot?' Werthen said in disbelief.

'Shame,' she said. 'Humiliation. Do you know what it feels like to be betrayed, gentlemen?'

Neither Werthen nor Gross spoke for an instant. Frau Steinwitz pulled a linen handkerchief out of a sleeve of the smock and dried her eyes. She forced herself to sit up straight like a subaltern coming to attention and breathed in deeply to control her emotions.

'He was going to leave me. Me and the children, for that, that ... creature.'

'You mean Herr Praetor.'

'Reinhold said he was in love with him. It was

awful. I could not let that happen to us. To the children. To the good name of Gutrum.'

Before Werthen had a chance to digest this shocking revelation, a commanding, gravelly voice sounded from the doorway to the sitting room.

'Valerie.'

An elderly gentleman stood there with firm dignity, dressed in a wool suit, but carrying himself as if he were in cavalry uniform.

'What are these men doing here?'

'Colonel Gutrum?' Werthen asked. He had not heard an arrival and assumed that the father had already been at the flat, perhaps lunching with his daughter.

'It is nothing, Father.'

'You look distressed. Are they bothering you?'

She began crying again.

The colonel looked at them with savage eyes. Old he might be, but the pistol he now drew from his suit coat pocket was quite new and appeared to be in fine working order.

'I want the pair of you out of here.'

Gross made to speak to the man.

'Now!' He cocked the pistol.

'I assure you, Colonel Gutrum,' Werthen said as he moved to the door, 'we have come here only to ascertain the truth of your son-in-law's death. Your daughter says she killed him. A matter of honor.'

The old man seemed not to listen or not to care. He pursed his lips and his leathery cheeks twitched as he worked his jaw muscles.

'Both of you must be gone in one minute or I

will not answer for my actions.'

Gross and Werthen moved quickly down the hallway, the colonel following them with the pistol at their backs. Out on the landing, the apartment door closed heavily behind them, echoing in the vast, empty hallway.

Of course, Werthen thought as they walked toward Schottenring. Praetor's 'someone important' whom the journalist's father had become aware of, was none other than Councilman Steinwitz. And Councilman Steinwitz also had his 'special friends,' as Kraus had mysteriously alluded. Discovering such a tryst had been too much for Frau Steinwitz. She killed them both out of rage and jealousy.

But this was hardly a crime of passion; she had evidently planned the murders over weeks. Not a crime of passion then, but cold-blooded murder. Yet would a court in the land bring in a guilty verdict against such a wronged woman? Werthen doubted it; the very mention of a homosexual affair would be enough to sway most jurors.

Still, they had to try, Werthen thought as they approached the Police Praesidium.

'I am afraid we need more than that to proceed,' Inspector Meindl said, a gnome of a man seated as usual behind his monumental desk.

'More than a confession?' Werthen said, bewildered at Meindl's statement.

'More than an emotional outburst,' Meindl said. 'The woman is the daughter of Colonel

335

Gutrum, after all.'

'Who threatened us with a pistol,' Werthen said.

'You were on private property,' Meindl said almost with disgust. 'One does not simply accuse the daughter of such a man.'

Werthen looked to Gross to intervene, but the criminologist seemed lost in his own thoughts.

'I know we could find evidence,' Werthen said. 'I mean, your men could find evidence. Send Detective Inspector Drechsler to the Steinwitz flat. Let him search through the lady's closet. There is sure to be a skirt or shoes with traces of blood on them.'

Drechsler, seated against one wall, made no comment to this suggestion. A faint smile only showed on his features.

'Because you have a theory? Please, gentlemen.' Meindl directed his attention to Doktor Gross. 'I have the utmost respect for you, Herr Doktor, but theories are hardly enough for a judge's order to search the Gutrum premises.'

'It is Councilman Steinwitz's premises we want searched,' Werthen said, but Meindl ignored this, continuing to stare at his former mentor, adjusting his tortoiseshell pince-nez and passing a forefinger along the tidy hairline over his right ear.

Finally Gross came out of his thoughts long enough to address the head of the Police Praesidium. 'There is the matter of the typing ribbon from Herr Praetor's flat.'

'Circumstantial only,' Meindl retorted.

'Not if we decipher the accompanying

336

message. I believe Herr Praetor was writing to confirm an appointment with Frau Steinwitz for the night of his death.'

'Beliefs, suppositions, theories.' Meindl spread his tiny and immaculate hands as if begging for more.

'She was seen leaving the scene of her husband's death,' Werthen reminded him, for they had appraised Meindl of all their evidence.

'Ah, that.'

Werthen did not like the sound of this response.

'Herr Kulowski was very clear about it.'

'Yes, well, the mayor's office has been in contact since. It seems that there may be some debate about this sighting. Herr Kulowski, it turns out, does not have very perfect eyesight. In fact, he should be wearing spectacles, as I do, but in his line of work, as the mayor explained, Herr Kulowski feels such apparel might make him appear less than imposing.'

'And the mayor offered this because...?' Gross said.

'He was afraid that Herr Kulowski's information might lead you two to the wrong conclusion about Frau Steinwitz. As it clearly has.'

Gross turned his head to look out the window to the gray and forbidding sky over the Schottenring. Werthen too refrained from comment. It was clear to him that Lueger had played a double game. The mayor, through Kulowski, had given the information about Frau Steinwitz in order to take suspicion off himself, and then proceeded to call it into question in order to keep the Gutrums in his debt. Politicians relished such machinations, Werthen knew.

Inspector Meindl took their silence as an admission of defeat.

'When and if you have more conclusive evidence, we will surely act, have no fear.'

Werthen read about it in the next day's *Neue Freie Presse*. It was under the society news.

Frau Valerie Steinwitz, née Gutrum, has been taken to a private clinic in Switzerland, there to recover from nerve attacks following the tragic death by suicide of her husband, Councilman Reinhold Steinwitz. The family attorney released a statement to the effect that Frau Steinwitz will remain incommunicado for the duration of her treatment, which could be lengthy.

Twenty

'So much for justice in the Habsburg realms,' Herr Meisner said. His recovery had been speedy and seemingly full. He was sitting up in his hospital bed, munching unhappily on dried toast with all the appearance of a martyr. Crumbs collected in his salt and pepper beard.

'Don't think about it, Father,' Berthe said, resting her hand on his, which lay on the counterpane. 'We should not have told you about it.'

'Nonsense,' he said. 'It is not as if I am an invalid. I simply bumped my head.'

'The doctor says you should not become overly excited,' Werthen told him, feeling a fool now for having mentioned the outcome of his case.

'You'll be coming home tomorrow,' Berthe said.

'About time, too.' Herr Meisner cast the piece of dried toast a baleful glance as one might a person expectorating in the street.

'And we are arranging the Aliya,' Werthen added.

Herr Meisner dropped the toast and reached a hand out to his son-in-law.

'It takes a bump on the head for this to happen?'

But it was said in good humor.

'As a matter of fact, it did. Life is simply too short for such quarrels.'

'You've made an old man very happy,' he said.

'Hardly old, Father. But this doesn't mean we are going to keep kosher.'

'Please,' Herr Meisner admonished her, 'do not even mention that word until after I get a good meal in my stomach.'

And so the Werthen residence returned to a semblance of normality as February passed into March. Werthen's parents did indeed depart for their estate in Lower Austria, though he was sure that the estate factotum, 'young' Stein – now approaching forty – would hardly be happy to have the old man back to bark out orders. And they held the naming ceremony as promised, Frieda taking the middle name of Ruth. Had his parents remained in the capital, Werthen would have maneuvered them into a christening instead of baptism, but without their presence it just did not seem important. Perhaps on their next visit.

At the office, Fräulein Metzinger was still observing a period of mourning, but Werthen no longer heard her sniffling mid-morning.

Werthen dreaded most speaking with Doktor Praetor, father of the murdered journalist. He did not want to tell the man that the murderer of his only son was beyond justice, for Austria and Switzerland had no extradition treaty. He had no idea how the man would react. Would he go to the newspapers? In which case Werthen could find himself in the midst of a nasty slander suit.

But the man deserved the truth. Both Werthen and Gross met with Praetor and explained the events.

'The daughter of Colonel Gutrum,' he said, almost in awe.

The surgeon appeared to be a realist; he understood how things worked in Austria and made no overt protests.

'At least we know,' Doktor Praetor said. 'But she is lying to you about the motive, mark my words,' he said with fierce vehemence. 'My son was no homosexual.'

Gross heard from Nagl in Czernowitz the day after Frau Steinwitz bolted. As suspected, Praetor was writing to confirm a meeting with her the very night of his death.

Additionally, Werthen happened to meet Oberbaurat Wagner again, this time in the company of Gustav Klimt. Out for a quick bite, he happened upon the artist and architect at one of his favorite eateries, The Red Stork, and accepted their invitation to join them at table. They exchanged pleasantries for a time, and then Werthen said, quite casually, that he was surprised to learn of the presence of Frau Steinwitz at the Rathaus the day of her husband's suicide. Wagner, who had discovered the body, merely shook his head.

'What is so surprising about a wife attempting to visit her husband at his place of work?'

'Ah, then you also saw her,' Werthen said, quite innocently. 'But of course you would have. Being first on the scene.'

'Of course I did,' Wagner said, taking offense.

'My eyes are perfectly fine.'

Werthen took this morsel of information as well as the decipherment of Praetor's typing ribbon to the Police Praesidium. Meindl, supplied with this evidence, merely shrugged.

'Still not very convincing. But in any case, she is out of our jurisdiction now,' he told them. 'As you well know, Switzerland failed to renew its extradition treaty with us last year.'

Werthen could not restrain his anger. 'Perhaps if Austria recognized the right of political asylum, then we might have such treaties with the rest of the civilized world and not just countries such as Russia and Prussia.'

Meindl smiled at him as if he had just made a bon mot. 'But when she returns to the empire, we shall take the matter up.'

Meanwhile the Steinwitz children were living with their grandfather on his estate near Vienna. Rumor had it that he was to adopt them and change their names to Gutrum.

After attending the Lawyers' Ball on Saturday, March 3, Gross and his wife Adele returned to Czernowitz for the spring semester. Ash Wednesday came on March 7, marking the end of the ball season.

He was suddenly awake, disoriented. Berthe was leaning over him.

'You were grinding your teeth again,' she said.

He brushed his hand over his face; it felt sweaty.

'Sorry.'

'You must stop thinking about it. There is

342

nothing you can do.'

'She killed twice and is free.'

'Not free,' Berthe said. 'She can never come back home.'

'And that is fitting punishment?'

'Go to sleep,' Berthe said, laying a soothing hand on his forehead. 'It's over.'

Next morning, Werthen was catching up on legal work. Fräulein Metzinger had been so dislocated by the tragedy of Huck that she had not been able to complete an urgent brief, so he was finishing it. But no sooner had he sat down with the brief than Fräulein Metzinger announced the arrival of a visitor, showing in a young man in clerical garb.

'Father Mickelsburg,' Werthen said when he finally recognized his visitor, the priest from the Theresianum whom he had earlier questioned about Hans Wittgenstein. 'An unexpected pleasure.'

The priest smiled as he took an offered chair.

'I have come for a bit of absolution, I am afraid.'

'Don't you have things reversed, Father?'

'You seem like a good man, Advokat Werthen.'

'I suppose I try to be.'

'I as well, though sometimes the flesh is weak.'

Father Mickelsburg looked suddenly miserable, as if he were suffering from an illness.

'What is it you have come to tell me, Father?' Werthen still found it odd to use the title with a man several years younger than him.

Mickelsburg produced a rosary from under his clothing, and began counting the ivory beads with a thumb, a gesture Werthen had seen often enough in cafés frequented by the Greek merchants of the city, but never by a Catholic priest.

'I understand you found the Wittgenstein boy, then. Hans?'

'Yes, quite soon after I spoke to you, as a matter of fact. Herr Praetor, his young friend, told me he had gone to the United States. The family received confirmation of that. You know of Herr Praetor's death, of course?'

Father Mickelsburg nodded. 'Yes. Ricus told me about your visit.' He stopped tallying the beads.

'Ricus?' Werthen said.

'I was not forthcoming with you when we met at the school, and I have felt badly about that ever since. He thought you were one of the "great pious ones."' Mickelsburg laughed lightly at the expression. 'It was Ricus's way of talking about the bourgeoisie, those who would not understand his ... our lifestyle.'

Werthen raised his eyebrows at this admission from the priest.

'You mean you and Herr Praetor were ... special friends?'

'Lovers,' the priest said. 'Let me finally use the word I would never use with Ricus himself.' A look of extreme pain passed over his face. 'You see, Advokat, I believe I killed him.'

'Nonsense.'

'I was also one of the "great pious ones" Ricus

railed against. I would not ... could not admit my love. Perhaps that is why he sought it elsewhere, why he was killed.'

Mickelsburg had obviously accepted the official explanation of young Praetor's death: a homosexual tryst gone wrong. Werthen was not about to disabuse him of that by accusing Frau Steinwitz of the crime. Apprising Doktor Praetor of the actual circumstances had been the least he could do, but Father Mickelsburg was owed no such honesty.

'Perhaps.' But his curiosity got the better of Werthen. 'I understand there may have been a relationship between Herr Praetor and Councilman Steinwitz.'

Suddenly Mickelsburg broke out into uncontrollable laughter. His body shook with the force of it and it took him several moments to regain his composure.

'I am sorry, Advokat, but that suggestion is, as you have witnessed, quite laughable.'

'How can you be so certain?'

'One simply knows these things. Did you ever meet the man?'

'I was his attorney for several years.'

'Well, then, did he strike you as someone who might fancy men?'

Werthen shook his head. 'But then, neither did you.'

Mickelsburg nodded at this riposte. 'I, however, am quite adept at disguises, Advokat. I met Councilman Steinwitz once in the company of Ricus, and I can tell you for a certainty that the man had no sexual designs on him. Councilman

Steinwitz was a deeply troubled man, but that had nothing to do with confused sexual identity. Rather, I think it had to do with his wife. He made a few pointed comments about her. I do not remember the exact words, but there was a feeling of disappointment from him.'

'Did Herr Praetor tell you the nature of his and Steinwitz's connection?'

'You mean exposing the scheme to sell the Vienna Woods? Of course. I was very proud of him.'

'Do you think you might be less than objective when you insist there was nothing more between them? After all, we all experience jealousy.'

'I assure you, Advokat, Councilman Steinwitz was not interested in men. If you have heard otherwise, somebody is trying to mislead you.'

He rose. 'And now, I have taken enough of your time, Advokat. But it has been preying on me that I was not completely honest with you before. Was not completely honest with Ricus.'

Werthen could not let it go. This new information from the priest gnawed away at him until finally he set out in the early afternoon to confirm his reawakened suspicions.

He went to see the journalist, Karl Kraus. When he and Gross had paid a visit to find out about Councilman Steinwitz's possible friends and enemies inside the Rathaus, Kraus had ended their conversations with that confounding remark about a circle of 'special friends' the councilman was rumored to have. At the time, this offhand remark did not seem important; now it seemed to scream at him for some kind of explanation.

Kraus was busy as usual with the latest edition of *Die Fackel*, but made time and space – clearing away stacks of old newspapers from the only available chair – for Werthen.

'I am sorry that my cryptic comment has given you pains,' he said after Werthen explained the reason for his visit. 'I should be delighted to expound on that, provided you assist me in another matter of curiosity.'

Kraus did not offer schnapps today; it sounded as if he might have a cold or a bronchial complaint. But despite illness, he still wore that Cheshire cat grin of his.

'I assume you refer to Frau Steinwitz?'

'Assume away, Advokat.'

'The newspapers say she is undergoing therapy in Switzerland.'

'Yes,' Kraus said. 'The newspapers say a lot of silly things.'

'This goes no further,' Werthen said.

Kraus assented to the request.

Werthen quickly outlined the case against Frau Steinwitz and the visit to her, which had elicited a confession.

'Could I not perhaps have gotten this from another source?' Kraus said after Werthen finished. 'Such a story needs publication.'

'Part of it is public record,' Werthen said. 'I am ashamed to say it, but I do not want my name attached to any of this, Kraus. Gutrum is the sort to bring a nuisance suit.'

'Yes, well, those hardly bother me. I have at

347

least three outstanding legal suits as we speak. It will be on my shoulders, Advokat. That I promise. But this truth must see the light of day.'

Kraus, busy enough before Werthen's arrival, seemed suddenly to redouble his efforts, pushing away the story he was working on, and finding several pieces of fresh paper.

'Aren't you forgetting something, Kraus?' Werthen asked. 'The special friends?'

Kraus looked up from the paper where he had already begun writing in a hand so minute and spidery that its decipherment would require the use of a magnifying glass by the printer.

'Ah, to be sure. The special friends. Well, there is a certain group of young ballerinas at the Court Opera that enjoy the company of powerful men. Steinwitz was among this group of men. I understand that the women are traded quite regularly, and that Councilman Steinwitz, whatever his scruples over selling off the Vienna Woods, had none when it came to matters of the flesh.'

'Young women, you say?' Werthen asked.

'But of course. The man was, by all accounts, quite a mastiff.'

Werthen's attentions were otherwise occupied for the next few days. With the collapse of the scheme to sell large portions of the Vienna Woods, the Rathaus recanted its demands on the Laab im Walde property. Werthen's estate agent, Grundman, notified him that there had been a renewed offer on the property from Herr Pokorny, the pharmacist whose wife had inherited it. The property was now offered, Grundman indicated, at a slightly reduced price.

'Herr Pokorny is, as we in the trade say, rather motivated now after all this business with taking it off the market and putting it back on.'

They were speaking by telephone, but Werthen could clearly discern a slight tinge of humor in the otherwise dour Grundman's voice.

Werthen told him he would let him know, but he was reluctant to get back into this business of the country house, having been so sorely disappointed to lose it before. However, discussing it with Berthe that night, he found that he actually began to consider such a purchase. Then, a visit to the property in the company of Herr Meisner renewed his enthusiasm for having a real home for Frieda to grow up in, if only for the summers at first. That very day he made an offer of fifteen thousand florins, the same that he had started with originally. Motivated or not, Herr Pokorny made the same counter offer as he had earlier and in the end the price was settled at sixteen thousand again. But Werthen was beyond caring, truly relishing the idea of getting the house in order for this summer's occupancy. They signed the final papers on March 10.

It was only after signing these that Werthen let his mind return to the business of Frau Steinwitz. This was accomplished by Kraus, who sent a blue flimsy pneumatic letter the same day to inform Werthen that his story on the death of Councilman Steinwitz would appear in the Monday edition of *Die Fackel*.

That Monday, Werthen lost no time in purchasing a copy on his way to the office. Photographs of Frau and Herr Steinwitz accompanied the text, a novelty for Kraus's magazine. Werthen read through the lead article once, then a second time, marveling at Kraus's ability to fill out the full story by innuendo, suggestion, and unattributed supposition. In fact, Kraus had created a miracle of modern journalism: a damning yet indirect brief against Frau Steinwitz for the murders of her husband and Herr Henricus Praetor, without writing one actionable sentence and without once mentioning the word, 'homosexual.'

Why, the man should have been a lawyer, Werthen thought.

Kraus's final sentence made Werthen reconsider the whole affair:

'One can only ask about the motive for these heinous crimes.'

'It's you again.'

'Very nice to see you, as well, Meier. I've come to see Herr Wittgenstein.'

'You were hardly welcome before, if you do not mind my saying, sir. Even less so now, I would assume.'

'Herr Wittgenstein, if you please.'

'Very well. I did warn you.'

Meier led the well-trodden path through the foyer and up the grand staircase to his master's study. Waiting outside, he heard Wittgenstein's voice boom at Meier, but could not make out what was said.

A slightly chastened Meier appeared. 'He will see you.'

Werthen entered the study, a fire in the grate once again pouring out waves of heat.

'Damn cheeky servant,' Wittgenstein said, volubly enough that Meier could hear himself referred to by that title. 'I'll decide whom I do and don't want to see. Now what in God's name brings you to my door again?'

'May I sit?'

Wittgenstein shrugged. 'As you wish. I confess, Advokat, to being somewhat impressed by your persistence. Others who have crossed me would hardly dare to come for such a tête-à-tête.'

'Should I fear for my life?' he said jocularly.

Wittgenstein turned suddenly serious. 'Others have.'

Werthen began to wonder for the first time if this were really such a good idea. Perhaps he should take Berthe's advice and simply let the matter go. But Frau Steinwitz's face, so eminently in control one moment and so suddenly broken the next, came to mind. He no longer believed that act. He needed to know the truth, regardless of the costs.

'I would like your help.'

Wittgenstein slapped his desk as he chuckled. 'Advokat Werthen, I must give you kudos for, as our Spanish friends say, your *cojones*. Why ever should I want to help you? You have cost me dearly.'

'I found your son,' Werthen said. 'And I saved you the embarrassment of being blamed for despoiling the Vienna Woods. The latter you may not believe just yet, but the former you know to

351

be true.'

'And I paid you handsomely for that service.'

'Indeed you did, sir. But I am talking about a deeper payment. In kind.'

Herr Wittgenstein cocked his head, examining Werthen closely. 'I am not sure if you are overly sincere or simply an idiot. Perhaps both.' Another chuckle. 'What help is it you require?'

'I would like to know if, among the list of fellow investors in the Vienna Woods project, was included the name of Colonel Adam Gutrum.'

Wittgenstein took in a large breath of air and blew it out between his lips, almost whistling.

'I think Colonel Gutrum might have enough on his plate with his daughter in a Swiss asylum. He does not need you dogging him, as well.'

'I have no intention of bothering the colonel, Herr Wittgenstein. That I promise you.'

Another appraising look. 'All right, since you ask. Yes. He was one of the major investors. Stood to make a packet if the deal went through. Does that conclude our business, Advokat?'

'Yes, sir. And I thank you.'

'Nothing to give thanks for. But I do believe our slate may be clean now.'

'*Tabula rasa*,' Werthen replied.

Outside on the Alleegasse he thought: We now have motive. She killed her own husband and Praetor to stop them from ruining the Vienna Woods sale, a venture that would bring a fortune to her father and, by inference, to her.

It was just as he and Gross initially thought:

352

someone involved with the sale had the most to gain by the deaths of Steinwitz and Praetor. But they could hardly be expected to focus on the wife as that person. Frau Steinwitz's tragic story of a shaming love affair between her husband and Henricus Praetor was just that – a story. A fabrication. She had killed for the basest of human motives, monetary gain. Which explained the missing notes of Councilman Steinwitz detailing the scheme, as well as the notebooks of Praetor where he kept transcriptions of interviews and the particulars of his investigation. Frau Steinwitz had surely destroyed those damning bits of evidence.

Werthen was walking along the street, lost in these thoughts, when young Ludwig Wittgenstein entered from the Karlsplatz in the company of a tall, thin man Werthen assumed to be his tutor.

'Another outing to the Natural History Museum, Master Ludwig?' Werthen asked as they approached one another.

'Yes, to be sure,' the boy said, smiling in recognition. 'Sorry I could not stay to talk the other day, but Mining would not hear of it.'

He meant at Huck's funeral, Werthen knew.

'Quite all right. Not a very happy occasion.'

'Master Wittgenstein,' the elderly and rather eunuch-like tutor said. 'We really should be on our way. It is a bitterly cold day.'

'It's fine, Traschky. Advokat Werthen is an old family friend. Go on if you like. I'll catch you up.'

'Don't dawdle, Master Wittgenstein. Latin

hour is next.'

Traschky, a wraith of a man, moved off like fog lifting on a summer morning.

Ludwig watched him go. 'He's not bad, actually. Bad breath, though.'

'How have you been?' Werthen asked.

'You mean about Huck's death?'

'I mean in general.'

'When asked that, Father always says, "I can't complain. No one would listen anyway." An interesting observation, don't you think, Advokat?'

'Very realistic, I should think. But in this case, I really do want to know.'

Ludwig ignored further attempts at solicitude. Instead, he pulled out the latest edition of *Die Fackel*.

'Have you seen this, Advokat?'

'What are you doing with that?'

'It's hardly seditious. Besides, Hans never stopped his subscription.'

Werthen now remembered seeing the red covers of the magazine on Hans's bookshelf and finding it odd that the son of Karl Wittgenstein would read it, considering the criticisms Kraus sometimes leveled at his father.

'So, three times a month I get to the postman before he delivers the mail and save this for myself. This Kraus fellow is really fabulous, don't you think?'

'Yes, I do,' Werthen agreed.

'There was an absolutely fantastic article this time about this woman who may have killed her husband and another chap, a journalist. She's hiding away now in a Swiss asylum, beyond justice.'

'I saw that article, yes.'

'You know the woman of course,' Ludwig said. 'I saw her at your office one day.'

Werthen now remembered. Frau Steinwitz had come to see him the day after he'd been beaten, the day Ludwig met Huck.

'You have a good memory, Master Ludwig.'

'Was she your client?'

Werthen shook his head. 'Her husband once was.'

'It's strange, you know. That day I met her at the office I thought I recognized her. And I was right. Seeing her photo again in *Die Fackel* and then reading the article by Kraus I realized I had actually seen her the night of this Herr Praetor's death. Only I didn't know until reading the article that he had died. In fact, I did not even know that he lived in the Zeltgasse. You see, I don't regularly read the newspapers yet. Such a lot of rubbish in them, Father says.'

Werthen felt at once a sudden sense of excitement and bewilderment at this barrage of revelations. 'You were at Herr Praetor's flat?'

'Not actually in his apartment. But at the building. We couldn't get in, you see. For some reason the *Portier* locked the front doors early.'

'Why were you there?'

'Mining was most mysterious about it. We were supposed to be at the Raimund play in the Theater in der Josefstadt. My tutor was very keen on me seeing *Der Verschwender*. But Mining said we had to visit someone first. I went

355

along with her. We all have our little secrets. Now that I've read the Kraus article, it makes more sense. He was a friend of Hans, right?'

'Correct.'

'The one, in fact, who told you Hans had gone to America.'

'Again, correct.'

'So maybe Mining was trying to find out more about Hans. Maybe they correspond.'

'Good surmise,' Werthen said, but thought it more likely that the older Wittgenstein sister had gone there to ensure that Praetor made no revelations to the press about his supposed homosexual relationship with Hans. Only something along those lines would account for her visiting under the guise of attending the theater.

'Well, you see, we rang the bell and could not get in. Mining and I waited several minutes and finally she just left in disgust, walking much faster than me. Like Traschky says, I am famous for dawdling. And it was then the house door opened, with Mining already around the corner, and out walks this woman. Frau Steinwitz.'

'You saw her clearly?'

'Very. We were not half a block apart.'

'And that means—'

'Yes. I know. That she saw me, too. And knew I had witnessed her leaving the scene of a crime. That is why I was so happy to see you just now. All morning long I have been trying to figure out how I could see you again, and here you are, like magic.'

'To tell me about Frau Steinwitz?'

356

'Yes. Well, and the rest. It's pretty clear, isn't it?'

The realization struck Werthen violently, like a physical blow. Of course, he told himself. I should have seen it before.

Young Wittgenstein continued, 'I mean, when she saw me again at your office she must have panicked. There is no way she could know I was ignorant of Herr Praetor's death. I was, in her eyes, the only witness to her crime.'

'She killed Huck,' Werthen finally said.

Ludwig nodded his head vigorously. 'That's what I think, too. It was the coat, you see. That night I first saw her I was wearing my loden coat with the fur collar. There's not another one like it in all of Vienna. At least Father says so. They tailored it specially for me. I was wearing it again that day at the office. And then Huck and I traded coats because I knew how fond he was of it.'

His boyish excitement was suddenly stilled, replaced by grief.

'She was following you. Looking for an opportunity to strike.' Werthen was thinking out loud.

'We went into the Karlsplatz *Stadtbahn* station to exchange coats. I left with Huck's coat on, hurrying to get home before I was missed. She must have thought I was Huck leaving and then followed him on to the platform thinking he was I. The coat was so bulky she never realized she killed the wrong boy.'

'And the fact that there was no mention of the tragedy in the press would not have bothered her,' Werthen thought out loud. 'She most probably thought your family was keeping the tragedy private.'

A blast of frigid wind blew down the Alleegasse, making them both shiver.

'She's an evil woman, Advokat. You aren't going to let her get away with it, are you?'

Twenty-One

What do you tell a ten-year-old boy to make him understand the ways of the world? How do you explain expediency, connections, and the perversion of power? How do you tell him that the world is not always – in fact seldom is – a fair place? That money and influence can trump justice?

Werthen did not bother to try. Instead he said, 'No, I won't let her get away with it, Master Ludwig.'

It was only later that he began to believe his own words.

'You can't let her get away with it,' Berthe said, echoing young Ludwig, when Werthen explained matters to her.

'I feel as angry as you do, my dear, but I do not see what is to be done. As long as she is in Switzerland—'

'That's it,' she said, excited.

'What?'

'You must get her out of Switzerland somehow. Kidnap her if you have to.'

Werthen said nothing, thinking of what his wife had just said.

They were lying in bed, their favorite place to

discuss matters since the birth of Frieda. Werthen was on his back and Berthe was nestled beneath his right arm, her head on his shoulder. She suddenly pinched him hard on the side.

'What was that for?'

'You are going to do it, aren't you?'

'I need a plan.'

'You need Gross.'

The criminologist arrived two days later, after Werthen sent off a telegram and after a trunk call that was most unsatisfactory, voices coming in and out of hearing like a fast approaching and then receding train.

Werthen met him at the station; Gross, who had arranged an emergency leave from his university, looked sullen after the all-night journey from Czernowitz.

'I believe I have an adequate plan,' Gross said by way of salutation. 'One problem only. We must first locate the woman.'

They headed to their favorite rendezvous, the Café Frauenhuber, by *Fiaker*, and over a late breakfast of warm *Semmeln*, fresh butter, a pot of apricot marmalade, steaming mugs of coffee with milk, and boiled eggs in freckled brown shells served in onion-ware egg cups, Gross explained his idea.

Werthen listened with rapt attention, stopping him once, then twice for clarification. They would quickly find out if such a plan would work when attempting to put the first parts of it into motion.

Gross was correct: the first thing they needed

to do was ascertain Frau Steinwitz's location, and Werthen had already begun work on that part of the mission.

Herr Otto presented them with the bill when it was apparent they were ready to leave.

'Did you notice our salvation?' he asked, his face an emotionless mask.

'How do you mean, Herr Otto?' Werthen asked, then realized that they were still seated on the wonderful Thonet café chairs that had been under threat. He had completely forgotten about the drive to modernize the Café Frauenhuber; about his promise to start a petition with others among the clientele to leave well enough alone.

'How did you accomplish it?' he asked the waiter in amazement.

'I am sure you know Herr Reichsrath Nadelman of the Finance Ministry. One of our more robust clientele?'

Werthen knew only too well of the man. He was of such an enormous girth that fellows at the café actually ran a lottery – in which Werthen took no part – to determine the man's exact weight. Another client of the café, Herr Bachman, was a functionary at the state stockyards in the Third District, and he invited Nadelman on a tour of the facility. The plan was that they would both mount one of the hoists used to weigh the beasts before slaughter, and then Bachman would simply subtract his weight from the total to determine that of Nadelman. In the event, however, the hoist broke; nothing to do with excessive weight, simply wear and tear. But the irony was not lost on the rest of the café clientele. Nadelman was thereafter referred to in whispers as the *Ochse*, or steer.

'What about him?' Werthen asked.

Herr Otto sighed, as if ready to report a death. 'I regret to say that Herr Reichsrath Nadelman had a nasty accident last week. You see, he was sitting down in one of the new, modern chairs and it sadly fell apart under him. Had a bit of a jolt, landing on the floor. One must be thankful he was not injured, but he did complain mightily to Frau Enghart.'

Werthen surveyed the room and saw only Thonet number fourteen chairs in attendance. Something was missing, however, or in this case, someone. Herr Bauer, the new head *Ober* whose idea it had been to modernize the premises, was nowhere to be seen.

'Unfortunate for Herr Reichsrath Nadelman,' Werthen said.

'Most,' Herr Otto agreed, his face still without expression.

'It seems to have done the trick, though. I assume Herr Bauer no longer has the ear of Frau Enghart?'

'Sadly, it was thought better that Herr Bauer seek his modernization at another establishment. He will be missed.'

They paid, leaving a handsome tip for Herr Otto.

On the way out Gross muttered, 'Remind me never to make an enemy of that man.'

They put Gross up in the rooms of the Hotel zur Josefstadt recently vacated by Werthen's parents. After a quick visit to Berthe and her father, Werthen and Gross set off for the Police Praesidium.

Detective Inspector Drechsler was in his cramped office going over reports. Greetings and small talk were kept to a minimum. They did learn, though, that Drechsler's wife was recovering nicely from her operation at the capable hands of Doktor Praetor.

'I suppose you've come about that little matter we spoke about?' Drechsler finally said.

Werthen told him that yes, that was the purpose of their visit.

'Any luck?'

'Easy enough,' Drechsler said. 'I have a Swiss colleague. I believe you met him, too, Doktor Gross, at the same conference where we met. Inspector Zwingl? A hefty sort of man with a left arm shorter than the right.'

'Ah, you mean the Kaiser?'

'Exactly.'

They did not explain, but Werthen assumed the nickname came from a similar affliction which the German leader, Kaiser Wilhelm II, shared.

'Very thorough, the Swiss. They do keep track of their foreign visitors.'

Drechsler pulled a card out of the middle drawer of his desk and handed it to Werthen.

The address meant little to him, other than that it was in the vicinity of Zürich.

'It's a noble spa really,' Drechsler said, 'not a clinic at all. In the town of Küsnacht. Taking the waters, she is.'

'Many thanks, Drechsler,' Werthen said.

363

'Just remember, gentlemen. Kidnapping is a crime.'

'Not you again. I thought you declared *tabula rasa* last time.' Herr Wittgenstein seemed in a fine mood, which was just as well. 'And you've brought a friend with you, I see. Does he need a favor, too?'

'Doktor Gross, at your service,' the criminologist said with great ceremony. 'And yes, I am in need of a favor. But first perhaps you would care to hear why you should help in this matter.'

Gross quickly outlined the case against Valerie Gutrum Steinwitz, putting special emphasis on the fact that she had attempted to kill Wittgenstein's own son, but killed another instead.

Wittgenstein's face became suddenly drained of color, his eyes squinted as if a powerful light were shining in his face.

'The damned she-wolf,' he said. 'I'll see she rots in prison for this.'

'Exactly what I hoped you would say, Herr Wittgenstein,' Gross said. 'And this is how you can make it happen.'

At Werthen's office they continued to marshal their forces. First Werthen found a gazetteer for Switzerland, noting that from the center of Zürich to the Park Hotel am See in Küsnacht was a matter of only ten kilometers.

A sudden ruckus sounded in the outer office, followed by the door to Werthen's office being thrown open. Fearing that the same thug had come to finish his work, Werthen jumped to his feet, brandishing a hefty brass paperweight from the desk like a mace.

Herr Beer charged into the room.

'I know what you're up to,' he said.

'I am sorry, Advokat,' Fräulein Metzinger said from in back of him. 'He would not listen to reason.'

'You should know about this, too,' Beer said turning to her. Then again to Werthen: 'You've found her, haven't you? The one who killed my boy?'

'I really do not know what you are talking about, Herr Beer. Now if you will excuse us, we—'

'I've been following you. Figured a man like you, he wouldn't let my boy's death go unavenged.'

Fräulein Metzinger put a hand on his shoulder. 'It was an accident. There's no one to blame.'

'Ask him,' Beer said, shaking off her touch. 'He knows different.'

She began to have doubts now. 'Advokat?'

Gross finally joined in. 'I think you can put that down now, Werthen.'

Werthen had not realized he was still gripping the paperweight.

'And you, Herr Beer, please be seated and tell us what you think you know,' continued Gross. 'You, too, Fräulein Metzinger. Our precipitate visitor is right in one regard: this does concern you.'

Beer took a proffered chair warily, as if handed a loaded gun. Once seated, he looked from one to the other of his interlocutors with a tight-

365

lipped grimace.

'It was the coat Heidrich had on when he died. I knew right off that was not my boy's coat. Then I saw you talking to that young swell near the Karlsplatz the other day.'

'Young Wittgenstein,' Werthen said.

'That's the one. Say what you like about the rich, but they aren't all bad. This young one was a bit scared when I approached him at the skating pond in the park—'

'You followed him, too?' Werthen was appalled.

'Don't get so high and mighty. I didn't mean him any harm. Waited till this walking cadaver he was with was busy with the skates, and then I told the boy my situation. That I am ... was Heidrich's father. That I had a right to know. And so, he told me.'

'Told you what?' Fräulein Metzinger asked, casting a brief glance at Werthen.

'It is a sad tale,' Gross said. 'We did not wish to involve more people in it than absolutely necessary.'

'Tell me.' It was an animal shriek.

Werthen told her the entire sordid story. She listened as one would to a requiem mass, hands held tightly in her lap, head bowed. When he finished, she looked up.

'Then Herr Beer is right,' she said. 'You are planning something.'

'We want to bring her back to Vienna to stand trial.'

'Rich folks' justice?' Beer sounded skeptical.

'There is a strong case against her,' Werthen

replied.

'Circumstantial,' Fräulein Metzinger said. 'Unless there is someone you have not told us about.'

She was right, of course. Werthen was well aware of that. Frau Steinwitz's confession to himself and Gross was a matter of hearsay; they were not officials of the court, merely private citizens who would claim to have heard one thing while Frau Steinwitz and her father would surely aver that no such confession had been made. Further, the Kulowski testimony had already been compromised, by none other than Mayor Lueger himself, no matter what Oberbaurat Wagner might say to the contrary about seeing Frau Steinwitz at the Rathaus the day of her husband's death.

Also, would Father Mickelsburg be willing to sacrifice his entire career for justice? He sought penance, but self-immolation might be too much to ask of the man. And Ludwig Wittgenstein? Assuming his father let him testify, would his sighting of Frau Steinwitz at the scene of Praetor's death be sufficient? Would jurors believe the transcribed note salvaged from Praetor's typing ribbon, suggesting a meeting for the night in question? Would they give credence to Frau Czerny's attestation to hearing a woman's voice from inside the flat that same evening? And would these same jurors put these facts together to accept the fact that Frau Steinwitz was also guilty of the murder of the hapless Huck?

Additionally, there was the fact of Gutrum being a major investor in the Vienna Woods deal, which provided Frau Steinwitz's motive in killing her husband and Praetor. But they had made a bargain with Lueger that that matter should be put to rest. Werthen knew Lueger would do everything in his power to quash such evidence. And he had powerful friends in every strata of the Viennese social, political, and judicial worlds. The gun in the case in the Steinwitz flat could be another circumstantial bit of evidence, that is, if it were still there.

Another factor was Frau Steinwitz herself. Confronted with her crimes, she would either deny them completely, or, if cornered, would opt for the defense of a *crime passionel*, as Werthen had earlier surmised. Then it would be the job of the prosecutor to show that both murders showed extreme premeditation. There was nothing of 'killing in the passion of the moment,' which is at the heart of a crime of passion. Yet demonstrating that depended on a clever prosecutor.

'You are absolutely correct, Fräulein Metzinger,' Werthen finally replied. 'The case is strong, not sure. But bringing Frau Steinwitz back to Vienna to stand trial is the best we can do.'

'Put me on the stand. I'll say I saw her shove my boy under the wheels of that *Stadtbahn* train.'

Gross was on his feet, a look of amazement on his face.

'Thank you, Herr Beer.' He grabbed the seated man's hand and shook it vigorously. 'You've struck on exactly the line of inquiry we have failed to pursue. The platform that day of young

Heidrich's death was of course crowded, for the trains had only just begun running regularly again after the heavy snowfall. We need to track those passengers down and show them photographs of Frau Steinwitz. Someone, perhaps several, must have seen her there. No one would suspect at the time, of course, that an elegantly attired woman would have pushed the boy. But I guarantee that some of them will remember her presence there; it is not every day that the rich and powerful subject themselves to the hustle and bustle of public transport.'

'The officer first on the scene must have taken names of passengers,' Werthen said without a pause, for this was exactly where his thoughts were going, as well. 'It is standard police procedure.'

'Perhaps Detective Inspector Drechsler can be of assistance one more time,' Gross said.

'I say we just kill her,' Beer muttered. 'You know where she is. I'll do the deed and smile on my way to the gallows.'

'Were we living several centuries ago, my good man,' Gross intoned, 'such a course of action would be the norm. Private settlement of accounts was an acknowledged method in the German-speaking lands. The authorities in such cases merely supervised these private settlements.'

'Please do not encourage him, Gross.'

'You seem an ardent man, Herr Beer,' the criminologist said. 'Perhaps you would care to join forces with us to see that justice is done?'

'Is that wise, Gross?' Werthen said.

'Done,' replied Beer. 'I am your man.'

Fräulein Metzinger merely shook her head at the entire enterprise. 'She will walk away from the courtroom smiling.'

Gross looked at her long and hard.

'I promise that will not happen, young lady.'

The private train Wittgenstein provided left from Wiener Neustadt, joining the rails of the Austrian train system a few kilometers to the west. If this was what it was like to be an industrialist, Werthen figured that he had chosen the wrong profession. The car they were traveling in was appointed as elegantly as one of the rooms in the Wittgenstein mansion. The walls were red plush, matching the well-stuffed fauteuils. Hunting scenes hung on the walls. At Werthen's side table sat a silver bell, which he picked up and jingled. Nothing happened. He jingled it more violently this time and heard the door open and close from the front carriage to theirs in the middle of the three-car train.

'Yes, sir.'

Werthen had never heard quite so much loathing put into two words before.

'Beer, I am only doing this for your benefit. You need practice at being a servant.'

Herr Erdmann Beer stood in front of him in deep-blue satin livery, his spindly shanks looking rather pitiful in the silk hose he wore. A sorrier version of Meier, the Wittgenstein house servant, but a real improvement over Beer's usual attire.

'What is it you require, sir?'

370

'Excellent, Beer. Now you sound like the real thing.'

Gross, seated in another chair closer to the rear of the car, put his evening edition of the *Neue Freie Presse* down and peered at Werthen over the edges of nonexistent bifocals.

'You're enjoying this, Werthen.'

'Yes, I am rather. What time will dinner be, Beer?'

'Sir, you can kiss me in the valley of wind.'

Which comment brought a mild chuckle from Gross, who once again turned to his newspaper.

Fräulein Metzinger entered from the other end of the car, from the rear of the train.

'I do believe you've missed your calling, Fräulein,' Beer said, looking approvingly at the gray and white-trimmed nurse's uniform she wore.

She blushed at the comment and then straightened her shoulders. 'I will take that as a compliment, Herr Beer.'

The private train hurtled through the early evening, as the four settled down to a meal together and final plans for the coming day.

Werthen awoke with sunlight in his eyes, pouring through the tiny window of his sleeping cubicle. He sat up in bed and looked at a brilliantly white world under an azure blue sky. In the distance were the Alps, tall, imposing, frozen. Off to his right he could see the icy blue tip of Lake Zürich and the high spires of churches in the city.

A good day for a kidnapping, he decided.

The four of them breakfasted as the train

371

bypassed Zürich, traveling southward along the Lake of Zürich sparkling and inviting under the rising winter sun. Vineyards lay thickly covered under a blanket of snow, grape arbors like stick men dotting the fields. They were attended in actual fact by none other than Meier, Wittgenstein's loyal servant, who could also be trusted, it seemed, to keep his mouth shut about any adventures he might be part of, as could the engineer driving the train and the brakeman, all loyal Wittgenstein men.

At ten after nine their private train pulled up at a siding near the station of Küsnacht. Out of the train they could see in the near distance their target, the Park Hotel am See. The grounds abutted the banks of the lake and the premises consisted of two large ornate buildings. The older, three stories high with turrets at both sides, fronted the lake; an enclosed portico connected that to another newer, but no less impressive hotel building farther back from lakeside. It stood five stories and had balconies surrounding each floor. Overall, this newer building was fitted out more in the alpine style favored by the builders of mountain lodges, while the older, original building had an air of gingerbread quaintness. Boat pads stood empty this time of year, but Werthen could imagine that in fine summer weather the lawns and launching pads would be a buzz of activity.

'You know your tasks,' Gross said to Beer and Fräulein Metzinger. 'If there is any sign of difficulty, however, you must simply cease and return to the train. We have not come to create more violence. Understood?'

Fräulein Metzinger – dressed in her nurse's uniform and standing next to a wooden wheelchair with blankets neatly folded in the seat – nodded, but Beer simply stared at the hotel buildings as if in a trance.

'Herr Beer?' Gross said. 'That is understood?'

'She's that close,' he said. 'The woman who killed my boy.'

'I promise you she will pay for her crimes,' Gross said. 'But not at your hands.'

'Whatever you say, Professor,' Beer replied, still gazing at the hotel.

Despite the low sun, the chill off the lake was intense. Werthen was anxious to get things under way. He handed Beer an overcoat that matched his uniform, both with the crest of the Park Hotel am See on them, another gift from Herr Wittgenstein, who seemed to have tentacles everywhere.

Their plan was for Beer to enter the hotel in the guise of one of the staff, then to go to Frau Steinwitz's room – the number of which was supplied by Drechsler – and to bring mid-morning coffee laced with sufficient laudanum to put her to sleep. Fräulein Metzinger, posing as a nurse, would then go to the room and she and Beer would administer diethyl ether sufficient to render her totally unconscious. Fräulein Metzinger had been advised in the technique by a doctor friend, having told him she was writing a penny thriller. The doctor was only too happy to contribute to her creative efforts.

Beer and Fräulein Metzinger would then put the lady into the wheelchair, bundled up so that no one could see she was unconscious, and wheel her to the waiting train. If noticed by staff or other guests, it would simply appear that she was being taken for an airing.

Gross and Werthen would be waiting in the grounds for their return, keeping an eye out for any watchers or bodyguards. It was, after all, possible that Colonel Gutrum would send someone to accompany his daughter.

'Good luck to you both,' Werthen said. 'And remember what Doktor Gross said. The first sign of trouble, you both get out of there. We will find another way to deal with her. Is that agreed?'

Agreement came from both, though with little enthusiasm.

Beer set off first, crunching through the snow. Five minutes later, Gross, Werthen, and Fräulein Metzinger followed.

It is finally under way, Werthen thought.

Werthen thought he might freeze while waiting. He knew it would take some time for the laudanum to work. Meanwhile, he tried to keep warm by walking back and forth along the small quay built in front of the hotel. Gross simply huddled in his heavy overcoat, his derby pulled down low over his face, and stared out into the icy waters of the lake. He was strangely quiet this morning, Werthen noticed, but perhaps that was because he was nervous about the success of their plan. Understandable enough. But he missed the criminologist's usual banter.

Werthen was about to try and bring Gross out when he heard the unmistakable crunch of wheels over frozen snow. There, coming down the path from the back building, were Beer and Fräulein Metzinger wheeling an inert Frau Steinwitz. They had done it. A wave of elation swept over Werthen.

'Gross. They're coming.'

The criminologist turned, and Werthen saw his expression turn from relief to alarm.

Werthen looked back and saw now that there was a fourth person coming down the same lane. He was large but agile, and though dressed in finer clothes than before, Werthen was sure it was the man with the broken nose who had attacked him and later Herr Meisner.

'Behind you,' he shouted to Beer, but too late, for the thug had already apprehended them and lifted Beer up by the front of his overcoat like a rag doll, shaking him. Werthen could hear Fräulein Metzinger scream. She attempted to push the wheelchair down the path, but the man grabbed her as well, throwing her to the ground like a bundle of old clothes.

Werthen was racing up the pathway toward them, followed by Gross. They had come armed, and as he ran he drew the revolver out of his coat pocket. He could hear Gross panting behind him as he pulled away. The thug had now taken the wheelchair and was returning toward the hotel. This altercation had not yet attracted attention from within the hotel; neither were there strollers about to witness events.

He reached Beer and Fräulein Metzinger, and though shaken, they both seemed unharmed.

'Let them go, Advokat,' Fräulein Metzinger

said, holding Werthen's arm. 'Remember your own rules. We try another day.'

Werthen wanted his own vengeance with the thug who had attacked him and his father-in-law, but knew she was right.

'Then let me,' Beer said, struggling with him for the revolver in his hand.

Gross had by now caught them up and wrapped his arms around the struggling Beer.

Ahead of them shots suddenly rang out. They all looked toward the sound and saw the large man topple in the snow. Then another pair of reports from the gun, and Frau Steinwitz slumped in her chair.

Werthen could hardly believe his eyes.

There on the path, gun in hand, was Doktor Praetor. He made no attempt to run away as panic broke out from inside the hotel. He dropped the revolver and simply stood there as a pair of beefy security guards came running down the path and held him. A woman screamed from the terrace at the sight of carnage.

Soon, Werthen knew, the area would be alive with policemen. For now, however, attention was focused on the dead and the perpetrator.

'We need to leave,' he said.

They did not run, but forced themselves to walk slowly away from the scene. Turning once, Werthen had the unmistakable sense that Praetor doffed his hat in their direction.

Epilogue

Frieda was wedged between pillows, playing with her silver rattle in the shape of a dreidel, the gift from her grandfather, who was seated next to her on the leather couch in the sitting room looking healthy once again.

'The one thing I do not understand about all this,' Werthen said, 'is how Doktor Praetor was able to track Frau Steinwitz.'

'Perhaps he went to Detective Inspector Drechsler,' Berthe suggested. 'After all, he had saved the man's wife and with no charge.'

Werthen took a sip of Frau Blatschky's wonderful coffee. 'I would never have thought he had it in him.'

Gross stirred in his chair. 'Doktor Praetor put up a front of formalism, denying that his son might have been a homosexual. Yet he loved Ricus deeply. It was clear to me that he would take matters into his own hands sooner or later. When we finally told him that it was Frau Steinwitz who had killed his son, his reaction was far too muted. I knew he was putting on an act for us. He would have his revenge, one way or the other.'

Werthen looked hard at his colleague. 'You told him, didn't you?'

377

'Karl,' said Berthe.

'No, no. It's quite all right, Frau Meisner. Your husband is correct.'

Herr Meisner's attention was taken away from his granddaughter by this discussion.

'But why?' the father-in-law asked. 'Playing God?'

Gross sighed; he suddenly looked very tired.

'As I said, I knew Praetor would seek personal vengeance. Were we to be successful in bringing Frau Steinwitz back to Vienna to stand trial, it is doubtful any jury in the empire would convict her of killing her unfaithful husband and his catamite. You knew that as well as I, Werthen.'

'True. But still—'

'And attempts to link her to the death of the unfortunate Huck are proving equally difficult. Drechsler has found three witnesses who can attest to her presence on the platform that day, but none who saw her shove Huck under the oncoming train. Beyond that, any defense attorney worthy of the name would be able to discredit those people by a simple reference to the picture in Kraus's *Die Fackel* article. How can one be sure after all this time where the witness saw Frau Steinwitz?'

'Also true,' Werthen averred.

'So, found innocent, Frau Steinwitz would surely have come into Doktor Praetor's sights at some time. Better then to end it in Switzerland than Austria.'

'I don't follow the reasoning,' Berthe said.

But Werthen did. It was suddenly clear to him. 'You mean because the Swiss banned capital punishment there a few years ago?'

'Exactly,' Gross said. 'My reasoning was that it is preferable for Praetor to stand trial for murder in Switzerland than in Austria. That is why I told him the whereabouts of Frau Steinwitz. Of course I had no way of knowing if or when he would arrive. I was only certain that he would try to take her life.'

'Unlike the gallant Herr Beer,' Werthen said.

'Beer played his role quite nicely, as did your Fräulein Metzinger,' Gross said.

'I still say you were playing God,' Herr Meisner said to Gross.

Gross ignored this. 'I have secured the best defense attorney in Switzerland for Doktor Praetor. A man well respected and well connected. I am also supplying the attorney with all our case notes on Frau Steinwitz so that he can plead extenuating circumstances and perhaps win a reduced sentence. It is better than facing the gallows here in Austria.'

At which point little Frieda emitted a burp of startling intensity.

Werthen looked from Gross to his daughter, and then to his wife. Were someone to harm them, who was to say what he would or would not do.

There are some things about which one would rather remain silent.

Two stonemasons were at work high up in the central spire of the Rathaus. They stood on a wooden platform over the huge clock and felt every vibration from the gears of the monumental timepiece. They had labored all morning carrying blocks of stone and mortar up the three hundred and thirty-one steps to the observation window, and they were now carefully laying stone upon stone to seal the opening.

'Seems a shame,' said one of the men, more loquacious than the other.

His companion made an unintelligible grunt at this comment.

'I mean, what a view from way up here. Like you was king of all Vienna. Why would you ever want to go and block it up?'

The other stonemason, a much older and stooped man, gazed out at the vision of Lilliputian Vienna beneath him. He shook his head.

'Lueger's the mayor,' the older man finally said. 'He knows best.'